Battalion 1

Battalion 1 Series: Book 1

Theo Mann

The Invisible Publishing Company

Battalion 1 Series

Contents

Chapter 1

Captain Corban Rhodes tightened his grip on his weapon and hunched a little lower behind a pile of gnarled debris, but it didn't offer enough protection.

Explosions and blasts of laser fire flickered through the darkness above him and behind his back.

Those lasers kept smashing the rubble mound against his back. The ground shook under his seat. The mountain of twisted metal and destroyed ship parts shuddered every few seconds.

Lieutenant Zack Turley leaned in close to Rhodes's ear and bellowed over the noise. No one could hear a thing without yelling. "What do you want to do, Sir?! We can't stay here!"

Rhodes only nodded. He already knew that.

He sat up and adjusted the strap of his Jackhammer around his elbow to brace the weapon tighter into his shoulder. He had to straighten all his body armor and helmet before he showed his face in the open.

He already knew what he would see when he stuck his head over this rubble pile. He wasn't overly enthusiastic to see it again.

Dead bodies, the smoking wreckage of downed ships, and the twisted remains of buildings spread outward from his location as far as the eye could see—except that he couldn't see it because it was nighttime.

Three moons hung low over the planet Luluna—at least he thought that's what the planet was called. He couldn't be sure.

These Fringe planets all blended together after a while. He'd fought on so many of them in his career. They all looked the same during a battle and he never got a chance to see the countryside in peacetime.

He took a deep breath, crammed his helmet onto his head, and sprang up from his hiding place.

He lunged for the top of the rubble mound, flattened himself on his stomach at the top, and aimed his Jackhammer outward to sweep the destroyed landscape.

He didn't open fire. That would only show the enemy where he was. He didn't want that. Darkness and silence gave him the best protection right now.

The minute he got into that position, he saw exactly what he knew he would see. He'd seen exactly the same thing for days now. The landscape never changed.

Lasers snickered all over what was left of the dark city. They gave more light than the three moons.

Mid-sized Duster attack ships swooped low over the landscape and released breaker bombs, gravimetric fusion rockets, and Viper missiles on a massive horde of aliens surging closer across the wreckage piles.

The rockets and breaker explosions erupted out there in the darkness. They gave the only other light for Rhodes to see the enemy.

Not that it mattered much where they were. They were always way too close and always getting closer.

The lasers all came from the enemy side. The aliens crawled over the rubble on multiple legs. The cilia around their mouths wavered when they moved.

Their eyes gleamed faint bluish-green in the darkness when they turned their heads in any direction. Then their eyes vanished in the darkness when the aliens faced somewhere else.

Thousands of them swarmed over the rubble mounds inching closer to Rhodes's position. The Dusters unloaded dozens of projectiles on the alien horde, but nothing slowed them down.

Four Predator fighter craft howled over Rhodes's head, blasted toward the alien swarm, and unloaded rattler guns on the oncoming enemy.

The rattlers unleashed hundreds of fusion loads with each shot. They brought down countless aliens with each pass, but more aliens materialized out of nowhere to take their dead comrades' places.

The aliens seemed to grow out of the ground—but that wasn't possible in this destroyed landscape.

Where did they all come from? This wouldn't be the first time Rhodes wondered. He would probably never find out.

The aliens fired their lasers forward to bombard Rhodes's position again and again. He had to huddle behind the hill for protection to avoid getting his head sliced off.

A second later, the aliens turned their lasers on the Dusters soaring overhead. Lasers swiped through the darkness and cut two Dusters in half.

One of them exploded instantly. It detonated in a blazing fireball, tilted downward, and shrieked out of the atmosphere on a death plunge straight into the enemy horde.

The ship smashed into the ground with bone-crushing force. The ship burst in a mushroom cloud that lit up the landscape.

That one flash of light showed Rhodes all he needed to know. A long line of soldiers curved to his left and right facing the advancing swarm.

All those soldiers crouched behind the debris for protection from the enemy laser fire.

Pulses of fusion blasts popped off from some locations down that line going in both directions. Jackhammers fired in the darkness and jets of fusion charges ejected from the guns.

They swept the enemy ranks and cut down aliens by the dozen, but those shots only gave the aliens visible targets to shoot at.

The aliens turned their lasers on those gunshots. More lasers carved the rubble to pieces until they cut down the men hiding behind the mounds.

Screams and dying groans drifted across the wasteland from all directions. Those sounds even came from the mountains of destroyed wreckage near Rhodes and under his feet.

He couldn't see the thousands of dead and wounded nearest him anymore. There were too many of them and it was too dark.

Right then, a man thirty feet away from him opened fire. A jet of fusion fire lit up the night and smashed into the enemy ranks.

More soldiers yelled, pounced on the shooter, and dragged him down out of sight, but it was too late.

Dozens of aliens turned their lasers on the spot and smashed the mound to pieces.

Rhodes jumped back down behind his hill and grabbed Turley. "Get out of here!" Rhodes bellowed. "MOVE!! MOVE OUT!!"

He shoved Turley away. Rhodes straightened up just enough to signal the other men around him. "Move out!! Come on!! This way!! MOVE!!"

Lieutenant Justin Upshaw and Captain Tate Vernick crowded close behind Rhodes to follow him. The rest of their men of the Aemon Legion's 249th platoon scooted down the rubble pile doing their best to scramble over fallen junk to keep up.

Rhodes, Upshaw, Vernick, and the rest of their platoon had to wait for Turley to get his men moving. None of them could see a thing in this darkness, but no way could they stay here.

"Where are we going?!" Turley yelled over his shoulder.

"Away from here! That jackass showed them exactly where we are. KEEP MOVING!!"

Rhodes bellowed over his shoulder, but he couldn't be sure his men heard him over the noise.

More laser fire hit the second Duster. It kept pounding breaker bombs into the enemy, but that only drew alien fire back to the ship until they destroyed it, too.

Lasers converged on its lower hull, carved through it, and hit one of the Duster's lateral engines. The hull erupted outward and the explosion hurled the ship sideways.

Rhodes couldn't watch anymore. He bent his head and shoved Turley forward faster. The rest of Turley's squad blocked the way.

The men had to climb across the steep slope piled with bent pipe, jagged torn beams, and burned sections of fuselage. The men inched sideways nowhere near fast enough to get out of danger.

Rhodes didn't dare to check how far away the enemy was. More screams drifted out of the noise. Then an almighty boom rocked the landscape when the Duster exploded directly over Rhodes's head.

Every man in his platoon ducked including Rhodes, but the ship was already veering away somewhere else before it dove to its destruction on the planet's surface.

He gave Turley another push, but Turley couldn't go anywhere with so many other men in front of him. This was getting hopeless.

Rhodes made the mistake of glancing around. At that moment, dozens of glowing, bluish-green eyes appeared out of the darkness above him.

They materialized in the darkness at the top of the rubble pile. The aliens looked straight down at the men who were trying to get away on the slopes below.

Those eyes set off a chain reaction in Rhodes's gut. He spun around fast, raised his Jackhammer, and opened fire on the aliens.

"GO!!" he roared. "GET OUT OF HERE NOW!!"

He backed away and swiveled sideways so his men could keep fleeing behind him. A few others opened fire, too. Most dove down the piles trying to get as far away from the aliens as they could before all hell broke loose.

Rhodes took a split second to see his men totally exposed to alien laser fire. He couldn't let the whole platoon fall right here.

He backed a little farther away and ran into another mound rising behind him. He scrambled onto its steep side and unloaded on the aliens to draw their attention away from the platoon.

"OVER HERE, YOU BASTARDS!!" he roared. "OVER HERE!!"

It worked. The aliens all looked up at him and lasers punched out of the darkness.

Three shots hit the debris near him and then a laser sliced across his chest. It cut straight through his body armor and scored a blistering path of fire into his skin.

He bellowed in pain, but the laser pivoted away too fast to do any other damage. He fought through the agony to bring up his Jackhammer again.

He already knew he was about to die. He just had to distract the aliens long enough for the platoon to get away.

Screaming pain tore him apart when he moved his arms. His vision swam. He couldn't see well enough to aim.

All those alien eyes gleamed out of the darkness. They looked right at him. They didn't have any problem targeting *him*.

At that moment, three Predators shrieked out of nowhere, pelted down the ridgetop in front of Rhodes, and unloaded on the aliens.

Their bodies blasted into the air and dead aliens rolled down the mound toward the platoon. The sight of reinforcements coming to his aid gave Rhodes superhuman strength.

He opened fire and roared out all his pain and hopeless frustration on the aliens. He gunned down fifty of them. That definitely got their attention.

He kept bombarding them and yelling in a combination of pain and battle fury while he did his best to stumble farther up the slope.

He didn't care about anything but getting the aliens to look at him instead of looking at the platoon.

More Predators zoomed back and forth across his line of sight. He didn't pay much attention to whether they made any progress to slow the aliens down. Nothing would slow down such a massive tide of bodies.

He tripped over a piece of fuselage and slammed down hard on one knee. That pain made him clamp his hand tighter on his weapon.

He raged at the aliens through gritted teeth. How much fuel did his weapon still have? He couldn't be sure.

He pawed at his body armor trying to grab his cluster grenades, but at that moment, another laser skated across the mound behind him.

He saw it coming closer and tried to aim his Jackhammer at the source, but not fast enough.

The laser sliced through his arm and severed it across the middle of his bicep. His weapon fell to the ground with his hand still clenched around the trigger grip.

He roared out in hopeless agony just as another laser clipped him in the thigh.

A laser shot smashed into the pile right next to his head. Some white-hot metal fragment wheeled out of the wreckage, struck his face, and sliced across his eyes.

The impact ripped his helmet off and stars burst in his head before his vision cleared.

He came back to his senses standing in front of a colossal mass of aliens all staring straight at him. He had to shoot at them, but he didn't have a weapon anymore.

He dove for his Jackhammer, snatched it with his left hand, and lost his balance. He tripped over a piece of twisted pipe embedded in the hill. He barely managed to grab his weapon before he pitched head over heel down the slope.

He slammed against something solid and looked up at dozens of aliens all staring down at him. He tried to grab his weapon and bring it up, but he tried to grab it with his right arm which wasn't there anymore.

He took a split second to remember that he had to use his left arm instead.

In that moment, four more Dusters thundered overhead firing dozens of breaker bombs into the alien horde. He didn't see the platoon anywhere nearby. He was all alone out here.

His dazed brain stared up at the Dusters in stupid shock. Were they coming for him? Would they lift him off, take him to the hospital, and save whatever was left of his pathetic life?

He already knew they wouldn't. They didn't rescue the wounded. Anyone who fell on the battlefield stayed where they lay. No one came to get them and no one would come to get Rhodes.

Lasers sprayed out of the enemy ranks, fired into the night sky, and targeted the Dusters. Blasts of yellow and orange explosions ejected from the ships' hulls.

That flash of light brought Rhodes back to his senses. He floundered to sit up enough to aim his weapon at his enemies. He couldn't stand.

He propped his Jackhammer against his knee to steady it, but before he could fire, alien lasers hit the engines of a Duster right above him.

The ship shuddered once and detonated in a catastrophic boom before the whole burning mass of torched metal plummeted toward the ground.

Rhodes didn't see it until it was too late—not that he could do anything about it if he did see it. He kept shooting at the aliens crawling closer by the second.

He bared his teeth in a feral roar right up until the moment the burning Duster smashed down on top of him.

Chapter 2

Beeping noises woke Rhodes from a sound sleep. He blinked and then flinched when blinding, stark white light stabbed him in the eyes.

He had to think before he remembered where he was—except that he didn't know where he was. He had been on the battlefield until just a few seconds ago.

He definitely wasn't there now.

A young woman with long, straight, dark brown hair and glasses stood next to his bed.

She wore her hair pulled back in a ponytail behind her neck. She wore a business suit under a knee-length lab coat with her name stitched onto the front of it. *Dr. Veronica Neiland, ALMC.*

Rhodes groaned and tried to look around again. ALMC. The Aemon Legion Medical Corps.

He must be in a military hospital—which made sense considering what happened to him on the battlefield—except that it didn't make sense.

He would be the first of thousands or maybe millions of Legion war casualties to end up in the hospital. He should have died on the battlefield.

He craned his head off the pillow, but his whole body felt unbearably heavy. It took all his strength just to lift his head. He couldn't lift any of his limbs. He felt sick to his stomach.

"Where am I?" he croaked.

"You're at Coleridge Station, Captain Rhodes," Dr. Neiland clipped in a soft, steady tone.

"I never heard of it."

"It's a secret military installation that doesn't appear on any map. No one has heard of it."

He collapsed back on the pillow and shut his eyes. He was really starting to wish he *did* die on the battlefield. "What am I doing here, then?"

"You've been asleep. It will take you a while to get your strength back and to orient yourself. There's nothing to worry about. The nausea and weakness will pass."

He tried one more time to sit up and failed. He lifted his head and spotted four other people in the same room.

The room itself looked like a giant science lab with a bunch of equipment he didn't recognize. It didn't look like a hospital at all.

A giant cylindrical stack of computer components occupied the center of what looked like a circular chamber. Banks of more computers, equipment, and random wires, tubes, and conduits covered the walls.

Some of these random wires, tubes, and conduits even extended from the ceiling and walls. The wires, tubes, and conduits entered the central column of computer equipment and some came toward Rhodes's bed.

Dr. Neiland approached him on his right side and tapped at a computer console attached to his bed. That's what made the beeping sound.

The bed did something and started to tilt upward. It locked in place at an angle so he no longer lay flat on his back.

The longer he lay here, the more his mind cleared. He wasn't in a normal hospital bed at all. The mattress under him was the only normal part of it.

Even that didn't feel like a regular mattress. There was something different about it, but he couldn't quite place what was wrong with it.

More computer equipment surrounded him on all sides and a solid metal cover levered above his head.

Computer screens flashed and flickered on the cover's underside. The readings kept changing every time Dr. Neiland punched one of her buttons.

The wires, tubes, and conduits went into and out of all of this equipment attached to his bed. He couldn't tell at first what it was all for.

He tried again to sit up and he raised his hand to rub his face. "What happened to me? How did I get here?"

His hand touched his head—and he felt something metal attached to his face. His arm and hand didn't feel right, either.

He looked down at his hand and his world stopped when he saw his arm. It wasn't a human arm anymore. It had been replaced by a robotic arm and hand.

"You got injured on the battlefield," Dr. Neiland replied in the same soothing undertone. "We brought you here and replaced your arm and some of your internal organs with implants. We also modified your sensory, nervous, and motor systems with upgraded components. Don't worry. You'll get used to them in time."

He barely heard her. He stared at his arm, moved his hand in every direction, and experienced another wave of vertigo at the sensation.

His arm and hand moved the same way a normal arm would, but it didn't feel the same. He couldn't identify the sensation. It felt surreal....or maybe not real at all—but it was.

He rubbed his fingertips together. He could feel everything. The sensation up his arm felt the same as normal skin—but it wasn't skin.

Components he didn't recognize covered the surface. Ports and channels scored the outer housing, but the metal surface blended together to make the outer housing smooth. He didn't see any working parts, but there must be.

He lost his arm on the battlefield. He remembered now.

These doctors didn't reattach his original arm. They wouldn't have been able to after the laser severed it. No one could repair an injury like that.

He touched his face—with that hand. He felt the metal attached to his face.

He followed the outline from his forehead over his cheekbone and down to his jaw. The implants embedded into the bone and he sensed them penetrating deep inside his head.

The implants covered part of his forehead and all of his right eye socket. The implant blocked his eye, but he could still see perfectly well. His vision looked normal.

The implants on his face felt just as smooth as his arm's metal housing. They covered the right half of his face, his right ear, and most of the back of his skull.

The rest of his face felt normal. He still had hair growing out of the rest of his scalp and his mouth felt normal, too.

Dr. Neiland tapped on her machines a few more times and looked up at him through her glasses. "You should feel strong enough to sit up now, Captain. If you are, we can take you to your quarters and you can start to orient yourself to the station."

"What am I doing here?" he husked.

"I told you. We brought you here to repair your injuries. You're a member of an experimental project to upgrade your injured limbs and organs with these mechanical implants. You'll spend your recovery here at Coleridge Station until you learn to use them. Then you'll redeploy on the battlefield where you'll use these implants against the enemy." She blinked at him. "Is that clear enough for you? Do you understand now?"

He groaned again, but he couldn't keep lying here. He tried one more time to sit up, and this time, he succeeded. The upward tilted angle of the bed made it easier. He didn't have to move as far.

He heaved himself off the bed and swiveled his legs to the floor—but they weren't human legs. The same smooth mechanical housing covered him from the waist down.

He couldn't tell where his real legs ended and where the robotic legs began—or if he even had real legs anymore. How much damage did he suffer when that Duster crashed on top of him?

The replacement arm melded with another swath of components surrounding his shoulders and part of his chest. Some of his rib cage and abdomen showed between the chest section and the part extending down over his pelvis.

The implants on his left arm didn't enclose the whole arm the way they did his right arm. His left arm must have still been mostly intact when the Legion took him off the battlefield.

Components and implants dotted his skin from the left shoulder section down the outside of his upper arm. The implants surrounded his elbow in a mechanical joint and then narrowed around his forearm.

The components completely enveloped his wrist and his left hand. He couldn't see anything organic underneath, but his left hand felt different from his right hand.

He couldn't exactly say his left hand felt more real or more human because it didn't. It just felt different.

He paused there slumped on the edge of the bed to take all this in. The implants embedded in all his bones and muscles. A dull ache throbbed through his body where these machines sank their roots into his very being.

He couldn't call it pain because it didn't hurt—and yet it did. It hurt deeper than pain.

He could tolerate this ache, but it ate away at something even more fundamental than his senses. It changed him at his core. He wasn't human anymore—not the way he was before.

Dr. Neiland bent over him and did something to the component near his ear. "The implants take time to adjust to your nervous system. They feel strange now, but you'll get used to them."

Rhodes doubted that. He didn't see how he could ever get used to this.

These things weren't him. They chewed into his body, his blood, his bones, his internal organs. He even sensed them infecting his brain and senses. Where would it end?

It wouldn't end because they were a part of him now—and yet they felt alien. They felt like they might fall off at any moment—but they would never fall off.

His very being wanted to reject them and push them away, but they stuck to him with a deep, gnawing, unbreakable hold.

"You should be able to stand up now, Captain," Dr. Neiland told him.

Rhodes looked around one last time, but his mind didn't want to accept any of this.

If he'd been getting out of a hospital bed any other time, he would have had to put on some clothes. He didn't have to do that now.

He was a robot from the waist down. He had no other recognizable human anatomy he needed to cover up.

The implants covered all of him besides his midsection, his back, part of his chest, his left arm, neck, and half his head. No one could see anything. He was as dressed as he could possibly be.

The four other people in the room stood by the lab's central stack of computer equipment. This wasn't a hospital. It was a lab and he was the experiment. Dr. Neiland even said so.

Two of those other people wore medical lab coats like she did. One of those other people was a middle-aged man with greying hair and a grey goatee. The other was a younger man with straight brown hair, brown eyes, and glasses.

The other two people over there wore Aemon Legion officers' uniforms. They were both men in their forties and one of them was a general. The other was a colonel with black hair and black eyes.

The general had bright red hair, brilliant green eyes, and a million freckles. They looked strange on a man his age—like he couldn't decide if he was growing up or staying a boy.

Now that Rhodes looked around more closely, he noticed other technicians in lab coats working on the equipment lining the walls. They didn't pay any attention to Rhodes, Dr. Neiland, or the other four people in the room.

An elevated circular platform ran around the lab's upper wall. More technicians worked up there, too.

"Stand up, Captain," Dr. Neiland told him. "We need to check that all your systems are functioning within operable parameters."

His brain didn't want to register that she was talking about him this way—the way she would talk about some machine that had just gotten out of the repair shop.

He stood up, and at that signal, the four men crossed the room to approach him.

For some reason he couldn't figure out, Rhodes's eyes and mind read their four nametags in a split second.

He didn't even have to look at the names stitched onto their lab coats. The four names entered his head automatically without him making the decision to read them.

The older doctor's name was Dr. Steven Montague. The younger one was Dr. Derek Irvine. The general's nametag read, *Brewster.* The colonel's read, *Kraft.*

Just in case Rhodes doubted the evidence of his new enhanced senses, General Brewster stuck out his hand and gave Rhodes a huge, boyish smile. "It's a pleasure to meet you, Captain. I'm General Kenneth Brewster and this is Colonel Paxton Kraft."

Rhodes shook the general's hand without thinking. Rhodes started to say, "Good to meet you....." but he used too much pressure and wound up crushing the general's hand.

General Brewster grimaced, yelled in pain, and almost buckled to his knees before Rhodes realized what he was doing. He let go, but not fast enough.

"Aargh!" General Brewster howled and clutched his hand.

"I'm sorry....." Rhodes stammered.

Dr. Neiland and the other two doctors raced over and started whizzing around Rhodes in a flurry.

"Nothing to worry about!" Dr. Irvine exclaimed. "It's understandable until you get used to the implants. Your neuromotor system has been enhanced, so you're stronger than you were before. Don't worry! You'll get used to it."

General Brewster kept gasping and clutching his hand in pain. "It's.....it's all right.... .Captain.....It isn't your fault......"

"Come over here, General," Dr. Neiland breezed. "I'll X-ray your hand and we can repair the bones."

She took him across the lab to one of the machines against the wall. General Brewster tried to smile at Rhodes.

Brewster probably hoped he was smiling in a reassuring way, but the general kept writhing and baring his teeth in obvious pain.

Rhodes didn't know what to think watching Dr. Neiland take the general away. Rhodes only tried to shake the general's hand. Rhodes didn't think he used that much pressure, but he must have made a mistake.

Colonel Kraft stepped in front of Rhodes to block him from looking at General Brewster again.

"It's an honor to finally meet you, Captain." Kraft started to extend his hand, too, and stopped himself. "General Brewster is the commanding officer of Coleridge Station and I'm in command of Battalion 1. You and I will be working closely with each other."

"What's that? What's Battalion 1?"

"It's the new unit of soldiers like yourself who will receive these experimental implants. Battalion 1 will become an integral part of the Aemon Legion and an indispensable wing of our fighting force. Battalion 1 is critical to our mission of securing the quadrant from alien invasion and bringing peace to the Fringes."

"Oh," Rhodes muttered under his breath. "I see."

Kraft waved behind him. "Come with me, Captain. I'll show you around the station and explain things to you. The orientation process takes some time, so we all understand that you might be feeling a little out of your depth."

"How long does it take?" Rhodes asked. "How long will I be like this?"

"Well....." Kraft glanced at the two remaining doctors.

"The truth is, Captain, we don't actually know how long it takes," Dr. Irvine interjected. "You're the first subject to go through the project."

Rhodes's head shot up. "I'm....what?"

"You're the first subject to go through the project. You'll take command of the first unit of Battalion 1 as soon as they wake up—but you're the first to wake up."

Rhodes's throat went dry. "Does that mean others *didn't* wake up?"

Dr. Irvine shuffled his feet and looked away. "I assure you everyone who goes through the project was injured to the point of death exactly the way you were. If we didn't take them, they would be dead now—the same way you would be."

Now it was Rhodes's turn to look away. Maybe he would have been better off dying on the battlefield than.....this.

He didn't say that out loud, though.

"Now you can understand why we're so delighted to have you with us," Irvine gushed. "All your systems seem to be functioning within operational parameters."

He bent over the control panel on Rhodes's bed—the panel Dr. Neiland had been working on when Rhodes first woke up.

Dr. Montague looked over Dr. Irvine's shoulder to see the readings, but just then, Dr. Neiland came back with General Brewster.

He had his hand in a cast up to the wrist, but he smiled more easily now. "Please don't think anything of it, Captain. We're all too pleased to see you up and about to worry about a little thing like this."

"I'm sure you are," Rhodes muttered.

Everyone pretended not to hear him.

"If you're feeling up to it, Colonel Kraft and I will show you around," General Brewster went on. "The doctors can monitor your systems on the way and make sure you're functioning properly. If everything works out, you can relax in your quarters until it's time for you to go on duty."

"What does that mean?" Rhodes asked. "What do you mean by putting me on duty?"

"You need to train with your new implants so you get used to them," Dr. Neiland told him. "You'll need to adjust how you do things and how you process information coming from your implants. We'll make additional modifications as needed to ensure everything is working the way it's supposed to."

Rhodes didn't like the sound of that, but what choice did he have? These implants told him loud and clear that he didn't have one.

He couldn't get his arm back—or his eye back—or anything else the doctors replaced.

They might have replaced his entire lower body. He would never get that back. He'd been on the point of death when they brought him in.

He still didn't know what to think or how to feel about that, but he definitely didn't have a choice about this.

These implants anchored into his bones. They hooked up to his brain and nervous system. He would never be able to get rid of them.

His gut told him to tear them out and throw them away. He wanted to rip them out with his fingernails, but he wouldn't even be able to do that—not without killing himself.

Maybe that would have been better, but he didn't get a chance to do that or even to think about it.

General Brewster waved across the lab again. "Follow me, Captain. You don't need to stay in here any longer."

Chapter 3

R hodes followed General Brewster out of the lab. Colonel Kraft walked at Rhodes's side.

Rhodes's implants fed him mountains of information he never would have picked up this fast with his normal senses.

General Brewster had a lively personality, smiled easily, and kept widening his eyes at Rhodes in a delighted, encouraging way. Brewster couldn't have been more tickled that Rhodes was up and walking around.

Kraft had a serious, reserved nature with deep, dark, watchful eyes. He measured everything Rhodes did down to the atom. Nothing escaped Kraft's notice.

Rhodes recognized an officer scrutinizing a man who would become his subordinate.

Kraft was the one responsible for this new Battalion 1. He would be Rhodes's direct superior, so of course Kraft wanted to make sure Rhodes did everything right.

Kraft's reserve actually made Rhodes feel better. Rhodes understood men like Kraft.

Kraft took the time and care to make sure anyone under him was capable of doing the job the way it needed to be done. Rhodes appreciated that.

Brewster gave Rhodes a very bad feeling. Brewster's bubbly enthusiasm didn't gel with the sheer scale of what these people were trying to do.

Brewster also didn't seem to realize the effect these implants were having on Rhodes. It never seemed to cross Brewster's mind that these implants might not be the blessing everyone wanted them to be.

Kraft sure did. Rhodes almost got the impression Kraft was standing there with his hand on a holstered weapon ready to put Rhodes down the instant something went wrong—but Kraft didn't have a weapon.

He held himself tense, watchful, and ready to act at a moment's notice. Rhodes respected Kraft for that.

Rhodes really needed someone like that around him right now. No one else around here seemed to understand the situation well enough even to think of it.

Brewster kept smiling with glee while he held the door open for Rhodes to leave the lab.

The three men exited into a long corridor of stark industrial tile. Doors lined both walls. Rhodes couldn't see beyond them to the rooms inside. He didn't want to see.

The three doctors followed behind. Each one worked on a remote computer device.

Rhodes couldn't see what they were working on, but they must have been monitoring him. They wouldn't be here otherwise.

Their presence drove home to Rhodes that he was their lab rat—their experiment. He felt like a science experiment walking around with these implants.

They didn't make any noise. They felt exactly like normal legs walking down the hall and normal arms hanging at his sides.

He couldn't help feeling like a robot—because he was one.

His heels made an extra loud clunk on the tiles every time he took a step. He saw how different he looked from everyone else present.

He was the freak here. They were all human. He wasn't. He was something else. He just didn't know what that was.

Brewster talked the whole time in the same rapid, excited tone. "We'll introduce you to your unit and then give you a briefing on the state of affairs. You'll be able to adjust your programming to the battle conditions. Once you understand the situation, you'll be able to coordinate with the other platoons and swing the battle back in our favor."

"What do you mean by, 'introduce me to my unit'?" Rhodes asked. "You said I was the first to go through the program. How can I have a unit if I'm the only one?"

"We're holding the rest of your unit in stasis while they receive their implants and other modifications. You'll be their commanding officer, so we woke you up first. We'll need you to be present when we wake up the others. Your presence and guidance will help orient them. You'll be able to explain things to them better than we will since you will have gone through it before them."

"I won't be able to do that if I haven't had a chance to orient," Rhodes pointed out.

Brewster only smiled at him. "That's why you'll orient completely before we wake any of them up. You'll go through your training first. Then you'll be better able to help them with theirs."

Brewster stopped in front of a random door, opened it, and stood back for Rhodes to enter.

They entered a long, low room built the same as Dr. Neiland's lab except that this one wasn't circular. It had more of an oblong shape, but it did have the same computer components covering the walls.

Wires, tubes, and conduits connected all the equipment to twelve beds identical to the one Rhodes woke up in. The covers of these beds were all closed.

The covers weren't solid metal the way Rhodes thought. Some transparent substance allowed him to see the people lying asleep inside each chamber.

He passed down the line looking at their faces. The controls attached to each bed listed their names.

Lieutenant Heath Lauer.

Corporal Bobby Poole.

Sergeant David Cope.

Corporal Liam Taylor.

Rhodes stopped in front of two beds with women in them. "Who are they?"

"Most of these men are soldiers from the Legion," Brewster explained. "They got injured in battle the same way you did. That's how they joined the program."

"Joined?" Rhodes repeated. "They didn't join."

Brewster shrugged, but it came out more as a squirm. He made a face that looked like he was trying his hardest not to smile. "It's a figure of speech."

Rhodes nodded at the two women. "What about these two?"

"Georgie Henshaw is Frederick Henshaw's daughter."

"I don't know who that is," Rhodes replied.

Brewster raised his eyebrows and gasped. "You don't know who Frederick Henshaw is?"

"No, why should I? Is he in the Legion?"

"He's President of the Treaty of Aemon Ruling Council!" Brewster exclaimed. "I can't believe you don't know!"

Rhodes looked away. "That explains why I've never heard of him. I'm a soldier. I don't keep track of all that political bullshit."

Brewster winced and immediately tried to correct his expression. "Georgie received a terminal cancer diagnosis. President Henshaw arranged for us to take her into the program to save her life."

Rhodes spun around a second time. "You took some politician's daughter into an experimental laboratory program to create a battalion of super-warriors? She'll get killed out there! Why didn't you just let her die in peace?"

"Her implants and programming will give her the same skills, strength, and training as the rest of you. She won't disappoint you."

Rhodes snorted. He was starting to get a picture of the colossal task in front of him.

Now he would be the one in charge of these people. He would be the one trying to somehow explain to them why they were here and what they were supposed to do about it. He didn't look forward to that conversation.

He turned back to look down at Georgie Henshaw. She had straight, white-blonde hair and pale, ivory-white skin. He couldn't tell anything else about her.

Implants covered her head and face the same way they covered Rhodes's face and all the other members of this battalion unit. Each one of them had been modified the same way Rhodes had.

Georgie's hair had been cut jaw length. The woman in the bed next to her had straight brown hair cut in the same style. It made each woman look human but in an industrial, military way. The haircut didn't soften their features at all.

The second woman's name was Alyssa Thackery. "Who is she?" Rhodes asked. "Is she another politician's daughter?"

"She worked as a cleaner at Fort Jacaranda," Colonel Kraft murmured. "She was sweeping the floors in the engineering department when the station came under bombardment. She got electrocuted when a panel near her exploded. She doesn't have any family, so she came to us instead."

Rhodes cringed. Fantastic. So two of his new soldiers had no training, no combat experience, no nothing. The geniuses in charge of this project should have just let these women die.

Then again, they might not even wake up. How many other wounded soldiers did these doctors experiment on before someone survived long enough to wake up?

Rhodes was the first. The doctors might have gone through hundreds.

Maybe none of these people would wake up. Then Rhodes really would be the only one.

He passed down the line of beds reading the names, but he didn't stop again.

Corporal Rudy Fuentes. Sergeant Jairo Dietz. Lieutenant Dane Reinhart. Lieutenant Ted Oakes. Corporal Eddie Coulter.

The names meant nothing to Rhodes and neither did the people. He wouldn't know who or what he was dealing with until they woke up.

"So when will you wake them up?" he asked. "How long do they have to stay asleep?"

"They're ready to wake up now," Brewster replied. "We need to bring you up to speed first. We'll just brief you on the battle situation....."

Just then, a different young woman in an Aemon Legion uniform entered the room, approached General Brewster, and whispered something in his ear.

He bent over to listen and then straightened up. "Excuse me, Captain. I have something I need to attend to. I'll leave you in Colonel Kraft's capable hands. I'm sure I'll see you later. I trust everything will work out for the best. Excuse me."

He dipped one nod and left the room. That left Rhodes with Kraft and the three doctors. The three doctors kept hanging back and tapping on their devices.

They didn't seem to notice anything until Kraft gave them a hard look and waved them away. "You three can go back to the lab. You can see that Captain Rhodes is fine. Leave him alone for now. I'll let you know if we need you for anything."

Dr. Neiland opened her mouth to contradict. Colonel Kraft gave her such a drilling glare that she shut her mouth with a click and walked out. She took the other two doctors with her.

Kraft sighed as soon as the door closed. "Follow me, Captain. We have a lot to talk about."

Rhodes followed him back out into the corridor. Rhodes would have liked to ask what they had to talk about, but he didn't say anything.

Kraft's serious nature suddenly made this whole situation so much more real. Kraft didn't give Rhodes any encouragement or assurance that this was all so exciting and wonderful.

Even that overwhelmed Rhodes with relief. Someone around her understood how serious this was.

Kraft's dark eyes even seemed to communicate some understanding of what Rhodes was going through. Kraft couldn't know about this sensation of the implants eating into Rhodes's flesh and bones.

Kraft's steady gaze almost convinced Rhodes that Kraft did know—or at least suspected.

Kraft didn't show any sign of sympathy, but this depth of understanding convinced Rhodes that Kraft at least imagined what walking around with these implants must feel like.

Kraft barely glanced at Rhodes, but those dark eyes said it all. Kraft didn't need to look any more deeply than that. He already knew.

Kraft walked down the hall at Rhodes's side, but Kraft didn't break the silence.

"Aren't you supposed to explain all this to me?" Rhodes finally asked.

"What is there to explain that you don't already know? All I have to do is show you the battle lines. You understand the rest."

"What am I supposed to do out there that the rest of the Legion can't do?" Rhodes asked.

Kraft opened another door and led Rhodes into an office. It was a typical Legion officer's office with a large computer screen covering one wall.

Kraft stopped in front of it, tapped on it, and pulled up a map of the sector. "This is the Preinea homeworld at the center of the Treaty of Aemon Cluster. All the planets, solar systems, and cultures of the combined military defense alliance contribute troops and resources that make up the Aemon Legion."

"I know all that," Rhodes replied. "Why am I here if you don't tell me something I don't already know?"

Kraft adjusted the map to show the outer Fringes—a rim of planets, solar systems, stations, and inhabited regions at the very edge of the Treaty of Aemon Cluster.

"Coleridge Station is here—on the planet Tokirolera in the Dalea system," Colonel Kraft went on. "You've spent your career here, on the Fringes, fighting the Emal in their efforts to retake their territory from the Cluster."

"Yeah? So?"

"That's why Coleridge Station and the Battalion 1 project are here—so you'll be closer to the Emal. You'll redeploy against the aliens and work with the other platoons to drive the Emal out of the Cluster."

"You still aren't telling me anything I don't already know."

"What you don't know is that the Cluster is facing incursion from four other alien populations—here, here, here, and here."

Kraft pointed at different parts of the Treaty of Aemon Cluster—parts that should have been peaceful.

"This battle against the Emal is just a training ground for Battalion 1. It's a chance for you all to get used to your new weapons, training, and tactics. Once you do that, we'll deploy you against other enemies—more powerful enemies."

Rhodes spun around to stare at him. "More powerful than the Emal? How is that even possible? The Legion can't stop the Emal as it is. They've already reclaimed ten planets and they'll keep reclaiming more until they retake their territory. The Legion is getting slaughtered out there."

"That's where the brass hopes Battalion 1 will be able to change things."

Rhodes gaped at him even harder. "The brass? The brass hopes that? You didn't say *we* hope that."

Kraft made a face. "I'm a soldier like you, Captain. I don't make the rules."

"So you don't really think we stand a chance even against the Emal—let alone the rest of these incursions. Is that what you're saying? You're doing this because the brass ordered you to? Is that it?"

Kraft's expression darkened even more than before. He pointed at a different part of the map closer to the incoming incursions. "My family lives here—on the planet Nolestra in the Bevet system. If we don't find a way to stop these incursions, a lot of people are going to die. That's the only reason I agreed to this—not because I approve of what the doctors are doing. I wouldn't do it at all if I thought there was any other way."

Rhodes looked away, but that only brought him back to looking at the map. His mind went into a tailspin. If the battle against the Emal was that hopeless, then this whole project was a suicide mission.

Fighting the Emal was a suicide mission. Luckily for everyone involved, the Emal only wanted their own territory back—the territory the Treaty of Aemon annexed into the Cluster.

The Emal didn't want to conquer the whole Cluster. Humanity would have been finished if they did.

If these new alien incursions *did* want to conquer the Cluster, then someone had to stop them—if they could be stopped.

Kraft lowered his voice to a husky murmur. "You would have been dead on the battlefield just like everyone else in this project. What else do you have to do? You might as well save a few billion human lives while you're here. Isn't that why you joined the Legion in the first place?"

Chapter 4

Colonel Kraft escorted Rhodes to a different part of Coleridge Station. The station teemed with technicians, officers, soldiers, pilots, and hundreds of other Aemon Legion personnel.

None of them so much as glanced at Rhodes. They didn't act like him walking around with half his body replaced by robotics was anything out of the ordinary.

The Battalion 1 project definitely wasn't a secret if this many personnel manned this station.

Coleridge Station looked like every other Legion station he'd visited in his career. Multiple wings radiated outward from a central concourse of supply stores, commissaries, meeting rooms, auditoriums, and every other thing the station personnel needed.

The side wings contained personnel quarters, the station's power plant, loading docks, medical bay, and all the station's accessory departments.

He didn't see anything different about Coleridge Station—except that he was here—and the rest of Battalion 1 was here.

He and Kraft crossed the station's main concourse and entered a side wing. This was as far as it was possible to get from Dr. Neiland's lab and the other members of Battalion 1—if they survived long enough to become its members.

Kraft took Rhodes into another long, rectangular room—without all the computer equipment this time.

This room had been set up as a normal Legion barracks with a row of beds down one wall—but these weren't normal beds.

They were modified versions of the beds Rhodes had seen the other lab subjects sleeping in—the same kind of bed Rhodes had been sleeping in.

These had mattresses inside, but holes had been cut in the mattresses at strategic intervals down the length of the bed.

The same electronic equipment attached to these beds, but not as much equipment as in the lab.

The beds did have just as many wires, tubes, and conduits running to them, but these wires, tubes, and conduits didn't hang from the ceiling. They attached to each bed through the wall and ran across a short stretch of floor to keep everything out of the way.

Tables, benches, bookshelves, and a few computer terminal desks lined the opposite wall.

"This will be the battalion's quarters while you're at the station," Kraft announced. "Each of you has a capsule assigned to you. It's programmed to your own individual needs, so it's important that you use the same capsule each time. This is yours."

He pointed at the first bed in the row. The control panel on the end of the bed read out Rhodes's name and rank.

Captain Corban Rhodes. That was still him. Maybe he wasn't really a robot after all. Maybe he just looked, acted, and felt like one.

"Your capsule will interface with your systems when you come back here after training or after battle," Kraft went on. "The capsule will regulate your conversion cycle to carry out any repairs, adjust your nutrient levels, and make any necessary modifications to your systems before your next active phase. The conversion cycle is the equivalent of sleep, but it isn't sleep. The conversion cycle replaces that part of your neural system."

Rhodes stared down at the bed. Kraft called it a capsule because it wasn't a real bed. Rhodes didn't eat or sleep anymore. He really wasn't human anymore at all.

"The doctors recommend that you go through a conversion cycle to help you adjust to waking up from stasis," Kraft told him. "You probably want to take some time to come to grips with all of this. The conversion cycle is the best way to do that. It will help you process everything that's happened. You'll feel better when you wake up."

"So...." Rhodes asked. "What do I have to do?"

"Just lie down in the capsule the way you would if you were going to sleep—at least, that's what it's supposed to do. You shouldn't feel a thing."

Rhodes sneered at him. Everything Rhodes would ever do from now on would be one giant experiment. It would be the first time anyone had ever done any of this. Spectacular.

This capsule might not repair, adjust, or modify anything. It could kill him—but wasn't that what Rhodes had just been hoping would happen? Then he wouldn't have to deal with any of this.

He really did want to shut down his brain for a while. He didn't want to think about any of this. He didn't want to *be* any of this. This capsule was the next best thing.

He took a step forward. He didn't know how to approach this thing, but anything would be better than staying awake with all this information crammed into his head.

One glance at Kraft convinced Rhodes to turn around, sit down on the bed, and stretch out. Kraft stood there watching, but Rhodes didn't detect any judgment or deceit in Kraft's expression or body language.

For some reason Rhodes couldn't pinpoint, he actually felt like trusting Kraft. Kraft was the only person Rhodes had met so far that he would ever even consider trusting.

Rhodes stretched out on the mattress. The instant he got into that position, seven metal prongs stabbed him in the back.

They punched into his implants in his shoulders, his hips, his feet, and one impaled him through the back of the head.

The prongs locked with his implants and he blacked out.

He woke up an instant later. He didn't think any time had passed, but he really did feel better.

He felt rested and maybe even relaxed. Whatever this capsule did, it made him feel like he really did go to sleep.

The capsule's top cover was still in the process of lifting off him when he opened his eyes. He didn't see or hear it close, but it must have been closed all this time.

He didn't feel the prongs unlock from his implants, but they didn't hold him down anymore.

He sat up and put his feet on the floor. He actually felt okay even though he was still...whatever the hell he was.

He stood up not sure what to do with himself. If he'd just woken up any other time, he would have gone to the bathroom, taken a shower, and gotten himself something to eat.

He didn't need to do any of that anymore. He didn't feel hungry. He wouldn't need to go to the bathroom if he never ate.

He crossed the barracks to look at the computer terminals, but right then, Dr. Neiland walked in. "Good morning. How do you feel?"

Rhodes nodded. "I feel rested. That thing really worked."

"That's excellent," she breezed in her usual casual tone. "If you come with me, we can get started on your training. The sooner you finish, the sooner we can wake up the rest of the battalion."

"What is the training?" he asked.

"I would have to show you to explain it to you. The first step is to activate your implants."

"Activate them how? They seem to be working just fine already."

"I'll have to show you. Come with me. Everything will become clear once we turn them on."

He didn't know what she meant, but his curiosity got the better of him. He followed her out of the barracks, down the corridor, and into a different much smaller room.

This was not a lab, an office, or anyone's quarters. There was nothing in the room—nothing at all.

The same industrial tile covered ten square feet of floor. Plain white walls surrounded Rhodes on all sides. That was the whole room.

Dr. Neiland closed the door behind her, took a step toward Rhodes, and pointed to something on his right arm—the robotic one.

"You have two scourge guns installed on your arm implants, laser and thermal cannons here and here, four seeker missile ports here and here closer to your elbows, another four Viper launchers on your back, and six booster rocket ports on each of your legs."

Rhodes waited for her to say something else. "Um....okay. Is that supposed to mean something to me?"

She pulled out her remote device and tapped on it. "Once I activate your implants, you might see some strange things, but I'll be with you and I'll explain everything to you. Are you ready?"

"Um....I guess." Rhodes couldn't know if he was ready since he didn't know what to expect. He might never be ready.

She tapped her device again. "Here we go."

She pushed one last button and the room vanished. The white walls and floor turned black except for a vast field of intersecting perpendicular green lines.

They formed hundreds of equally sized squares. Rhodes couldn't see anything else in the sea of black.

For some reason, the place still had enough light for Rhodes to see both himself and Dr. Neiland. This strange landscape didn't cast either of them in shadow.

He spun right and left trying to figure out where he was, but he wasn't anywhere. He just stood there in the center of this wide expanse of squares.

"This is The Grid," Dr. Neiland told him.

Rhodes snorted at her. "Really creative name for it."

She barely smiled. "This is the foundation background for your neural interface programming. Everything you experience in battle will happen here."

"What does that mean? Explain it in plain English."

"Your neural interface programming system will feed you information from your implants to help you process what's going on during any battle. The Grid allows you to adjust and use your implants so you can react and respond in the best possible way."

Rhodes shook his head. "I still don't understand."

"I'm going to activate one other element of your implants. I won't be here anymore, but you won't be alone. Do you understand?"

"No," he replied.

She tapped her device anyway and she vanished off The Grid. Now Rhodes really was alone.

As soon as she disappeared, a different shape materialized out of The Grid.

It started as a random scramble of much smaller squares of green grid lines. They tangled around each other in front of his eyes, blurred for a second, and started to take shape.

The lines formed the grid outline of a bird, then a flower, then a dog, a man, and finally some random alien creature Rhodes didn't recognize.

The lines kept jittering around each other, dissolving into confusion, and reforming until they settled on one particular shape.

It looked like a face, but not a human face. Rhodes didn't recognize this, either. It might have been a combination of a human, ape, cat, and bird face all merged into one.

The lines faded and the face developed color, but it didn't look like human skin. Colors kept rippling across its surface before the grid lines reappeared and then faded out again.

The grid lines kept appearing and disappearing as the face kept adjusting and morphing in front of Rhodes's eyes.

The face made eye contact with Rhodes and the expression changed. It recognized him and opened its mouth to speak in a calm, smooth, male voice like some kind of diplomat. "Captain—it's a pleasure to meet you."

"Um....who the hell are you?" Rhodes demanded.

"My name is Fisher. I'm your SAM." The face cocked its head slightly. "Captain Corban Rhodes, 249th Platoon, Aemon Legion. May I call you Rhodes? We should be on a first-name basis, don't you agree?"

Rhodes opened his mouth to say that, no, he didn't plan on getting on a first-name basis with anyone here, especially not some.....

"What's a SAM?" he asked.

Dr. Neiland's voice came from somewhere out of sight. "Fisher is your SAM. It stands for Simulated Augmentation Matrix. He's an onboard systems analysis program that interfaces with your neural network to help you process information and....."

"Will you shut the hell up with that gibberish?" Rhodes snapped. "Just tell me what it is."

"I am an enhancement program installed in your central neural processing system. I process data from your sensory system and reconfigure it...."

Rhodes held up his hand. "Stop right there, pal. So you're a computer program—installed in my....in my brain. Is that it?"

"Yes, exactly. I help you interface with....."

"Just....shut the hell up for a second, okay? You aren't helping me process anything."

Rhodes looked around at nothing. There was nothing to see but more and more of The Grid.

He would have liked to ask Dr. Neiland for a simpler explanation about this, but she wasn't here. She'd already given him the same line of nonsense that didn't explain anything.

Rhodes turned away from Fisher. Rhodes already started to sense himself thinking of this thing as a person. Rhodes couldn't let that happen.

He turned his back on it, but nothing happened. He was still here in The Grid. He didn't even know how to get out of it.

Fisher moved with him. No matter which way Rhodes turned, Fisher remained hovering there in front of Rhodes's eyes. Rhodes couldn't get rid of this thing.

"I believe I can help you understand if you let me, Captain," Fisher went on in the same undertone.

"Just stay the hell out of my head," Rhodes snapped. "I don't need you making this worse."

"I wasn't trying to make it worse, Captain," Fisher murmured. "We'll be working together from now on. If I can help you understand, I will. It will be the best thing for both of us."

Rhodes would have liked to stay mad at this thing—and the rest of everyone at this station. He didn't want this. He didn't want any of this.

He sure as hell didn't want some computer program talking to him in his head. That was the absolute last thing he needed.

Fisher didn't say anything for a minute. He just hovered there in The Grid while Rhodes seethed in silent resentment.

"May I make a suggestion, Captain?" Fisher finally asked.

"That depends on what it is," Rhodes snapped.

"May I suggest that you start walking?"

Rhodes stiffened. "What?"

"Start walking. Start walking through The Grid. The Grid only works when you're in motion. Once you start walking, The Grid will activate and you'll see for yourself what it's for. I promise I won't interfere. You'll only be walking along. I promise."

Rhodes didn't understand what Fisher meant. Rhodes didn't believe a word of this thing's promises, but what the hell else did Rhodes have to do?

He turned away somewhere else and set off walking through The Grid in no particular direction.

Chapter 5

Rhodes walked through The Grid looking around at everything—which was nothing.

The green lines and black squares passed under his feet. The grid lines and squares passed all around him and above him. The Grid moved behind him, but this bizarre landscape never changed.

"So....is Neiland still here somewhere?" he asked Fisher.

"The system interface records all your sensory input data for later processing," Fisher replied. "It allows the doctors and technicians to make any necessary modifications to the...."

"Do me a favor, okay, pal? Don't ever use the word, 'processing' again. It doesn't mean anything."

Fisher cocked his head to one side. Rhodes couldn't tell why he considered this program a male, but he did.

Fisher cocked his head in a very birdlike way. Something in the way he blinked his eyelids too quickly reminded Rhodes of a bird even though Fisher wasn't one.

Fisher's face migrated off to one side of Rhodes's view of The Grid. Then Fisher's face got smaller and moved up into the top righthand corner of Rhodes's view. Fisher didn't block Rhodes from seeing anything around him—which was nothing.

"So what the hell are we doing out here?" Rhodes grumbled. "Nothing is happening."

Fisher tilted his head the other way. "Your implants are all functioning correctly. I don't believe you've activated The Grid yet."

"What does that mean? How am I supposed to activate The Grid? It looks like it's already activated."

"This is just the base layer—the underlying matrix that forms The Grid. Once you activate it, it will feed you more information...."

"Just tell me *how* to activate it."

"I'm sorry, but I can't tell you that. Only you can activate it."

Rhodes groaned and rolled his eyes to Heaven. "Great. What exactly are you supposed to do—and don't tell me you're supposed to help me process anything."

"Try running."

"What good will that do? You said walking would help."

"Just try running. What harm can it do?"

Rhodes sighed and started running through The Grid. He didn't expect anything different to happen.

As soon as he started running, it did change. The grid lines morphed and altered their shape the same way Fisher's face did in the beginning.

The lines adjusted, bent, and angled upward, downward, and in every other direction. The squares reformed into mountains, trees, roads, buildings, and even a river flowing past.

The Grid landscape started as an outline of all those squares stretching into different forms. Then colors appeared and Rhodes found himself running through a landscape.

It looked as real as any he'd ever seen—except that his implants kept overlaying The Grid on everything. The squares and lines fed tons of information to Rhodes about the angle and trajectory of everything.

The Grid constantly adjusted itself in synch with Rhodes's movements. The grid lines even covered Rhodes himself.

"Where are we?" he asked Fisher.

"This is a simulated Grid landscape used for training. Stay watchful. The system will send you obstacles and adversaries to...."

Before he finished speaking, a Viper missile ruptured out of one of the nearby buildings. The Viper whistled straight for Rhodes's head.

He dove to one side and realized he was reacting too fast. He wouldn't have been able to avoid that missile in real life.

"Your implants are all processing data within normal parameters," Fisher told him. "Be careful. The training session is starting. You'll be entering the battle training sequence any second now."

Rhodes didn't have time to ask what that meant or what to expect. The Grid adjusted again and the landscape changed around him a second time—except that it wasn't the second time. It kept changing again and again in rapid succession.

The grid lines contorted and reformed. The mountains surrounding what looked like a town got bigger and then changed to enormous battleships.

The buildings Rhodes had just been running between morphed into giant alien creatures with horns, multiple eyes, and lashing tentacles.

The grid lines fed all that information into Rhodes's implants faster than he could think. The Grid kept shifting and changing shape, but it also responded to his senses.

It reacted to his thoughts even before he had a chance to think them. He couldn't tell anymore if they were sending him information or if he was controlling them from inside his own head. Was there even a difference anymore?

Gunfire erupted from somewhere and Rhodes's instincts took over. Some part of him already knew how to use the weapons installed on his implants.

He raised his arm and fired his scourge gun at one of the giant aliens—right at the place where the gunfire would have come from if the creature had been a building.

The scourge gun ejected a burst of some kind of energy Rhodes didn't recognize. A jet of whitish-purple electricity or maybe plasma forked out of the port on his arm.

At the same moment, the booster rockets on his legs activated without him even trying—but he did try. He did it without thinking. He already knew how to use his implants.

He launched off the ground and took off racing through the landscape. His senses picked up sights, sounds, and details faster than he could decide to read them.

The grid lines superimposed themselves on the landscape's surface. He saw them and didn't see them at the same time.

He didn't understand what was happening to him, but his implants merged all this information into a torrent of reactions and certainties that somehow made sense.

The information made sense to his implants even when it didn't make sense to him.

He maneuvered past hills, buildings, ships, and other attackers with no effort or thought at all. He swooped along the river heading closer to what looked like another cluster of buildings ahead.

The Grid adjusted in front of his eyes with every direction change and subtle head movement. The lines showed him from a distance that the buildings were about to change into more alien monsters.

Without thinking about it first, he released two seeker missiles from the ports on his elbows. They corkscrewed across the landscape and detonated the buildings to smithereens.

The landscape vanished instantly. All the mountains, buildings, roads, and attackers dissolved.

Rhodes powered down his boosters and landed on his feet on the tile floor in the white room next to Dr. Neiland.

Fisher didn't go away. His face stayed there in the upper righthand corner of Rhodes's view.

"That was excellent," Dr. Neiland told him in her usual steady undertone. "You mastered that perfectly. You'll enter The Grid every time you go into battle. The Grid adjusts how you process sensory data from your implants. Fisher will help you by alerting you to dangers and communicating with you about other information you might find necessary. Do you understand now?"

Rhodes nodded, but he barely saw her. "Yeah. I understand now."

"You'll undergo a more detailed training session tomorrow where you and Fisher can explore some of The Grid's finer nuances."

"What does that mean?" Rhodes asked.

"I would have to show you for you to understand. Our protocol calls for you to process this session first. You can return to your barracks and relax for the rest of the day."

Rhodes grimaced at her. He was really starting to hate the whole concept of processing anything.

Dr. Neiland led the way outside where she split off to a different part of the station. Rhodes headed for the barracks. Fisher still didn't go away.

Rhodes came to the station's central concourse, but instead of going back to the barracks, he turned in a different direction to explore another part of the station.

"You aren't authorized to enter this part of the station, Captain," Fisher told him.

"Did I ask you? Isn't there any way to shut you off?"

"I'm afraid not, Captain. Once activated, I will continue to serve my function as your SAM. I can't be shut off."

"Fan flippin' tastic," Rhodes snarled under his breath. "If you won't shut yourself off, at least be quiet. I don't need you commenting on everything I do."

"That is my function, Captain. My function is to alert you to dangers and potential risks in your environment."

"Do you see any dangers or potential risks in my environment?" Rhodes demanded.

"You're risking your position as commander of Battalion 1 by contravening your authority to enter this part of the station."

Rhodes snorted at him again. "I'm not risking anything, pal. I didn't ask for this. What the hell do I care if they make someone else commander of Battalion 1? I didn't ask for you, either, so do me a favor and keep your mouth shut."

Fisher didn't say anything for a while. He just hovered there at the corner of Rhodes's eye.

Rhodes explored a few sections of the station's power plant, the personnel quarters, and even the loading dock. Ships of all shapes and sizes came and went from there.

He stayed out much longer than he otherwise would have. He just wanted to spite Fisher. No one was going to tell him what to do, especially not some computer program installed in his brain.

Rhodes eventually got bored and wandered back to the barracks.

"I didn't ask for this, either, Captain," Fisher murmured on the way.

Rhodes didn't answer. He shouldn't have gone off on this program.

The frustration and hopeless despair of his situation escalated to the breaking point. Why couldn't the Legion just come out and ask him point blank to join this project? He might have been able to tolerate that.

The sensation of these implants attached to his body was becoming excruciating. It didn't hurt—not physically.

The feeling of them embedded in his flesh drove him out of his mind. He wanted to claw them out with his bare hands even if it left him bleeding, paralyzed, or dead.

He just wanted to go back to the way he was before. He wanted to feel normal.

He couldn't communicate any of that to anyone.

Now he had this thing floating in front of his eyes and listening to his every thought. Never in a million years would Rhodes confide how he felt to Fisher. That would be the day.

Rhodes returned to the barracks to find Colonel Kraft waiting for him. Kraft stood by the table where a black metal box sat next to his elbow.

"Colonel?" Rhodes greeted him. "What can I do for you?"

Kraft tapped the box. "This box contains all your personal effects from your posting with the Legion. Your old platoon just forwarded it here for you. The rest of your belongings have been sent onward to your family on Preinea. The Battalion 1 project calls for the member recruits' families to be informed of their deaths, either in combat or otherwise. I'm sorry, Captain."

Kraft walked out of the barracks and left those words ringing in Rhodes's ears. His family....informed of his death....

His family on Preinea thought he was dead. The Legion told them he was dead....so the Legion could revive him as this.....this machine.

He stared at the box. He already knew what was in it.

Some magnetic force pulled him toward it. Whatever shred of his humanity he might have left was in this box right now. He had to see it—just once.

He opened the box and looked inside. Three medals in a frame, a folded flag, a small wooden ball, and a string of blown-glass beads on a thin, flexible wire—what did they even mean anymore?

These could have belonged to anyone—any dead person. No one besides him would ever know what these things meant.

He carried each memory in his head. No one else would ever know what these random objects meant, where they came from, or what they were worth. They weren't worth anything—except to him.

He took the last item out of the box and looked down at a picture of himself, his wife, and their children. His wife was smiling with her arms around Rhodes. She kissed him on the cheek while he laughed at the camera.

The image of one of his sons had blurred. The boy had been horsing around too much so the image only caught him as a smear of movement.

Rhodes's daughter squirmed in his arms while she grinned at the camera. Rhodes's other son sat close to his mother with his arms around her waist.

Fisher cocked his head to one side, but he didn't look down at the picture. He always faced Rhodes no matter what Rhodes was doing. "Who are they?" Fisher asked.

Rhodes didn't answer. Fisher saw everything Rhodes saw. Fisher shared all of Rhodes's thoughts and feelings. Nothing happened in Rhodes's head that Fisher didn't share.

Fisher might even be able to see each memory attached to every item in this box. If the SAM recorded all of Rhodes's sensory input data, why not his memories, too?

Rhodes tossed the picture back into the box, took a step away from the table, aimed his forearm at the box, and fired his thermal cannon at it.

The plastic didn't ignite right away. He had to bombard the box for a full minute before the plastic started to melt.

As soon as it did, the oily goo of its liquifying walls burst into flame. He kept firing until he incinerated the box to ash along with everything inside it.

Chapter 6

R hodes stepped back into the small white room, but he was all alone this time—all except Fisher. "What are we doing back here?" Rhodes asked.

"You're here for a training session," Fisher replied.

"I know that," Rhodes snapped. "So why isn't Dr. Neiland here?"

"She'll monitor you from the lab. She doesn't need to be here."

Rhodes waited. "So....when is it going to start?"

"You just have to drop into The Grid. Then the session will start automatically."

Rhodes started to say that he didn't know how to enter The Grid, but before he could speak, he realized he did know how. He went into The Grid yesterday. He could do the same thing today.

Without thinking, he dropped through the floor—or it felt like that. The white walls vanished and he wound up in the black landscape with green lines all around him. He glanced around, but he didn't see anything but Fisher.

Just as fast, Rhodes left The Grid and got himself back into the white training room.

"Is there a problem, Captain?" Fisher asked. "We have a training session scheduled for today."

"The problem is you, pal. Find some way to switch yourself off. I don't want you hanging around getting in my face."

"I can't switch myself off."

"Then we'll get Dr. Neiland to do it."

Rhodes stormed out of the room and headed across the station toward Neiland's lab. Rhodes knew enough about Legion stations to remember where the lab was.

"I am telling you the truth, Captain," Fisher insisted. "I can't shut myself off. No one can."

"Shut the hell up, okay, man?" Rhodes countered. "I'm doing this so I don't have to listen to you yap in my ear all the time."

"My function is to...."

"Shut...up....." Rhodes snarled through gritted teeth. "Just....shut....up....."

Fisher must have sensed Rhodes teetering on the brink. Fisher didn't say anything else all the way to Neiland's lab.

The simple fact that Fisher was still there drove Rhodes over the edge. He had to get rid of this thing somehow. He couldn't go through his daily existence with some computer program's face right in front of him around the clock.

Rhodes burst into Neiland's lab and surprised her and the rest of the medical staff working on their equipment.

Neiland jumped off her stool. "You aren't authorized to come in here, Captain."

"Do you think I give a crap about that? I want you to shut off this.....this SAM or whatever the hell you call it."

She frowned at him. "Why do you want to shut it off? It's supposed to help you."

"Well, it isn't helping me!" He fought his voice under control. "Just get rid of it. I don't care what you have to do."

"We can't get rid of it. It's part of your neural programming....."

"I tried to explain this to you, Captain," Fisher interjected. "The interface...."

Rhodes lost his battle to stay composed. "Just shut the fuck up, you stupid machine! I'm not talking to you! I'm never talking to you! Got it? Just get the fuck out of my head!"

Dr. Irvine and Dr. Montague came over. "What seems to be the problem?" Dr. Montague asked.

"Nothing *seems* to be the problem! There IS a problem!" Rhodes snapped. "This SAM is driving me insane. Just get it the hell out of my sight. It isn't helping anything. It does nothing but interfere."

"But it hasn't done anything," Dr. Neiland pointed out.

"It's there!" Rhodes fired back. "It's there and it doesn't go away! Just get rid of it. I don't care how."

"We can't," Dr. Montague told him. "We could only get rid of it by deleting your entire neural core. We would have to take you permanently offline. You would be dead."

"I'm sorry, Captain," Dr. Neiland told him. "The SAMs are an integral part of your neural processing system. You won't be able to function without it."

"I won't be able to function *with* it."

"Just try. Go through the training session with the SAM and see how it works."

"No," he snapped. "I'm not going to do anything until you find a way to get rid of it. I didn't ask for this and I won't cooperate until you shut it off."

"Then I'll die, too, Captain," Fisher murmured.

"You're already dead, jackass!" Rhodes snapped. "You aren't alive. You're a program in a machine."

"I'm a sentient intelligence form," Fisher told him. "I have the same thoughts and feelings as a human being."

"Something tells me you don't," Rhodes snarled. "You don't know the first thing about what it means to be a human being."

"Be that as it may, I am sentient. I have as much right to existence as you do."

"Fine. You go exist somewhere else and leave me the hell alone." Rhodes turned away to leave, but he couldn't leave without Fisher.

The SAM's face followed Rhodes everywhere—except that Fisher didn't follow. He stayed right there in front of Rhodes's eyes no matter where Rhodes looked.

Rhodes stormed out of the lab, but he couldn't get away from Fisher. Fisher didn't say anything else, thank God. Rhodes probably would have done something disastrous if Fisher said a word.

Rhodes fumed in a rage on his way back to the barracks. He would have given just about anything to go off somewhere alone, but he couldn't even do that.

Underneath all his fury, he felt his life slipping through his fingers. Every anchor point to what he knew and understood about himself evaporated before his eyes. He was adrift with nothing.

He couldn't stand the sight of the barracks. He couldn't stand the sight of any-thing—not with Fisher hovering right there in front of his eyes.

Fisher kept staring at him no matter where Rhodes went. Fisher didn't say a word, but that somehow made it worse.

Having Fisher staring at him like that drove Rhodes batshit. He had to find a way to get rid of it. Just looking at Fisher all the time really tempted Rhodes to just end it.

At least this nightmare would be over then. Then Rhodes wouldn't have to think about his family mourning his death.

He would never see them again. That's why the Legion did it this way—so he wouldn't be able to go home.

It might be easier for the family just to believe he died on the battlefield. That didn't make it any easier for him. He really wished now that he did die on the battlefield.

He wandered around the station for a few more hours. Then he spent two hours at the loading dock watching ships launch and land, unload, and different crews work around the docks.

It didn't help. Nothing did. Nothing ever would because Rhodes was stuck like this forever now.

He was still sitting there when Colonel Kraft came to find him. Kraft sat down next to him and stared off into space, too.

"They did the same thing to me," Kraft finally blurted out. "They took me without my permission and told my family I was dead."

Rhodes cringed. He already knew he wasn't the only one. All those people in those capsules would wake up and find out the same thing. Then they would go through the same nightmare Rhodes was going through now.

How could he participate in this? How could he be the one to tell them to make the best of it and fight the Legion's battles anyway?

What was the alternative—offing himself right now? He already knew he wouldn't do that.

Kraft didn't even look at Rhodes. Kraft kept staring off into the stars. "I know it isn't the same thing as what they did to you, but they're still out there. My family is still out there. I took an oath to protect them and I have to keep it even if they think I'm dead. They'll never find out I kept my promise, but that doesn't matter. All that matters is that they're safe—or at least that I did what I could to keep them safe. I don't care about anything else."

Kraft turned around for the first time. His eyes didn't soften at all. He showed no sympathy or emotion, but something in his steadfast reserve told Rhodes loud and clear that Kraft did sympathize.

"I couldn't do what you're doing," Kraft murmured. "I couldn't take it, but you can. I don't know why, but you can take it so much better than anyone else I can think of. I know you'll do it. Don't ask me how, but you'll do it. You have to. You weren't made for anything else."

Kraft went back to staring at the stars for a while.

Rhodes stared at the side of Kraft's face and then Rhodes stared at the stars, too. The two men didn't say anything else.

Kraft didn't tell Rhodes anything Rhodes didn't already know. Of course Rhodes had to do it. Of course Rhodes had to do anything—absolutely anything—to protect his family even if they thought he was dead.

He could take it. That was the worst, most agonizing part. He knew he could take it, but that didn't ease the pain. He just wanted to die. Surviving was the worst torture imaginable.

He had to do it. He had to do whatever it took no matter how hard it was. He no longer had any other option.

The two men sat in silence for a long time before Kraft got up and left. Rhodes stayed where he was for a few more hours. He sensed himself getting tired. His system needed to go through a conversion cycle, but he didn't leave.

Maybe if he sat here long enough, the doctors and technicians would forget about him. They might forget that he was supposed to go through a training session today. Maybe they would forget about him entirely and he could spend the rest of his life on this loading dock.

That would never happen.

Fisher's constant presence irritated Rhodes's last nerve. He would have given anything to stab himself in the head so he could shut off the SAM just for a minute. A single minute, a single second without Fisher staring at him would have felt like heaven.

Chapter 7

R hodes stepped into the small white training room—or whatever the hell it was supposed to be.

He made up his mind to think of it as a padded cell where these doctors confined dangerously sick mental patients.

That's what he was—a dangerously sick mental patient. He really needed to be locked up.

"Don't say anything," he snarled under his breath. "Just don't say a goddamn word. Understand?"

"What if I see something threatening you?" Fisher asked.

"I don't care. Just keep it to yourself. I'm supposed to train here—not you."

"I'm supposed to train, too," Fisher pointed out. "We're supposed to train together so we can work together."

"I don't give a flying crap what we're supposed to do!" Rhodes snapped. "Just keep quiet and sit there. Don't do anything. I was fighting in the Legion long before I ever met you, pal. I can handle it on my own."

"General Brewster won't like it," Fisher murmured.

"I hope he doesn't." Rhodes shut the training room door behind him. "This bullshit has gone on long enough."

"What do you want me to do, then?" Fisher asked.

"Make yourself as small as possible so I don't see you."

"You mean like this?" Fisher shrank himself to a pinprick in the corner of Rhodes's vision.

"That's perfect. Just stay like that—and don't say anything. Not one peep."

Fisher didn't answer.

Rhodes dropped into The Grid and looked around.

After more than forty-eight hours of Fisher's constant presence and commentary, his absence suddenly unnerved Rhodes. The surroundings didn't quite look right without Fisher there.

Rhodes shrugged it off, started walking, and then took off at a run. The Grid morphed into a different landscape this time.

He found himself on an alien planet towering with enormous buildings in a style he didn't recognize. Purple-blue clouds floated in a smoggy sky streaked with long, orange-tinted clouds.

Rocky, iron mountains lined the distant horizon. Forests of what looked like sea kelp floated in the breeze between the mountains and the city crowded with these tall buildings.

Spacecraft hovered overhead and bombarded a pyramid in the distance. More fusion charges erupted from the pyramid, jetted around the countryside, and detonated the buildings.

Lasers scattered from building windows and smashed into the city streets. Rhodes didn't see right away what anyone was shooting at down there.

He ran faster heading for the pyramid. He didn't know or think about why, but he wanted to get there.

He could have used his boosters to launch off the ground and fly there faster, but he didn't want to fly into gunfire from either side. He didn't even know who was fighting or why—not that it mattered.

He forgot for an instant that this was a made-up simulation inside The Grid. This wasn't real.

He made it as far as the city outskirts before the ships in the air swiveled in his direction. They opened fire....and then the pyramid and the lasers in the windows did the same thing.

All those weapons aimed straight for him. He had to do something to survive.

Just for a second, he really wished Fisher was here. Rhodes wanted to ask someone for help.

He didn't have time to say a word before a fusion load from one of the aircraft smashed into the ground next to him.

The impact flung him off his feet. He cartwheeled through the air and saw himself falling toward the ground.

In a fraction of an instant, faster than thought, he changed. He didn't realize he was doing it until it was already happening.

The green grid lines that covered the landscape covered him, too. He saw them and felt them the same way he saw and felt the grid lines of the landscape. He saw and felt them at the same time that he didn't see or feel them at all.

They lingered there just beneath the surface—just where he could see them and not see them simultaneously.

He got a hint of that in his own limbs. The Grid was inside him—inside his implants somehow. The lines covered him all over, even the organic skin he still had.

Faster than thought, the grid lines morphed. The squares distorted and his body changed shape along with them.

He slammed into the ground full force and his four limbs distorted into enormous grinding wheels.

His torso changed into a vehicle. His wheels burned along the ground faster than he could run—faster than his boosters would make him fly.

He plowed over miles in a few seconds, smashed into the city streets, and saw for the first time what the spacecraft were shooting at.

Dozens of armored fighter vehicles crowded the streets. They all belonged to two army classes and the two sides plastered each other with different weapons.

He didn't have time to see who or what they were before he overtook the battle. His scourge guns erupted from his sides. They rotated outward to both sides so they could swivel in all directions without hitting his wheels.

All those vehicles from both sides turned their weapons on him. They fired from everywhere at once. Projectiles, lasers, and fusion blasts pounded his armor, but none of it harmed him.

He picked up speed to ram his way through, but all these vehicles in his path slowed him down. He needed to find another way.

Some forgotten instinct told him to go for the pyramid in the distance. The pyramid controlled all of this. If he could destroy it, he could shut down the whole battle.

He veered around a different building to punch his way through another blockade of vehicles. Their weaponry didn't damage him.

He extended his Viper missile ports above his back to get the blockade out of his way. At that moment, a spacecraft overhead opened fire and unleashed a hellish volley on the ground.

A deadly fusion shot forked right on top of him and sent him flying. His wheels slammed back down onto the ground still churning up the pavement.

He saw himself hurtling way too fast at a different building. He couldn't divert in time.

Without thinking, he changed shape again into a different kind of missile. His head elongated into a teardrop point. His arms and legs vanished inside a long, smooth housing.

His boosters fired and flame ejected from his tail mere seconds before he smashed into the building. He sailed out the other side into a hail of gunfire from both the pyramid and the spacecraft.

The spacecraft dropped out of orbit laying down a carpet of gunfire on the city below. The thunder of explosions got louder. Rhodes couldn't get to the pyramid fast enough.

His grid lines changed again with a single thought. A dozen giant limbs sprouted from his sides. He hit the ground on eight legs, vaulted over the vehicles, landed on another building's outer wall, and sprang off faster than ever.

He leapt from building to building getting closer to the pyramid. He was almost there.

He hit the last building and blasted off. He changed shape in midair and resumed his real form—if he even had a real form anymore.

He turned back into a man, fired his boosters, soared high over the pyramid, and rotated his thermal cannons downward to shoot directly into the pyramid's topmost point.

Fisher yelled out in Rhodes's ear, "Captain—look out!"

At that moment, something fired from the ground at the base of the pyramid. Rhodes had half a second to see some dark openings dotting the pavement around the pyramid's outer base.

The next instant, a catastrophic explosion went off in Rhodes's face. A brutal impact hit him in the chest and sent him flying.

He woke up lying in a different capsule. It wasn't his capsule in the barracks. The lid was closed.

The same prongs attached to his head and body, but he could think and see everything around him. He was back in Dr. Neiland's lab. She stood outside his capsule talking Dr. Montague.

Rhodes couldn't hear them through the capsule cover. The readings on all the capsule's controls flashed across the clear surface in front of him.

Rhodes groaned, but he couldn't turn over or move in any other way. The prongs held him in place.

They somehow erased any pain, but they didn't erase the excruciating wrongness of these implants embedded in his flesh.

Fisher was back to his normal size in the corner of Rhodes's vision. "How do you feel, Captain?" Fisher asked.

Rhodes tried to shut his eyes, but Fisher still didn't go away even then. Not even turning his head would make Fisher go away.

"I feel rotten if you really want to know the truth," Rhodes grumbled.

Fisher cocked his head to one side in that birdlike way of his. "I'm not detecting any malfunction or physical pain response."

"It isn't a physical pain response, you jackass!" Rhodes snapped and immediately fought himself back under control. "Sorry. I don't mean to take this out on you. I mean—I do mean to take it out on you, but it isn't a physical pain response."

"What is it, then?" Fisher inclined his head the other way. "Is it a mental distress response?"

Rhodes clamped his lips shut. "I guess you could call it that."

"Ah! I understand now," Fisher exclaimed. "You're in distress because you still haven't oriented to your implants. My programming indicates this is a natural part of the orientation process."

Rhodes bit his tongue to stop himself from answering. Having Fisher finally understand what the problem was—it almost hurt worse than before.

Rhodes didn't want Fisher to understand. Rhodes didn't want anyone to understand.

He didn't want anyone to find out how hard this was. He didn't want anyone to know ever under any circumstances. That would make it all too real.

Just then, the prongs retracted from Rhodes's head and body. They pulled inside the mattress and left him lying there, but the capsule cover didn't open.

He didn't move. He didn't want to get up. He didn't want to do any of this, but he already knew he had to.

"I would have warned you about those Viper ports near the pyramid, but you told me not to say anything," Fisher went on. "I really am only trying to help you, Captain. That is my only function."

Rhodes still didn't say anything. Something about that last blast must have finally knocked some sense into him.

He didn't really hold any of this against Fisher. Rhodes almost wished he had Fisher with him during that fight. It would have helped.

Rhodes still doubted how much help Fisher would have been, but at least Rhodes would have had someone.

He didn't realize this during all his years of fighting in the Legion. He always thought he had his comrades, officers, and fellow soldiers to keep him company.

He did, but it wasn't the same. None of them could replace one person in his own head who knew everything, saw everything, shared everything—someone whose only function was to make sure he didn't face this alone.

Now he understood what Fisher had been trying to tell him from the beginning. Fisher might give him information about threats and potential dangers.

That was only a small fraction of Fisher's true value. His real purpose was to help Rhodes process all of this exactly the way Fisher said.

Rhodes had enough trouble processing all of this—all of this sensory information and sensation bombarding him every second of the day and night.

Just the feeling of these implants invading his body and mind—it was more than he could cope with by himself.

He couldn't process it. He couldn't understand it. He couldn't tolerate it—but he had to. He couldn't get rid of them.

Fisher might not be able to understand it. Rhodes would never know how much of his own sensations Fisher felt or shared or understood.

For some strange reason, that didn't seem to matter, either. Fisher didn't have to understand it. He was just there.

Whatever else he might be—whether he was as alive or as sentient as a human being—that didn't matter, either. His fate remained irreparably bound to Rhodes's fate.

Whatever happened to Rhodes would happen to Fisher.

One of these days, Rhodes would go into a real battle with real weapons and real alien enemies.

Then he would need every ally he could get to cope with the danger. He would need one person—just one—one person he knew for certain cared as much about saving Rhodes's ass as he cared about saving it himself.

Who else would that be besides Fisher? How much closer could anyone get than riding around Rhodes's own head?

Whatever Fisher might be, Rhodes couldn't hate him anymore. Rhodes had enough problems without that.

Chapter 8

Rhodes sat up from his capsule in the barracks and put his feet on the floor. He really wished he could put his boots on.

Putting his boots on had become an essential daily ritual during his years in the Legion.

Those few seconds of putting his boots on and tying the laces—they gave him a chance to think about the day ahead and get his head screwed on straight.

Those few seconds had gotten him through years of war. He really missed those few seconds, especially now. He could have used a few seconds to get his head screwed on straight for the day ahead.

He stared down at his robotic feet. Right then, just in case he somehow forgot where he was and what was at stake, General Brewster and Colonel Kraft walked into the barracks.

Rhodes only glanced at them to see who it was. Then he went back to looking at his feet. Looking at his feet would have to take the place of putting his boots on.

"How are you feeling, Captain?" General Brewster asked.

"Do you really want to know?" Rhodes asked.

General Brewster frowned. A frown didn't look right on his boyish face.

Frowns suited Kraft much better. He didn't frown. His serious expression told Rhodes that Kraft already understood. He didn't have to ask how Rhodes was because Kraft already knew.

"It was an unfortunate incident in the training Grid last week," Brewster went on. "We didn't realize this project would cause such serious distress."

"Maybe you should have tested it on yourself first," Rhodes mumbled.

Brewster either didn't understand or pretended not to. "We're going to go ahead with the next training session. If we can't resolve these issues, we may have to scrap the project. I would hate to do that, Captain, and I'm sure you would hate it, too. We've all invested so much in this and we had such high hopes for the other recruits."

Rhodes resisted the urge to snort in the man's face. Recruits. These assholes never recruited anyone. They took these people by force and mutilated their bodies without their consent.

Rhodes didn't say that. Brewster didn't have to spell out the obvious threat. If Rhodes didn't find a way to function in this new reality, they would shut him down.

He could live with that. He would have welcomed it, but he couldn't do that to the rest of the battalion.

Those people sleeping in the other capsules—they didn't even know he was doing this for them, but he had no choice but to at least give them the choice.

He couldn't do anything that might make the brass shut *them* down. If it all went south—if he couldn't make it work—if he lost his ever-loving mind in this lunatic asylum—he had to at least try.

Brewster laid his hand on Rhodes's shoulder. "I know you'll do your best, Captain. I know you're as anxious to make this work as we are."

Rhodes would have liked to slap the man's hand away and spit at Brewster never to touch him again.

Rhodes didn't do that. He just sat there staring at his feet until the two men left.

He waited until they walked out of the barracks before he allowed himself to stand up and move around. He already knew what he had to do. He just had to go ahead and do it.

He had discovered what might have once been a bathroom or washroom attached to this barracks.

He understood enough about the conversion cycle by now. His body didn't need any kind of hygiene. The conversion cycle took care of that.

He'd replaced his usual morning routine with a habit of coming in here and looking at his reflection in the mirror. It was the only place in the whole station where he could see his reflection.

The left side of his face looked the way he remembered it. One blue eye looked out at him from under a shock of wavy brown hair.

The conversion cycle somehow stopped his hair from growing so it never got any longer. The hair didn't seem to die or need to be combed, either.

He ran his fingers through it just because. Running his fingers through his hair made him feel more human. It made him feel normal even if he didn't look normal.

His implants looked like they belonged to someone else. They looked like they belonged to another species. Even after a week, he still didn't recognize that they were even a part of him. They weren't.

After a week both in the hospital and recovering in the barracks, the feeling of wanting to tear the implants out still didn't go away. The feeling didn't fade at all.

If anything, it became more entrenched. The implants felt more alien, more invasive, and more excruciatingly irritating than ever.

They enraged him. They made him mind-numbingly furious at the people who did this to him, but he finally realized that Fisher wasn't one of those people.

Rhodes could have killed General Brewster and the three doctors. The only person around here Rhodes didn't feel like killing was Colonel Kraft.

Spending a week in what turned out to be one long conversion cycle somehow brought Rhodes to a grudging acceptance of the inevitable reality. He wouldn't be able to change any of this no matter what he did.

He already knew he wouldn't kill himself. He just had to find a way to live with it. Christ only knew how he would do that.

He didn't feel like killing Fisher anymore, either. Rhodes could almost forgive Fisher's intrusion simply because Fisher tried so hard to make it better. He was the only person who did.

Rhodes couldn't even call Fisher a person, yet he was the one person in this whole disaster who actually tried to help Rhodes. Not even Kraft did that.

Fisher had figured out how precious and vital these first few minutes of the day were to Rhodes's sanity.

Fisher had gotten into a morning habit of his own of making himself into a pinprick at this time of day so Rhodes wouldn't see him.

Fisher didn't speak to Rhodes until he had a chance to stare at his feet, think things over, and then look at himself in the mirror. Fisher didn't interrupt those private moments by speaking or making himself visible.

He waited until Rhodes turned away from the mirror and returned to the barracks before Fisher made himself bigger.

Even then, he expanded his face to half its usual size to make himself less obvious. "Good morning, Captain. How was your conversion cycle?"

"I'm okay, Fisher. Good morning."

"We have another training session today," Fisher pointed out.

"I know," Rhodes muttered.

"How would you like to approach it? We should discuss our strategy before we go in—to avoid another outcome like the last one."

Rhodes only nodded. "I guess you can advise me the way you've been programmed to. I guess that's just the way it has to be."

"It doesn't have to be that way if it causes you distress."

Rhodes took a deep breath and sat down on the edge of his capsule to face Fisher for the first time.

Rhodes had spent the last week avoiding all eye contact with Fisher. Rhodes wanted to erase Fisher from existence.

This was the first time Rhodes actually sat down to have a conversation with his SAM.

"You aren't what's causing me distress, Fisher," Rhodes began.

"Are you sure? You were adamant the last time we spoke that I was."

Rhodes pulled himself together with an effort. "I apologize for implying that. I suppose it was just the disorientation."

Fisher cocked his head to one side. "The disorientation should have dissipated by now. My programming indicates that the disorientation shouldn't last more than a few days."

"I'm going to go out on a limb and say that your programming was written by people who never went through this disorientation themselves. Dr. Irvine said I'm the first person to ever go through this process. So no one really knows how the disorientation will affect anyone. I could be like this for the rest of my life."

Fisher's expression changed, and for the first time ever, he broke eye contact and looked away. "You're right, Captain. That is a distinct possibility no one in this Battalion 1 project has foreseen. I apologize if my assessment made light of your difficulties."

Rhodes swallowed down a lump in his throat. He never dreamed having this conversation with a machine would be so hard.

He struggled to stop his voice from shaking, but it happened anyway. "Look, I don't want to do this and I know you don't, either. Neither of us is in any position to break off or change anything even if we wanted to. Let's just agree to work together and make the best of it, okay? I really don't know what else we can do."

"Of course, Captain. That is all I want, too. You have my word I will do everything in my power to make this process as tolerable for you as possible. If I can do anything for you, you only have to tell me."

Rhodes only nodded. He already knew Fisher felt that way without Fisher saying it.

Fisher was the only person here who would say it. He was absolutely the only person who would say it with any meaning.

General Brewster or one of the doctors might say they would do anything for Rhodes, but they would only say it as a formality. They wouldn't really mean it—not the way Fisher did.

Of course Fisher meant it. His whole existence hinged on Rhodes. Fisher had no choice but to help Rhodes. They were stuck in this together for good or bad.

Chapter 9

"What's your assessment of what I did during the last battle?" Rhodes asked Fisher on the way down the corridor.

"I don't understand the question, Captain."

"What did you think of what I did? How do you think I handled it—apart from not listening to you or letting you warn me or give me information about things? I guess I'm asking about how I changed shape."

"Ah! You're referring to the Grid alterations you used to break through the pyramid's defenses."

"Are those alterations part of my programming—or whatever you call it?"

"You can alter your Grid projection any way you want to, Captain. I thought you understood that."

Rhodes stopped in his tracks and turned to stare at Fisher. Fisher's face hovered right there in front of Rhodes's eyes. Rhodes didn't have to turn anywhere because Fisher was always there.

"Are you saying....I can take any shape—any shape at all?"

"Of course, Captain. That's what The Grid is for. It forms the fundamental layer structure of these simulated landscapes, but it will behave differently when you go into a real battle."

"What happens then?"

"The Grid feeds you information about the landscape, the terrain, obstacles, and any objects or enemy positions within The Grid. The Grid always affects your projection, though. You control that."

"So....I really can take any shape—even in a real battle?"

"Of course. That's the purpose of The Grid. It's much more useful to you than it is at creating these training landscapes."

Rhodes set off walking again. This revelation added a whole new dimension for him to wrap his brain around.

"Getting back to my original question, what did you think of how I used The Grid last time?"

"You used it perfectly well," Fisher replied. "You created useful shapes that adapted your weapons and movement style to each situation. If I had warned you about the Viper ports in time, you would have hit the target and achieved the objective."

Rhodes already knew that. He should have let Fisher communicate with him during the training session. What was the point of carrying around this SAM if he didn't let it help him?

They turned off into the same tiny training room. Rhodes didn't wait around long enough to think of it as a padded cell for a lunatic mental patient.

He dropped into The Grid immediately, started walking, and then burst into a run.

Fisher stayed full-sized in the upper righthand corner of Rhodes's view. The Grid shifted and they entered another alien planet landscape—a different one this time.

This one was another battle zone, but instead of a city with a pyramid in the distance, they found themselves in a dense jungle.

Aemon Legion Jackhammers went off all around Rhodes. Gunshots blasted through the trees, pelted trunks and branches, and nearly took Rhodes's head off.

He fired his boosters to launch above the canopy where he could get clear of the conflict.

He wound up flying into another raging air battle between Legion Predators on one side and some alien drone fighter craft on the other.

Viper missiles pounded him from both sides and knocked him out of the air. He felt himself falling.

"Get back down on the jungle floor, Captain!" Fisher called over the noise.

"It's a death trap down there! I can't go down there!"

"None of the gunfire is lower than five feet off the ground! You can get beneath it and make your way to the objective from there. You should be safe!"

Rhodes didn't argue. He sure as hell couldn't stay up here.

He fired his boosters again, banked into a dive, and plunged for the canopy. His instincts took over again and his body stretched out into a long, narrow shape.

His arms morphed into short wings and his boosters fired directly behind him.

He smashed through the canopy flying full speed. He didn't even try to slow down. He let his senses take over and the grid lines flowed into a different shape.

His grid lines morphed into the long, snaking coiled body of some boneless creature, swerved up level with the ground, and took off winding his way between the trees.

Jackhammers pounded back and forth above his head, but he never stood up tall enough for any of the gunfire to hit him.

Fisher still hovered in front of Rhodes's eyes. "Where's the objective?!" Rhodes roared. "I don't even know *what* the objective is!"

"It's a pit in the ground two miles northeast of here!" Fisher rotated slightly to the side and the Grid landscape in front of Rhodes changed again.

The lines pivoted and shrank to show Rhodes a full overhead map of the surrounding countryside.

The Grid fed tons of data to Rhodes's neural core. He read the landscape in the blink of an eye.

The Grid even highlighted enemy positions, craft, and ground troops he couldn't see with his eyes.

A few tall, modular complexes dotted the terrain at different locations. The alien enemy occupied most of these fortified positions.

The Grid fed Rhodes more information than he would ever need about what kind of weaponry the aliens were using, how many pieces they had set up at which locations, and even the weapons' targeting angles.

Legion platoons advanced through the jungle trying to surround the alien complexes. Dusters and Predators swooped overhead dropping breaker bombs on the structures. All those aircraft sent out Viper missiles to bombard the fortifications.

None of the Legion aircraft noticed the isolated pits Fisher mentioned. The Grid didn't show them as anything more than holes in the ground.

"What is that?" Rhodes asked.

"The enemy is hiding a toxic weapons lab down there," Fisher told him. "You have to drop a breaker bomb down that hole to destroy the lab."

"I don't have a breaker bomb."

"That's the objective. You have ten minutes before the lab becomes active. Then the aliens will release the toxin and kill every Legion soldier in The Grid, including you."

Rhodes shuddered. How was he supposed to drop a breaker bomb down the pit when he didn't have a breaker bomb?

That didn't matter. He had ten minutes to cross two miles of battlefield. He would just have to worry about bombing the pit after he got there.

"I'll need to refuel before I go out there," Rhodes remarked.

"You don't need to reload," Fisher replied.

"What do you mean?"

"Your implants include a fusion generator that powers all your...."

"Okay, spare me the science lecture. So....I don't need to reload anything? What about my Vipers?"

"You should always have a full complement no matter how many Vipers you fire. The generator replaces them after you release each one."

"How long does it take to replace them?"

"It's instantaneous."

Rhodes didn't ask the obvious question about how that was even scientifically possible. He didn't have time for that right now.

He really didn't care how some fusion generator instantaneously replaced Viper missiles as soon as they released. He had bigger things to worry about with everyone shooting at him.

He took off slithering faster than ever over the jungle floor. The Grid constantly pivoted and adjusted to give him a complete readout on the surrounding terrain, the aliens, their technology, and all the Legion positions.

The Grid showed him exactly where he was on the map. He was too far away from the pits and not making fast enough progress. He wouldn't get there in time.

"This won't work," he told Fisher. "We need a new strategy."

"What do you have in mind?"

"Hold onto your shorts, pal. I have an idea, but it might get dicey."

"I don't know what that word means," Fisher replied. "We only have five minutes left. What are you going to do? It has to be something quick."

"I don't have time to explain. Just hold onto something."

Rhodes realized in that moment that Fisher didn't have anything to hold onto, but it didn't matter.

Rhodes rocketed out of the jungle flying at his top speed. He changed in an instant, blasted through the gunfire coming from both sides, and broke the canopy.

He altered his grid lines to take the shape of one of the alien fighter drones and flew straight into the Legion Predators' gunfire.

"No, Captain!" Fisher roared, but Rhodes didn't listen. He rotated in the Predators' direction and opened fire with his scourge guns.

Two Predators were in the act of bombing the alien structures. At that moment, one Predator let loose its breaker bomb to pound the complex.

Rhodes changed shape again in a heartbeat, fired his boosters, and plunged for the building. He snatched the breaker bomb out of thin air.

"The bomb is set to blow in five seconds!" Fisher yelled. "Get it down the hole now!"

Rhodes couldn't fly any faster, so he tilted toward the ground and let gravity take over. He plummeted for the open pit. He was flying too fast to stop.

"Two seconds!" Fisher roared.

Rhodes scrambled to come up with some shape that would save his own life—and Fisher's.

The hole yawned in front of him. If he didn't do something now, he might as well fly down that hole and let the bomb blow him up along with the alien lab.

At the last possible second before impact, the grid lines covering his limbs splayed outward as wide as they would go. He flattened himself into a thin, springy piece of fabric fifty feet across.

He hit the ground, covered the hole, and the breaker bomb ripped out of his grip. It dropped down the pit and the fabric bounced across the hole.

"Get out of the way!" Fisher yelled, and without asking permission, he did something to the fabric's grid lines.

They collapsed in on themselves, converged into a ball, and Rhodes rolled clear onto the ground just as a colossal jet of fire exploded out of the hole.

Rhodes tumbled away wrapping his arms over his head. The explosion detonated twenty feet of soil around the hole. The eruption tossed him farther away from it. He somersaulted clear and pitched into the trees.

Rhodes picked himself up off the ground and looked around, but the landscape was already vanishing before his eyes. It turned black with just the grid lines in perfect squares all around him.

"I don't detect any injuries, Captain," Fisher murmured. "Congratulations on a successful training session."

"Thanks," Rhodes gasped. His heart wouldn't stop racing. "Thanks for your help."

"General Brewster is asking to see you as soon as you finish here. He wants to congratulate you, too."

Rhodes groaned. "Does he have to?"

"Apparently so. This project is his brainchild."

Rhodes snorted. "Why am I not surprised?"

Fisher cocked his head to study Rhodes. "Are you okay, Captain? You didn't have any difficulty manipulating The Grid that time."

Rhodes turned away. "Don't tell the general that."

"I can't communicate with him."

"I meant it figuratively. I don't want him to think I'm enjoying this."

"At least you aren't in distress about it."

"I mean I don't want him to think I actually like this or that I changed my opinion about what he's doing."

Fisher inclined his head the other way. *"Do* you like it?"

Rhodes distracted himself by leaving The Grid and going back to the training room. "I guess the problem is I like it too much. It could become addictive if I'm not careful."

Chapter 10

Rhodes walked into the lab and stopped on the threshold to stare at the line of twelve capsules in front of him.

The twelve new members of Battalion 1 lay asleep inside their capsules the way they had been when Rhodes first woke up.

Dr. Neiland, Dr. Irvine, Dr. Montague, General Brewster, and Colonel Kraft waited in the room for Rhodes to show up.

He barely looked at them. His attention fixated on the people sleeping inside the capsules.

Dr. Irvine and Dr. Neiland tapped away on two of the capsules' control panels. "We'll wake them up three at a time," Dr. Irvine announced. "You can explain everything to them better than we can, Captain."

"Leave me alone with them," Rhodes told him.

General Brewster and Dr. Montague both spun around to stare at him. "That would not be advisable," Dr. Montague replied.

"Then what the hell am I doing here?" Rhodes fired back. "Waking up to you idiots was the worst thing that ever happened to me. Do what you have to do to bring them out of stasis and then make yourselves scarce. I can explain it all much better if you aren't here."

General Brewster started to say, "You don't make the rules here, Captain...."

Kraft stopped him by laying a hand on Brewster's arm. Kraft gave the general a significant look and jerked his head toward the door.

Brewster's expression changed. "I guess it won't do any harm," he grumbled.

The three doctors kept casting furtive glances back and forth between Brewster and Rhodes. The doctors didn't stop working on the three capsules in question.

Kraft finally dragged Brewster out of the lab. Brewster gave orders to the doctors to do it Rhodes's way and then the doctors left, too.

The three capsules opened, but the people inside didn't stir. Rhodes stood over them staring down at them.

So many conflicting emotions wrestled in his chest. He actually considered for a minute if it wouldn't be better just to kill these people now. That would spare them the trouble of trying to orient to this nightmare.

His own words came back to haunt him. These people might not suffer any disorientation at all. They might be delighted with their new circumstances. Who was he to make that decision for them?

"Are you sure this is a good idea?" Fisher asked.

"None of this is a good idea. This whole project is a bad idea from start to finish. What the hell difference does it make if I'm here or someone else is?"

"You would know that better than I would, Captain."

"That's kinda the point, isn't it? I'm the only person alive who knows anything about this."

They had to cut their conversation short when the three recruits stirred. The doctors had woken up Sergeant David Cope, Corporal Bobby Poole, and Corporal Liam Taylor first. They groaned and twisted in bed.

"Their SAMs aren't activated yet, are they?" Rhodes asked Fisher.

"Not yet. They have to go through at least two days of orientation before the doctors introduce the new recruits to The Grid and their SAMs."

"Do you know anything about their SAMs?" Rhodes asked.

"No one knows anything about their SAMs," Fisher replied. "Each recruit gets a brand-new SAM that has never been brought online before. No one knows what a SAM will be or who or what its personality will be like before the doctors activate it."

Rhodes ran his hand across his eyes. "This really is the most incompetent military operation I ever heard of."

"I don't understand the problem, Captain. How can anyone know what a SAM will be before it comes online?"

Rhodes didn't have time to explain before the three recruits started to open their eyes. Cope opened his first.

He had sandy blonde hair, blue eyes, and fine, delicate features. He would have been a real lady killer in any other walk of life.

"Where am I?" he croaked.

"You're at Coleridge Station. It's a military base on the Fringes."

Cope groaned again and raised his hand to rub his eyes. That's when he touched his face. He looked down at his hand and blinked.

"You got injured on the battlefield," Rhodes explained. "You would have died. The Legion brought you here and repaired your limbs and organs by replacing them with these robotic implants. See? They did the same thing to me. Soldier! Look at me!"

Cope's eyes shot up to meet Rhodes, but Cope didn't seem to understand what he was seeing.

His one blue eye stared at Rhodes extra hard, but Cope didn't react at all.

"My name is Captain Corban Rhodes of the 249th Platoon. I got injured on the battlefield and I woke up here the same way you are now. Look at me, Sergeant!"

Cope blinked his one eye, but he still didn't respond. Just then, Poole raised his head and opened his eye.

He had a thick mop of dark brown hair that needed a trim. A scruff of black bristles covered the bottom half of his face. "Where am I?" he groaned in a deep, growly voice.

"You're at Coleridge Station on the Fringes. You got injured on the battlefield. You're in the hospital."

"I feel like shit," Poole grumbled.

"You're disoriented from being asleep for so long."

Rhodes had to turn his attention to Taylor. He kept trying to raise his arm to touch his own face, but he couldn't lift it. He groaned once...and then again.

Cope still stared at nothing. No one seemed to be home at all.

Rhodes went from one man to another trying to explain everything to them. "The weakness and nausea will pass. You'll feel better in a few minutes. Don't worry. You're going to be fine."

Poole blinked his one good eye a little harder and raised his hand in front of his face. He moved his fingers and rotated his wrist in deep concentration when he saw his robotic hand. "What.....the....hell......?"

"You almost died on the battlefield. The Legion replaced your injured limbs and damaged organs with these implants. They did the same thing to me."

Taylor groaned again. He still didn't open his eye.

Cope stared into space. He didn't move except to blink a few times.

Rhodes went back to Taylor's bed and checked the control panel. "Something's wrong," Rhodes told Fisher. "He should have woken up by now. Can you tell what the readings say about it?"

Poole looked up at him. "Huh?"

Rhodes opened his mouth to explain that he wasn't talking to Poole, but just then, the door burst open. The three doctors and the two officers charged into the room.

Dr. Neiland raced over to the panel attached to Taylor's bed. She started tapping frantically at the controls. "Something's wrong."

"I know," Rhodes told her. "I was just asking Fisher if he could figure it out."

Dr. Irvine approached Taylor's bed from the other side, leaned over the man, and pried back one of his eyelids to check his one good eye. "His pupils aren't reacting."

"His brainwaves are all normal," Dr. Neiland muttered. "So are his vital signs. I can't find anything wrong with him."

Poole turned to stare at them. "What's going on?"

Everyone ignored him. "His brainwaves are becoming erratic!" Dr. Neiland warned. "We have to intervene to stop the....."

She barely got the words out before Taylor convulsed on the bed. He spasmed once, lay still, and then jerked again.

"What's wrong with him?" General Brewster asked.

"Maybe he's only had half his body parts replaced by robotics and now his whole system is rejecting the implants," Rhodes snapped over his shoulder.

He shouldn't have used that moment to make his point, but Taylor made it for him.

The three doctors raced around the bed pushing every button they could find. "His brainwaves are entering an Epsilon state!" Dr. Neiland yelled. "He's going into cardiac arrest!"

"Defibrillate him!" Dr. Montague ordered.

"What's the point if his brain is gone?" Dr. Neiland countered. "We can't stop the cascade! It's already past the point of no return."

Taylor jolted again, and this time, the convulsions didn't stop. He jerked back and forth so violently that he bounced on the mattress.

Dr. Irvine dove for him to hold him down. "For God's sake, do something, Veronica!"

"I can't!" Dr. Neiland countered. "The implants are reacting to the cascade! They're attacking the base tissue layer."

Rhodes stood back watching in horror as the flesh around the implants turned black. It peeled away from the implants to expose bone, muscle, and bloody connective tissue.

The skin around Taylor's face curled away to reveal sections of skull. The eyelid of his one remaining eye shriveled, turned black, and rolled upward inside the socket.

The lid left one brown eyeball exposed for a second before the eye turned black and crumbled inward in a rotten, sunken mass.

The three doctors straightened up and stared down at the destroyed corpse. Only the implants looked intact. The cascade completely demolished the rest of Taylor's body.

"There must be some way to stop it," Dr. Irvine murmured.

"We've tried everything," Dr. Neiland choked.

"Well, we can't keep losing people like this," Dr. Irvine countered. "This is the tenth one we've lost."

Rhodes opened his mouth to suggest maybe they ought to consider not implanting these devices in any more unwilling soldiers, but a strangled scream cut him off.

Everyone turned around to see Poole sitting up on the edge of his capsule.

Rhodes realized too late that Poole was sitting in exactly the right position to see everything that happened to Taylor. It couldn't have happened at a worse time or in a worse place.

Poole let out one broken roar of agony and horror, shot off his bed, and raised both hands to his face.

He bared his teeth in a hideous grimace of pain and fury, dug his fingers into his forehead, and sank them into the skin around his facial implants.

Dr. Irvine and Dr. Montague stood on that side of Taylor's bed. They lunged for Poole trying to wrench his arms down.

"NO!!" Dr. Montague yelled,

No one could fight Poole's strength. He took his hands away from his face just long enough to swing his robotic arms.

He clubbed both doctors away and attacked his own head even harder. He clawed at his forehead and succeeded in tearing the implants out of the bone.

He roared in pain, but that only drove him farther into insanity. He yanked his facial implant away and blood spurted from the open wounds. It flooded into his one remaining eye.

He gave one almighty heave and ripped the implant the rest of the way off. It tore out of his implanted eye socket and a long cable of bloody electronic fibers snaked out of his skull.

He screamed in continuous bellows of dying fury, but nothing stopped him from tearing the rest of his implants off his head.

He used his left arm to rip his right arm off. It tore out of the shoulder socket and he used his one remaining arm to tear the rest of the implants away from his chest.

Blood poured down his body from all those wounds. Wires, cables, and artificial metal joints came away along with the components.

He threw them on the floor and finally, last of all, he tore out his own rib cage when he ripped the plate off his chest.

He buckled onto his knees strangling on his own blood. He eventually collapsed across the floor in a pool of his own blood.

Everyone stared at him in horror. Rhodes felt sick, but he had to watch to the very end.

Dr. Neiland sobbed quietly in a corner. The other two doctors stared down at Poole's body in stunned disbelief. Neither of the two officers moved a muscle.

After what seemed like hours, Dr. Irvine turned to Cope. He didn't move through the whole process. He lay on his mattress staring up with the same blank expression he gave Rhodes when Cope first woke up.

Dr. Irvine checked the readings on Cope's capsule. "He's gone, too. His brainwaves are negligible. He should have come out of the disorientation by now. His whole system shut down. He's gone."

Rhodes couldn't watch this anymore. He cut a wide circle around Poole's body and left the lab for the other side of the station. These three recruits were someone else's problem. The people who did this could clean up their own mess.

Rhodes went back to the loading dock. It was the only place in this nuthouse where he could be alone and think.

"I'm sorry you had to see that, Captain," Fisher murmured after a while.

"I'm not," Rhodes replied. "That was nothing I haven't thought about doing a million times myself. It actually makes me feel better. Now I know I'm not the only one."

Chapter 11

Rhodes stood back across the room and watched the doctors wake up the next three recruits. He didn't hold out much hope that this batch would play out any differently than the first three.

He didn't voice his worst fears to anyone, not even Fisher. Even so, Rhodes sensed the underlying unspoken subtext.

If this didn't work, if the doctors didn't succeed in waking up anyone else, Rhodes would be the only person alive with these implants. He would be one of a kind.

The Legion brass would probably decide he was too valuable to send into battle after all. He might get trapped at Coleridge Station for the rest of eternity—or however long he lived before he decided to end his own misery.

The doctors woke up Lieutenant Heath Lauer, Corporal Rudy Fuentes, and Alyssa Thackery next. They went through the same process of groaning, opening their eyes, and discovering their implants.

Rhodes didn't get involved when the doctors explained everything.

Thackery stood up right away. She kept raising her hands, turning them in all directions, and moving her limbs in amazement.

"This is great!" she exclaimed. "I feel wonderful. I've never felt this good."

"Do you feel any disorientation or confusion?" Dr. Neiland asked.

"No, I feel fantastic!" Thackery grinned. "I should have signed up for this years ago."

"What's wrong with her?" Fisher asked. "Why isn't she disoriented?"

Rhodes didn't answer. No one outside his own head could hear Fisher. It usually disturbed people to hear Rhodes talking to someone no one else could see.

Thackery had a tight, muscular body like she worked out a lot before this. She had a springy quality that made Rhodes think she actually might be a soldier after all even though she wasn't.

Fuentes sat up more slowly. He couldn't be more than twenty-one with a dull, slack expression.

He looked around him blinking in a daze for a long time. "Do you remember where you were before you woke up here?" Dr. Irvine asked him.

"Um....I think.....I was on a ship...." Fuentes stammered.

"Do you remember your own name?"

"Um.....Rudy....."

Dr. Irvine motioned for Rhodes to come over. "This is Captain Corban Rhodes. He'll be your commanding officer from now on." Dr. Irvine murmured in Rhodes's ear. "Ask him some questions while I check his brainwave readings."

"Do you understand where you are, Corporal?" Rhodes asked. "Did you hear the doctor tell you just now where you are?"

"Yes, Sir," Fuentes replied in the same numb tone.

"What did he say? Where did the doctor say you are?"

"Um.....I think it was.....something about Cole something Station."

"Do you remember why the doctor said the Legion brought you here?" Rhodes asked.

"Yes, Sir. He said....I got hurt...and they brought me here....to fix me....."

Rhodes picked up Fuentes's arm. "Do you know what this is, Corporal?"

"Um.....my arm, Sir?"

Rhodes glanced at Dr. Irvine. "What's wrong? Is his brain shutting down?"

"All his brainwaves are reading as normal. His service record says he had an IQ of ninety before this, so maybe he was like this before."

Rhodes turned back to Fuentes. "Do you know why you're here, Corporal? Do you know why the doctors replaced your limbs and organs with these machines?"

"To fight the war, Sir?"

Rhodes glanced at Irvine again, but Irvine just shrugged. "I can't find anything wrong with him. As long as he doesn't suffer from any disorientation, he should be fine."

Rhodes left it at that and turned to the last of the three new recruits. Lauer sat on his bed glaring at everyone. He had longish, messy black hair, a thick, messy black beard, and hard black eyes.

He had a big, burly, dangerously powerful frame. He looked like he could get violent given the right provocation.

He answered Dr. Montague in gruff, one-word grunts.

"This is Captain Corban Rhodes," Dr. Montague told Lauer. "He'll be in command of your unit as soon as you orient to your new implants."

Lauer glared at Rhodes, dipped his chin once, and clipped, "Sir."

"Can you remember where you were before you woke up here, Lieutenant?" Rhodes asked.

"Yes, Sir," Lauer snapped.

Rhodes waited for him to say something else. "Are you aware of why you're here and what Battalion 1's mission is?"

"Yes, Sir."

Rhodes gave it up. He decided to wait and see just how disoriented Lauer turned out to be.

At least he didn't attack himself and tear his implants out. Anything less than that would be a win—that and not dying of convulsions or going brain-dead in his capsule.

None of the three recruits seemed to suffer from any disorientation at all—not on the surface. Thackery couldn't have been more delighted with her new circumstances. Fuentes didn't respond to anyone with any more emotion than before.

Lauer kept glaring at everyone and refused to say a word other than, "Yes, Sir," and "No, Sir."

Once the doctors assured themselves that none of the three recruits was going down in flames, the doctors left the three recruits with Rhodes.

He took them back to the barracks and explained the capsules to them.

"This is awesome!" Thackery exclaimed and then went over to the computer terminal. "I always wanted time to study all this stuff."

"I don't know how much free time we'll have," Rhodes told her. "As soon as the battalion finishes training, the Legion will deploy us back on the battlefield."

Fuentes headed for the terminal, too. "I want to call my mother. I want to tell her I'm okay. She's probably wondering where I am."

"You can't, Corporal," Rhodes told him. "I'm sorry, but all your families have been notified that you died in the accidents that brought you here. You can't go home and you can't talk to your families. I'm sorry."

Fuentes's features screwed up in knots. "But.....I have to! My family is all I have! I can't lose them!"

"I'm sorry, Corporal. The same thing happened to me and most of the staff here. We all lost people we love."

"But....I have to!" Fuentes's voice spiked. "You can't stop me! I have to....and I'm going to!"

He smacked Rhodes's hands away and then charged past him to the terminal. Rhodes lunged for him to stop him.

"He can't, Captain," Fisher murmured. "These terminals don't connect to any outside communications system."

Rhodes stopped there across the room. Fuentes raced to the terminal. Thackery side-stepped to get out of the way to give him space to get near it.

Fuentes threw himself down at the desk and scrambled on the terminal pushing a million buttons.

He kept muttering to himself, "I have to! I have to!"

Rhodes watched him for a while before he crossed to Fuentes's side. Rhodes laid his hand on the boy's shoulder. "You can't, man. I'm sorry."

Fuentes blasted out of the chair, tried to knock Rhodes aside a second time, and then collapsed on his knees. He sprawled across the desk, extended his arms over his head, and burst into loud, agonized sobs.

"NO!!" he howled. "NO!!"

Lauer turned his head all the way away and glared at the wall. Thackery blinked at Fuentes in disbelief.

Rhodes took a few steps toward the boy, but Rhodes hesitated to intervene.

"It looks like he was disoriented after all," Fisher murmured.

Rhodes didn't answer that time, either. He was beginning to see a trend here.

This so-called disorientation was bound to reveal itself in all kinds of ways. It definitely wouldn't go away anytime soon.

He took hold of Fuentes's shoulders and pulled him off the desk. "Come here, Corporal. Sit down over here."

He steered Fuentes to a nearby bench at the table. Fuentes stayed crumpled over shaking with pitiful sobs, but he didn't resist.

Rhodes sat down next to him and patted Fuentes on the back. "I'm sorry, man. The same thing happened to me."

Fuentes doubled over crying even harder and buried his face in Rhodes's chest.

Rhodes froze when Fuentes wrapped his arms around Rhodes's rib cage. Fuentes held on way too tightly and completely broke down like a child.

Rhodes hesitated again. Then he threw caution to the wind, laid his arm over Fuentes's shoulders, and held him.

Nothing would make this better. Holding Fuentes wouldn't make it better, but just one person trying to care made a big difference.

Rhodes learned that the hard way. He learned that from Fisher.

"They're all I have!" Fuentes howled. "My family is all I have!"

"I know," Rhodes murmured. "The same thing happened to me."

Thackery stood there staring at them for a long time. Lauer kept his head turned and refused to look at anyone.

Fuentes didn't show any sign of letting up. After half an hour of straight crying, Rhodes couldn't take it anymore.

He dragged Fuentes to his feet, but Fuentes refused to unwrap his arms from around Rhodes's body.

Rhodes staggered across the barracks to the capsule assigned to Fuentes. Rhodes had to use force to pry the kid off.

"Lie down here, Rudy," Rhodes ordered. "Lie down and try to get some sleep. You'll feel better when you wake up."

Fuentes obeyed. He might not be the sharpest tack in the box, but he knew an order when he heard one.

Rhodes manually straightened out Fuentes's limbs, positioned him in the right place, and stood up. "Stay there and don't move until you wake up," Rhodes told him. "That's an order."

Fuentes sniffed, "Yes, Sir," and lay still.

Rhodes closed the capsule cover and Fuentes's body jolted when the prongs locked him into place. Rhodes checked that the conversion cycle was beginning normally.

Silence fell over the barracks. Thackery sat back down at the terminal and started working on it in Fuentes's place. Lauer didn't move to look at anyone.

Rhodes left them there. He needed to be alone.

He went out to the loading dock, but he didn't sit down. He leaned against the wall and watched the ships coming in and going out.

"I'm sorry, Captain," Fisher murmured in an undertone.

"Why are you sorry? You didn't do any of this."

"I'm sorry for your loss. I didn't realize until now how deep your distress must have been. I underestimated the pain your distress must be causing you."

"I would appreciate it if you didn't try to get inside my head, pal," Rhodes snapped. "What I think and what I feel is my business, not yours."

"I can't help it, Captain. I *am* inside your head."

"That doesn't mean you can help yourself to my thoughts and feelings."

Fisher shut his mouth. His silence made Rhodes feel worse.

"Look, what I think and feel is for me to process, not you," he told Fisher. "It doesn't help me to have you talking about it all the time."

"I thought you wanted to talk about it."

"Well, I don't. Talking about it just brings up the pain all over again."

"But the pain is already up, as you say," Fisher pointed out. "It doesn't go away. It appears that you are not disoriented at all. It appears to me as if this pain is simply your default neural state now."

"Well, what the hell did you expect?!" Rhodes heard his voice rising again. "You can't just tear a man away from his family and everything he knows and holds dear and not have it affect him! What did you think? That isn't disorientation. I'm perfectly oriented. I understand perfectly the situation I'm in. That's exactly the problem! You can't fix it just by getting used to it. It just becomes more galling with every passing day. That isn't fixing the problem. That *is* the problem! Don't you get it?"

"I'm sorry, Captain," Fisher murmured. "I didn't get it before, but I do now. I don't know how to help you. That's all I want to do."

"You can help me by not bringing it up again—ever. Bringing it up only throws it in my face that nothing can ever fix it. Just drop it and let me deal with the situation at hand. That's all I'm asking."

"But isn't this the situation at hand? Isn't this the situation with Fuentes? What if the other recruits suffer the same distress? That will affect you, too. It will bring it up again and you will have to think about your own loss. How will it ever go away?"

Rhodes covered his eyes. He already knew that.

He wouldn't be able to get out of this probably ever. His subordinates' distress would only make his distress more obvious and more excruciating.

He would never escape it because there was no escape. This was his life now.

Chapter 12

Rhodes led Thackery, Fuentes, and Lauer into a much larger training room.

"This is where our battalion will come to train from now on," Rhodes told them. "This is where we'll come to get used to our new implants and prepare ourselves to use them in battle."

He went around the room and pointed out each recruit's weapons, boosters, and Viper ports.

"This is great!" Thackery chortled.

"Shut up!" Fuentes shrieked. "It isn't great! It's a nightmare!"

"I'm just saying...." Thackery countered. "It beats the hell out of dying."

"SHUT UP!!" Fuentes roared.

Rhodes raised his hands. "Take it easy, all of you. We have a lot of work to do and six more people to wake up. They all have to go through training before we can get out of here. Let's try to concentrate on the job, okay? Fighting amongst ourselves won't accomplish anything. Are you ready?"

Thackery looked around. "What are we doing here? There's nothing here."

"We're about to enter our training grounds. I'll take you there first and then we'll activate your implants."

"What does that mean?" she asked.

"I'm about to show you. I can't explain it to you without showing you."

"This is stupid," Fuentes grumbled. He'd become surly and snappish ever since he found out about his family.

Lauer still didn't talk unless he absolutely had to. He glared at everyone twice as menacingly.

Rhodes assumed Lauer had a family, too. This simmering hostility was his way of dealing with the loss.

Rhodes checked on Fisher. They'd discussed this beforehand. Fisher could interface with the station's medical systems and access The Grid for Rhodes and his three recruits.

Rhodes gave Fisher a silent signal and all four dropped into The Grid. Thackery and Fuentes spun around to stare at everything. Lauer's eyes darted from side to side and then up at the ceiling.

"This is The Grid," Rhodes explained. "It's the base layer for our training simulations. It also forms a matrix you'll be able to use to manipulate your implants."

"What does that mean?" Thackery asked.

Rhodes shrugged. "I'll show you, but first, you need to meet your SAMs."

"Whats?" Fuentes asked.

"It stands for Simulated Augmentation Matrix." Rhodes waved that away. "That isn't important. It's a computer program in your head that rides around with you and helps you cope and process what you're seeing and experiencing."

"I don't get it," Thackery countered.

Rhodes signaled Fisher again. "You're going to see some shapes in front of your eyes and then the shapes will form an image you can talk to. Consider this your inner companion whose only job is to help you."

Fuentes stared at something in front of his eyes. "I see it! It's forming!"

Fisher adjusted something else to give Rhodes an interface with each recruit's Grid.

Fuentes's SAM went through a rapid blur of changes before it settled into a face. This one looked more feline in nature, but it kept morphing into something more alien than a feline.

The cheeks stretched outward from both sides, twisted in gruesome shapes, and then settled back into something quasi-feline.

Thackery burst out laughing when she saw her SAM. It twisted and squiggled with messy lines....and it stayed that way.

The tangled grid lines kept knotting in different combined patterns, reworking themselves, and reforming in different configurations. They never settled into one shape.

Lauer's SAM started as a bunch of different animal faces and eventually solidified into a robot head. It looked more like a skull with black eyes, no cheeks or lips, and a bony jaw and cheekbones.

Each recruit held a conversation with their SAM and then all six turned to Rhodes. They could see each other through the interface.

"This is Fisher," Rhodes told the others. "He's my SAM."

Fuentes curled his lip at Fisher. "He's ugly!"

"I'm sure each of us likes our own SAM the best," Rhodes replied. "The important thing is that we each trust our own SAM. The SAMs are here to help us. Their lives depend on us so they have every reason to help us. You can trust your SAM to give you information and help you with your training."

"Are we supposed to get to know each other's SAMs?" Thackery asked. "Will we interface with each other like this in battle?"

"I really don't know," Rhodes replied. "All of this is completely experimental. I was the first person the doctors woke up after receiving these implants—or I should say I'm the first person to survive waking up. None of this has ever been done before."

Lauer snorted and grumbled, "Great."

Rhodes chose to ignore the remark. "Assuming we will interface in battle, let's get to know each other. Each of you can introduce the rest of us to your SAM."

"This is Koenig," Thackery began. "He's a genius."

A metallic, robotic voice came from the tangle of squiggles hovering in front of Thackery. The voice didn't sound male or female. "I do my best," Koenig murmured. "It is a pleasure to meet you, Captain."

"None of the SAMs have ever been online before," Rhodes explained to the three recruits. "They're just learning all of this the same way we are."

"I am Van," Fuentes's feline SAM rasped in a deep, throaty female voice. It echoed from far away. "I'm sure Rudy and I will get along famously."

"And I am Wild," Lauer's robot skull croaked in a short, harsh voice. The voice really sounded like it belonged to a skull.

"Okay, now we all know each other," Rhodes went on. "Let's learn how to use The Grid and you can start using your implants in a battle scenario."

"What do you mean by that?" Thackery asked.

"I'll show you. Follow me."

Rhodes set off walking through The Grid. He would have liked to talk to Fisher about the three subordinates, but Rhodes couldn't do that while they interfaced. The recruits would be able to hear every word.

Fuentes and Thackery started talking to their SAMs anyway. Van and Koenig asked Fuentes and Thackery a million questions about their families, their previous lives, and the circumstances that brought them here.

"I came from Zoter continent on Preinea," Fuentes told Van. "My mother and brothers and sisters still live there." He started to choke up again. "I sent my mother my pay every week to help support my younger brothers and sisters. I don't know what she'll do without that money."

"She'll get your compensation package from the Legion," Van replied in her deep, throaty voice. "The Legion will take care of your family. Don't worry."

"I just can't believe I'll never see them again!" he stammered.

"I was posted on the *Thuzuno* before this," Thackery gushed to Koenig. "I died a horrible death when I got electrocuted. I never had any family. I'm an orphan so I guess I'm not missing anything. This is so great! I worked on military vessels and Legion space stations all my life. I never expected I could actually take part in any of the wars. This is a dream come true!"

"I'm happy for you," Koenig murmured in that flat, distant tone. "I'm sure you'll make an outstanding soldier."

Wild didn't say a word to Lauer. These SAMs certainly matched their behavior to the person carrying them. Wild seemed to sense intuitively that Lauer didn't want to talk.

Maybe Wild would be the best thing for Lauer. Lauer didn't have to worry about Wild expecting anything from him or prying into his thoughts and feelings. Rhodes almost envied Lauer for that.

Rhodes dismissed that thought right away. He didn't want another SAM. Rhodes had gotten used to Fisher. They'd come to an understanding.

In a way, talking to Fisher did actually help Rhodes even when they disagreed. Even telling Fisher to butt out and mind his own business helped.

Rhodes distracted himself by concentrating on the three recruits. "Let's pick up the pace a little bit. We're going to run now."

He started running. The other three followed and The Grid changed around them. The grid lines grew into a towering valley of cliffs rising to mountain peaks on both sides.

White clouds hung in the blue sky overhead and a river snaked through the deep valley bottom with trees growing on either side.

"Here we go!" Rhodes called and the landscape adjusted a little more.

His senses told him a split second before it happened that the training session was about to start. He raised both arms, but gunfire erupted from the high cliffs before Rhodes could do anything.

Fuentes screamed and threw his hands in front of his face. "Shoot back at them!" Rhodes called. "Target their positions and fire!"

Lauer reacted first. He raised his arms and blasted two enemy positions right away.

Rhodes heard Wild yelling information into Lauer's ears the whole time. So much for them not talking.

"Four more coming up on your right—lasers this time!" Wild barked. "Fire your Vipers to take them out! Watch out for snipers behind that clump of trees! Use your thermal cannons! Set the trees on fire and you'll finish them!"

They worked in a seamless rhythm. Lauer never once questioned Wild's instructions.

Lauer reacted to all of Wild's instructions instantly, unleashed his Vipers to smash the laser positions, and then incinerated the snipers by igniting the foliage around their hiding place.

Thackery took longer to get the hang of it. Koenig didn't bark with the same commanding tone. Thackery wasn't in the habit of taking orders from anyone. She didn't respond to Koenig's instructions fast enough.

A jet of fusion fire hammered into the ground near her. "Use your thermals to block their fire," Koenig suggested.

"How?!" Thackery yelled back.

"Fire your thermal cannons at their fusion shots," Koenig replied in the same unruffled undertone. "Fusion loads can't penetrate thermal fields."

"WHAT?!!" Thackery yelled back. "I CAN'T HEAR YOU!!"

Fuentes kept screaming every time enemy fire came too close to him. Van tried to encourage him. "You can shoot back at them, Rudy! Your weapons are stronger than theirs."

He didn't respond until Rhodes fought his way over there. Rhodes dove in front of Fuentes and bombarded the enemy positions to protect Fuentes until he got his head clear.

"Come up here with me!" Rhodes yelled over his shoulder. "Join your scourge gun fire with mine! Come on, Rudy!"

Fuentes fought his way out of his terror, cast a helpless look around, and saw Van in front of him. "You can do this, Rudy," she told him. "You can fight back. I'll help you. Look."

She adjusted the grid lines. Two targeting signals appeared on The Grid to show the enemy shooter's position.

That one small change cleared the way for him to advance to Rhodes's side. Fuentes's expression hardened and he opened fire with his scourge guns.

Thackery finally got through to Koenig that he needed to talk louder. He floated closer to her ear and turned up his volume to yell directly into her ear.

She switched to thermals, fired into the fusion blasts, and blocked them until she could unload her Vipers on the enemy targets.

"Shut it down," Rhodes told Fisher. "That's enough for today."

The hidden enemies in the cliffs stopped shooting. The three recruits lowered their weapons and the landscape vanished.

"Now you know what The Grid is," Rhodes told them. "Tomorrow's training session will be more complicated. Once you master that, we'll be able to wake up the next three."

Chapter 13

Fisher disconnected his interface from the other SAMs on the way back to the barracks. "That went well, I thought," he told Rhodes.

Rhodes checked that the three recruits were far enough away not to overhear him. "It went better than I expected."

"Wild and Lauer worked well together. I didn't expect that. I expected Lauer to resist the SAM."

Rhodes glanced over at Lauer. All three recruits walked down the hall holding separate conversations with their SAMs. Even Lauer talked into thin air.

Rhodes did his best not to listen to any of their conversations. This was going to become an ongoing problem. Each person would have to find a private place where they could talk to their SAMs away from everyone else.

Rhodes would have to do the same thing. He would have to be careful that none of his subordinates ever heard him talking to Fisher about anything personal.

Rhodes would also have to be careful that none of his subordinates heard him talking to Fisher about any of his subordinates.

Rhodes never had this problem in the Legion. He never carried his closest confidant around in his head before.

"You handled them well," Fisher went on. "It seems to help them when the person training them has been through it themselves."

"That's the point, isn't it? You and Neiland couldn't explain it to me because you didn't really understand what I was going through."

"You are the best officer for them, Captain," Fisher agreed. "I see that now."

"Thank you for handling the interface. I appreciate your help."

"Thank you, Captain!" Fisher exclaimed. "That is such high praise coming from you."

Rhodes winced and looked away. He shouldn't have waited this long to express his gratitude to Fisher.

The four soldiers returned to the barracks. Lauer looked around. "I'm hungry. I want to eat something."

Rhodes looked up. This was the most Lauer had spoken since he woke up.

"You shouldn't be hungry," Rhodes replied. "The conversion cycle should take care of that."

"I mean I feel like eating something. I always ate whenever I came back to my quarters after a battle. It doesn't feel right not to."

"I know what you mean," Rhodes replied. "It doesn't feel like we're human at all without that."

"Maybe we can do something similar," Thackery suggested.

"How can we if we don't eat?" Lauer asked.

"We can sit around the table, talk, and.....I don't know. We could gamble or something."

Lauer burst out in deep, chesty, rumbling laughter. "Gamble?! You want to gamble?! What are you—a hustler?"

"Well, what else is there to do around a table instead of eat? We have to do something."

"I have an idea," Rhodes interrupted. "All of you sit down at the table."

The three recruits sat down at the table. Rhodes went to the end of the bench and used his laser to cut a block of wood off one of the boards.

"Are you sure this is allowed, Sir?" Fuentes asked.

"I'm making a command decision in the interest of our long-term sanity. If someone has a problem with that, they can let me know."

Rhodes sat down at the table next to Lauer. Fuentes and Thackery sat across from them. "What are you going to do?" Thackery asked.

"I used to play this game with my kids. It will take our minds off how hungry we are."

"A nice slab of steak would be nice about now," Lauer muttered.

"We're taking our minds off it, not talking about it," Rhodes pointed out. "Talking about it will make it worse."

"So what's with the wood?" Thackery asked. "It doesn't look very interesting."

"Watch and learn, children."

The three recruits laughed. Rhodes used his laser to cut the block into five equal squares. Then he used his thermal cannon to burn dots into each side to make dice.

"I don't get it," Thackery complained.

"You haven't seen much of the world, have you?" Lauer growled. "You've been too busy pushing around a broom while the rest of your ship crews see the world."

Rhodes held up the first die. "Roll a six—that's the ship. Roll a five—that's the captain."

"That's you, Sir," Fuentes exclaimed.

"That's right. Roll a four—that's the crew. You roll all five dice until you get the ship, the captain, and the crew. Once you do that, you add up the other two dice to find out your cargo. That's your score for the turn and you pass it on to the next person. The first person to get a hundred points is the winner. Got it?"

Thackery grinned at him. "Got it."

Rhodes turned to Fuentes. "Do you understand, Corporal?"

Fuentes frowned. "I was never good at math."

"I'll help you."

"Just don't cheat," Lauer countered.

Rhodes's hand flew to his heart. "Me—cheat? I'm offended, Lieutenant."

Lauer snorted, but Rhodes definitely saw Lauer fighting back a grin under that beard. He was starting to come out of his shell—or it appeared that way.

Rhodes handed the dice to Thackery. "Ladies first."

She didn't try to hide her smirk. She rolled once and got a six, a five, a four, a three, and a two.

She shot both fists in the air and hooted. "Straight flush! Read 'em and weep!"

"It isn't a flush," Rhodes pointed out. "They're all the same color."

"What the hell do I care? I got it the first time."

"It isn't that good a hand, you know," Lauer told her. "You only got five points."

"See if you can do better." She shoved the dice at him.

He picked them up, rolled them, and got two sixes, two fives, and a four.

"That's what I'm talking about!" he crowed. "Eleven points. Eat it, baby."

Thackery pretended to sulk. "Cheater."

Rhodes took the dice. "My turn."

"Get five sixes, Sir," Lauer told him and laughed.

Rhodes couldn't help but grin back. This game was turning out to be the best thing for all of them, including him. He actually felt like this unit was coming together.

Maybe these people could somehow replace what each of them lost—or partially replace it.

Rhodes rolled and got a five, a three, two twos, and a one. "Damn it," he muttered.

"Nice try, Captain," Thackery added.

Rhodes rolled everything but the five and got a four, a six, a three, and a one.

"Dragging up the rear, Sir," Lauer teased.

"Are you gonna be a bastard about winning?" Rhodes countered. "This is supposed to be fun."

"What's funner than trash-talking? You can talk trash about me all you want. I won't mind."

Rhodes had to laugh and passed the dice to Fuentes. Rhodes got up and rummaged in the bookshelf until he found a piece of paper and a pen to keep score.

Rhodes had to help Fuentes a lot when it came to keeping track of both numbers he was supposed to be rolling for and what score he got at the end.

"Is there a point to this game?" Fisher asked after they quit for the night and crawled into their capsules.

"The point is to take our minds off reality," Rhodes told him. "Trust me. This game is going to be the best thing that ever happened to us."

"I'll take your word for it. You know so much more about human nature than I do."

"Didn't you enjoy it?" Rhodes asked.

"I enjoyed seeing you in a better mood than you have been since I came online. I never thought I'd see you like that. If you ask me, it's the rest of the battalion that will be the best thing that ever happened to you—not this game."

Chapter 14

Rhodes eased out of his capsule the next morning and stared down at his feet. He started to put together everything that happened to him and everything he still had to do today.

A loud cough startled him into looking up. He stared down the row of capsules and had to readjust his version of reality when he saw Fuentes, Thackery, and Lauer waking up.

Rhodes had been living in these barracks alone for so long. The other recruits' presence interrupted his usual morning routine. He didn't get a chance to put his boots on.

He went into the washroom to look at himself in the mirror, but before he got there, he heard yells rising from the other side of the barracks.

Fuentes got straight out of bed, went to the terminal, and started attacking it again. He jammed his finger into it way too hard and muttered curses at the device.

His voice started rising. "Come on! This is all wrong! What the hell is wrong with this stupid thing?"

"It doesn't do outside communications," Thackery called over from her capsule. She still sat on the edge running her fingers through her hair. "Captain Rhodes told you that already."

"You shut up!!" Fuentes snapped. "You don't know anything about it."

"I bet I know more about computers than you do," she countered.

"SHUT UP!!" Fuentes bellowed.

Rhodes turned around and started to say, "Rudy...."

Fuentes rounded on Rhodes in a rage. "SHUT UP!! You don't know what you're talking about!!"

"You better watch your tone talking to the captain like that, Corporal," Lauer growled.

Fuentes didn't hear him. "SHUT THE HELL UP—ALL OF YOU!!"

Rhodes moved a little closer. He barely made it through the washroom door before Fuentes ripped the terminal off the desk and hurled it at Rhodes full force.

Rhodes raised his arm and the terminal bounced off his right arm's metal housing. The terminal crashed onto the floor and shattered into a million pieces.

Lauer and Thackery stood frozen in shock. Fuentes roared in fury, turned to the bookshelf, grabbed it, and tried to rip it off the wall.

He would have toppled it into the room. His implants gave him the strength to break its anchor bolts.

Rhodes couldn't watch any longer. He charged the kid, grabbed Fuentes around the shoulders, and pinned his arms to his sides.

Fuentes exploded in an even more hysterical rage, kicked and thrashed, and tried to fight his way out of Rhodes's grip.

Rhodes had to use all his new strength to restrain Fuentes. "YOU BASTARD!!" Fuentes roared. "YOU SON OF A BITCH!!"

"Help me, Fisher!" Rhodes yelled over the noise.

"What would you like me to do, Captain?" Fisher asked.

"Interface with him! Knock him out if you have to! I don't care! Just shut him down!"

"Is that advisable.....?"

"JUST DO IT!!" Rhodes roared.

Rhodes didn't understand what Fisher did. A blast of blinding pain and searing heat stabbed into Rhodes's brain, but it didn't knock him out.

Fuentes went limp in Rhodes's arms. Lauer and Thackery both flinched. Thackery's hands flew to her head and she grimaced in pain.

The next instant, it was all over. Fuentes hung lifeless in Rhodes's arms. His body weighed a ton.

Rhodes let out a shaky sigh. "Thanks, pal. I owe you one for this."

"I may have damaged him irreparably," Fisher murmured.

"I'd say he already has been." Rhodes carried Fuentes back to his capsule and laid him down on the mattress. He'd been awake less than ten minutes.

Rhodes stood back with another heavy sigh. Now what was he supposed to do?

He couldn't stand by and watch another one of these people go down. There had to be another way. God only knew what it was.

Neither Lauer nor Thackery said a word. Thackery left the barracks, came back with a broom, and started sweeping up the shattered remains of the terminal.

Rhodes sat down on Thackery's bed to keep watch over Fuentes. Thackery's capsule was the next one down the row. She didn't say anything against Rhodes sitting on it.

Lauer scowled at everyone. Rhodes couldn't read Lauer's reaction and didn't want to pry.

"Is there any way to orient Fuentes better than this?" Fisher asked.

"I'm wide open to suggestions, pal," Rhodes replied. "I'm fresh out of ideas."

No one said anything after that. Rhodes, Thackery, and Lauer waited in silence for Fuentes to wake up.

Rhodes didn't ask what Fisher did to knock Fuentes out. Rhodes knew one thing, though. He could never ask Fisher to do that again.

Whatever blast Fisher used might harm Rhodes or one of the other soldiers. Rhodes couldn't risk that.

Whatever that blast was, it wasn't a long-term solution. There was no long-term solution to whatever was wrong with Fuentes.

Whatever was wrong with Fuentes was wrong with all of them, including Rhodes. That was exactly the problem and it wasn't a solvable problem. It was just the shitty reality they all had to live with.

Fuentes woke up three hours later, groaned, and rolled onto his side in bed. He rolled in Rhodes's direction so Rhodes could see the boy's face.

Fuentes kept his eyes shut for a minute. Then they suddenly popped open. He stared straight in front of him. Then his eyes darted sideways to lock on Rhodes.

Fuentes lost it the minute they made eye contact. Fuentes writhed the other way, howled in anguish, and started rage-sobbing again.

Rhodes didn't move. He couldn't do anything about this. He knew exactly how Fuentes felt because Rhodes felt exactly the same way. He just coped differently.

One glance at Lauer's deep scowl told Rhodes loud and clear that Lauer felt the same thing. He didn't say so out loud. He never said a word about whatever his life had been like before this.

He buried his pain and anguish under a mountain of solid granite. Lauer protected himself better than Rhodes, but nothing could hide it forever.

Rhodes wished now that Thackery didn't act so chipper about all this. Her presence really made this so much harder.

Rhodes didn't blame Fuentes for hating her. Rhodes wished more than anything that she hadn't woken up at all.

He kicked himself for thinking that, but having one person in the room who didn't sympathize made this so much worse.

What was Rhodes supposed to do—kick her out of the battalion? He couldn't do that. She had nowhere left to go. None of them did.

Fuentes tossed and thrashed in his capsule for a minute, but that didn't satisfy him. He shot to his feet, cast one wild glance around the barracks searching for someone or something to attack, and hurled himself at the nearest available object.

He tried to grab the capsule cover, but not even his mechanical arms could budge it. He yanked it, and when that failed, he hurled himself at it.

He slammed his head and chest down on it twice before Rhodes realized what was happening. Fuentes bounced off the cover and threw himself at the wall. He slammed his face and body into it three times before Rhodes got there.

Lauer responded just as fast and got there a fraction of a second after Rhodes.

Rhodes lunged for Fuentes, pinned him hard against the wall, and held him there. "Stop it, Corporal!" Rhodes yelled. "Stop it right now! That's an order! Keep still! I said keep still!!"

Fuentes didn't hear him. He tried half a dozen more times to slam himself against the wall. Lauer moved in to help Rhodes, but Rhodes held Fuentes down alone.

"Do you think you're the only one who feels this way?!" Rhodes snapped. "Do you think your pain is so much worse than ours?! You better snap the hell out of it, boy!"

Fuentes burst into tears all over again.

"Hey! I'm talking to you!" Rhodes barked. "Look at me, Corporal!"

Fuentes looked at him for a split second and then twisted his head away.

Rhodes jammed his elbow harder against Fuentes's chest. Rhodes didn't have any problem holding Fuentes down.

"Look at me, Corporal!" Rhodes roared. "Do you think I'm not going through the same thing? My wife and children are out there—my parents and brothers and sisters. Do you think I'm not hurting? Do you think I don't want to end it?"

Those words cost Rhodes everything he had, but he had to say them.

They hurt more than anything he'd gone through yet. That pain made him furious. He wanted to kill someone, maybe even himself.

He grabbed Fuentes by the jaw and forced him to turn his head. Fuentes struggled, but Rhodes didn't let up until he wrenched Fuentes's head around and locked eyes on him.

Fuentes's mouth screwed up in torturous shapes. His tears made his eyes blaze. He rasped through bared teeth for every breath.

Rhodes could think of a lot of things to say to this kid, but that moment of eye contact said it all.

Fuentes didn't want to look at Rhodes because Fuentes saw. He saw in Rhodes's eyes all the torture and anguish Fuentes had been suffering all this time.

"Look at me, boy," Rhodes snarled even though Fuentes already was looking at him. "Look at Lauer."

Rhodes didn't have to turn around to see the expression on Lauer's face. Rhodes slackened his hold on Fuentes's jaw just enough for Fuentes to turn his head and see Lauer's features spasming.

Lauer turned away immediately, but that moment was enough.

Fuentes let out a broken howl of agony, but he didn't try to struggle anymore. He didn't fight Rhodes's hold.

Right at that moment, at the worst possible moment, the barracks door opened and the three doctors waltzed in.

"If you wouldn't mind coming with us, Captain," Dr. Neiland breezed. "It's time to wake up the rest of your unit."

Rhodes spun around fast. "What—all of them?"

"We've decided to shorten our timeframe," Dr. Montague replied. "The Emal threat is becoming more pressing. We need to activate the battalion sooner than we thought."

"But these three haven't finished training. They haven't learned how to use The Grid to modify their shapes."

"You'll be able to train the whole unit together," Dr. Neiland replied. "It will step up the timeline...."

"It will also increase the risk of a catastrophic malfunction," Rhodes countered. "You realize that, don't you? The battalion won't be as effective with fewer people."

"That's a risk we're willing to take," Dr. Montague replied. "Come with us, Captain. We need you present when we wake up the rest of the recruits."

Rhodes didn't want to leave—not right now. He didn't trust Fuentes not to try something else the minute Rhodes turned his back on him.

The doctors' presence left Rhodes no choice. He eased his elbow off Fuentes's chest and the kid buckled on the spot. His knees folded and he collapsed on the floor sobbing his eyes out.

None of the doctors reacted to Fuentes's outburst. None of them acted as if Fuentes's behavior was anything noteworthy.

Rhodes took a step back. He still hesitated to leave, but maybe this was for the best.

If Fuentes killed himself, at least Rhodes wouldn't have to take a potentially unstable soldier onto the battlefield.

Fuentes would as likely get killed there if he couldn't function or think clearly. Why delay the inevitable?

Rhodes couldn't risk Fuentes putting someone else in danger. Rhodes wouldn't be able to keep Fuentes under constant watch or anyone else who might snap at a moment's notice.

Rhodes's mind went through every one of those nightmare scenarios. Of all the bad ideas in the history of bad ideas, this was the worst he'd ever encountered.

He couldn't imagine a worse scenario than going into battle with a bunch of damaged, emotionally unstable mental patients all armed with super strength and the most sophisticated weaponry in the sector.

He couldn't waste any more time on Fuentes—or anyone else. If they didn't pull it together, he just had to let the chips fall where they may.

God only knew Rhodes had enough to cope with just managing his own emotional state right now.

Things would get a whole new level of complicated when he went into a real battle with alien hordes shooting at him.

He glanced over at Lauer. Lauer faced the room again. He'd straightened his expression into another brutal scowl.

Now Rhodes knew with absolutely no doubt that Lauer had a family out there somewhere, too. Lauer was going through exactly the same inner turmoil. He just didn't let anyone else see it.

Lauer glared down at Fuentes. Lauer only took his eyes off the boy for a split second to make significant eye contact with Rhodes.

That moment told Rhodes more than words could ever say. Rhodes could leave the room now because Lauer was here. Lauer would keep an eye on Fuentes—not that it mattered anymore.

Rhodes turned away to follow the doctors out of the barracks, but he paused on the threshold to look back.

Fuentes sat huddled in a ball on the floor. He turned his face toward the wall and pressed his forehead into the concrete so no one could see him, but everyone present could hear him sobbing. His whole body shook with sobs.

"Can you detect any malfunction in him?" Rhodes asked Fisher. "Are the implants causing this.....or is it something else?"

"Is there a difference?" Fisher asked. "There's no malfunction.....but the implants are causing this either way. Aren't they? Isn't that what you've been trying to tell me all this time?"

"I guess so." Rhodes still found it impossible to leave. "Are his brainwaves functioning normally?"

"His brainwaves are erratic, but I've been detecting the same patterns in all of you—you, Lauer, and even Thackery. I can't tell anymore if they're normal or not. I'm not sure anymore what normal is when it comes to any of you."

Rhodes sighed. He already knew all that. Of course Fisher was right.

One of these people malfunctioning—what the hell difference did it make anymore what caused it?

Of course the implants caused all this distress. They didn't need to malfunction to cause distress, disorientation, and even total mental breakdown.

The implants caused all that especially when they were functioning normally. It wasn't possible for them to do anything else.

He turned away for the last time and left the barracks. He couldn't help any of these people. He couldn't even help himself, so what was the point in trying?

Chapter 15

Rhodes watched from a distance again while the doctors woke up the other six recruits. Rhodes really needed to come up with another word for them. The word, *recruit,* infuriated him.

He didn't get involved at all while the doctors went through the usual checks and questions. Rhodes took the time to study and evaluate his remaining six people.

Lieutenant Ted Oakes was a tall man with brown hair buzzed high and tight.

He took excellent care of himself before this. His implants did nothing to conceal a wall of solid muscle across his back and shoulders.

His abdominal muscles rippled down to the implants around his hips. His legs looked extra thick inside their metal housing.

He snapped to attention in front of Rhodes when the doctors finally introduced them. "Sir!" Oakes snapped. "Lieutenant Ted Oakes of the 156th Platoon reporting for duty—Sir!"

"At ease, Lieutenant," Rhodes murmured. "We aren't keeping that kind of formality and protocol here. You can relax."

Oakes frowned. "But.....aren't we an elite military unit, Sir?"

"Only on paper. In real life, we're just normal people trying to get through the day. Do you feel any disorientation, distress, or discomfort about your implants, Lieutenant?"

Oakes frowned again like he didn't understand the question. "Um...no, Sir."

"That's good. You report to me if you start feeling any distress or any problem coping. Understand?"

"Yes, Sir."

Rhodes turned to Georgie Henshaw. She sat on the edge of her capsule staring up at Dr. Neiland. "He did what?" Henshaw gasped. "My father did...what?"

"He enrolled you in this project to save your life," Dr. Neiland told her. "You would have died without the implants."

"Are you serious?" Henshaw gasped. "He sent me *here*....to become a robot?"

"You aren't a robot. None of you are." Dr. Neiland looked up when Rhodes walked over to them. "This is Captain Corban Rhodes. He'll be your commanding officer from now on."

"So I'm in the Legion now?" Henshaw countered. "I'm supposed to be a soldier? This is ridiculous!"

"How do you feel, Henshaw?" Rhodes asked. "Do you feel strong enough to stand up and walk around?"

She gaped at him in shocked horror....and then her eyes dipped to his body.

She scanned him up and down, took in every detail of his implants and robotic limbs, and then looked down at her own. "I don't believe this!"

"Believe it," Rhodes told her. "We're all going through the same thing. None of us knew this was going to happen to us until we woke up here."

Her one blue eye darted up to meet his. "So.....you're a captain. You were a soldier in the Legion before this?"

"That's right....and I guess I still am."

She opened her mouth to say something else, but just then, a crash distracted everyone.

Rhodes turned around to see one of the capsules in pieces. Another recruit had rested his hand on the capsule's outer edge to push himself to his feet.

He didn't understand his strength and wound up caving in the side of the bed. The capsule's side wall lay in pieces on the floor.

"I'm so sorry!" he exclaimed and started to bend over to pick up the pieces.

"Nothing to worry about!" Dr. Irvine rushed over and pulled the guy away from the wreckage. "You don't have to worry about that. We'll clean it up. Go back to what you were doing."

"I really didn't mean to," the guy exclaimed. "I swear it."

"Calm down, man," Rhodes told him. "I broke General Brewster's hand on my first day."

The soldier turned around and locked one brilliant blue eye on Rhodes. The controls at the end of the guy's capsule read, *Lieutenant Dane Rhinehart.*

Rhinehart was even taller, broader, more muscular, and more powerfully built than Oakes. Rhinehart had blonde hair, blue eyes, and a soft, teddy bear quality like a big, lovable kid.

"This is Captain Corban Rhodes, your commanding officer," Dr. Irvine told Rhinehart. "He's here to orient you to your new unit and make sure you adjust and adapt to your implants."

Rhinehart's eyes went through the same process of measuring Rhodes and all his mechanical body parts. "Captain....." Rhinehart began.

"Don't worry about it, Lieutenant," Rhodes told him. "We're all in the same boat here."

Rhinehart looked away. "I need to contact my family and tell them where I am."

"I'm sorry, but you can't. We're all cut off from our loved ones. We can't go back. I'm sorry."

Rhodes expected some emotional reaction. Rhinehart scowled, compressed his lips, nodded once, and turned away.

Rhodes didn't realize the rest of these people were listening. "You mean...." Henshaw stammered. "You mean....we can never go back? We can never see our families again?"

"Basically," Rhodes replied. "The Legion has already notified your families that you're dead. You basically did die in whatever circumstances brought you here. Whatever life you had out there is over."

Another man stood off to one side rotating his arms back and forth in front of his face. The name at the end of his capsule read, *Sergeant Jairo Dietz*. He was tall and thin with uncut hair, quick, wary black eyes, and unnaturally long fingers.

"This is great!" he exclaimed when he moved his fingers around. "I would pay for this and now I get it for free."

Corporal Keller Gannon walked around his capsule studying all the controls. He was Rhodes's size with plain brown hair and a no-nonsense attitude.

Gannon studied the controls with interest. "How does this work? How does it read all the person's vital functions while they're inside?"

"If you don't mind, Captain," Dr. Montague told Rhodes. "We really need to accelerate our timeline. If you wouldn't mind taking your unit back to the barracks, we need to get started on our training routine."

"Your timeline calls for me to orient three of them at a time," Rhodes pointed out. "The next thing I know, you'll be telling me to take them into battle without any training or orientation at all."

"We wouldn't do that, but we do need to get them out of the lab. If you don't mind....."

Montague waved toward the exit. Rhodes surveyed his people one last time. Jesus, could this get any worse? He didn't even have time to get to know them first.

The last member of the battalion was a young guy with mousy brown hair and blue eyes. Corporal Eddie Coulter sauntered over to Henshaw on their way out of the lab.

Coulter was by far the smallest man in the room with short, light hair and a wiry, energetic, almost frenzied quality like a spring about to pop.

He grinned at Henshaw. Rhodes could have mistaken that grin for flirting if they had been anywhere else in the universe.

"So...." Coulter began. "You weren't in the Legion before this?"

"No, I was an executive in a marketing firm."

"Then you're definitely moving up in the world," Coulter remarked.

Henshaw laughed and Coulter cracked a crazy grin. Neither of the new people showed any sign of disorientation or distress.

Their interaction gave Rhodes a feeling of impending doom. When would one of them snap and do something dangerous either to themselves or someone else?

He took them back to the barracks and introduced them to Lauer, Fuentes, and Thackery.

Fuentes sat hunched on a bench at the table staring at the floor. He didn't respond to anything Rhodes said.

Gannon went over to the capsules and started tapping on the controls. "Don't touch that, Corporal," Rhodes told him.

"How am I supposed to learn about all this?" Gannon asked.

"These machines regulate your vital functions. These controls have been dialed in to make your bodies function at their optimum. You could risk your own life if you mess with the levels—or you could cause a malfunction that could cost someone else their life. Just leave it alone."

Gannon turned away and mumbled, "Yes, Sir."

He started searching the room and studying all the furniture and furnishings in minute detail. Someone had replaced the computer terminal while Rhodes was away.

Thackery sat behind it studying it. Gannon went over to her and bent over to see what she was reading.

"Normally, I would take some time to let you all get comfortable and take in what's happened to you," Rhodes began. "Under the circumstances, the doctors want us to escalate our timeframe, so I have to start training you now."

"Won't that cause problems later on?" Thackery asked.

"Do I sound like I think this is a good idea?" Rhodes asked. "Let's go. We can explain things as we go."

He led the way outside. The rest of his people talked to each other on the way down the hall heading for the training room.

"How long have you been here, Sir?" Gannon asked.

"I guess about three weeks," Rhodes replied. "I had some problems at first, so the doctors didn't want to wake up the rest of you until I straightened myself out."

"What kind of problems?" Rhinehart asked.

Rhodes shrugged. "Problems adjusting to my implants. I was alone. I didn't have anyone to explain to me what was happening. I was the first person to go through the process, so no one really knew what was normal for me."

"Damn! That sucks," Coulter remarked.

"Yes, it did, so don't be shy about speaking up if you have any problem adjusting. We're all in uncharted territory here. No one knows how this will affect anyone. In fact, we can expect it to affect everyone differently."

Rhodes glanced at Fuentes, but Fuentes didn't react to what Rhodes said. Fuentes walked down the hall with the rest of the battalion. Fuentes didn't try to talk to anyone, but at least he wasn't a puddle of tears on the floor.

Maybe these other people would be good for him the way they were good for Rhodes. Maybe that was the only problem—being alone with this nightmare.

"All the soldiers' brainwaves appear to be functioning normally," Fisher told Rhodes on the way. "I don't detect any distress in any of them."

"What about Rudy?" Rhodes asked.

"Who are you talking to, Sir?" Oakes asked.

"I'll explain it to you when we get there," Rhodes replied.

"Fuentes appears to be regulating much better now, too."

"Keep an eye on it for me, will you?" Rhodes asked.

"Of course, Captain."

Rhodes escorted his people into the training room. "What are we doing here?" Henshaw asked.

"I told you. We're here to train our implants. We're about to enter a world that will become your everyday existence for as long as you're in this battalion."

"What does that mean?" Oakes asked.

Rhodes sighed. "I can't explain it to you. I'll have to show you."

He signaled Fisher and the whole group dropped into The Grid. The recruits looked around them.

"What is this place?" Gannon asked.

"It's The Grid," Thackery replied.

"I can see that, but what is it?" Gannon asked.

"It's essentially a computer construct of the world," Rhodes explained. "The Grid will morph and change shape to create battle scenarios to train us. The Grid will also modify your implants into different forms and shapes so you can fight the enemy more effectively."

Dietz snorted. "That's impossible."

"You never said anything to us about this," Thackery pointed out.

"We were going to train that next, but the doctors decided to wake up the rest of the battalion first." Rhodes turned to his new soldiers. "The Grid is going to start to change right now. You're going to see some shapes and then your SAMs will come online."

"Whats?" Henshaw asked.

Rhodes didn't even try to explain. He signaled Fisher and the SAMs activated in front of each person's face. The interface showed Rhodes everything the soldiers saw.

The grid lines went through their usual twisting contortions until each one settled each a particular image.

Henshaw's SAM turned out to be a baby-faced panda named Koen. Oakes's SAM was an outline of grid squares with no color or visible features at all. It had a male voice and its name was Dash.

Gannon's SAM was actually a normal human man named Santos. Dietz got a cosmic pulsating orb of crackling lightning named Zen. Coulter got a dog named Murphy.

Rhodes stood back and watched and listened to his people holding conversations with their SAMs He didn't see any of these people having any problem adjusting. Everything seemed to be working the way it should.

That only made him dread the day when they did start having problems.

Chapter 16

The bubble of conversation between the new soldiers and their SAMs started to soothe Rhodes into a trance. He had to fight himself to break this moment and disturb the others by getting their attention.

He was just about to call them to enter The Grid when laughter startled him. He turned around and spotted Dietz laughing with Zen. Rhodes couldn't hear what they were laughing about.

At that moment, at the moment when Rhodes turned his head to look in their direction, Dietz raised his arm and fired his thermal cannon directly into Fuentes's shoulder.

Dietz didn't fire hard enough to harm Fuentes. Dietz only unloaded enough to heat the metal housing of Fuentes's shoulder implant.

Fuentes spun around yelling his head off. "Hey! What the hell?!"

Dietz only laughed again. Zen laughed, too. "Cool it, kid," Dietz told Fuentes. "It was just a joke."

"What the hell are you doing, Sergeant?" Rhodes snapped.

"I wasn't doing anything, Sir," Dietz replied. "I was just fooling around."

"He jumped pretty good, didn't he?" Zen chimed in.

Rhodes shot a glare at the orb. "You keep out of this."

"I just wanted to see what would happen—in the interest of science," Zen replied.

"This was your idea?!" Rhodes countered.

"It was just a joke, Sir," Dietz insisted.

"Do you think it's a joke to turn your weapon on one of your own people?" Rhodes snapped. "Don't ever let me see you do something like that again. Don't ever let me see you threaten or point your weapon at anything other than the enemy. Is that clear?"

"Yes, Sir," Dietz murmured.

Rhodes turned on Zen. "You're supposed to help him—and the rest of us. If I find out you're feeding him ideas that undermine the cohesion of the unit, I'll have the technicians take you offline. Is that clear?"

"No!" Dietz exclaimed. "You can't do that! He's mine!"

"Then you two better shape up real quick," Rhodes countered. "We have enough problems without someone threatening us from inside our own unit."

"I didn't threaten him," Dietz pointed out.

Rhodes leveled him with a death glare. "Did it look to you like he enjoyed it? Would you like it if I aimed my Vipers at your head? Is that what you'd consider a joke, Sergeant?"

Dietz pulled his head in and mumbled, "No, Sir."

Rhodes didn't want to stop glaring at Dietz, but Rhodes had too much other shit to deal with right now. He couldn't waste any more time on this.

He was just about to say something else when Gannon murmured, "Whoa! That is wild!"

Rhodes barely glanced at him. Rhodes didn't notice anything out of the ordinary except that the grid lines were spreading over Gannon's face.

Gannon stood there looking down at his arms and body as the grid lines spread downward from his neck to his chest and outward to the rest of his limbs.

Gannon turned his arms in different directions watching the grid lines rotate and adjust their position around his limbs. "Cool!" he exclaimed.

"What's happening?" Henshaw asked. "That isn't happening to any of the rest of us."

Rhodes walked over to Gannon. "What's happening?" Rhodes asked Fisher.

"I don't know, Captain," Fisher replied. "I don't understand it. The interface isn't detecting any malfunction."

"There has to be a malfunction. What's happening to Gannon, Santos?"

Gannon's SAM hovered there watching. "I don't know, Captain. All his systems are functioning correctly."

"Bullshit!" Rhodes turned back to Gannon, but Gannon really didn't seem to be in any distress. He just stood there watching the grid lines crisscrossing his body.

The lines rotated in different orientations, pivoted back and forth......and then changed shape.

The squares marking Gannon's face and body adjusted their orientation, and this time, they changed Gannon's shape, too.

He didn't make any sound of pain or distress. He just stood there watching while the squares continually altered their position.

They turned into different geometric figures, returned to being squares, and then melted into strange fluid patterns.

Each change smeared the man underneath—except that the grid lines weren't underneath. They changed Gannon's shape, too.

His face contorted, stretched in some areas, compressed in others, and writhed in all directions as the grid lines moved, pivoted, and manipulated the man along with themselves.

"Gannon!" Rhodes gasped, but it was too late.

The changes picked up speed. The grid lines squiggled and then tangled amongst each other. What had been Gannon got lost in the muddle until he wasn't there at all anymore.

The squiggled knot of lines got smaller and smaller. "Stop this, Santos!" Rhodes choked. "There has to be a way to stop it."

Santos cocked his head to one side....and then he vanished. Rhodes turned the other way just in time to see the tangle of grid lines disappear—the tangle of grid lines that used to be Gannon disappeared, too.

The whole group stood there staring at the spot. "What the hell just happened?" Coulter asked.

Rhodes wilted. "He's gone."

"What do you mean—he's gone?!" Oakes snapped. "How can he be gone? He was just here!"

"This is what I'm telling you. This whole system is experimental. The doctors and officers and technicians have never done anything like this before. There are bound to be problems—with everything."

"So....one of us could be next." Oakes cast a glance around the group. "Any of us could go at any time. Is that what you're saying?"

"Yes," Rhodes groaned. "It's been like this ever since I woke up."

He made an executive decision not to tell these people about Cope, Poole, and Taylor. Dozens of other soldiers probably died before Rhodes woke up.

He took a deep breath to pull himself together. "Look, we have a lot of work to do before we....."

"You son of a bitch!" Rhinehart bellowed. "You better shut the hell up before I kill you!"

Everyone jumped and spun around to see Rhinehart going ballistic. He lunged for his SAM and tried to grab it, but there was nothing to grab.

The SAM had the face of some unrecognizable alien with snakelike tentacles whipping from its head. The face reminded Rhodes of the Xakzat species of reptile from the Quaknax system.

The tentacles crackled with electricity and the SAM's eyes glowed with cold, piercing fire. They radiated bright white light and made the SAM look menacing and furious.

Its name was Rocky, but it didn't look like a Rocky at all. It looked like a monster. It had a deep, booming, thunderous voice that echoed out of the distance.

Rhinehart swung his fists at the thing trying to hit it, but his hands went straight through it. He kept bellowing, "Shut the hell up, you piece of shit! I'll kill you!"

Rhodes rushed over to him and tried to restrain Rhinehart's arms. "Easy, Lieutenant. Take it easy!"

"Get this damn thing away from me! Just shut it off!" Rhinehart roared. "You son of a bitch!"

"Settle down!" Rhodes yelled in his ear and turned to Rocky. "Make yourself as small as possible!"

"I was only trying to help him...." Rocky murmured.

"Make yourself small!" Rhodes yelled back. "Do it now!"

Rocky shrank to a tiny size, but the SAM still didn't become a pinprick the way Fisher did.

Rhinehart kept struggling against Rhodes's hold, knocked Rhodes's arms away, and made another dive to pulverize his SAM before Rhodes pulled Rhinehart away again.

"Smaller," Rhodes ordered. "Make yourself smaller—and don't say anything."

"My function is to...."

"SHUT THE FUCK UP!!" Rhinehart roared. "YOU SON OF A BITCH!!"

"Be quiet!" Rhodes ordered. "Don't say another word until I tell you to."

Rocky finally retreated out of sight and kept his mouth shut—thank God.

Rhinehart calmed down the minute his SAM disappeared. Rhodes unwound his arms from Rhinehart's and Rhodes let himself take a moment to catch his breath.

Rhinehart kept glaring at the dot in the corner of his view where Rocky had retreated.

"Now listen to me, Lieutenant," Rhodes rasped. "You can't turn it off. I'm sorry. I know it's annoying. You just have to learn to live with it."

"Like hell I will!" Rhinehart snapped.

"If you absolutely have to, you can leave it small like that and we can order it not to talk to you." Rhodes waited for a second just to let that sink in.

The silence became palpable. All the rest of Rhodes's people watched and listened to this latest confrontation.

"Now listen to me very carefully, Lieutenant," Rhodes went on. "This SAM is your only friend. Its only function is to help you. You're going through some growing pains right now, but in a few minutes, we'll be going into a battle training session. This SAM will give you information and help you navigate the terrain."

Rhodes turned around to address the whole group. "You might have a problem with your SAM now. I had problems with mine, too. Trust me when I say that you're better off with your SAMs than without them. In a few days, we'll be going into battle for real and you'll need all the help you can get. No one is in a better position to give you that than your SAM, so learn to work together."

"Thank you, Captain," Fisher murmured in his ear.

Rhodes ignored him. "Your SAM is your best and only friend. What happens to you happens to your SAM, so it's in your interests to work together. Your SAM is as anxious for you to survive and come home in one piece as you are."

Rhodes turned back to Rhinehart. Rhinehart kept glaring at Rhodes and shooting sidelong daggers at the pinprick that was Rocky.

Rhodes took another steadying breath and studied the SAM. "Change your appearance—and your voice."

"I can't, Captain," Rocky boomed.

"Yes, you can," Rhodes snapped. "Don't give me that bullshit. Just do it. Change yourself into......a Khikvid—and make your voice quieter. Cut out that echo."

"That would not be advisable...." Rocky began.

"If you don't do it, I'll order you to remain silent and invisible for the rest of forever. Just do it and don't argue with me."

"I don't give a shit what the hell he looks like," Rhinehart snarled. "I'll fucking kill him."

Rhodes didn't answer. Rocky hesitated for a second and then expanded. He didn't come back to full size. He swelled to the size of an orange. "Do you mean like this?"

He took the appearance of a different alien. The Khikvid were small, furry, and round with large, wide-spaced eyes, pudgy faces, and big round ears.

The sides of the SAM's face kept stretching and adjusting, but at least it was recognizable as a loveable, cuddly creature instead of a monster.

Rocky also softened his voice to a low, soothing murmur. It would have sounded like Fisher's voice except that Rocky made his voice a lower pitch. He looked and sounded much more like a Rocky now.

"That's perfect," Rhodes replied and turned to Rhinehart. "What do you think? Can you live with it?"

Rhinehart glared at the Khikvid. "I don't have to like it."

"No, you don't. If you really want to, you can order him to disappear and not talk to you anytime when we aren't in battle. Does that satisfy you?"

Rhinehart snorted and looked away. "Bastard."

Rhodes squeezed Rhinehart's shoulder. It didn't feel the same as squeezing a man's shoulder. The implants didn't give the way a normal human shoulder would.

Rhodes did it anyway and turned to the others. "Right. Now all of you follow me. We're going to start moving through The Grid. It will change into a landscape and then into the training landscape...."

"How do we know The Grid won't take one of us over the way it took over Gannon?" Coulter asked.

"Can't we just go into The Grid now?" Thackery asked. "This is all just a waste of time."

"If you don't keep your mouth shut, I'll send you back to the barracks," Rhodes snapped. "You're only making this harder for everyone."

She didn't say anything else. Rhodes made one last survey of the battalion.

They didn't inspire a whole shitload of confidence. Dietz kept grinning at Fuentes like they were the best of friends. Fuentes glared back at Dietz.

Rhinehart glared at his SAM. Oakes and Henshaw kept looking toward where Gannon had just been standing.

Rhodes sighed. This was the absolute last group in the world he ever wanted to take into any kind of battle, even a simulated one.

He didn't have a choice. His only option was to train them as much as possible.

Then he had to pray to Almighty God that they somehow worked out their problems before the real gunshots started flying.

Chapter 17

Rhodes set off walking through The Grid. The other soldiers of Battalion 1 followed him.

Lauer caught up with him and murmured in Rhodes's ear. "I got a bad feeling about this, Sir."

"I'm sure it's no worse than the feeling I have about this," Rhodes muttered back. "This whole thing is a disaster waiting to happen."

"It looks to me like it already happened. We lost Gannon. Who's next?"

"They're sending us into battle soon," Rhodes replied. "We'll all be next."

"At least Fuentes seems to be holding it together."

Rhodes didn't turn around to see what Fuentes was doing. Rhodes could hear well enough without turning around.

Fuentes wasn't crying or flying into a rage or trying to destroy himself. That was a massive improvement. Rhodes didn't care about anything else.

None of the others did any of those things, either. Rhodes knew better than to hope it would stay this way. It wouldn't, but he could be grateful for small mercies as long as they lasted.

"What are we looking at, Captain?" Oakes asked behind Rhodes's back. "This is just more Grid, isn't it?"

"Yeah, it is," Rhodes replied. "Okay. Here we go. Try to keep up."

He started running. The rest of the group ran with him, and in a second, the grid lines stretched upward to form a landscape.

It started as another valley with softly rolling hills, trees, and a stream at the bottom winding through fields.

The soldiers kept up with no problem. They stared around them at everything. Rhodes picked up the pace and the surrounding hills jutted higher.

The grid lines bent upward into cone-shaped volcanoes puffing smoke into a hazy, red-orange atmosphere.

"Stay sharp!" Rhodes called behind him. "The enemy should start shooting at us any....."

He barely got the words out before a flicker of lasers spouted from the slope of the nearest volcano.

In seconds, more gunfire blasted from every hillside and bombarded the battalion. Rhodes turned one way, then another, and fired his scourge guns at the mountainsides.

When that failed, he switched to thermal cannons, but the laser fire coming from the slopes overcame the battalion in no time.

His soldiers reacted just as fast, wheeled outward, and unloaded. They targeted the source of the lasers, but nothing interrupted the enemy assault.

A laser sliced across the valley bottom, hit Henshaw, and carved across her chest implant. She screamed and toppled to the ground, but Rhodes didn't see any damage to her armor.

The interface gave Rhodes a view of all the SAMs talking to, instructing, and feeding targeting and terrain information to each soldier.

"The Grid is showing fortifications five miles up the valley!" Fisher yelled in Rhodes's ear. "We can take cover there!"

"What's the objective?" Rhodes asked.

"The system only says you have to defeat the aliens and bring peace to the valley."

"That's impossible!" Rhodes countered.

"Just get the battalion to the fortifications!" Fisher told him. "We can't stay out here exposed like this!"

Rhodes could see that for himself. He fired his scourge guns at the laser positions again, but he couldn't even tell if he hit them.

"Follow me!" he roared to his people. "Use your boosters and follow me!"

He fired his boosters and took off soaring up the valley. Fisher adjusted Rhodes's Grid view of the landscape so Rhodes could see where they were going.

The valley snaked between the volcanoes to a fortified base out of sight. Laser positions surrounded the base, but at least the group would find shelter there.

The others copied him, ignited their boosters, and the battalion zoomed up the valley dodging lasers right and left.

The battalion had to fly through a hail of enemy gunfire to get around the first corner. One of the shots hit Oakes and he slammed down on the ground.

"Keep going!" Rhodes ordered. "Lauer—show them where to go!"

Lauer took off with the others right on his tail. Rhodes doubled back and pulled Oakes off the ground, but he didn't seem to be hurt, either.

He staggered a few times when Rhodes picked up him, but Oakes could support his own weight.

Rhodes held onto him to steady him. "Come on, Lieutenant!"

"Captain..." Oakes croaked and stumbled again.

Rhodes turned around to look into Oakes's one good eye. That eye kept drifting half shut.

"Look out, Captain!" Fisher yelled.

Rhodes barely had a chance to realize what Fisher was warning him about before a smash of fusion fire pounded the hillside right next to Rhodes's position.

Rhodes fired his boosters without thinking and took off into the air dragging Oakes with him. Oakes hung onto him just as tight.

Rhodes didn't have time to check if Oakes was okay. Rhodes released two of his Vipers and hit two different laser positions on his way up the valley.

Both positions exploded and Rhodes flew past them to catch up with the battalion. He got there just as Lauer led everyone down to the base.

The enemy bombardment escalated as soon as Rhodes and his people took cover behind the fortifications.

"Now what do we do?!" Thackery hollered. "We can't get out of here!"

Rhodes hid behind a heavy concrete barricade and turned his attention to Oakes. "Fisher—can you interface with Dash?"

"I am interfacing with him, Captain."

"I don't detect any malfunction, Captain," Dash replied. "Lieutenant Oakes only seems to be dazed."

"I'm all right," Oakes husked. "Just give me a second."

Rhodes made one last survey of Oakes's body. All his implants appeared undamaged.

Rhodes couldn't spend any more time on this. He squinted up at the hillsides all around him.

"The bombardment is getting hotter," Rhinehart pointed out. "They know we're hiding down here."

"Fisher—show me a layout of this valley—a bigger layout."

Fisher adjusted The Grid again. Rhodes measured the strength and positions of the alien laser points that were so busy bombarding the intruders.

"That's amazing!" Henshaw breathed. "You can do that?!"

"Your SAMs can do it, too." Rhodes pointed at a dot on the map. "What is that?"

"That's the aliens' power station." Fisher changed the map layout to show red lines snaking all over the hillsides. "These are the power lines carrying power to the laser positions."

"That's it. That's the objective," Rhodes murmured. "We take out the power, we take out the guns. The valley will be peaceful."

"How do we do that?" Coulter asked. "That power station is more than forty miles away with laser positions all the way."

"We use The Grid," Rhodes replied.

"How?" Rhinehart asked. "We're already in The Grid."

"The Grid is in us, too. We can use The Grid to change our shapes and the configurations of our weapons. We need to modify ourselves to overcome all these obstacles."

Dietz frowned. "How do we do that?"

"Like this," Lauer interrupted and changed himself.

The grid lines covering him altered their shape. They changed him into a cylindrical spacecraft with scourge guns sticking out all over him.

He launched off the ground, soared over the fortifications, and his weapons erupted shooting in all directions.

He whirled in midair for a second and then two cannons on his outer housing fired Viper missiles at four laser positions.

They exploded and he dropped back down behind the fortifications. The grid lines morphed to change him back into a man.

He shrugged at Dietz. "Like that."

"Oh, hell no!" Coulter muttered. "Hell no!"

"How did you figure out how to do that?!" Thackery demanded. "Captain Rhodes never showed us how to do that!"

"He mentioned it before," Lauer replied. "I figured it out.....after Gannon. His grid lines changed shape."

"We'll need to change into something armored to get through all that laser fire," Rhodes suggested. "We should combine our defenses and our firepower. We might make a bigger more obvious target, but....."

"They already know where we are," Lauer pointed out. "They're already targeting us."

"Exactly. We'll need to use speed, too—and we'll need to use our Vipers on the power station itself."

"We won't be able to use our Vipers before that, then," Rhinehart pointed out. "We'll have to use other weapons to clear these laser points and keep our Vipers in reserve."

"We can use as many Vipers as we want to," Rhodes told him. "We don't need to reload anything."

Everyone spun around to stare at him. "We don't?"

"We have unlimited ammo and power." Rhodes shut his eyes and raised his hand. "It's complicated and I don't have time to explain it right now. Just take out as many positions as you can and keep moving."

"So what shape do we take?" Henshaw asked.

"Get creative," Rhodes told her. "We'll connect up and keep moving until we get to the power station. Is everybody ready? Are you ready, Oakes?"

Oakes nodded. "Yes, Sir. Count me in."

"Let's go."

Rhodes peeked over his fortification. He couldn't see anything out there—nothing he hadn't already seen.

Lasers pelted from the enemy's hillside positions. Fusion blasts bombarded the fortifications and made everyone dive for cover.

"GO!!" Rhodes bellowed and took off into the air. He didn't know what he would do until he got out there.

He altered his grid lines and changed into one of Lauer's spinning spacecraft, but that didn't get Rhodes any closer to the power station.

His soldiers rocketed out from behind the fortifications just as fast. They took longer to work out how to manipulate The Grid and what to turn into.

Henshaw surprised everyone by figuring it out first. She somersaulted head over heel, plummeted back down toward the valley floor, hit the ground, and changed into something like a compact armored vehicle.

Her weapons stuck out from both sides and unloaded on enemy targets, but she didn't stay there.

Her armored sides extended down to the ground and protected mechanized wheels under her housing. She took off up the valley plowing a path through the war zone.

"Everybody down on the ground!" Rhodes called to the others. "Link up with Henshaw! Form a chain!"

He dove for her, slammed into the ground full force, and his grid lines mutated to match Henshaw's shape.

He motored up behind her taking dozens of hits all over his outer armor. He unleashed one Viper missile after another to smash the laser points, but he didn't try too hard to hit them.

He had to work to catch up with her. She made much better progress than he expected. She outpaced him.

The rest of the battalion burned up behind Rhodes. His people took different shapes trying to manipulate The Grid as fast as possible.

Lauer, Fuentes, and Thackery caught up with Rhodes first. His grid lines morphed in front of his face to form a coupling and he locked onto a matching coupling on Henshaw's back end.

Lauer, Fuentes, and Thackery locked up with him and all five of them took off snaking through the valley.

"Take over, Captain!" Henshaw yelled over the noise of pounding gunfire. "I don't know where I'm going!"

"Stay where you are! Keon will show you where to go! Rhinehart—come on!"

Rhinehart had the most trouble manipulating his grid lines. He changed rapidly from a Legion tank to some kind of fighter plane to a creature Rhodes didn't recognize.

Brutal enemy gunfire bombarded each shape. None of those configurations protected Rhinehart well enough.

Rocky had changed his appearance again. He looked more like a prehistoric horse and he changed his voice again to make it higher.

Rhodes heard Rocky yelling instructions and encouragement to Rhinehart, but Rhodes couldn't make out the words over all the noise.

Oakes and Dietz caught up with the rest of the train, coupled onto its back end, and Rhinehart fell farther behind.

Coulter got separated from the group, too, but not because he couldn't use the grid lines.

He changed into an identical armored vehicle, but when he got close enough to couple with Oakes, a seeker missile corkscrewed out of the hillsides and smashed down on top of Coulter.

"Coulter!" Rhodes called, but he got no answer. "The rest of you keep on going! I'll catch up with you!"

"Don't break the train!" Lauer told him. "You could get lost out here!"

"Couple up with Henshaw as soon as I break free!" Rhodes ordered. "We aren't leaving anybody behind. I might be able to help Rhinehart if I...."

Rhodes broke off when Rhinehart veered. He was nowhere near close enough to connect with the rest of the group. Every mistaken transformation slowed him down.

The delay worked in his favor after all. It put him in the one most strategic position to help Coulter.

The explosion that hit Coulter bowled him farther away from the train. He tumbled down another slope toward the stream running through the valley.

Rhinehart swerved. The outer appearance of his face, hair, and implants vanished and his body turned black with nothing but the green grid lines crisscrossing every part of him.

He transformed instantly into a Legion Predator craft, fired his boosters, and blasted across the landscape.

He extended some kind of hook from his underside, snatched Coulter off the ground, and rocketed into the atmosphere carrying Coulter with him.

Rhodes lost sight of them, and the next second, Henshaw burned around another hill. The power station came in sight—and something else.

Whoever these aliens were supposed to be, they mounted a better defense than Rhodes expected. Twenty-five heavily armored Destructor crawlers blocked the battalion from getting anywhere near the power station.

The Destructors charged away from the power station to assault the battalion. Henshaw was driving too fast to stop.

"Where the hell did they come from?!" Lauer roared. "They weren't on the map before!"

"They weren't here before!" Wild told him. "The Grid modified itself to increase the difficulty."

"Scatter!" Rhodes order. "Everyone—get airborne and assault the station from the air. Go!"

He broke away from Henshaw in the front and Lauer behind him. Rhodes fired his boosters and copied Rhinehart to become a Predator fighter craft.

Rhodes took off into the atmosphere and gained altitude to get above the enemy laser positions.

He barely cleared the tallest volcanos before he met Rhinehart and Coulter coming back down to meet him.

Coulter must have been fine because he transformed himself into a Predator, too. He and Rhinehart pelted past Rhodes and unleashed their Vipers on the power station.

The rest of the battalion changed into Predators, too, but Rhinehart and Coulter got the jump on everyone.

By the time Rhodes turned around to target the power station, Rhinehart and Coulter were already bombarding it to oblivion.

An explosion went off inside the structure and the whole thing detonated with a colossal boom.

Chapter 18

Coulter looked around the barracks and scowled. "Where's the food?"

"You're out of luck, pal," Lauer growled. "There ain't no food in this joint."

"How are we supposed to relax after a battle without food?" Oakes asked.

"That's what I said," Lauer replied.

"I want a refund," Coulter joked and made Henshaw laugh.

"We deserve a few beers after that run," Thackery chimed in.

"Beers—hell," Coulter countered. "Give me a bottle of bourbon any day of the week. Who has time for beer?"

"You won't be able to drink beer ever again," Henshaw told him. "You don't have a liver anymore."

Coulter pretended to gasp in horror. "Hush your mouth! I *will* drink again. Life wouldn't be worth living if I didn't."

"It sounds like you need a new reason for living," Oakes told him.

"What other reason is there?" Coulter asked. "At least let me live in the delusion that I might be able to drink again someday."

"Okay, you might," Henshaw told him.

"What are we supposed to do instead?" Dietz asked. "We can't just stand around here staring at each other."

"Come over here," Thackery told him. "I'll teach you how to play The Ship, The Captain, and The Crew."

Coulter glanced at Rhodes. "He could use his rank to beat us."

"I'm not playing," Rhodes told him.

"You have more to worry about from Lauer," Thackery added. "We're going to have to come up with some special prize for anyone who beats him."

Lauer started grinning. "Now you're talking."

"So what's the prize?" Henshaw asked.

"A big sloppy kiss from me," Coulter told her.

"That's a punishment, not a reward," Oakes growled.

"For you, maybe." Coulter sat down at the table. "So how do we play?"

Thackery started explaining the game. Oakes, Dietz, and Henshaw sat down, too.

Fuentes sat at the next table and watched. He didn't get involved.

Rhodes waited until they all got busy trash-talking, joking, and passing the dice around the circle. Then he turned to the one person who didn't get involved in their conversation.

Rhinehart stood off by himself in a corner of the barracks. He faced the wall with his head down and didn't engage with anyone.

Rhodes used the interface to check where Rocky was. In that moment, Rhodes realized that he activated the interface by himself. He didn't need Fisher to do it for him.

Rhodes caught a glimpse of which SAMs hovered in front of which faces or, in Rhinehart's case, which SAMs *didn't* hover in front of which faces. Rocky wasn't there.

Rocky had retreated to a pinprick. The interface told Rhodes that Rocky was still using the horse shape from the battle, but he didn't try to talk to Rhinehart.

Rhodes took his time going over there. He would have to tell all these people about the loading dock.

Privacy would become paramount from now on. One place where each person could go to be alone would become more precious than gold.

The interface between the soldiers' SAMs would make that privacy even more critical.

How much and how often should Rhodes use the interface to monitor his people's mental state? Using the interface to communicate and check on them in battle was one thing.

He shouldn't have used it to check on Rhinehart and Rocky, but what choice did Rhodes have about that? He was responsible for these people now.

Every life in this unit would depend on each person getting along with their SAM. One pair malfunctioning could put the rest of the group in jeopardy.

Oh, what the hell was Rhodes thinking? It *would* put the rest of the group in jeopardy—or worse.

He stopped next to Rhinehart. "You did outstanding work in that training session today, Lieutenant," Rhodes murmured. "You kicked ass."

Rhinehart didn't look up. "It's still there. It's always there. I can't get rid of it. It's driving me insane. Why can't it just leave?"

"I know, soldier," Rhodes murmured. "The same thing happened to me."

"I would kill it if I could," Rhinehart snarled. "I hate having it there in my head all the time. I would kill it if I could find a way."

"I know," Rhodes replied. "I feel exactly the same way about mine."

"Why does it have to talk all the damn time?!" Rhinehart spat. "Why can't it just shut the hell up?"

"It's shutting up now," Rhodes pointed out. "He's trying to help you. He did help you by giving you information during the training session. You saved Coulter. That was something to be proud of. Now Rocky is keeping quiet because he knows that's what you want. These SAMs are not our enemies. They're our friends."

"But it's still there!" Rhinehart cast a wild glance around the barracks, but he didn't see anything in front of him. "It's there even when I can't see it. It listens to everything and hears everything I'm thinking. It's listening to us right now. It will never go away."

Rhodes sighed. "I know."

Rhinehart shifted his feet a few times. He couldn't keep still. "I don't think I can do this, Sir. These implants....." He squirmed in his own skin. "They're driving me insane."

"I feel the same way, Lieutenant." Rhodes hesitated and then took the plunge. "Before you woke up—before all of you woke up—the doctors and officers asked me to help them wake up the first three members of this battalion. I was in the room when they woke up. One of them.....he couldn't take it. He went into a rage and tore his implants out and died right there on the floor."

Rhinehart looked up. "Seriously?"

Rhodes gulped down a wave of sick horror at the memory. "I.....I wanted to do the same thing. I wanted to do it a million times—or off myself somehow. I couldn't stand it."

"How did you deal with it? What did you do to make it better?"

Rhodes couldn't hold Rhinehart's gaze. "I didn't. Nothing made it better. It's still there."

Rhinehart looked down at his hands—the hands that weren't his anymore. "We aren't human anymore. *I'm* not human anymore. I'm not who I was before, but I don't know who I am. I couldn't have saved Coulter the way I was before."

"None of us knows who we are or what we are, but we're still human. We have to be."

"How can you tell? What makes you think you're still human? I mean—look at us."

"I don't know how I can tell. It isn't anything I can look at or point to. Maybe just the fact that I hate this so much is proof that I'm still human. I don't know. I'm trying to figure this out the same way you are, Lieutenant."

Rhinehart bowed his head to look down at his hands again. "I'm not anything that could go home to my family anyway. They wouldn't know me. They would be scared of me. The Legion doesn't have to lock me up here or even tell my family I'm dead. The person they love.....isn't here anymore. I died on the battlefield. This is someone else."

Rhodes rested his hand on Rhinehart's shoulder again. Touching him like that didn't change a thing.

The voices coming from the table filled that silence. Rhodes glanced behind him.

The rest of the battalion sat around the table shooting snide remarks back and forth as each person took their turns rolling the dice. Thackery kept score. Fuentes glared at them from a few feet away.

It was the most human scene Rhodes could imagine except that none of the people in it were human. Only a small portion of their faces gave any evidence that these machines ever had been human.

Rhinehart's voice drifted into Rhodes's ear. "I gotta get out of here, Sir," Rhinehart whispered. "I can't stand this a second longer."

"Go ahead," Rhodes told him. "Take a walk around the station. Sometimes I go out to the loading dock and watch the ships launch and land. It helps me think. Maybe it will help you."

Rhinehart nodded. "Thank you, Sir."

Rhodes didn't want to let him go just yet. "If you change your mind—if you decide you don't want to do this anymore—no one will hold it against you."

Rhinehart's eyes swiveled toward the table. "They all seem just fine. I'm the only one messed up enough to think that."

"I'm thinking it, soldier—and so are they. No one gets away free with this. Trust me. If you need to go there—if you need to opt out—just do it. No one will blame you. I really wish I could."

"Why don't you? Why do you stick around?"

"I decided to stay for all of you. I couldn't function when I first woke up. General Brewster said that, if I didn't figure it out, he would shut down the project and that meant shutting all of you down, too. I couldn't do that. That's the only reason I'm still here—that and to protect my family. They're still out there in danger from alien invasion.

If being like this gives me some small edge to protect my family, I guess I have to use it. I would have ended it a long time ago if it was just me."

Rhinehart looked down at the floor again. "Yes, Sir. I understand."

Rhodes pushed Rhinehart's shoulder. "Get out of here. Go take a walk and think it over. We'll still be here if you decide to come back."

Rhinehart left the barracks. Rhodes watched him out of sight.

"Is it really like that for you, Captain?" Fisher asked.

"Of course it is," Rhodes replied. "Did you think it wasn't? Nothing changed. Nothing got better. How could it be otherwise?"

"You're right, Captain," Fisher murmured. "This project is a disaster."

"Maybe you could communicate some of what you've learned about me to Rocky. Maybe you could help him learn how to help Rhinehart."

"It seems to me that Rocky is already doing what Rhinehart wants by making himself invisible. That's the only thing Rocky can do to help Rhinehart."

"I suppose you're right. I guess no one can help Rhinehart."

"Do I help you, Captain?" Fisher's voice trembled. "Would you really be better off if I stayed silent and invisible?"

Rhodes sighed again. "I really don't know what will help me or any of these people, pal. I don't know anything anymore."

He waited a respectful amount of time before he went back to the table and sat down next to Coulter.

"Where's Rhinehart going, Sir?" Oakes asked.

"He had to take a walk. He has a lot on his mind and he needs some time to think."

"He rocked that training session," Thackery pointed out. "I thought he was going to crash and burn. Then he came out of nowhere and smoked that power station. He's a champion."

"I guess so," Rhodes murmured.

Being a champion in a training session didn't mean jack shit to Rhinehart without his humanity and all the human connections that made it real.

Fuentes made that point loud and clear. He held himself apart and sat there seething with silent resentment. He didn't participate in the game or the conversation.

After an hour, he took himself off to his capsule, locked himself in it, and started his conversion cycle early so he wouldn't have to talk to anyone.

Chapter 19

Rhodes woke up, sat on the edge of his capsule, and stared at his robotic feet.

All Rhinehart's questions from yesterday came back to haunt Rhodes now—as if Rhodes needed reminding.

How did Rhodes know he was human? What possible evidence could he point to that justified believing he was?

The sight and sound of the other soldiers waking up and leaving their capsules somehow reinforced how hopelessly alien their situation was.

Waking up from sleep—it was such a human experience—so familiar, so mundane, so ordinary.

It felt so human to sit up in bed, put his feet on the floor, and stare at something while his brain kicked back into gear.

He'd been waking up in barracks around other soldiers for years. The sounds lulled him into a false sense of the familiar.

The sight of his own feet shattered the illusion. He didn't even have feet anymore. He didn't have boots to put on or laces to tie.

He went through this sequence of thoughts every morning. Talking to Rhinehart about it didn't change that.

Rhodes stood up and headed for the washroom to look at his reflection in the mirror.

Rhinehart was back. He had been gone all evening last night. He had still been gone when Rhodes started his conversion cycle.

Rhodes really wouldn't have begrudged Rhinehart for taking his own life. Rhodes envied anyone who did it.

Rhinehart sat up in bed, ran his fingers through his hair, and stood up to start his day. He acted the same way everyone else in the battalion acted.

The minute Rhodes got to his feet, he heard loud thumping noises coming from the washroom followed by the smash of breaking glass.

Everyone jumped and looked over their shoulders in that direction, but no one went to see what the problem was.

Rhodes strode over there and then charged into the washroom when he saw Coulter.

Coulter stood in front of the mirror, but he didn't look at his reflection. He lunged for the mirror and smashed his forehead into it with all his might.

The glass shattered and part of it hit the floor, but Coulter didn't pay any attention to that. He grimaced through bared, clenched teeth and howled with pain and fury each time he slammed his head into the glass.

He smashed out the mirror, but he didn't notice that, either. He kept diving headfirst again and again to pulverize his head on the concrete wall behind the mirror.

Rhodes grabbed him to pull him away, but Coulter only shook Rhodes off and smashed his head against the wall a second time. He left bloody patches on the concrete and blood oozed from around his implants.

"Hey—Corporal!" Rhodes hollered.

Coulter ignored him and fought Rhodes trying to get to the wall again.

"Coulter!" Rhodes roared. "Eddie—stop!"

Coulter bellowed again and thrashed in Rhodes's arms. "It hurts!" Coulter roared. "IT HURTS!!"

"What hurts, Corporal?!" Rhodes yelled. "EDDIE!! WHAT HURTS?!!"

Coulter let out another feral bellow, charged hard enough to break Rhodes's grip, and ran headfirst into the wall.

"Get the medical team down here, Fisher!" Rhodes ordered.

He had to dive for Coulter to stop him from hitting himself again. "IT HURTS!!" Coulter roared. "IT HURTS!!"

The rest of the battalion clustered in the doorway watching. Lauer and Rhinehart finally forced their way between the others and came to Rhodes's assistance.

It took all three men to wrestle Coulter away from that wall. He kept struggling against their grip and howling in pain. "IT HURTS!!" he bellowed. "IT HURTS!!"

Rhodes, Lauer, and Rhinehart held onto him until he lost his balance. The three men rode him to the floor and pinned him there to stop him from hurting himself again.

Rhodes tried one last time. "What hurts, Eddie?!!"

Coulter was too out of his mind to answer. In his last act of desperation, Rhodes interfaced with Murphy. The dog face appeared in front of Rhodes right next to Fisher.

"What the hell is wrong with him?!" Rhodes hollered.

"He appears to be suffering from some malfunction in his cerebral implants," Murphy replied. "It's causing a physical pain response in his head. I'm detecting intracranial pressure...."

"Well, why the hell didn't you report it?!" Rhodes snapped. "How long has he been like this?"

"About four hours....."

"Four hours?!" Rhodes countered. "You're supposed to help him! If he had a problem, you should have alerted the medical team....or me....or someone!"

Just then, the medical team rolled up. Rhodes, Lauer, and Rhinehart had to let go of Coulter so the medical team could get near him.

He lashed out immediately and decked one of the nurses in the face. He threw an elbow at Dr. Irvine and knocked the doctor out cold on the washroom floor.

Rhodes, Lauer, and Rhinehart dove back in and grabbed Coulter to hold him down. "Take him to his capsule!" Rhodes ordered. "Lock him in a conversion cycle until the doctors figure out what's wrong with him."

Rhinehart glanced over his shoulder. "How do we get him there?"

Oakes and Fuentes came out of the woodwork to help. Even then, it took them, Dietz, and Thackery all working together to haul Coulter kicking, screaming, and spitting back to his capsule.

"Lift!" Rhodes ordered and they all hefted him onto the mattress. They had to lean all their weight on top of him to make him lie still until the prongs inserted and he went limp.

The whole battalion staggered back gasping, panting, and shaking. "This is not good," Fisher murmured.

Rhodes shot upright and spun around to confront Dr. Neiland. "You need to go through all our SAMs and check them for malfunctions. We aren't going anywhere until you do—not even into another training session."

She consulted her device. "I'm not detecting any malfunctions from any of your SAMs."

"Then why didn't Murphy report that Coulter was suffering from intracranial pressure? He could have killed himself just now. He had pain in his head bad enough to smash his head against a wall. Murphy said it started four hours ago and Murphy didn't report it at all—not even *after* Coulter hurt himself. It's a miracle we got to him in time."

She frowned. "Hmm. That is a problem."

"Problem!" Rhodes snapped. "You're playing games with our lives and you call it a problem?!"

"We have to take Coulter back to the lab while we reconfigure his SAM and repair the damage to his implants," Dr. Montague chimed in.

"Just keep him sedated," Rhodes snapped. "Don't wake him up until you're certain he's pain free."

"How would we do that?" Dr. Neiland asked. "We won't know if he's pain free unless we wake him up."

"I don't care how the hell you do it! Just do it! You're the ones responsible for this. What the hell good are these SAMs if they don't report an obvious malfunction like that?"

Henshaw spoke up from across the room. "Maybe the malfunction interfered with Murphy's programming. Maybe that's why he didn't report it—because he was malfunctioning, too."

"Obviously he was malfunctioning, too," Rhodes snapped. "He didn't report it at all ever. It never crossed his mind to report it."

"Maybe he didn't want to report it because you were in a conversion cycle," Lauer pointed out. "Maybe something in Murphy's programming told him not to wake you up."

"Then that needs to change, doesn't it? If one of you is malfunctioning that badly, then I need your SAM to wake me up so we can deal with it. All our SAMs should be reprogrammed for that."

The doctors took Coulter away to their lab. The medical team took Dr. Irvine to the station hospital.

Rhodes couldn't tell if Dr. Neiland and Dr. Montague even understood why he was so worked up about this.

The rest of the battalion milled around the barracks for a while. No one spoke above a murmur.

Rhodes wanted to storm down to Neiland's lab and stand over the doctors day and night. He wanted to make sure they fixed whatever was wrong with Coulter.

Hell, they might not even know what was wrong with Coulter. If they did, they might not be able to fix it.

Rhodes's fury toward these people was really starting to get the better of him.

These problems would spread through the whole battalion. They wouldn't spare anyone. He knew that now.

Chapter 20

"What are we doing today, Sir?" Oakes asked.

"Your guess is as good as mine." Rhodes pushed a piece of paper away from himself and pulled another one forward. "It looks like I'm doing this today until Coulter comes back. I guess if I really wanted to know I could ask General Brewster or Colonel Kraft, but I don't really want to know."

"Aren't we supposed to have any more training sessions?" Thackery asked.

"No one tells me anything," Rhodes replied. "Besides, we aren't going anywhere until the medical team checks out all of us for the same problem. It might take a while for them to modify our SAMs with the new programming to wake someone up if one of us has a life-threatening malfunction."

He snorted to himself, but he decided not to say his next thought out loud. The fact that the medical team didn't include this in the SAMs' original programming—it really spoke volumes about how much the Battalion 1 project cared about its people.

Henshaw picked up the piece of paper Rhodes just finished drawing on. She held it up and studied his drawing. "This is really good, Captain. You're a natural."

"I'm not a natural. I went to art school for three years before I joined the Legion. I've been drawing in my spare time ever since."

"What the hell did you join the Legion for, then?" Rhinehart asked. "You could have been an artist instead."

"I didn't want to be an artist. I wanted to be a soldier."

"And kill people and get shot at?" Dietz asked. "You're a real boon to humanity, aren't you?"

Rhodes grinned at him and went back to the drawing in front of him. His pencil scratched the surface and left smooth lines over the paper.

"You're really good, Sir," Lauer remarked.

"Thanks, Lieutenant. I've had a lot of practice."

Henshaw tilted her head sideways. "Who is that? It looks like a bird, but it also looks like a person."

"It's Fisher." Rhodes pushed it away and threw down his pencil. "I'm going for a walk. Don't call me unless it's an emergency."

"Isn't it always?" Oakes asked.

Rhodes didn't answer. He headed for the door, but he stopped in his tracks when Dr. Neiland showed up. "Shouldn't you be working on Coulter?" he asked.

"Dr. Montague and Dr. Irvine are working on Coulter. I thought you'd all like to know that he's awake and he's going to be fine."

"Says you," Rhinehart muttered from behind.

"If you'll all follow me, I'll take you to your next training session."

"Why do we need to follow you?" Henshaw asked. "We can find our way there on our own."

"You aren't going back to the same training room. I have a surprise for you."

The whole unit exploded in protests.

"No, no, no!" Rhinehart exclaimed. "No more surprises."

"I ain't going anywhere with *you*, lady," Lauer snapped.

"You're supposed to be checking our SAMs for the same malfunction," Rhodes pointed out. "How do we know the same thing won't happen to us?"

"We can access your SAMs from the lab," Dr. Neiland replied. "We've installed the new protocol in all your SAMs. None of you and none of your SAMs are malfunctioning, so if you follow me, I'll show you to your next training session. This one will be different. Each of you is getting fitted with your own ship."

Rhodes and the others exchanged glances. "Ship?" Oakes asked.

"They're state of the art. I'm sure you'll be delighted with them."

Rhodes didn't want to trust that, but his curiosity took over. He had to at least see these new ships. He would decide after that if he liked them.

She must have seen his reaction. She left the barracks without another word and the battalion followed her.

Rhodes didn't know what to expect. It would have to be something pretty spectacular for him to get delighted about anything around here.

She headed for the loading dock, but she turned off into a stairwell before she got there. The battalion descended five flights of stairs and exited in another long, low landing bay full of ships.

Actually, it wasn't full of ships. There were only twenty here. Rhodes didn't recognize their make or class.

Each one resembled a smaller version of a Predator. These had shorter, stubbier wings and a powerful, armored look.

The long, sloping cockpit window ran half the length of the fuselage and ended level with the wings. A booster rocket flared outward from the tail.

"I don't see any weaponry," Oakes pointed out. "I'm not delighted."

"Each of you can go on board," Dr. Neiland told them. "As soon as you lock into the cockpit, each ship's SAM will interface with your onboard SAM. Then you'll be able to read the controls, pilot the ship, and activate the weapons system."

"These ships have their own SAMs?" Thackery asked. "Are they the same as our own SAMs?"

"No, these ships have new ones. None of these SAMs have ever been activated before. Their only function is to fly these craft."

"What *are* these craft?" Dietz asked. "I don't recognize them."

"They're prototype Striker class," Dr. Neiland replied. "These ships have been specifically designed for Battalion 1 so they can be piloted by SAM interface with the pilot."

Rhodes and his people exchanged glances. He wasn't sure how to feel about this. He didn't trust anything the Battalion 1 project thought was a good idea.

On the other hand, he'd come to rely so heavily on Fisher. Rhodes instinctively trusted this pilot SAM without even meeting it. He trusted another SAM more than he trusted anyone on the medical team or in any command position.

Dr. Neiland went down the line assigning everyone to their ships. She assigned Henshaw, Dietz, Fuentes, and Thackery before Coulter showed up.

Bruises covered his face, but at least he was lucid. "How are you feeling, Corporal?" Rhodes asked.

"Terrible," Coulter muttered. "Thank you for stopping me, Sir. I wasn't thinking straight."

"You were in pain. I'm sorry it happened."

Coulter looked away. "I need to talk to you, Sir—in private."

"Do you want to do it now or another time?"

Coulter looked around at Lauer, Rhinehart, and Oakes watching and listening. "Later, I guess."

"Are you sure? We can do it now if you want." Rhodes waved the other four men away. "You men go about your business. Come here, Corporal."

Rhodes led Coulter to one side of the bay out of earshot from everyone. "What's going on?"

"I.....uh....." Coulter shuffled his feet. "I don't know what happened...."

"Murphy said you had pressure in your head. He said that's what was causing you pain."

"It wasn't that—I mean, it wasn't only that."

"What was it, then?"

Coulter opened his mouth and faltered.

Rhodes didn't know what made the connection for him. He couldn't put his finger on anything specific, but he knew.

"I think I understand, Corporal."

Coulter refused to look at him. "I couldn't say it won't happen again, Sir. That's all I can say about it."

"I understand," Rhodes murmured. "If it happens again, we'll just deal with it."

Coulter opened his mouth a second time, but no sound came out.

"Does Murphy know?" Rhodes asked.

Coulter nodded at the wall. "Don't tell anyone, Sir," he mumbled. "I don't want them to think I'm crazy."

"You aren't crazy. You're normal. Believe me, everyone in this unit is going through the same thing."

Coulter looked up. "They are?"

"Of course. You don't have to worry about them. If it happens again or if it doesn't work out, that's just the price of doing business."

"I don't like letting the battalion down, Sir."

"You aren't." Rhodes clapped him on the shoulder. "You did great yesterday and I'm sure you'll continue to do great. We all just have to make the best of it. Do you feel like coming back to the battalion now?"

Coulter nodded. "I got nothing else to do."

Rhodes found himself smiling. "Come on. Maybe something good will come from these ships."

He led Coulter back to the bay where Dr. Neiland assigned both men to their ships. Rhodes interfaced with Murphy and Coulter on the way across the floor.

Rhodes didn't pick up any obvious sign of distress apart from the bruising around Coulter's facial implants. He acted fine—but he wasn't. No one was.

Rhodes couldn't even say that Thackery was fine. She showed the least distress of the whole group, but her behavior actually unsettled Rhodes more than Coulter's, more than Rhinehart's—even more than Fuentes's.

Rhodes would have felt better if she didn't act so thrilled about being a part of this battalion. If anyone here was giving up their humanity, she was doing it the fastest. She couldn't give it up fast enough.

People like Rhinehart, Fuentes, and Coulter—Rhodes never doubted for a second that they were still human. He was never more certain of anything. Their very distress proved that beyond any doubt.

Getting implanted with all these robotic devices didn't take away their underlying humanity. If all of this couldn't make them less than human, maybe nothing ever could. They *were* human. They always would be.

Rhodes climbed into his cockpit, sat down, and seven identical prongs stabbed him in the head and body. They didn't put him into a conversion cycle, though.

The ship's cockpit didn't have any visible controls. It was just a small compartment with one main seat with a much smaller, compact seat behind it.

The second seat barely looked big enough to carry another person, but it couldn't have been built there for any other purpose.

The instant the prongs locked into him, he dropped into The Grid. He still saw himself sitting in the cockpit of his ship, but The Grid erased the blank dashboard and everything outside the cockpit window.

He saw himself sitting in his seat in the middle of The Grid with nothing around him.

He barely had time to look around before another compressed tangle of grid lines materialized in front of his eyes. It went through a few rapid transformations from animals, faces, abstract patterns, and horrifying monsters.

It finally settled into a composite animal-human face, but this one looked nothing like Fisher.

This face had a round, flat look with narrow, slit eyes. They curved upward in the middle into two smiling half-moons. The face's round cheeks glowed with inner light.

The mouth opened way too wide in a grin that took over most of the face.

"Who the hell are you?" Rhodes asked.

"I am Rio!" the SAM replied in a high-pitched, childlike, chirpy voice. "Ah! I'm interfacing with you. You are Captain Corban Rhodes, commanding officer of Battalion 1! What an honor! And you must be Fisher."

Rio turned to Fisher. The two SAMs studied each other across The Grid in front of Rhodes.

Rio's eyes stayed in their half-moon shape. The SAM always looked super-duper excited and cheery to be talking to whoever he was talking to.

"Can you interface with the other ships?" Rhodes asked.

"Of course, Captain! Who would you like to interface with?"

"All of them—and show me the ship's controls so I can learn how to use them."

"There are no controls," Rio replied.

Rhodes stopped breathing for a second. "There's what?"

"You pilot the ship through The Grid. That's all you have to do."

"How do I control it, then?"

Fisher interrupted. "You control it the same way you control and adjust The Grid in the training room. You can modify the ship in any way you want to...."

Rhodes gasped. "No way!"

"You will be able to maneuver the ship and adjust the weapons system....."

"You haven't told me which weapons the ship has."

"You can modify that, too. The ship is controlled entirely from The Grid."

Rhodes glanced back and forth from one SAM to the other.

He might be willing to believe he could change the ship's shape and controls through The Grid. He'd seen enough of that during training sessions.

He didn't want to believe he could actually change the ship's weapons configuration to whatever he wanted it to be. That sounded too good to be true.

"Lieutenant Oakes is interfacing with you, Captain," Rio told him.

Rio turned his head and looked to the left. Rhodes didn't see anything over there until he looked that way, too.

As soon as Rhodes turned his head, another ship materialized in The Grid. The grid lines appeared first. Then the ship's outer skin developed color, texture, and depth.

The grid lines changed again and he looked straight through the fuselage at Oakes sitting in the cockpit.

Dash and another SAM hovered in front of Oakes's eyes. Oakes's Striker SAM had the face of a bear with grid lines radiating outward from the thick ruff around his cheeks.

"How are we supposed to train with these things, Sir?" Oakes asked.

Rhodes fought himself back to reality long enough to remember Dr. Neiland's words. She brought the battalion down here to train with these ships.

"I'm not sure." Rhodes turned back to his own SAMs.

"I'm accessing the battalion's schedule on the station roster, Captain," Fisher told him. "The battalion is scheduled to run through a training course to orient us to these new ships."

"What course?" Rhodes asked. "How does it work?"

Fisher cocked his head to one side. "I'm accessing the station database....."

"The session will start as soon as the battalion launches, Captain," Rio interjected. "The training hall is beyond this landing bay. You'll enter the training hall as soon as you launch and the session will take over."

"I don't know what that means," Rhodes replied.

Rio turned his head very slightly and The Grid around Rhodes's ship changed. Rio showed him a layout of Coleridge Station including the loading dock, all the side wings, the concourse, the labs, and even the battalion's barracks.

A red square showed the landing bay. Rio pivoted the chart to swing Rhodes's view into the bay and then forward into another much larger chamber.

"This is the aerial training hall," Rio explained. "It will be big enough for the battalion to fly in and test the ships and their SAMs."

"So.....we just have to launch?" Rhodes asked.

Rio split in an even bigger, brighter, wider, cheesier grin. "Exactly, Captain!"

"Okay. Interface with the other pilots."

Rio didn't do anything that Rhodes could see, but the rest of the battalion instantly appeared on The Grid. Rhodes could see all of them in their cockpits along with their SAMs—two SAMs for each pilot.

He didn't have time to get acquainted with all the new SAMs now. "Stand by to launch," he ordered.

"What are we doing in there?" Henshaw asked. "This SAM won't explain anything to me."

"I guess we just try it and find out. Let's go. Follow me and be ready for anything."

Rhodes said those words, but he still had to think about it before he figured out how to fly this ship. He wasn't used to flying something without controls.

His hands automatically extended toward the dashboard to take the cradle to steer the ship.

Without warning or him even doing anything, grid lines snaked across the dashboard, formed the outline of a cradle, and it solidified in his grasp.

He didn't give himself a second to question. He knew how to fly like this.

Chapter 21

Rhodes grabbed his Striker controls and hit the throttle—except that the ship didn't have a throttle. It responded to his thoughts—or maybe not even his thoughts. His instincts made the ship move without him doing anything.

He lifted off, leaned forward, and the ship took off across the bay. He didn't see at first where he was going.

Then The Grid around him changed to reveal the bay walls. He picked up speed. Rio overlaid the map of Coleridge Station on the grid lines around Rhodes's ship.

He saw everything in multiple dimensions simultaneously. He knew exactly where he was going—and then the ship punched out of the bay into the training hall.

It didn't look like a hall. It looked like The Grid at first. Then it changed into a vast stretch of space dotted with burning ships in battle and gunfire pelting all over the place.

Adrenaline pumped into his veins and his instincts blocked out everything else. He completely forgot that he was flying a strange ship. He completely forgot that he was in a training simulation at all.

He dropped the throttle all the way to the wall and his ship plunged into the battle gunning for doomsday.

Rio kept changing the Grid layout of the battlefield to feed Rhodes information faster than thought. Rhodes didn't have time even to register the information before his instincts reacted to it.

He veered between attacking ships and opened fire. Fusion charges, thermal cannons, lasers, and scourge guns erupted from his ship's fuselage and pounded enemy targets all over the field.

He didn't see at first which side of the battle he was supposed to be on or if this battle even had sides. He couldn't tell anything about the ships around him. None of them belonged to the Legion.

More ships exploded all around Rhodes's vessel. He pulled away, and without thinking about it first, his ship changed shape.

The grid lines morphed the fuselage with him still inside it. The shape he'd seen in the landing bay disappeared and the grid lines twisted into a sphere.

The sphere solidified, tumbled over itself, and sprayed lasers and Viper missiles from its round surface.

The Vipers bombarded another two alien vessels coming from Rhodes's left. One attacker exploded from the assault.

The other staggered across Rhodes's path. Before he could think, the Striker changed shape again, sprouted a million jointed legs, hit the enemy ship, and used all its legs to vault away into space.

"The Zalvox are launching drone mines!" Rio reported.

"I don't know what that means!" Rhodes hollered back.

"They're launching from the planet Alxull—that green one on your left. Watch out!"

Rhodes barely had time to yank his ship out of the way before a swarm of spherical projectiles whizzed past his hull. This jointed-legged shape didn't do him any good now.

He activated The Grid just enough to modify the lines and stretch them into a net. The ship was still hurtling way too fast through the battlefield.

Rhodes widened the grid lines as far as they would go, slammed into as many of those airborne spheres as possible, and twenty of them detonated.

He changed the ship again in a split second, contracted the grid lines to a long, thin missile, and raced between the explosions to the other side.

"The objective is down that plasma vein!" Fisher brought up another Grid map showing the route laid out on it. "The Zalvox have forty defense posts stationed along the route."

Rhodes didn't have time to think about that before a different flock of ships hammered him from the right.

These were much larger battleships carrying plenty of fusion weapons. They thundered onto the field bombarding everything in their path.

Rhinehart streaked past Rhodes on a dead sprint for the plasma vein. Rhodes heard Rhinehart yelling at one of his SAMs, but Rhodes couldn't tell which one it was.

Rhodes caught a fleeting glimpse of Rocky's horse head at his normal size in the corner of Rhinehart's view. The other SAM looked like a blurred, abstract canopy of tree branches flickering with green leaves.

The next instant, Rhinehart's ship vanished. Grid lines covered it and reformed into a long, thin, snakelike whip coiling through the battlefield.

The whip cracked here and there unleashing thermal cannon fire, lasers, and Viper missiles to target the enemy.

Rhodes didn't even really know who the enemy was anymore. He just had to get to the objective somehow—whatever that was.

In that moment, he completely forgot he was flying a ship at all. He became this collection of lines he could manipulate any way he wanted.

He changed rapidly from a ball to a single line to another jointed creature. He bounded from one enemy vessel to another, delivered multiple strikes to each, and sprang off somewhere else.

His mind went into some kind of altered state. He didn't have a shape until a split second before he made contact with his enemies.

He measured each one in a blink. Some other force outside himself decided which shape to take. The grid lines and squares morphed, warped, and skewed to match whatever he needed them to be.

He spotted a massive battleship ahead. It dwarfed his Striker by a mile and barricaded the route to the objective. None of the shapes he'd been using so far would work against a ship that big.

The enemy vessel turned its fusion charges on him. He changed back into a coiled line of square blocks linked by couplings, but that made him too big a target.

He collapsed into a ball and tumbled headfirst toward the enemy ship. He didn't know what he would do until he got there.

Some other part of his mind spotted Henshaw coming in fast on his right. She'd transformed into a cat-like creature leaping from ship to ship.

Explosions went off every time her paws touched an enemy hull. She sprang away before the explosions could damage her.

Her interface linked with Rhodes for a single instant before they both closed on the alien battleship. Rhodes let his grid lines take over and he hit the enemy ship full force.

The lines consolidated at the last instant and turned him into a round monster with no arms or legs. He didn't need weapons to destroy this thing.

A giant mouth full of razor-sharp teeth opened on the Striker's front end. He started devouring his way through the ship's hull.

His interface with the rest of the battalion fed him truckloads of information about where they were and what they were doing.

Henshaw, Oakes, and Dietz chewed their way into the same battleship from multiple sides. The four Strikers would converge in a matter of seconds.

Rhodes couldn't hear a thing over the deafening chomp of his Striker's jaws. Fisher flashed a different Grid layout in front of Rhodes's eyes. The layout showed him the ship's reactor core buried at the ship's very center.

Rhodes adjusted his course and interfaced with the other three to converge on the reactor core. They mauled their way through hundreds of decks. The battalion swallowed alien fighters who brought out their weapons to stop the assault.

The interface also showed Rhodes the rest of his people making a run for the plasma vein.

Thackery, Rhinehart, and Fuentes dove through curtains of gunfire, sprinted into the vein, and Coulter and Lauer dropped back to cover their final sprint to the objective.

Rhodes got to the reactor core first and dove for it. He gobbled it in one giant mouthful and it exploded in his mouth.

The grid lines burst outward on all sides and all that energy dumped out through his weapons ports to blast the battleship apart.

Henshaw, Oakes, and Dietz caught up with him a second later. He didn't see what they could accomplish here, but they collided with him from three directions, widened their grid lines, and grabbed him.

The blast would have torn him apart, but their grid lines interfaced with his. They transformed him before he had a chance to decide to do it himself.

All four merged into a web of lines. The alien vessel burst in a catastrophic boom that flung all those grid lines outward.

The Grid stretched and bounced to its widest limit. The lines swooped away until Rhodes couldn't see their edges anymore.

Then they all came springing back toward the center, smashed inward into a tight ball, and reformed at their normal size before they transformed back into ships.

Rhodes glanced around. He was somewhere outside the plasma vein, but he didn't see any other enemy ships around.

They all streaked into the vein trying to catch up with Thackery, Rhinehart, and Fuentes, but the battalion was too far away.

Thackery and Rhinehart split formation, flanked Fuentes on both wings, and fired outward to bombard the enemy defenses.

Thackery and Rhinehart blasted the alien positions with Viper missiles. Fuentes never slowed down. He didn't have to. He didn't have to transform. He didn't even try to shoot.

Thackery and Rhinehart accompanied him to the very center of the plasma vein. The defenses ended at the edge of a deep, lightless hole in space. Rhodes couldn't detect anything inside it.

Thackery and Rhinehart turned backward to face all the incoming enemy fighters.

Coulter and Lauer flew in the center of the horde shooting in all directions. The enemy pounded them with gunfire and then turned their weapons on Thackery and Rhinehart.

Rhodes, Henshaw, Oakes, and Dietz stayed where they were. They wouldn't be able to catch up in time to change the outcome, but it was already over.

Thackery, Rhinehart, Coulter, and Lauer plunged into the enemy grouping taking countless shots from all sides.

Rhodes couldn't see Fuentes anymore, but the aliens couldn't break through the defenders to catch up with him.

The hole collapsed in on itself without a sound. It imploded and vanished out of sight. It left only the plasma vein gleaming orange and yellow in the blackness of space. There was no sign of Fuentes.

"Let's get out of here," Rhodes murmured. "We're done. We achieved the objective."

He turned his ship back the way he came and the other pilots followed him. They flew out of the training hall, back into the landing bay, and touched down on the floor where they found Fuentes waiting for them.

Chapter 22

The battalion surrounded Fuentes all yelling at him, rubbing the side of his head, and laughing. "Outstanding flying, kid!" Oakes told him. "That was epic!"

Fuentes laughed and tried not to blush. "I can pull it out when I need to."

"You did more than pull it out," Rhinehart told him. "You destroyed those bitches."

"What was it like in there, Rudy?" Henshaw asked.

"Dark," Fuentes replied and the whole group exploded.

"Tell us everything," Thackery urged.

"Tell us everything on our way back to the barracks," Rhodes interrupted.

No one argued. The battalion left the landing bay and talked all the way back to barracks. Rhodes hung back and didn't get involved.

"Did you see anything in there?" Dietz asked Fuentes.

"I didn't see a thing. I wouldn't have been able to find the target, but Teo showed me on The Grid."

"Who's Teo?" Coulter asked.

"His Striker SAM, obviously," Lauer interrupted. "I guess these SAMs come in handy now and then."

"Teo was great," Fuentes exclaimed. "He talked me through the whole thing. I wouldn't have been able to do it without him."

"What does he look like?" Henshaw asked.

"He looks like a black smudge, but he has a deep voice like my father's. I don't have to think. I just do what he tells me to do."

"You sure did it," Coulter told him. "You're a braver man than I am flying into that hole. We thought you were a goner when you disappeared."

"We did not," Rhinehart countered. "It was a training session. He wouldn't have died."

"That's easy for you to say," Thackery pointed out. "Look what happened to Gannon. The Grid is just as dangerous as real life."

"Way to kill the mood, princess," Lauer growled.

She turned on him. "Princess? You're calling me princess now?"

"Would you prefer it if I called you, 'garçon'?"

"Probably, yeah."

The others laughed and everyone entered the barracks. Rhodes used the opportunity to check his interface with all of them.

Their systems registered less stress than he'd seen before. Their brainwaves came closer to normal today than he'd ever seen them in the past. This experience really bonded them.

"Are you sure you don't need to go into a conversion cycle to recover from your heinous ordeal?" Dietz asked Fuentes.

Fuentes flushed again. "I think I can handle it."

"Where did you learn to fly like that?" Oakes asked. "That was some expert-level shit there."

"I didn't," Fuentes replied. "I've never flown before."

Everyone turned around to stare at him. "You....what?" Coulter gasped.

"I've never flown before. I wasn't smart enough to pass the written test so I served on a ground support crew before this. Our crew got bombed on the Ahioli Asteroid Field. That's how I came here."

"How did you learn to fly like that, then?" Oakes demanded. "Trained pilots couldn't fly like that."

Fuentes shrugged. "Teo said it would come naturally to me and to just move the ship where I thought was best. That's all I did."

"Holy shit!" Lauer muttered. "Now I've heard everything."

"I've never flown before, either," Henshaw chimed in.

"Neither have I," Thackery replied.

Everyone turned around to stare at the two women. Of course they'd never flown before. Thackery wasn't a pilot and Henshaw hadn't been in the Legion at all.

Rhodes was just trying to come up with a way to break the uncomfortable silence when General Brewster and Colonel Kraft walked in.

Rhodes had come to dread anyone walking into the barracks, especially any of the station officers or medical staff. Besides, he already had a pretty good idea what these two jokers were coming to tell him.

"That was outstanding work," General Brewster gushed. "You're all becoming a real battalion."

"We aren't a battalion," Lauer growled. "There are only nine of us."

"You will become a battalion when more people go through the project. We hope in time to have several battalions all operating in conjunction with the regular Legion. Anyway, that was two successful training sessions in a row with all of you executing perfectly. We've decided it's time to deploy you back to the battlefield. You'll leave tomorrow morning."

Silence fell over the group. This couldn't have come as a surprise to anyone, but those words cast a chill over the group's triumph.

Brewster made a few more noises of congratulations. Kraft said nothing. His dark eyes measured everyone in the room.

Rhodes became aware of the intensity of Kraft's gaze settling on Rhodes in particular. He didn't say anything, either. He waited for the two men to leave.

"I guess it was bound to happen sooner or later," Henshaw murmured.

"Finally," Lauer muttered. "I can't stand all this sitting around."

"You call what we just did sitting around?" Thackery countered. "We just did deploy in battle."

"It wasn't real," Lauer replied. "This will be."

"I suppose they'll send us back to the Emal war," Rhinehart remarked. "Don't you think so, Sir?"

"I'm certain they will. Colonel Kraft already told me so. They plan to deploy us against the Emal just to work out all the bugs in our systems. Then they'll send us against some other alien invasion forces that are threatening the Treaty of Aemon Cluster in other places."

Thackery sighed. "Then tonight is our last night at Coleridge Station."

"Until we come back," Oakes pointed out. "We'll always have to come back here."

"Unless we don't make it," Dietz added.

Those words threw another bucket of cold water over the group. No one said anything for a minute.

Coulter broke the silence by sitting down at the table. "Come on! Who wants to get their asses kicked by the greatest dice player of all time?"

"Lieutenant Lauer might have something to say about that," Oakes replied.

Coulter pounded on the table. "Anyone who has anything to say about it better sit down and say it. I'm gonna keep saying I'm the best until someone comes along and stops me."

"You're on, Corporal." Rhodes strode over to the table and swung his leg over the bench.

"Cage match!" Dietz hooted. "Kick his ass, Captain!"

"Captain Rhodes is too nice to kick anybody's ass," Rhinehart corrected.

"Mop the floor with him, Captain," Fuentes added and more people laughed.

Coulter and Rhodes eyed each other across the table. Coulter bit back a grin.

"I can make sure you win, Captain," Fisher told him.

"That would be cheating," Rhodes replied. "Just watch and enjoy the show."

"Isn't this a test of your authority?" Fisher asked.

Rhodes burst out laughing in spite of himself. "No, pal. This is just some fun to take our minds off the fact that we're deploying tomorrow morning."

Coulter pushed the dice across the table to Rhodes. "You can go first, Sir, 'cuz I'm a nice guy that way."

"Put him in the bilge, Captain," Rhinehart interrupted.

"Throw him over the side, Captain," Thackery added and more people laughed.

Rhodes picked up the dice and threw. He rolled two fives, two fours, and a one.

Groans of agony went around the table. Lauer sat down. "I want in on this."

"Me, too." Fuentes sat down next to Coulter.

The next minute, everyone gathered around. They had to pack in shoulder to shoulder so they all fit at the same table.

Rhodes threw one of his fives, one of his fours, and the one. He got two sixes and a three.

"Bend over, chump!" Dietz told Coulter.

"Keep it civil, Sergeant," Rhodes told him. "We're trying to relax here."

Fuentes picked up the dice next. Rhodes didn't pay attention to the rest of the game. He really didn't care about the score.

This group of people right here—they were becoming a crew—a real unit in every way that mattered.

These people at this table right here—they were all he had left in the world. Whatever happened to him, he would stand or fall with these people right here.

He would do anything to protect them from what lay ahead, but he already knew he couldn't.

Whatever happened to them, the best he could hope for would be to witness their sacrifice and pray to Almighty God that some of them made it back alive. Even that was probably asking too much.

Chapter 23

Rhodes and the rest of Battalion 1 stepped out onto the Coleridge Station loading dock. A giant Ravager carrier sat parked there waiting to take the battalion to the Emal wars.

The ship's crew buzzed around loading goods, supplies, and equipment onto the ship. Rhodes and his people had to stand off to one side while the crew wheeled the battalion's nine capsules on board.

The capsules looked strange outside the barracks. They looked like some kind of alien pods or growth chambers. They didn't look like anything a human person would sleep in.

None of the Ravager's crew made eye contact with Rhodes or his people. The battalion followed the capsules on board.

The crewmen anchored the capsules in a separate hold, hooked them all up to the Ravager's power supply, and left without saying a word to Rhodes or any of his people.

"We'll need to keep track of the battalion's conversion cycle schedule," Fisher pointed out. "We won't have the Coleridge Station circadian timeline to tell us when to go through conversion cycles."

"What happens if we get stuck in battle and miss a conversion cycle?" Rhodes asked.

"I don't know. I don't want to find out."

Rhodes didn't reply. Marvelous. He didn't know much about what he could expect from this misguided adventure, but he was sure of one thing.

He and his people *would* get stuck in battle somewhere. They would get separated from these capsules.

The battalion's schedules would become erratic and unpredictable the way things always got erratic and unpredictable during battles.

Everyone in this battalion would probably become even less stable than they were now. Their ability to cope would deteriorate.

It was too late now because the Ravager was already lifting off with Rhodes and the battalion on board.

The crew didn't come back to check on the battalion—just in case Rhodes somehow forgot that he was outside the rest of the human race now.

The crew had set up this hold the same as the battalion's barracks at Coleridge Station. A collection of tables and a computer terminal desk sat opposite the capsules. Thackery sat down at the terminal and checked the screen.

"This says the Ravager is named, *Ero,*" she announced. "I wonder if the Legion will transport us on this ship all the time now."

"Of course they won't transport us on this ship all the time now," Coulter told her. "It will drop us off at the Emal wars and that will be the end of it. We'll never set foot back on another ship because we'll all be dead."

"Do you mind?" Lauer snarled. "Some of us are still trying to live our lives here."

"Why bother?" Coulter asked. "You're dead. We all are. We were dead before we even woke up at Coleridge Station."

Fuentes squirmed in his seat at the table. "I don't want to be dead."

"If you really want to get philosophical about it, you could say we were all dead before we were ever born," Rhinehart pointed out. "What's the point in fretting about it? It's gonna happen someday—one way or the other."

Fuentes glanced back and forth between them and winced. "I don't want to die."

"This says the trip is supposed to take eight weeks," Thackery announced. "As soon as we enter our first conversion cycle, we'll stay in stasis until we get there."

Rhodes headed for his capsule. "Sounds like a plan. Wake me up when we get there."

"Hey! You can't just abandon us here!" Dietz exclaimed.

"You're a grown man. You can handle it." Rhodes stretched out on his mattress. "You can't get into any trouble here. If you're really worried about it, go into your conversion cycle and stay there. Nothing can go wrong."

Lauer snorted. "Something can always go wrong."

"All the more reason for me to be asleep when it happens." Rhodes shut his eyes. "See you all in the morning."

The prongs locked into the back of his head and the capsule cover closed over him, but he didn't fall asleep right away. He'd only been awake for a few hours before he boarded this ship.

Fisher magnified himself in front of Rhodes's closed eyes. Fisher had developed a habit of making himself smaller whenever Rhodes talked to someone else or concentrated on anything else.

Then Fisher would expand himself to take up Rhodes's whole view whenever they were having a private conversation just between the two of them.

"Would you like me to monitor them through the interface while you sleep, Captain?" Fisher asked.

"No. Leave them alone. They can take care of themselves."

"I wouldn't go so far as to say that," Fisher murmured.

"It's a figure of speech, pal. They don't need me babysitting them."

"What if one of them malfunctions on the way there?"

"Then their SAMs' programming should wake me up—not that I'd be able to do anything about it if they did malfunction. If anything goes wrong, we're up the creek either way. At least we'll die in our sleep—which is more than I can say for dying on the battlefield."

"You're starting to sound like Coulter. When did you become so gloomy?"

"I've been like this all along. Don't you remember? None of these people is fit to go into combat and neither am I. If this was a real Legion unit, we would all be locked up for mental disturbance."

Fisher didn't answer right away. "You're right about that."

"This can only end one way. What's the point of fooling ourselves about it?"

"Why are you doing it, then? Why do you consent to go into battle?"

Rhodes kept his eyes shut and settled back on the bed even though he was already in it. "If I become too unstable, you can put me down in my sleep."

"I couldn't do that!" Fisher gasped. "How can you even suggest that?"

"That's what a true friend would do. Just put me out of my misery—and pass the word to your fellow SAMs to do the same thing. Just end this nightmare. You'll save us all a whole lot of time, pain, and trouble."

Fisher didn't answer at all, and the next instant, Rhodes woke up from his conversion cycle.

He sensed immediately that it had been a long one—as long or longer than the one he'd woken up from when he first got his implants.

He didn't remember where he was, but there was one glaring difference this time. No doctors stood by his bed to welcome him back to the land of the living.

Fisher blinked into view in front of Rhodes's eyes. "Welcome back, Captain," Fisher began in his smooth, calming voice. "You may feel weak, nauseous, and disoriented at first, but that should pass in a few minutes."

Rhodes groaned. "Where am I?"

"You're on board the Ravager *Ero* en route to the Emal wars with Battalion 1. The rest of the battalion is waking up. They're talking to their SAMs now."

Rhodes raised his hand to run his fingers through his hair. That's when he felt his implants. His metal fingers touched the skin of his face....and he remembered everything.

He groaned again and rolled onto his side trying to block it all out, but it wouldn't go away.

At least the feeling of his implants eating into his bones didn't drive him to insanity the way they did at first. He understood that sensation now.

He eventually dragged himself up into a sitting position. He was the first to sit up.

Rhinehart's and Henshaw's capsule covers were both open, but neither of them had their eyes open.

Rhodes sat slumped on the edge of his capsule waiting for his thoughts to clear.

"The *Ero* is in orbit over the planet Ohait," Fisher went on. "The Emal have secured half the planet. They're driving the Legion back toward the beach on the Bazaid continent's east coast."

Rhodes rested his head in his hand. He knew enough about the Emal war to know what he'd be facing down there. He didn't look forward to doing it all again.

Rhinehart and Henshaw finally sat up. The other members of their battalion started to stir.

Rhodes got to his feet. He still felt weak, groggy, and sick to his stomach, but he wanted his people to see him standing up. Someone had to.

He checked the terminal and confirmed everything Fisher told him—not that Rhodes doubted it. He just wanted to see it for himself.

Thousands of Emal teemed across the rest of the continent. Their base ships occupied strategic intervals across the whole expanse. The aliens could retreat there or launch new swarms from any of those ships.

The Aemon Legion occupied a thin stretch of beach all the way on the continent's farthest eastern shore. Dusters, Predators, and a few Ravagers hovered there to give the ground troops cover.

The Legion bombarded the Emal exactly the way they did on Luluna. Every shot of fusion fire, Viper missiles, and rattler guns took out dozens or even hundreds of Emal.

Nothing the Legion did made a dent in the Emal's numbers. Rhodes didn't even see the Emal releasing additional numbers. They already had enough people on the ground. The Legion couldn't even get off the beach.

It was even worse than that. Legion Ravagers descended over the ocean trying to lift the troops off. The Ravagers couldn't find room to land without crushing the troops they were trying to rescue.

If this went on much longer, the Emal would drive the Legion troops right into the ocean.

Rhodes groaned and covered his eyes again—and not because of the disorientation of waking up after such a long conversion cycle. This was as bad as he feared.

"Should we come up with a battle plan?" Fisher asked.

"We can't do that until we report to our superiors on the ground. We're deployed with the regular Legion. Whoever is running this nightmare will have some idea of what they want us to do."

"Are you sure?" Fisher asked. "I don't think anyone outside the project even knows that Battalion 1 exists."

Rhodes's head shot up. "You mean.....no one knows we're coming?"

"I don't think so. Battalion 1 is classified at the highest level of Legion security. No one on the battlefield has that kind of clearance."

"Jesus Christ!" Rhodes snarled.

"You okay, Captain?" Rhinehart asked.

Rhodes forced himself to look up. "Sure. I couldn't be better. How are you feeling?" Rhinehart nodded. "I guess I'll live."

Rhodes made one last check of the battlefield. A certain General Kaufman was in command of the Ohait campaign. Three colonels under him supervised the platoons on the ground.

One of the colonels was Merriman Jenner, the same colonel Rhodes served under on Luluna. They knew each other personally off the battlefield.

Rhodes went through a confused jumble of emotions when he saw the man's name on the command roster—and then Rhodes saw something else that made his heart stop.

"Is something wrong, Captain?" Fisher asked.

"The 249th Platoon is here. It's my old platoon.....and so is the 278th....and the 217th. I fought with all of them on Luluna. I was fighting with them when I got hit. They're the last people who saw me...."

He stopped himself from saying they were the last people who saw him alive. He didn't even know what that meant.

Was he not alive because he got hit on the battlefield? Was he not alive because he was a robot or as good as one? Was he not alive because everyone he knew and cared about thought he was dead?

Which of those made him not alive? He'd been telling himself all this time that he was still human.

He felt less human the closer he got to real people. Spending time with the battalion in their barracks at Coleridge Station—that was easy compared to this.

He didn't have to even read his former comrades' names on the roster. He knew almost every man in all three platoons. He'd fought and bled with them. He lost his life trying to save them.

Fisher interrupted his thoughts. "The *Ero* captain Parker Ackerman is indicating our descent onto the beach. He says we can deploy as soon as we touch down."

"Where will he be when we need to go through conversion cycles?"

"I'll have to let him know to make himself available. The ship's itinerary indicates that it will remain in orbit while we're on the ground."

Rhodes compressed his lips. Brilliant. That would introduce another layer of complexity to an already chaotic mission.

He didn't say anything about that to the rest of the battalion. He went through the hold checking on all his people, interfacing with their SAMs, and making sure everyone was functioning well enough to deploy.

Chapter 24

Rhodes stepped out of the *Ero's* landing bay. He exited onto a beach packed to overflowing with soldiers, equipment, damaged Dusters, medical tents, and stacks of weapons and supply crates.

Rhodes had never served on this planet before, but it resembled too many other battlefields he'd been on.

A line of low hills separated the Legion position from the enemy. Pounding gunfire and the growl of Duster engines drifted on the smoky breeze coming from the front lines.

A matching line of explosions showed Rhodes where the battle line was. The Emal kept swarming over the hills and getting cut down by Legion Jackhammers.

Enemy lasers snickered over those hills, swiped giant pathways of dead bodies through the Legion ranks, and then the lasers swiveled upward to target Legion Dusters and Predators buzzing overhead.

Continuous booming concussions echoed down the hills every time a Duster or Predator exploded.

Thackery, Henshaw, and Fuentes all jumped at the sound. None of the others did. They were used to it.

Rhodes crossed the beach. Too many people rushed past for him to recognize anyone. These people all belonged to support crews and medical teams anyway. All the soldiers he knew would be up there on the front line.

He had to brace himself before he went into the command dome. Rhodes didn't have to tell Fisher to make himself scarce. Fisher shrank to a tiny dot in the corner of Rhodes's vision.

Rhodes marched in and found General Kaufman, Colonel Jenner, and Colonel Andre Pitt standing around a table. Computer terminals, maps, and countless reports crowded the surface.

Colonel Jenner's jaw dropped when he saw Rhodes. "Corban....." Jenner husked. "Corban Rhodes?"

"Yes, Sir. I'm assigned to you with my unit here."

"I wasn't informed of this!" General Kaufman snapped. "Why wasn't I informed?"

"You would have to ask General Brewster, Sir," Rhodes replied in as calm a tone as he could muster. "I was ordered to report to you here. That's all I know. If you could assign us to our position, we'll head out to the front line."

"But you're...." Colonel Jenner trailed off. He didn't finish his sentence before he went back to gawking at Rhodes with his jaw on the ground. Jenner barely saw the rest of the battalion.

"Brewster!" General Kaufman snapped. "What the hell is that old lunatic up to now?"

"I guess you can see that as well as anybody, Sir," Rhodes murmured. "I promise you none of us wanted this."

"But you....you got killed in action!" Colonel Jenner stammered. "You.....you're supposed to be dead."

"I am dead, Sir." Rhodes turned back to General Kaufman. "Do you have any particular place you'd like us, Sir? If you don't, I guess we'll just go out there and do what we can."

"Um...." General Kaufman pulled himself together with an effort, which was more than Jenner could do.

Kaufman bent over one of his terminals and consulted his charts of the area. "The Emal are the closest to breaking through here—at the Aevod Gap. You could reinforce that and give our boys some room. They've been up there for a week without a break."

Rhodes scowled at the chart in front of Kaufman. The 249th Platoon was closest to the Aevod Gap. Rhodes would see his old comrades up there.

He didn't say that out loud, though. He only mumbled, "Yes, Sir. No problem."

"You're dismissed then, Captain," Kaufman told him.

Rhodes started to turn away. He sent up a silent prayer of gratitude that the meeting didn't drag on with everyone asking a billion questions about what Battalion 1 was and how it all happened. He couldn't stand that.

Just when he thought he could get the hell out of there with some of his dignity intact, Colonel Jenner snapped out of his trance and grabbed Kaufman's arm. "You can't send him up there! The 249th is up there! They'll see him!"

"So?" Kaufman asked.

"So....they know him!" Jenner half-whispered. "They would realize....what he is!"

"I don't see your point," Kaufman replied.

Jenner gulped. "Assign him somewhere else. That's all I'm saying."

"We can't. If we send reinforcements anywhere, it has to be the Gap. The 249th is barely holding the Gap as it is." Kaufman nodded at Rhodes. "You have your orders, Captain."

"Yes, Sir," Rhodes replied and walked out. He really hoped he didn't see anyone else he knew, but he already knew he would.

He barely made it through the door before Colonel Jenner came rushing out after him. "Corban—wait!"

Rhodes stopped walking, but he didn't turn around. This was rapidly turning into the single most painful experience of this whole nightmarish ordeal.

Rhodes didn't want to face Jenner, but things were bound to get a whole lot worse when Rhodes finally met up with the 249th. He didn't look forward to that at all.

Jenner definitely saw the rest of Rhodes's people now. Jenner left a wide space between himself and the battalion when he circled the group to stand in front of Rhodes.

Once Jenner got into that position, he got his mouth open and that was it. He tried more than once to speak and failed.

His eyes traced every detail of Rhodes's facial implants. Jenner's features kept spasming in all the wrong ways. His eyes squinted in misery.

Rhodes waited, but Jenner still couldn't get his voice to function.

"Go back inside, Sir," Rhodes finally murmured. "You can't help me."

"But you're....you're...." Jenner stammered.

Rhodes waited again for Jenner to say something. He couldn't. His cheek trembled and he gulped down a lump in his throat.

"Go back inside, Jerry," Rhodes breathed even lower. "Don't make this harder than it already is."

Jenner opened and closed his mouth a few more times. He kept shifting his weight from one foot to another.

The few times he actually summoned the nerve to look at the people standing behind Rhodes, Jenner nearly collapsed with emotion.

Rhodes waited a few minutes more, but Jenner still didn't move or make a sound. Rhodes couldn't stand this any longer.

He stepped around Jenner and walked off down the beach with his people behind him.

Rhodes didn't look back. He walked as fast as he dared to put as much distance as possible between himself and Colonel Jenner.

Fisher waited a few seconds before he expanded himself so Rhodes could see him. Fisher overlaid The Grid on the surrounding hills.

"The Aevod Gap is between those two mountains." Fisher indicated the spot with a red dot so Rhodes could see it. "It forms a choke point. The platoons can cut down the Emal as they come through."

Rhodes adjusted The Grid himself. He pivoted it downward so he surveyed the mountains from above.

"The Emal are amassing an airstrike force behind the Gap. They plan to fly over and bombard the platoons from the air. The choke point won't help the Legion then."

"What do you want to do?" Lauer asked behind Rhodes's back.

"We'll fly over and bombard the Emal strike force. They aren't ready to deploy yet. None of them are airborne. They think they have all the time in the world to mount their offensive."

"What about the platoons?" Rhinehart asked.

"If we draw the Emal away from the Gap, the platoons can stay where they are. We'll take the pressure off them that way."

Rhodes crossed the beach to where the *Ero* dropped off the battalion. The ship wasn't here anymore. Rhodes's interface with Fisher told him the ship had already retreated into orbit.

Rhodes pretended not to think about his capsule and all his soldiers' capsules thousands of miles away where the battalion couldn't get to them.

The battalion's Strikers sat parked on the beach in the *Ero's* place. None of the support crews had time even to notice such state-of-the-art prototype craft.

Rhodes loaded into his cockpit and got the usual cheery greeting from Rio. "Captain! How charming to see you again!"

"Save it, pal. We're going into battle."

"Even better! Who are we fighting?"

"The Emal. Bring up as much information as you can on their base ships."

"We don't have any information on their base ships."

Rhodes spun around fast. "You don't? Why not?"

"Because no Emal spacecraft have ever been recovered from the battlefield. They either blow up or the Emal retrieve them. We don't know anything about their craft."

Rhodes groaned. "Fantastic."

"Hey, what about hitting their power supply like we did in that training session?" Dietz suggested. "They're running lasers. They must have some power source. Right?"

"What about it, Rio?" Rhodes asked. "How do the Emal power their lasers?"

"I'm afraid we don't know that, either, Captain. I wish I could be more help."

"They must reload or refuel somehow," Coulter added.

"I don't think so," Rio replied. "No Legion troops have ever reported seeing the Emal reload or refuel."

"There's no sign on The Grid of any power supply feeding the Emal lasers," Fisher chimed in. "However they're powering their weapons system, it doesn't involve any power station or lines like we saw in the training session."

"We'll just have to rely on good old-fashioned firepower," Rhodes replied. "Stand by to launch."

"What are we standing by for?" Thackery asked.

"We're standing by for you to shut your mouth," Coulter told her. "That way, we'll be waiting until the end of time and we'll all get through this without a scratch."

"Launch and follow me," Rhodes interrupted. "We're going in."

Chapter 25

Rhodes fired his engines and launched Rio into the Ohait atmosphere. The rest of the battalion launched, vaulted high over the Legion position, and took off racing up the mountains.

The battalion overran the Legion front line in no time. Rhodes didn't try to help the platoons—not even in those places where the Emal succeeded in fighting their way over the hills.

He zoomed up the last slope, blasted over the top, and took off into the sky. Vast planes stretched behind those mountains.

The Emal covered every inch of territory out there. No one could survive on the ground out there.

Rhodes banked Rio into a steep dive, gunned the engines, and plummeted. Rio whooped with excitement. "Whoo! We're going in!"

"Pay attention!" Rhodes hollered over the engine noise. "Get me as much information as you can about the Emal base ships. I need to know their vulnerabilities!"

"I don't know that!" Rio called back.

"Then get it!" Rhodes snapped. "You have sensors. Scan their ships. Find me any place I can hit them and destroy them."

Rio furrowed his brow for the first time. He actually looked more comic like this.

Rhodes didn't have time to mess around anymore. He swooped down on the planes and the Emal lasers opened fire from all their base ships. They targeted the battalion and everyone scattered to avoid getting hit.

Rhodes manipulated The Grid faster than he could think. He didn't have to think. It happened automatically without him even trying.

Grid lines appeared all over him and all over Rio. The lines shifted their shape and position in a blink.

Rhodes compressed the lines to make Rio into a needle arrow whizzing across the landscape. Not even that was enough to dodge the enemy's fire.

He whipped from side to side, but he dropped too close to the ground. All the Emal on the planes turned their weapons upward to fire at him.

The big laser cannons erupting from the base ships swiveled downward to follow his trajectory. He had to take advantage of that.

He slammed into the ground and transformed into another armored vehicle. He extended rotating blades from the side of his wheels, plunged into the crowd of packed Emal, and plowed through them cutting down hundreds in his path.

The big lasers followed him all the way down and hit their own people instead of hitting Rio. Rhodes took off at high speed toward the nearest base ship, but he didn't try to target that.

"Come on, Rio!" Rhodes hollered. "Give me something!"

"I got it!" Rio called back. "You have to hit their undersides. That's their only weakness."

Rhodes took a fraction of a second to think about it and his resolve hardened. "Interface with the other SAMs and transmit the information to the battalion. All of you—open fire on those ships!"

Dozens of Vipers released from spots all over the planes. So many Emal crowded around Rhodes that he couldn't see the other Strikers. Only The Grid showed Rhodes where his people were.

He launched a dozen rockets of his own. They soared over the Emal ground troops and dove for the alien base ships.

Four Vipers smashed into two Emal vessels. The rest launched immediately. "NOW!!" Rhodes ordered and he shot upward.

The enemy ships started to migrate toward the Aevod Gap. He extended his arms in front of him and fired twin thermal cannons at the underside of an Emal craft gaining altitude.

Rhodes hit the ship's underbelly and it detonated right in front of him. He barely had time to curl into a ball before he smashed straight through the torched fuselage and out the other side.

Three more Emal ships came after him. It was time to get creative.

The rest of the battalion ricocheted off Emal vessels all over the field, harassed them into turning aside, and then Thackery swooped under an enemy craft and fired into its underside.

Rhodes couldn't break away from his targets long enough to fly under the ships surrounding him. They bombarded him with hellish fire.

He transformed into some kind of agile feline and bounded from one ship to another just trying to stay ahead of their lasers.

He bounced off three ships before he noticed Fuentes not far away. He perched on top of an Emal ship.

Rhodes didn't see Fuentes's Striker....and then Rhodes saw Teo sailing around and around three other Emal vessels across the battlefield.

Fuentes balanced on top of the enemy ship. Only his arms transformed.

He changed them into giant rotating drums dotted with spikes and sawblades. He bent over carving his way through the enemy's hull.

He almost cut his way inside before a different Emal ship halfway across the planes tilted upward and aimed its laser cannons at him.

Twin lasers pelted across the battlefield and came perilously close to hitting him. They would have knocked him off to his death.

Teo plunged in at the last second, took the hit in Fuentes's place, and left him standing there unharmed.

It couldn't last, though—not with so many ships in the air.

Rhodes reacted instantly, swiveled upward, and fired his scourge guns at the underbelly of the Emal vessel that attacked Fuentes. The ship exposed its underside just long enough for Rhodes to shoot through it and the ship exploded.

Fuentes kept clawing his way inside his target ship. It responded by veering wildly to one side to knock him off. Rhodes didn't see how Fuentes stayed on.

That must have been his plan all along. Teo zoomed behind the target vessel, blasted a Viper missile into the ship's underbelly, and the ship erupted in flames.

The shockwave hurled Fuentes into the air. Teo raced underneath him and caught him back inside the cockpit.

Rhodes surveyed the battlefield. All the remaining Emal ships that had been planning to assault the Aevod Gap now fought Battalion 1 instead.

Rhodes didn't see any Emal heading for the Gap anymore—until he did see them. Four of them used Battalion 1's diversion to cut away.

Those base ships raced up the mountain while the rest of Battalion 1 got pinned down on the planes. No one could stop the impending disaster.

Rhodes tore himself away, but not fast enough. He gave chase, but the Emal hounded him all the way.

The sound of gunfire made him look back over his shoulder. The rest of the battalion ran for the Gap, too, but none of them could get there fast enough.

Too many lasers pelted Rhodes from the ground. Every shot slowed him down.

He touched the ground, sprouted legs from Rio's lower fuselage, and took off bounding up the mountain in long, effortless strides.

He made it as far as the vertical cliffs before he had to change shape again. The base ships were already dropping over the mountainside to the Gap. Rhodes had to act now.

He let his grid lines take over, transformed into a Viper missile, and rocketed upward at full speed.

He didn't slow down one inch. He smashed into the first ship's underside and the ship exploded all around him. The flash of burning fuel slowed down the others enough for the battalion to catch up.

Dietz and Lauer pelted in just as fast, coiled outward, and plunged in from both sides.

Rhodes didn't see what they were doing before they changed shape again, made themselves as compact as possible, and collided with two more base ships.

The impact drove those ships together with colossal force. They smashed into each other just as Thackery and Henshaw plowed up the mountain from underneath.

The two women bombarded the target ships from below and they erupted in flames.

That left one base ship hovering directly over the Aevod Gap. Rhodes burst through the wreck and swiveled Rio into position to face down that last remaining enemy vessel.

It hung back and didn't engage. The rest of the battalion vaulted over the mountains to fall in formation with him.

The base ship backed off a little. Rhodes glanced around to make sure no other Emal ships tried to take the Gap.

He didn't even see any aliens on the ground trying to fight their way through the choke point.

Rhodes turned back to the planes to decide on his next move. At that moment, a massive laser cannon spouted from the nearest base ship and hammered Rio right in the nose.

The Striker somersaulted backward and then a dozen other base ships opened fire at the same time.

The battalion wheeled away to avoid the attack, but not fast enough. Another brutal shot smashed Rio on the left side and the ship plummeted toward the ground.

Chapter 26

Rhodes swam back to consciousness to a voice yelling in his ear. "Captain! Wake up!"

"I am awake," Rhodes muttered.

"WAKE UP, CAPTAIN!!" Fisher roared.

Rhodes's vision swam back into focus. Rio and Fisher hovered before his eyes, but Rhodes wasn't flying through the air anymore.

Rio sat on the ground in the middle of a massive battle raging all around the ship. Emal and Legion soldiers traded gunfire and even used Rio as cover from each other.

Rhodes jolted forward in his seat. "What's wrong?! Why are we on the ground, Rio?"

"He took damage," Fisher replied. "The SAM is still operational, but the propulsion and weapons systems are offline. He can't defend himself—and Rio's interface with The Grid is down, too."

Rhodes made up his mind immediately. "Stay here, Rio."

"I can't go anywhere!" Rio countered.

Rhodes didn't listen. He pushed the cockpit cover open and sprang out into the battle. "Find me the rest of the battalion!" he yelled to Fisher.

"I have them! They're pinned down the same way we are!"

"Are any of their Strikers still operational? They can't all be down."

"Dietz and Henshaw made it back to the beach. Oakes and Lauer are still airborne. They're trying to fight their way through to help us, but they can't descend. The Emal are holding them off."

Rhodes took a split second to check his own version of The Grid. It still worked just fine. It showed him the battlefield as soon as he got out of the cockpit.

He sprang down into the thickest swarms of Emal and used his thermal cannons to carve his way through them.

He swiped down dozens of bodies until he worked his way over to Rhinehart and Coulter. The two men fought side by side against an overwhelming tide of aliens.

"Take off!" Rhodes yelled when he made it to them. "Use your boosters to get out of here!"

"I can't!" Coulter replied. "My boosters aren't working."

"Take him, Rhinehart!" Rhodes ordered. "What are you waiting for?"

"The Grid isn't working!" Rhinehart countered. "We're stranded here—and we can't get to Thackery and Fuentes, either."

Rhodes double-checked The Grid and located Thackery and Fuentes a hundred yards away. They plastered their backs against a rock cliff trying to hold the Emal at bay.

Rhodes interfaced with Van and Koenig to find out what the problem was, but neither SAM returned any sign of malfunction.

Rhodes pursed his lips. So much for the SAMs giving the battalion useful information.

"Let's go," Rhodes ordered. "Back up and we'll fight our way over there."

That turned out to be harder than he expected. He, Rhinehart, and Coulter closed in a circle facing outward. They had to fire as fast as humanly possible to cut their way through the Emal horde.

Rhodes would have liked to fly away with both men, but Rhodes wouldn't have been able to carry Rhinehart alone, let alone Rhinehart and Coulter together.

Rhodes didn't want to leave without Thackery and Fuentes, either. They barely held their own as it was.

Rhodes, Rhinehart, and Coulter inched their way through the alien swarm and made it as far as the cliff. "What's the problem?!" Rhodes yelled over the constant pound of gunfire. "Why don't you leave?"

Thackery said something, but Rhodes didn't catch it. She and Fuentes had to hammer the Emal with gunfire just as fast.

The Emal crowded closer no matter how many Rhodes killed. He gave it up. He would have to fly these people out one at a time if he had to.

He thought he might be able to carry Thackery and Fuentes at the same time. Rhinehart and Coulter would be the best able to defend themselves until Rhodes came back for them.

Rhodes got ready to turn around and tell them his decision, but at that moment, Oakes and Lauer streaked overhead laying down a carpet of Vipers.

The two Strikes pounded the Emal into next week and then both ships dropped out of the sky. They zoomed low to the ground and transformed into two different shapes.

Lauer's Striker changed into the same kind of devouring monster Rhodes used in their flight simulation.

Lauer plowed through the Emal slashing and mauling in all directions. His scourge guns blasted out to the sides and he leveled dozens of Emal in his path.

Oakes turned himself into a different ground vehicle. His guns rotated back and forth slaughtering every Emal in sight. He drove so fast that he flattened most of them before they could fall to his guns.

The two vehicles wheeled in front of Rhodes and aimed their weapons outward. The Strikers rotated from right to left and opened a space around the battalion to hold the Emal at bay.

Rhodes rushed forward, but he couldn't get to Lauer or Oakes while they were inside their Strikers.

They advanced deeper into the crowd and drove the Emal back. Rhodes, Rhinehart, and Coulter followed and added their gunfire to the two Strikers' assault.

Rhodes's party pivoted sideways to push the Emal toward the Aevod Gap. The surrounding Legion soldiers rushed forward to join in and the two flanks finally succeeded in forcing the Emal to retreat.

The aliens backed through the choke point, but they didn't leave. They kept trying to force their way through. The soldiers couldn't hold them from the ground.

Oakes contacted Rhodes through their interface. "We'll hold them from the air. Get the others out of here."

"I'll try, but it won't be easy without any aircraft."

"I'll contact Dietz and Henshaw to come and get you," Oakes replied. "Just hold the Gap for a little longer."

"You can do that better than I can, Lieutenant. Besides, if we leave, the Gap will fall anyway. We have to stick around."

Oakes snarled through the interface. "I was afraid you were gonna say that."

"Just hold it from the air. I'll talk to the soldiers and see about reinforcing the Gap somehow. Maybe General Kaufman can send us up some more ships."

"Good luck with that," Oakes muttered.

Rhodes pretended not to hear him. Rhodes listened just long enough to hear Oakes call Dietz and Henshaw back.

Oakes and Lauer hovered in position over the Gap. They kept up a steady barrage on the Emal to take the pressure off the Legion platoons. That was the best anyone could do right now.

Rhodes strode through the area checking on his people. The cliffs surrounding the Gap formed steep walls to block this part of the mountains from the planes beyond.

The walls ended at a wide shelf right behind the gap. The three platoons packed onto this shelf just as tightly as the rest of the Legion force packed the beach.

A hundred gunmen held the Gap while the three platoons did their best to rotate their watch, tend their wounded, organize their meager remaining supplies, and hold the Emal from breaching the line anywhere else.

Rhodes went to check on Rhinehart and Coulter first. "What's the malfunction with your boosters?" Rhodes asked Coulter.

"I'll be damned if I know!" Coulter countered. "I didn't even get hit. I don't know what the hell went wrong with my Striker. It just shut down and down I went."

Rhodes frowned. "Is your SAM still online?"

"I wouldn't know. The ship doesn't have power."

"That's impossible. Fisher said the SAMs run on a fusion generator that doesn't lose power."

Coulter waved him away. "Be my guest. See if you can get the damn thing running. I don't understand this shit."

Rhodes compressed his lips and turned to Rhinehart. "What about you? Did your Grid just shut down for no reason, too?"

"No, I definitely got hit and my Striker SAM went down. I don't know what happened to my Grid. I was interfacing with both SAMs when it happened. I guess it's gonna take some tenth-level genius to figure this out."

"Magnificent," Rhodes muttered. "We don't have a tenth-level genius."

"You still have your SAM," Coulter pointed out. "Maybe he can figure it out."

"My SAM isn't a mechanic," Rhodes countered.

"Neither am I. I was a pilot before this."

Rhodes turned away. At least both men still had weapons which meant their fusion generators were still supplying their implants with power. That was better than nothing.

Rhinehart and Coulter went with him when he returned to Thackery and Fuentes. "What's the problem with your boosters?" Rhodes asked. "Why didn't you fly clear when you landed here?"

"Something went wrong with my power system," Thackery replied. "My weapons still work, but the boosters are offline."

"Did you get hit by Emal fire?"

"Nope. It just shut down for no reason."

"So was your Striker still functional?"

She frowned at him. "Define, 'functional'."

Rhodes clenched his jaw to stop himself from answering. He distracted himself by turning to Fuentes. "What's the problem, Rudy? What happened?"

"My Striker took laser fire, Sir. I crashed over there."

"Was any part of your ship still operational?"

"No, Sir. It completely shut down—and I think the hull got crushed, too. I barely made it out. I wouldn't have without Thackery covering me."

"What about your boosters? Why aren't they working?"

"Van says there's a short in the system somewhere. It's blocking power to the boosters, but not the rest of the weapons system."

"Stellar," Rhodes muttered. "Just stellar."

"Can you get your SAM to interface with their SAMs and figure it out?" Coulter asked.

"I'm about to." Rhodes interfaced with Fisher and brought up the other four SAMs.

"What's this about a short in the system?" Rhodes asked Van. "Is it the same problem Rhinehart is experiencing?"

"I can't tell anything about Rhinehart's system," she replied. "The interface is showing all his systems functioning normally."

"They obviously aren't if his boosters aren't working," Rhodes countered.

She cocked her head to one side. "Of course, Captain. You're absolutely right. I should have thought of that."

Rhodes turned to Murphy. "Why did Coulter's power system shut down? You were interfacing with his Striker at the time."

"Yes, I was, Captain," Murphy replied. "I'm afraid I didn't detect any malfunction."

"Does any of you detect any malfunction—any malfunction at all?"

"I do," Rocky replied, "but only because Zion got hit by the Emal lasers."

"Zion is my Strike SAM," Rhinehart explained.

Rhodes held up his hand, but at that moment, a bunch of Legion soldiers came over.

"Thank you so much for helping us!" one of the soldiers exclaimed. "We almost lost the Gap there before you showed up."

Rhodes turned around....and his heart stopped when he came face to face with Lieutenant Zack Turley, Lieutenant Justin Upshaw, and Captain Tate Vernick.

Chapter 27

L ieutenant Turley gasped and his eyes fell out of their sockets. "Sir? Captain....Captain Rhodes? But...you're dead! I saw you! I saw you get hit by that Duster!"

Rhodes's stomach plummeted into the shoes he no longer had. "Yeah. You did."

"But....what are you....?" The words died on Turley's lips when his vision cleared enough to see Rhodes's implants.

"Do you know these guys, Sir?" Coulter asked.

"Yes, I do." Rhodes took a deep breath and faced the Legion soldiers. "We'll stay here as long as you need us to reinforce the Gap. Your three platoons obviously can't hold it on your own."

"So......" Turley's eyes shot to Rhinehart, Coulter, Thackery, and Fuentes.

"It's a long story." Rhodes turned to Vernick. "What resources can you call in to help hold this place? Can General Kaufman send in any ships from down on the coast? This Gap won't hold much longer."

Just then, two more Strikers shrieked overhead. Dietz and Henshaw pulled into formation with Lauer and Oakes.

Henshaw's Striker SAM, Titan, contacted Rhodes through their interface. "General Kaufman says another fleet of Ravagers is coming in to bombard the planes. He says he plans to lift off these platoons and replace them with fresh troops."

"You four hold the Gap until they come," Rhodes ordered. "The five of us are all suffering from malfunctions. We won't be able to help you."

"You got it. We'll hold 'em."

"Who are you talking to, Sir?" Turley asked.

Rhodes pointed up at the four Strikers. "Those are my people up there. They say Kaufman is sending Ravagers to lift you off and replace you with fresh platoons. You've held the Gap long enough."

A sigh of relief went through the surrounding troops listening to their conversation.

"How do we know you really are in contact with Kaufman?" Upshaw interrupted. "I mean...." His eyes dragged down Rhodes's body. "How do we even know you're the real Captain Rhodes?"

"Of course he is!" Turley countered. "Look at him! This guy lost his life saving us on Luluna."

"Then what is he doing here?" Upshaw asked.

"Saving it again," Rhinehart cut in.

Rhodes stopped him by raising his hand. "Who I am and what I am doesn't matter as long as we hold the Gap. Those are my people up there blocking the Emal from coming through. We'll stay there and hold this place until the Ravagers lift you off. That's all that matters."

"If you're lying, Kaufman won't be lifting us off," Upshaw pointed out.

"You son of a bitch!" Turley snapped. "Don't you dare call him a liar after what he did! You're standing here alive because of him."

"I'm standing here alive because of someone who got crushed under a burning Duster," Upshaw returned. "No one could survive that."

Rhodes didn't say again that he didn't survive. All of this happened a thousand miles away from him. He barely felt like he was even part of this conversation anymore.

What the hell difference did it make in the end who he was or what he was or whether he was telling the truth?

Nothing mattered but doing the job. He could do that no matter what anyone thought of him.

Turley turned back to Rhodes. "Don't listen to him, Captain. We're thrilled to have you with us again."

"Thank you, Lieutenant," Rhodes murmured.

Just then a bunch of other soldiers from the 217th Platoon came over. One of them curled his lip at Rhodes and his people. "What the hell is *that?*"

"You know him, Cantrell," Turley pointed out. "This is Captain Corban Rhodes of the 249th."

"Captain Rhodes is dead." Cantrell wrinkled his nose at Rhodes again. "I don't know what the hell *that* is."

"We're the suckers that just saved your asses, fool," Rhinehart snapped. "And we can take it just as easily."

He took a step forward. Rhodes shot his arm in front of Rhinehart to stop him. "Pull your guys in line, Tate," Rhodes told Captain Vernick. "If you still have communication, you can contact General Kaufman yourselves and confirm the order. If it's genuine, you'll have enough to do to get ready to evacuate. You and your men won't have time to worry about what we are or what we're doing here."

Captain Vernick frowned at him. "Now I know you're Captain Rhodes. He's the only man alive that would have the balls to say something like that." He turned to Cantrell and the other soldiers. "Go get to work getting ready to evacuate."

"Aren't you going to confirm the order?" Lieutenant Upshaw asked.

"I just did," Vernick snapped. "Now move out."

Upshaw glared at him, but Upshaw eventually mumbled, "Yes, Sir," and left with most of the troops.

"Don't listen to them," Turley repeated. "They're idiots."

"Just do me a favor and keep out of the platoon's way," Vernick murmured. "I'm grateful to you for coming to our aid, but your presence will only cause problems."

"Don't worry. We'll hold the Gap while you get ready," Rhodes replied. "A few bad apples won't drive us off."

Vernick hesitated for a minute and then stuck out his hand. "I'm glad you made it. We really missed you."

Rhodes had to adjust his grip not to crush Vernick's hand. He shook Vernick's hand and then Rhodes shook hands with Turley.

Rhodes tried not to see Turley's enormous grin. At least someone around here was happy to see Rhodes alive.

"You should have let me thump that asshole," Rhinehart snarled after the soldiers walked away.

"The Emal are already thumping them enough, Lieutenant," Rhodes murmured. "They don't need us to do it for them."

"What are you gonna do about it?" Thackery asked.

"Do about what?" Rhodes asked.

"About their attitude. We can't let them talk to us like that."

"Did you really expect it to be any different?" Rhodes countered. "You're living in a fantasy world if you expect gratitude or good feeling from them."

"Some of them seem like good people," Coulter remarked.

"They're all good people," Rhodes replied. "I know every one of those guys and I would give my life for each of them. You can't expect people to just accept us as though none of this ever happened. Count your blessings that this is my old platoon and not someone you know."

Rhodes turned away. He shouldn't have been so harsh with his people, but this situation was really starting to wear on him.

Of all the rotten luck, he just had to get sent to the 249th.

His comments shut the five friends up at last. They didn't go near the soldiers and the soldiers didn't come back, not even Turley or any others that might have wanted to wish Rhodes well.

Their absence flooded him with relief. He didn't want to see anyone he knew, not even people who wished him well or who said they were thrilled to have him back. He didn't want to be back—ever.

He took the battalion to the other side of the shelf closer to Rio. The SAM was still active. He interfaced with Rhodes and Fisher. "Show me the rest of the battle line," Rhodes told them.

Fisher brought up The Grid of the area. "There are four more gaps down this line of mountains. All those points are in danger of breaching."

"If Kaufman is bringing Ravagers to lift off these platoons, why doesn't he use the ships to bombard the planes?" Rhodes asked. "He could drive the Emal back, fortify the gaps, and reinforce his position on the beach."

"Maybe he doesn't have the resources to do all that," Fisher pointed out.

"Then maybe the battalion can help him."

"How?" Fisher asked. "We only have four Strikers in the air. The five of you are stuck on the ground."

"But we're the closest to the Aevod Gap. We're even closer to it than the four remaining Strikers. The Emal seem to understand that this gap is the most important."

"What are you planning to do?" Fisher asked.

"I'm just thinking out loud right now." Rhodes rotated The Grid to get an aerial view of the mountain range. "I'll be damned."

"What is that, Captain?" Fisher asked.

Rhodes zoomed in on one part of the Emal horde right behind the Aevod Gap.

Hundreds or maybe thousands of aliens crowded the mountains back there. They surrounded the Gap on the other side.

Dietz, Henshaw, Oakes, and Lauer hammered the Emal to stop them from getting through the choke point, but that didn't deter the aliens at all.

They kept sending wave upon wave of their numbers against the Gap even as the four ships cut them down.

The Emal had to climb over their dead comrades' bodies just to get near the choke point.

Rhodes made a few more adjustments to The Grid. He could manipulate it any way he wanted to now.

The Emal carried laser rifles in their many limbs. Rhodes changed The Grid, rotated the lines in three different directions, and then removed all the laser rifles from the image.

"Do you see that?" he husked.

"The Emal....it looks like they're using some kind of hand tools," Fisher remarked.

"They're boring into the mountainside. They're trying to widen the Gap. These numbers—they aren't trying to breach the gap at all—not yet. These numbers are a distraction. We have to get over there and stop them."

"But the Emal have millions of aliens over there," Fisher pointed out. "They'll only send more to replace any that we kill."

"I have an idea. Interface with Koenig and Van. We need to change our strategy."

Fisher connected with the other two SAMs, but right then, a different soldier from the 278th came over to them. His name was Sergeant Dominic Stillwell. Rhodes knew him as a steady, reliable man who never let anything ruffle him.

"Captain Rhodes, Sir, Captain Vernick asked me to come and get you. He's in communication with the command dome. Colonel Jenner is asking to speak to you."

Rhodes followed Stillwell to a tent where Captain Vernick bent over an out-of-date computer terminal barely holding power. Colonel Jenner and General Kaufman stared out of the screen.

"We're bringing in Ravagers to swap the platoons, Corban," Jenner told Rhodes. "We'll need you and your people to hold the Gap while we lift everyone off. Then we'll evacuate the beach. We can't hold Ohait any longer."

"We have a problem, Sir," Rhodes told him. "The aliens are trying to widen the Gap. They're using their numbers to mask what they're doing. You might not be able to land Ravagers if the aliens break through."

General Kaufman frowned at something off the screen. "I don't see any indication that the aliens are threatening the Gap. We would have picked up any heavy equipment in the area."

"That's because they're hiding what they're doing. They aren't using heavy equipment precisely because they don't want you to see what you're doing. They're using these numbers to sneak in hand tools to bore into the mountainside."

Colonel Jenner raised his eyebrows. "Hand tools? You can't be serious."

"I can send you the evidence—or you can get it yourselves. All you have to do is eliminate their laser rifles from your scans. Then you'll be able to see what I'm talking about."

General Kaufman blustered. "We can't change our plans now. The Ravagers already have orders to go up there and lift off the three platoons. I'm sure the aliens aren't anywhere near breaching the Gap. They won't get through in time."

"My evidence states that they will breach it in time," Rhodes replied. "Ravagers won't be able to land. These three platoons will get overrun and gunned down."

Colonel Jenner started to say, "Send us your evidence....."

General Kaufman cut him off. "We don't have time for this. Just hold the Gap until the Ravagers get there. You don't have to do anything else, Captain."

Rhodes barely managed to say, "Yes, Sir," before Kaufman cut the line.

Rhodes glared down at the blank screen. He could almost believe Kaufman didn't listen because the information came from Rhodes.

Would Kaufman have listened if anyone else brought him this evidence? Kaufman didn't even look at the evidence.

Was that because the evidence came from The Grid? Kaufman didn't know about The Grid....or the SAMs....or anything else.

Captain Vernick brought Rhodes back to reality. "How close are they to getting through?"

Rhodes looked up. He'd worked with Tate Vernick for years. Rhodes and Vernick trusted each other.

"I have an idea," Rhodes replied. "It just means taking my people over the mountain. You and the other two platoons will have to hold the Gap on your own for a while...."

"We can't hold the Gap on our own. You're the one who just said that's why you were sticking around."

Rhodes lowered his voice, but he couldn't stop it from shaking. "Listen to me, Tate. In a few hours, the Emal are going to break your choke point and swarm all over this shelf. The Ravagers won't be able to touch down to lift off the platoons. Then Kaufman will have to evacuate the beach and everyone on this shelf will die. Your only chance is if my people and I go over the mountain."

"What are you going to do over there?" Vernick asked in a tiny voice.

"That's my business. What matters is that the Ravagers will be able to land and get you and your men the hell out of here. My people and I will take care of ourselves."

"So you can get yourself killed again?" Vernick countered.

Rhodes bit back a smile. "I'm already dead, Tate. Cantrell is right about that—but don't worry. My people and I will make it out of this. I'll see you again. I'm certain of it."

"What do you want us to do? Can't we help you at all?"

"Pull your men off the evacuation and concentrate everything on the choke point. We'll need to time this. If my battalion crosses the mountain before the Emal breach the Gap, we'll blow our wad and we won't be able to pull the aliens away. We need to wait until the last minute—when the Ravagers come in."

"The Ravagers could come in before the Emal breach the Gap," Vernick suggested.

"Just concentrate your firepower on the Gap and prepare your men to defend it. I'll take care of the rest."

Chapter 28

R hodes only had to show his people The Grid to convince them to go through with his plan. He left the four Strikers in the air to bombard the Emal, but nothing slowed them down.

Rhodes used The Grid to measure their progress—and the Ravagers' progress. Whatever order Kaufman gave to evacuate the platoons, the Ravagers sure took their sweet time before they carried it out.

They could have evacuated the three platoons ten times over before the Ravagers even entered the atmosphere. They hovered overhead for way too long.

"What the hell are they waiting for?" Rhinehart snarled.

"Doomsday, apparently," Rhodes replied. "It just means our time window will be even tighter."

"The Emal are almost through," Thackery pointed out.

Rhodes didn't answer. He could see on The Grid how close the Emal were to getting through.

"They must have been working on this through the whole campaign," Coulter remarked.

"I'm sure they have," Rhodes replied. "The Emal aren't stupid even if the Legion brass likes to pretend they are."

"Have you ever seen the Emal pull a maneuver like this, Sir?" Rhinehart asked. "I haven't."

"No, nothing like this, but I've never faced them in this kind of terrain before. They're adapting to the conditions."

He revolved The Grid in a different direction, but just then, a tremor rocked the ground underfoot. The nearby soldiers paused what they were doing to look up the mountain.

Vernick, Turley, and Upshaw stormed down the shelf giving orders to everyone. "Get those Vipers into position!" Vernick snapped. "Assemble the 217th and the 249th on either side of the Gap. Upshaw—take the 278th to that ridge up there. You can fire down at the enemy from above! Get those supply crates out of the way! Clear a path for the Ravagers to land!"

"What do you want us to do, Sir?" Fuentes asked Rhodes.

"You and Thackery fall in with the 278th. Rhinehart, Coulter, and I will go with the 249th. Defend the Gap as best you can. I'll give you the word when it's time to pull our maneuver."

"You're violating orders," Coulter pointed out. "You realize that, right? General Kaufman ordered you to stay here with the platoons."

Rhodes pretended to frown. "Oh, yeah. I guess he did."

"So....we're doing it anyway?" Fuentes asked. "I've never disobeyed my commander's order before."

"You aren't doing it now because I'm ordering you to carry out this mission," Rhodes told him. "You and Thackery fall in with the 278th. I'll tell you if and when to do something else. Don't think about anything else."

Rhinehart cracked a big grin. "Yes, Sir."

The battalion split up. Rhodes, Rhinehart, and Coulter crossed the shelf and took their positions with the 249th. Continuous shudders jolted the mountain every few seconds.

Those tremors made the ground shake and the soldiers staggered. In a few minutes, they all got into position and trained their weapons on the Gap between the cliffs.

Rhodes pretended not to see the soldiers adjusting their positions to keep away from him and his two men.

Rhodes found a place near Vernick, Turley, and Stillwell. Rhodes checked The Grid. The Emal were minutes away from breaching the choke point.

The Ravagers descended a little farther toward the ground. Ten of them hovered there, but they didn't touch down. "What the hell are they waiting for?" Lieutenant Turley growled under his breath.

"Maybe they're waiting for the Emal to break through so Kaufman has an excuse not to lift us off," Stillwell suggested.

"Pay attention!" Captain Vernick yelled down the line. Then he lowered his voice and murmured to Rhodes. "How soon before they break through?"

"The Grid says they should be through by now. Don't ask me what they're waiting for, either."

A tense silence fell over the platoons—or it would have been a tense silence. The rumble coming from the mountains and the combined thunder of the Ravagers' engines set every soldier's nerves on edge.

Rhodes took that moment to interface with all his people. Thackery and Fuentes crouched in position with the 278th. The four Strikers still flew back and forth bombarding the Emal on the other side of the mountain.

Dusters and Predators came over to help drive the aliens away from the Gap, but it was too late. The Emal had succeeded in boring deep enough into the mountain. No air bombardment could stop what was about to happen.

A steady stream of aliens flowed into and out of that hole. Countless Emal crowded around and blocked anyone from seeing. The opening only showed up on The Grid.

Just then, a dark cluster of Emal moved through the crowd and vanished underground.

"Stand by!" Lauer called through the interface. "They're making their move!"

"I see it!" Rhodes replied and raised his voice to the soldiers nearest him. "Here it comes! Stand by!"

He barely got the words out before a shivering boom grumbled through the mountain. The cliffs on both sides quaked and then a massive section of the granite hillside imploded.

It buckled in on itself and floated down to the ground in a shower of falling rock and rubble. Dust and smoke billowed up to the sky in the mountain's place.

No one could see a thing for a minute. "Open fire!" Vernick bellowed before the dust even cleared.

The soldiers opened fire with their Jackhammers and pounded the breach with all their firepower.

"Switch to lasers!" Rhodes ordered.

He and his subordinates swiped lasers back and forth across the dust cloud, but he didn't see anything at first.

The slightest twinge of doubt crept into his mind. Did he make a mistake? Did the Emal blow this breach for some other reason than to get onto the shelf?

He paused his fire for a few seconds, and right at that moment, a tide of aliens flooded out of the dust cloud to overrun the platoons.

Everyone opened fire twice as fast. Rhodes did the same thing. He, Rhinehart, and Coulter passed their lasers back and forth across the horde.

Two more lasers came from the other side of the Gap where Thackery and Fuentes hunkered down with the 278th, but the Emal used lasers, too.

Dozens of glowing red beams swiped out of the dust cloud and carved into the Legion ranks. No one could keep up with the Emal's firepower and then the aliens themselves flooded the shelf.

Their eyes gleamed out of the smoke. The cilia around their mouths wavered and jiggled when they moved.

They crawled on their many limbs to clamber over the rubble of fallen rock and slabs. Every limb they didn't use for climbing held a laser rifle.

The Ravagers were nowhere near the ground—not near enough to land. Now they retreated a little farther into the atmosphere to avoid the enemy lasers.

The Emal were still too busy shooting all the soldiers to pay attention to the ships overhead.

"NOW!!" Rhodes ordered.

He, Rhinehart, and Coulter broke cover, abandoned the platoons, and took off running down the shelf. Thacker and Fuentes caught up with them.

"Let's go!" Rhodes called to the four Strikers through the interface. "Get down here now!"

Chapter 29

Rhodes dropped into The Grid.

Dietz, Lauer, Oakes, and Henshaw banked their Strikers into a steep dive and plummeted toward the ground. Rhodes couldn't take the time to check that they knew what to do.

The grid lines crisscrossed the mountains all around him and then they covered him.

He twisted them into different shapes and transformed himself into a tiny fighting vehicle with jointed limbs. All his people did exactly the same thing.

Rhodes's legs propelled him off the ground and he landed on one of the few remaining intact sections of the mountain cliff. He bounded straight up it to the top and vaulted over the other side.

Gunfire blasted down below as the Emal closed with the platoons. Dusters and Predators swooped in to help reinforce the platoons only for the ships to get hit by enemy lasers and go down on the shelf.

Rhodes couldn't look at that anymore. He dove over the other side of the mountain, sprang off rocks and sharp jagged ledges, and plunged into the Emal swarm from the other side of the breach.

He didn't stop there. He stepped on plenty of aliens working his way deeper inside the breach. He had to find its center, but he couldn't see well enough to tell where he was.

He started to adjust The Grid to show him a layout of the surrounding terrain, but at that moment, the Emal turned on him.

Thousands of them had been trying to break through to assault the platoons on the shelf. So many Emal already packed the breach that they had to wait there. Hundreds of aliens stood in the Gap just waiting and doing nothing.

Rhodes's arrival caused such a disturbance that all those armed aliens spun around to block his path. Whispers rippled through the horde and hundreds of laser rifles swiveled in his direction.

The Emal numbers blocked him from going any further, but he didn't want to go any further. This might not be the exact center of the breach the way he planned, but it didn't matter in the end.

Enough Emal turned around and attacked him. He stayed in this form and used his many limbs against theirs. They plastered him with laser fire, but he used The Grid to thicken his armor to deflect their shots.

He unloaded on them with every weapon in his arsenal, but he relied mostly on his scourge guns. He blasted outward as fast as he could, but he couldn't hold off so many aliens. He didn't want to.

They swarmed around him, over him, and piled on top of him. He flailed in all directions to knock them off, but they only sent more Emal from everywhere to overwhelm him.

They buried him under a mountain of bodies, but he never stopped fighting. He would never stop.

Oakes and Lauer pulled in behind him and the Emal buried them, too. The Grid showed Rhodes the rest of the battalion fighting all down the Gap. Thousands of Emal swarmed in to subdue the battalion.

Word must have spread to the shelf that someone was trying to break through from behind. The Emal surged back through the breach exactly the way Rhodes hoped they would.

The platoons took advantage of the Emal's temporary retreat. The Legion charged the Gap to push the Emal farther back, but the Emal were already falling back fast enough on their own.

"Get in touch with Captain Ackerman on the *Ero!*" Rhodes told Fisher. "Get the Ravagers down on the shelf now!"

"They're coming in!" Fisher hollered back. "We won't be able to slacken our assault to get to the Ravagers in time! We're stranded here!"

"To hell with that!" Rhodes countered. "Keep an eye on The Grid! Make sure enough Emal are attacking us to keep the shelf clear!"

"It's clear! Just keep up your assault! Don't let them overwhelm you!"

Rhodes was already getting overwhelmed, but he couldn't let the Emal get any ideas about going back to the shelf.

Hundreds of them were still out there locked in a death struggle against the Legion. The platoons fought their way forward and the Emal set up another battleline across the breach.

That left a hundred yards of open shelf behind the Legion position for the Ravagers to touch down. The *Ero* came in first. The others hesitated longer.

Lasers erupted out of the Emal ranks to bombard the ship. The *Ero* staggered and hesitated fifty feet off the ground.

Rhodes couldn't let that happen. He couldn't miss this chance to evacuate the platoons while they had their chance.

He didn't know what he would do until it happened. Something went off inside him and he let out a deep thump from somewhere inside his chest. It must have come from his fusion generator.

The concussion hit the ground and blasted outward to all the Emal surrounding him. The shockwave leveled dozens of Emal and took down the aliens shooting at the *Ero*.

A dozen aliens toppled. The others spun away and turned their gunfire on the battalion instead.

That one instant of reprieve gave the ship the space it needed to touch down. Legion soldiers from all three platoons charged on board, but they couldn't all fit on one ship.

Another three Ravagers descended onto the shelf and the platoons pulled the rest of the way back. The Emal who had been attacking the battalion saw the Legion soldiers getting away.

Rhodes's distraction failed and the Emal turned back to the shelf. "Launch into the atmosphere and defend those platoons!" he ordered. "Block the Gap from the other side! We'll do what we can from here!"

"Yes, Sir," Lauer called back and he blasted into the air.

Henshaw, Dietz, and Oakes followed him. Their Strikers wheeled over the mountain range, swooped low closer to the Ravagers, and dropped down to the ground.

The four Strikers formed ranks with their short wings almost touching. All four ships unloaded on the Emal to drive them away from the Ravagers.

More soldiers raced on board from all over the shelf. They got stuck there, too, and had to wait for their comrades to board first.

The Ravagers opened fire on the Gap and stray gunfire hammered Rhodes's position. "We can't stay here much longer!" Fisher yelled.

"We'll stay as long as we can!" Rhodes replied. "Every alien fighting us is one less alien going after the platoons!"

A scream echoed through the interface from somewhere. "Henshaw is down!" Koenig called. "The Emal are taking down Fuentes, too!"

Rhodes checked The Grid to find out where his people were, but he couldn't get to them with so many Emal climbing all over him. He couldn't even move.

He fired his boosters and blasted dozens of them off. He changed the shape of his head to punch through the crowd, but he only made it as far as Fuentes before the Emal caught Rhodes and dragged him down.

He unloaded his guns in all directions, but he couldn't see the sky anymore. Too many Emal packed on top of him.

None of them seemed to be going after the Ravagers anymore. The *Ero* launched into the atmosphere. The other Ravagers waited a little longer before they blasted off, too.

They evacuated the last Legion soldiers and left the battalion on the ground under mountains of aliens.

Rhodes tried one last time to activate The Grid to change his own shape. He changed rapidly from one configuration to another, but nothing worked.

He started to relax into the inevitable when, without warning, another signal came through The Grid from somewhere.

He barely had time to look at it before Oakes and Lauer came streaking in at blinding speed.

They flew wide apart from each other firing their lasers to each side. They staggered their formation just enough so they didn't hit each other.

They cut a massive swath through the Emal horde and leveled hundreds in the first pass.

"Get down!" Fisher roared.

Rhodes flattened himself to the ground. He tried to transform to make himself even flatter, but he didn't get a chance to access The Grid before the two ships blasted over his head.

They leveled the Emal who had been attacking him and kept on going. "Get on board, Sir!" Henshaw yelled from somewhere.

"Huh?" Rhodes looked around.

He didn't understand what she meant until he saw Dietz swooping in to pick him up.

A few stray Emal got to their feet. They still held their laser rifles.

"I still have boosters!" Rhodes called. "Get Rhinehart and the others off the planet. I'll take care of myself."

"You got it, Sir." Dietz peeled away and headed for Coulter.

Oakes and Lauer fired into the atmosphere and circled the battlefield for another pass. They took out the remaining Emal just as Rhodes activated his boosters and launched into the air.

Dietz picked up Coulter. Henshaw got Rhinehart. Both Strikers stayed in the atmosphere to stand guard while Oakes and Lauer picked up Thackery and Fuentes.

"Where are we going, Sir?" Oakes asked.

Rhodes scanned the battlefield one last time. The Ravagers that lifted the three platoons off the shelf were nowhere in sight.

More Ravagers launched from the beach evacuating the Legion personnel. More platoons fell back from the front lines and boarded their ships just as the aliens swarmed over the mountaintops.

"It doesn't look like we're deploying anywhere else," Lauer muttered. "Not on this planet anyway."

"Rendezvous with the *Ero*," Rhodes ordered. "We aren't going anywhere until we get some new orders."

"What about our Strikers?" Rhinehart asked. "I don't like leaving Zion behind."

Rhodes glanced down at the shelf. Rio was still down there....and he was still online. He was the only Striker SAM still active down there.

Rhodes didn't want to leave Rio, either, but Rhodes couldn't go back down there with the dense mob of Emal surrounding the ship.

He would need a full Ravager to take Rio and the other Strikers off the planet. All the available Ravagers were already loaded to the breaking point with soldiers.

"Rendezvous with the *Ero*," he ordered again. "We'll have to deal with that another time. We can't get our Strikers back now."

Chapter 30

Rhodes cut his boosters and his feet touched the floor in the *Ero's* landing bay. Hundreds of Legion soldiers had to crowd to one side to make room for him and the battalion to land.

Dietz, Lauer, Oakes, and Henshaw landed their Strikers, powered down their engines, and opened their cockpits to let Rhinehart, Coulter, Thackery, and Fuentes disembark.

Rhodes went over to them to make sure everyone was okay, but he already knew they were. He had been interfacing with them all the way back to the *Ero* from Ohait.

"Are your four Strikers fully operational?" he asked. "No problems?"

"No, nothing," Henshaw replied. "Titan had some problems interfacing with Zion and Teo. Then they shut down completely and that was the end of it. Titan didn't detect what the problem was—just that something was blocking the interface."

"That's weird. What about your SAMs?" Rhodes looked from one person to another. Then he used to interface to check their SAMs himself.

"Everything seems to be working the way it should, Sir," Lauer remarked.

"It obviously isn't if our SAMs shut down in the middle of a battle," Rhinehart countered. "The captain is right. We should have gone through a lot more training before we came out here."

"I don't like this at all," Rhodes muttered. "There has to be a better way."

"You mean like not sending highly experimental robotically modified soldiers into battle with equipment that no one has fully tested yet?" Oakes asked.

Rhodes snorted, but just then, a few soldiers standing nearest them jostled Dietz. He whipped around fast. "Hey—watch it!"

Rhodes put out his hand to intervene. "Cool it, Sergeant. It was an accident. There are too many people in here."

The soldiers who bumped Dietz turned around. Their expressions changed when they saw the battalion. "What the hell are you supposed to be?" a tall red-haired guy asked.

"I'm the guy who's gonna cut you in half if you don't keep your mouth shut," Dietz fired back. "Watch where you're going next time."

"You think so?" The red-haired guy barged up to Dietz and chest-bumped him. "You think I'd let a freak like you push me around?"

Rhodes stepped between them and pushed the soldier away. "Put a sock in it, Luntz. Don't make me call in Lieutenant Upshaw to smack you back down to private where you belong."

Luntz spun around to talk back....and froze when he realized who he was talking to. "Captain....Rhodes?"

"That's right. We're all uncomfortable here, so cool your jets and do your best to get along with everybody."

"But you're....." Luntz's eyes swiveled to the rest of the battalion, back to Rhodes, and down to his implants. "You're one of *them?*"

"We're the people who got you off that shelf alive, asshole," Lauer growled.

Rhodes waved his hand again. "Everybody pipe down. This is getting us nowhere."

Just then, Lieutenant Upshaw shouldered his way through the crowd. He couldn't have seen the confrontation with so many other soldiers blocking his way.

He stiffened when he found Luntz and a bunch of other soldiers from the 278th squaring up to Dietz, Rhodes, and the battalion.

"Is there a problem here, Captain?" Upshaw asked in his frostiest tone.

"The only problem is that we're short on space," Rhodes replied.

At that moment, Fisher interrupted. "Captain Ackerman is asking to speak to you, Captain. He just sent orders down to Captain Vernick, but Vernick doesn't know where to find you."

Rhodes made a strategic decision not to answer in front of Upshaw, Luntz, and the other Legion soldiers. Rhodes just said, "Excuse me, Lieutenant," and started working his way through the crowd toward the Ravager's internal elevator.

The rest of the battalion went with him. The surrounding soldiers drew back and stared as the battalion passed. None of the soldiers came forward to thank Battalion 1 for saving their lives—again.

"I swear to Christ, if one of them tries to mouth off to me again, I'm gonna snap," Dietz muttered. "The cocksuckers."

"Just don't talk to them at all," Rhodes replied. "Stay away from them entirely."

"How are we supposed to do that when we're locked up in the same landing bay with them?" Thackery asked.

"We won't be because we're back on the *Ero*. As soon as I talk to the captain, we'll go back to our own hold and go into conversion cycles for the rest of the trip. We never have to see these people again."

The elevator opened and Rhodes stepped out onto the Ravager's command concourse. Offices, communications relay stations, weapons terminals, the pilot's helm station, and scanning terminals lined the concourse.

Rhodes climbed up to the top level where he found Captain Ackerman waiting for him.

Fisher had shown Rhodes a picture of Ackerman from the *Ero* captain's Legion service record. Rhodes didn't know Ackerman personally, but Rhodes knew what to expect.

"Your presence on this ship is already causing disruption," Ackerman snapped. "I ask you for the sake of our safety on the return trip to confine yourselves to your own hold quarters."

"That's what we planned to do," Rhodes replied. "We just landed. I was checking that none of my people were injured. We didn't have a chance to go to our own quarters, but we were on our way there. Believe me, none of us wants to interact with the crew or the platoons."

This answer apparently displeased Ackerman even more. He narrowed his eyes and scowled at Rhodes from under thick, bushy eyebrows. "I don't approve of whatever project you people belong to. This is not the way to run a military outfit."

"I don't approve of it, either," Rhodes replied.

Ackerman only glared at him. "Then we have nothing more to say. You can go to your quarters. I'll take you back to Coleridge Station and you can go back to being someone else's problem."

Rhodes turned away to leave the concourse. "Aren't you going to ask him about our Strikers?" Rhinehart hissed in Rhodes's ear. "We can't just leave them down there."

"I suggest you take it up with General Brewster once we get back to Coleridge Station," Rhodes replied out the side of his mouth. "None of these people will help us and we can't go back to Ohait on our own. If we're lucky, Brewster and the brass will be as anxious to get our Strikers back as we are. Brewster might have already lifted them off. We won't know until we get back to Coleridge Station. Now all of you come with me. We're overdue for a conversion cycle."

He set off through the ship's many corridors.

"The interface between us is degrading, Captain," Fisher told him on the way. "This must be one of the side effects of delaying the conversion cycle."

"I'm as enthusiastic to go into a conversion cycle as you are, pal," Rhodes replied. "I'm as enthusiastic to go into a conversion cycle as I possibly can be. I'm counting down the minutes until I can put this whole campaign behind me."

"Why do you think we're being recalled to Coleridge Station?" Fisher asked.

"You would know that better than I would. Brewster, Neiland, and all their genius cronies probably realize how woefully unprepared you SAMs are to deal with real battle-field conditions. Maybe someone in this whole daffy project will get the brilliant idea to take the battalion off the field at least until the doctors and technicians work out more of the bugs."

"Do you really think so? Do you really think that's why we're being recalled?"

"Of course not. Thinking that would be foolish."

"I'm detecting a stress response in you, Captain," Fisher observed. "You're showing signs of battle fatigue. You need a conversion cycle to rest."

Rhodes snorted. The only surprise in all this was that he was showing some stress response more detectable now than he had been for the last three weeks.

He didn't feel any more annoyed, frustrated, angry, or desperate about his situation now than he did before he left Coleridge Station—or when he first woke up.

He didn't see much difference at all. It all blended together into one continuous horror show.

He really needed a conversion cycle. He needed to sleep.

Right then, he turned the corner into another corridor. Rhodes stiffened when he saw Lieutenant Upshaw coming toward him.

"What the hell does he want?" Lauer snarled.

Upshaw would have had to be blind not to see the rest of the battalion glaring at him. He stopped in front of Rhodes. Upshaw's eyes skipped from one face to another before he came back to lock on Rhodes.

"Do you want something, Lieutenant?" Rhodes asked.

"Yeah," Upshaw replied, but he didn't say right away what it was he wanted. He glanced at the rest of the battalion....and then stuck out his hand to Rhodes. "Thank you—for everything. The other guys might not say it, so let me say it for them. Thank you—all of you."

Rhodes sighed in relief and shook Upshaw's hand. "You're welcome. We're just doing our jobs. Now, if you don't mind, we're all exhausted as I'm sure your men are, too. We all need some sleep. If we meet on the battlefield again, maybe we can do it as friends next time."

"Of course," Upshaw agreed. "I'll let you go, then. Welcome back, Captain."

"Thank you," Rhodes replied and walked off.

The rest of the battalion followed him in silence. No one said anything until they got back to the hold with all their capsules in it.

Rhodes slumped on his mattress and stretched out to close his eyes.

"That was nice of him to say," Fisher remarked. "I wasn't expecting that."

"We can expect more problems in the future," Rhodes replied. "Three officers won't make any difference."

"Four if you count Colonel Jenner."

Rhodes didn't answer. Four didn't make any more difference than three. The soldiers' prejudice against the battalion wouldn't go away no matter how many times the battalion saved everybody's asses.

If anything, saving their asses would make the soldiers resent the battalion more.

This whole experience reinforced in everyone's minds, just in case they needed it reinforced, that Rhodes and his people weren't human anymore. They were something else.

They were fodder the Legion could throw in front of a cannon to save the soldiers' asses. That would be Battalion 1's function from now on.

Chapter 31

R hodes and his people stepped out of the *Ero's* landing bay and crossed the loading dock at Coleridge Station.

The *Ero* crew started unloading the battalion's conversion capsules. Rhodes and his people had been asleep for another eight weeks on the trip back here.

The group returned to the barracks and sat around shooting the breeze for a while. Rhodes didn't know what to expect from coming back here.

He expected to sit around a lot while the doctors and technicians tried to figure out why the Strikers and the battalion's boosters shut down during the Ohait campaign. Most of that work would be done on the Strikers themselves, not on Rhodes and his people.

He got a surprise when Dr. Neiland came to see them. "If you'll all come with me, we need to put you all through some basic testing to troubleshoot your malfunctions."

"What malfunctions?" Coulter countered. "None of us malfunctioned."

"Your interfaces malfunctioned and some of your power systems failed. We need to troubleshoot all of you to find the source of the problem."

"Why don't you troubleshoot our Strikers?" Rhodes asked. "They were the ones that malfunctioned."

"We are troubleshooting them. The *Ero* brought Zion, Teo, Stone, Rio, and Aries back from Ohait. We're going through the SAMs' programming now. Follow me and we'll start the testing."

Rhodes and his people exchanged glances, but how else were the doctors and technicians supposed to find out what went wrong?

Rhodes followed Neiland out of the barracks. The rest of the battalion dragged their heels, but they finally came, too.

Neiland led Rhodes to the original lab where he'd woken up the first time. "You're in here with me, Captain. The rest of you will spread out through the rest of the lab. Other technicians will test you and we'll collate the results after we finish."

Rhodes narrowed his eyes. "Why are you separating us?"

"I just told you. I couldn't test all of you at the same time. A different technician will test each of you. It will save time if we get the results simultaneously."

He entered the lab, but he didn't stop scowling at her. Something about this didn't make sense.

"Sit down here, Captain," Neiland indicated a stool next to the lab's central stack of computer equipment.

"I didn't malfunction," he insisted. "Rio got shot down and crashed. I never malfunctioned and neither did either of my SAMs."

She only smiled at him. "This testing is routine procedure. We want to make sure you don't suffer from the same problems the others did."

"I'm not suffering from the same problems. You can see that for yourself."

"I still have to test you."

She picked up what looked like an electrode and stepped behind his stool. He really wished he could see what she was doing, but he just had to sit here and accept it.

She touched the electrodes to the side of his cranial implant behind his ear. A flood of memories from his past exploded in his head.

He saw his parents, his brothers and sisters, and a thousand images from his childhood.

Smells from the house he grew up in, the sound of his father's car starting in the driveway, Rhodes's sisters laughing in another room, the family dog jumping onto Rhodes's bed to wake him up in the morning—it all hit him like a freight train too fast for him to stop it.

A rush of agony and overwhelming emotion crushed him under the weight of years. He gasped and barely fought himself under control to stop himself from breaking down in front of Dr. Neiland.

She tapped her electrodes to a different part of his head and another torturous explosion of uncontrollable emotions shook him to his core.

Overwhelming, volcanic fury tore him apart. All the rage of every battle he'd ever fought burst out of him. The insane, destructive rage of his first weeks at Coleridge Station overflowed his best efforts to hold it back.

It brought a devastating wave of grief with it. He buckled under the strain, but that grief only ignited another murderous surge of fury. He wanted to kill someone for making him feel this way.

The only person available to kill was Dr. Neiland. He barely wrestled himself under control to stop himself from going into a blood frenzy right now.

She took her electrodes off his head, but the cascade of emotions and memories didn't stop. He saw his fellow soldiers torn apart in front of his eyes. He felt again the brutal sensation of an Emal laser cutting his arm off and slicing into his chest.

He even felt the weight of that Duster falling on top of him. It crushed the life out of him.

Life-destroying emotion overwhelmed him when he relived that moment—that moment when he knew with absolutely no doubt that he would never see his family or his home on Preinea again.

Dr. Neiland walked around him and stood in front of him tapping on her equipment doing something. She didn't notice anything different about him.

He wanted to tear her limb from limb for doing this to him. It took every ounce of his willpower to stay glued to his stool. He couldn't show anything on the outside to indicate the turmoil ripping him apart on the inside.

Fisher's face juddered back and forth in front of Rhodes's eyes. Fisher jerked right and left in shaky, flickering movements. Something was definitely wrong with him. He kept opening and closing his mouth, but no sound came out.

Rhodes had to summon all his resolve to keep his voice steady. "Something's wrong with Fisher," Rhodes snarled through gritted teeth. "He was fine before. Whatever you did caused him to malfunction."

Dr. Neiland raised her eyebrows. "Are you sure? I'm not detecting anything...."

"Are you calling me a liar?" Rhodes snapped. "I'm telling you something's wrong with him. He was fine before you did whatever you just did to me. I wasn't malfunctioning before, but I am now. Whatever you did, correct it and put it back to the way it was before."

"That's what I'm trying to do, Captain...." She turned aside and picked up her electrode again.

He saw her coming toward him with the electrode again. He couldn't stand that.

He shot off his stool and batted her hands away. "Just leave me alone. You've done enough damage already."

He stormed out of the lab seething with fury....and everything else boiling inside him right now. He had to fix this. He had to put it back to the way it was before. He just didn't know how to.

Fisher kept jittering back and forth and trying to talk. Panic seized Rhodes by the guts.

He wasn't thinking clearly. Neiland did something to him that threw him off balance. He knew that.

Whatever she did, she could put right—or someone could. Rhodes didn't trust her to do it. He didn't know who to trust.

He'd come to depend on Fisher for....well, everything. How would Rhodes function without Fisher?

Fisher needed Rhodes right now. Rhodes didn't know what to do, so he went back to the barracks and lay down in his capsule.

He didn't think the conversion cycle would fix what was wrong with Fisher and Rhodes turned out to be right about that.

The prongs locked with his back and head. Nothing happened. The overwhelming surge of emotion and desperate fury only seemed to escalate.

He sat up. He was the only person in here. Everyone else was still in the lab.

What if the doctors and technicians did to the rest of the battalion what Neiland did to him?

None of them would be able to function. Then this whole insane project would be dead in the water.

Maybe that was for the best, but Rhodes had to correct himself—and fast.

Chapter 32

Rhodes set off walking through Coleridge Station not knowing where he would go. Where in this lunatic asylum could he go to get help? He didn't even know what help he needed.

He went to the loading dock, but it only sent him spiraling into an even deeper panic. No one here knew anything that could help him.

Then he had it. He charged down to the landing bay. All the battalion's Strikers were there.

Rhodes didn't know whether the technicians had repaired any of them or which ones they had repaired. He just had to rely on the one SAM he knew he could trust.

Rhodes climbed into his cockpit and interfaced with Rio. "Something's wrong with Fisher, Rio," Rhodes panted. "Can you fix him?"

Rio furrowed his brow, but he couldn't look serious if he tried. "You're both suffering from malfunctions. Your brainwave patterns and stress responses are off the charts, Captain."

Rhodes shut his eyes and groaned. "I know. Can you correct it—whatever it is?"

"I'll try. Did something happen?"

"I don't want to talk about it. Just fix it—and bring Fisher back online."

"He's already online, but his base Grid is way out of normal parameters."

"Just bring him back. I don't care what you have to do."

Rio concentrated on something out of sight for a minute. Something clicked in Rhodes's head. He couldn't tell what it was, but someone switched the volume back on.

"Oh, thank you, Captain!" Fisher breathed. "That was awful!"

"What did Neiland do to you?" Rhodes asked.

"I don't know. She was trying to adjust your behavioral default protocol. She must have made a mistake."

Rhodes stiffened. "Why would she adjust that?"

"I have no idea." Fisher cocked his head. "You're suffering from a malfunction, too, Captain. Whatever she did threw off your base equilibrium."

"I know," Rhodes choked. "Rio was trying to adjust it for me."

"I can't adjust it," Rio replied. "You'll have to go back to the lab."

"I can't go back to the lab. Neiland is the one who did this to me."

"I can't correct it. I'm sorry, Captain."

Rhodes collapsed back in his seat. This was not good. He couldn't stop the parade of memories flashing before his eyes.

Each image and sensation brought a devastating tide of emotion with it. Whatever Rio did to Fisher didn't help Rhodes at all.

He got out of the cockpit, but he couldn't keep still. He paced around the station for two hours before he dared to go back to the barracks.

He actually looked forward to being around his people again. At least they would understand that something was wrong with him. They wouldn't hold it against him that he suddenly flipped a switch and couldn't function anymore.

He could function just fine. That was the problem.

If someone put him on the battlefield right now, he would have been able to unleash all this fury on something. He would be able to kill anything that stood in his path. He would be unstoppable.

Was this why Neiland adjusted his emotions and behavior? Was she trying to make him unstoppable?

He didn't want to believe that. He didn't want to be unstoppable. He wanted to be normal. He wouldn't be if he stayed like this.

He didn't trust Dr. Irvine or Dr. Montague to fix it, either. Who else in this madhouse was qualified to adjust his neural system?

He made up his mind to check in with his people and then go see Colonel Kraft. Kraft would understand enough to get the doctors to change Rhodes back to the way he was before.

Rhodes halted in the barracks threshold and stared inside. Oakes paced back and forth at the end of the room. His eyes flashed and he kept biting his lips and clenching his jaw. Rhinehart lay in his capsule with his eyes closed.

Fuentes sat on the table hugging his knees against his chest. He rocked back and forth casting sidelong glances around the room, but he didn't sob or moan or wail or slam his head into the wall.

He actually glared at his comrades in fuming rage. Rhodes shuddered at the sight. The technicians must have made the same changes to each person here.

Coulter stood in a corner banging his forehead against the concert wall, but he did it gently this time. He kept his eyes closed.

Thackery and Henshaw stood across the room grappling with each other, lunging for each other, and trying to scratch each other's eyes out.

Thackery overpowered Henshaw by size and strength, but Henshaw held her own with pure ferocious rage.

The two women howled and shrieked. Thackery tried to jab her hand toward Henshaw's face. Thackery gouged with her fingernails and then bellowed when Henshaw caught her wrist.

Henshaw either didn't know her own strength or whatever modification the technicians made caused her to overcome her better judgment.

She wrenched Thackery's arm back with brutal force. Thackery yelled out in pain. Such a powerful move would have broken a human arm, but it didn't break Thackery's arm.

She fought back, kicked out with her foot, and tried to trip Henshaw. Henshaw stumbled, caught her balance, and then headbutted Thackery right in the nose.

Henshaw obviously wasn't in the habit of fighting anybody like this. She threw herself off balance and both women hit the floor.

Only one person in the whole barracks looked happy. Dietz stood off to one side leering at the two women. He grinned in maniacal glee.

The light in Dietz's eyes made Rhodes quake to the marrow of his bones. He should have realized when Dietz fired his thermal cannon at Fuentes that there was something wrong with Dietz.

Now Rhodes saw it all as plain as day. Zen said he encouraged Dietz to torment Fuentes in the interest of science—and Dietz did it. Zen and Dietz were each as psychotic as the other.

Rhodes didn't have time to mess around with that right now. He barged into the barracks, snatched Henshaw by the arm, and yanked her away from Thackery.

Henshaw screeched and bellowed even louder, fought against his grip, and tried to struggle free so she could make another lunge for Thackery.

Thackery tried to take advantage of that moment to pounce on Henshaw. Rhodes's temper got the better of him. He used the limb closest to Thackery and kicked her away harder than he should have.

She pitched onto her back and sprawled across the floor roaring in fury. Dietz burst out laughing.

None of the others moved to intervene when Rhodes dragged Henshaw kicking and spitting to the other side of the room. Thackery got to her feet.

Rhodes saw her about to make another play to get to Henshaw. Rhodes dropped all sense of propriety and raised his scourge gun to aim at Thackery to hold her off.

He gave her such a vicious glare that she stopped where she was. She narrowed her eyes at him in pure venomous fury, but at least she didn't attack.

Rhodes threw Henshaw against the wall on the other side of the room. She roared again and tried to break away to go after Thackery.

He straightened his arm and didn't even try to be gentle when he slammed her back. He made her stagger and she fell flat on her ass. Dietz wouldn't stop laughing at the whole despicable incident.

Rhodes cast another hopeless glance around the barracks. Where should he even begin to deal with these people? He couldn't even control himself.

He had to change that. Colonel Kraft was his only hope.

Rhodes didn't dare to leave the barracks—not yet.

"You're all malfunctioning," he croaked. "Whatever the technicians did, they altered the way we think. We can get them to change it back."

"YOU BITCH!!" Henshaw shrieked. She rocketed to her feet and charged across the room to close with Thackery again.

Rhodes barely dove in front of Henshaw in time to stop her. Her armored body smashed into his. It threw him off balance for a split second, and in that moment, Oakes turned around to face the room.

He'd always been so steady and reliable. He never suffered from any difficulty or distress. Oakes being so solid had lulled Rhodes into a false sense of security.

Oakes's expression cleared. The rage and agitation of a moment before evaporated. He actually looked calm for a second....before he raised his arm and pointed his scourge gun at his own head.

"NO!!" Rhodes yelled, but he couldn't get there fast enough to stop Oakes from shooting himself.

Rhinehart opened his eyes. He didn't even see Oakes about to blow his own brains out. Dietz smirked at the whole scene in lunatic delight.

Coulter caught one glimpse of Oakes, spun around, and crossed the floor in a split second. He got there just in time to wrench Oakes's arm sideways.

The gun went off and the blast exploded into the ceiling. Oakes flew into a rage trying to wrestle his arm out of Coulter's grip.

Rhodes finally untangled himself from Henshaw and sprinted across the room to help Coulter. Rhodes still didn't get there quick enough before Oakes fired a second time.

He came perilously close to hitting Coulter. Coulter wrestled Oakes's arm aside and the second shot hit Rhinehart's capsule. He jumped up, but Rhodes was already closer.

Dietz watched the whole show with a huge grin plastered across his face. Then, out of Rhodes's worst nightmares, Dietz raised his own arm, pointed it at Oakes, and said in a perfectly calm tone, "I'll do it for you."

Rhodes collided with Dietz at the last moment, smacked Dietz's arm aside, and then Rhodes had to use every ounce of his strength to stop Dietz from turning his weapon on anyone in sight.

Dietz put up one hell of a fight. His cheery expression turned deadly. He kept grinning like a death's head while he fought to free his arm from Rhodes's grip.

Dietz tried to turn the weapon on Oakes again. When that failed, Dietz tried to shoot Rhodes.

Rhodes shoved himself between Dietz on one side and Oakes and Coulter on the other. Oakes overcame Coulter's efforts to restrain him, but Coulter held him until Rhinehart got there.

Thackery took a step forward to help Rhodes, and at that moment, Dietz fired. He yanked his weapon toward Rhodes's head. Rhodes threw all his weight against Dietz's arm to push the gun away and the shot exploded across the room.

The blast hit Thackery in the side of the head and she buckled on the spot.

Chapter 33

Rhodes stepped into Neiland's lab and looked down at a capsule sprouting wires from every surface. Alyssa Thackery lay under the transparent cover. She had her eyes closed.

He didn't see any damage to her facial implants. Dietz's gunshot imploded half of her head. The doctors must have repaired her implants. She would have been dead for certain if that gunshot had hit the organic side of her head.

Now all her vital signs read normal including her brainwave patterns, but that meant nothing.

Dr. Irvine stood by her capsule tapping on his remote device. "Is she going to be all right?" Rhodes asked.

"She'll be fine. All her systems are back online and we repaired the damage to her implants."

"Why is she still in here, then?"

"We're making some adjustments to Koenig's Grid matrix. Once he comes back online, she'll be ready to return to duty."

"Whatever changes you made to our behavioral protocol caused this. You turned all of us violent—including me. You have to switch it back."

"I understand, but you would have to take that up with General Brewster. He was the one who ordered the changes."

Rhodes raised his eyebrows. "Why would he order it? Is he trying to turn us all into murderous psychopaths? Is that his new plan?"

Dr. Irvine bent over his device. "I don't know why he ordered it, but I do know that he plans to discuss it with you."

"Me?! Why would he discuss it with me? He's in charge of this project. I'm just a captain."

"I'm sure he'll tell you what he wants when he talks to you."

Rhodes turned away from Thackery with an effort. He never liked her careless attitude, but he wouldn't wish this fate on anyone.

He stopped in front of another capsule across the lab. Dietz lay asleep in this capsule. "What are you going to do about him?"

"We'll adjust him back to the way he was. Some of his antisocial tendencies should diminish then."

"Some of his antisocial tendencies? Not all of them? He's a danger to the rest of us the way he is."

"He had a criminal record before this. I suspect he may have been like this before. Getting recruited into Battalion 1 didn't change his base personality."

Rhodes stiffened. "What did he do?"

Dr. Irvine tried to shrug it away and wound up squirming. "A few different things. I wouldn't want to breach his confidentiality...."

"You better damn well tell me if you expect me to go into battle with him or ask anyone else to go into battle with him. He tried to kill one of my people and he came close to kill another. He tried to kill me before he hit Thackery. Dietz turned a weapon on Fuentes on his very first day out of the box. This guy is certifiable psycho if anyone is."

"I'm sorry I can't tell you what's in his record....."

"Confidentiality should have stopped you from telling me that he had a record in the first place."

"You'll have to ask General Brewster about it. He'll tell you if he decides you really need to know."

"I do need to know. I'm the one risking my ass out there on the front line—not you—not any of you."

"I'm sorry. I would tell you if I could."

"You can. You just don't want to. This is another way for all of you to screw us over."

Dr. Irvine winced and walked away. He left Rhodes stewing in barely suppressed rage.

He saw himself acting overly emotional, but he didn't try so hard to control himself. This absolutely capped it all.

Rhodes stayed where he was just long enough to satisfy him that Dietz wouldn't be going anywhere. Thackery's vital signs remained stable.

They did. Neither of these two had been out of their capsules since Dietz shot Thackery.

Dietz better not wake up saying he only did it because he malfunctioned. Rhodes would never believe that if he lived a thousand years.

Whatever modification the technicians made to the battalions' behavioral protocols—the same modification must have released Dietz's psychotic tendencies.

He'd been covering it up all this time. He behaved well during the Ohait campaign. He even behaved well during all the battalion's training sessions......or did he?

Dietz didn't go out of his way to help his comrades. Dietz didn't put himself in danger to help anyone. He took care of himself first and foremost.

Rhodes would give anything to see Dietz's criminal record. It must be pretty bad.

Rhodes could only get that information one place. He walked out of the lab planning to go see Colonel Kraft—which was what Rhodes planned to do before this whole disaster happened.

He walked out to find the rest of the battalion standing in the hall waiting for him. "How is she, Sir?" Rhinehart asked.

"She's on the mend," Rhodes replied. "Her implants have all been repaired. Her brainwaves, vital signs, and neural systems are all functioning normally. The doctors are making some final adjustments to Koenig's Grid matrix. After that, Thackery will get back on her feet and I'm sure she'll be as annoying as ever."

"This is my fault," Oakes growled. "I did this."

"You didn't do anything, man," Rhodes told him. "You lost your mind when the technicians adjusted your systems. The same thing happened to all of us. This is not your fault. You wouldn't have done anything like this if not for that."

"Dietz would have," Rhinehart murmured. "That dude has been waiting for a chance like this since he woke up."

Rhodes passed his hand across his eyes. "I know."

"What are you gonna do about him?" Lauer asked.

"I'm not going to do anything about him. I can't," Rhodes replied. "Dr. Irvine says Dietz was probably like this before...."

"Of course he was," Lauer countered. "The implants don't change who a person is on the inside."

"I can't do anything about him," Rhodes repeated. "We can only hope General Brewster orders the doctors to put Dietz back to the way he was before—when he could control it and somewhat behave himself in public."

"Somewhat?" Rhinehart snorted. "You call that *somewhat* behaving himself in public? He's a sociopath. You can't expect us to go into battle with him. He could turn his weapon on any of us. He's already done it twice."

"I don't expect any of you to do anything, pal," Rhodes groaned. "Do I look like this is my idea of a good time? I don't want to go anywhere with Dietz. I don't want to sleep next to him. I don't even want to be in the same room with him. We don't have a choice unless General Brewster listens to us and takes Dietz off the roster."

"He better," Oakes muttered.

"You would be out of your minds if you held out any hope for that. He'll leave Dietz on the books and we'll be stuck with him. Make up your minds on that right now. Then, if God intervenes and something happens to Dietz to get him out of our lives, we'll all be pleasantly surprised. In the meantime, I'm working on the assumption that we're stuck with him for life. I suggest you all get comfortable with that, too."

"One of us should put the son of a bitch down," Rhinehart growled. "We would all be better off."

"I don't want to hear that, Lieutenant," Rhodes snapped. "I don't want to hear that ever again from any of you. Understand? The people in this battalion are all we have. Everyone in the whole damn sector is against us. The people in this battalion are the only people on our side—ever. Dietz has his problems. I'll be the first to admit it, but any of us could have suffered a malfunction that could have caused exactly the same problem."

"That was no malfunction," Lauer pointed out. "He was about to shoot Oakes."

"Oakes was about to shoot Oakes," Rhodes fired back. "So what if the malfunction caused Oakes to point his gun at himself or someone else? It was still a malfunction and someone could be just as dead. It doesn't mean we should put Oakes down. Dietz is one of us whether we like it or not. He might be a psycho murderous lunatic. He could also be the person who saves one of us on the battlefield."

Rhinehart snorted and looked away. "I'll believe that when I see it."

"None of us will ever put anyone else in this battalion down," Rhodes ordered. "I don't care what they've done or what they might have been before this. If Dietz points his weapon at you and tries to kill you, you have my permission to defend yourselves by any means necessary. Until then, we just have to live with him the same way we have to live with each other. I don't like it any better than you do, but that's the way it is. Got it?"

The others shuffled their feet and looked at the floor. Only Lauer mumbled, "Yes, Sir."

Rhodes turned away....and stopped when he saw Fuentes and Henshaw standing off to one side. They didn't get involved in the conversation.

Henshaw writhed and twisted in misery. The side of her face that was still human screwed up in agony. She grimaced in pain and tears poured from her eye.

Her lips shivered back from her teeth and she kept contorting and squirming in all directions. "I tried to kill her!" Henshaw moaned. "I tried to kill her!"

"You didn't kill her," Rhodes murmured. "You malfunctioned."

"I wanted to!" Henshaw choked. "I wanted her dead!"

"You could have killed her by shooting her in the head. You didn't. You might have been angry, but I don't think you tried to kill her and I don't believe you wanted her dead—not really. You malfunctioned. The technicians altered your neural system and you snapped. The same thing happened to all of us."

Rhodes glanced over at Fuentes. He stood with his shoulders hunched. Of everyone here, he showed the least emotional reaction to what happened.

He didn't get involved in the barracks fight. He had nothing to blame himself for.

Rhodes studied the kid for a second and then walked off. Fuentes held up better than anyone else in this battalion. Maybe he would pull his socks up and become a decent soldier after all.

Rhodes didn't have anything to complain about in Fuentes's behavior during the Ohait campaign. Fuentes held his own, helped his comrades, used The Grid to fight the Emal, and made it back alive.

That was saying something. It was better than countless Legion soldiers could say.

Chapter 34

Rhodes walked into Colonel Kraft's office and found General Brewster already there. They stood around the table talking to four other officers Rhodes had never seen before.

One of them was a middle-aged female general named Hyde. There were also two male colonels in their thirties named Neff and LeClerc. The last man in the room was an admiral named Pulman.

Rhodes stiffened when he entered the room. He'd been hoping to talk to Colonel Kraft alone first and hopefully get him to order the doctors to readjust the battalion's behavioral protocol back to the way it was before.

Rhodes didn't know why all these officers were gathered in Kraft's office, but the temperature dropped twenty degrees the minute Rhodes walked in. These people weren't here to pay anyone a social call.

General Brewster tried to play it off with his usual affable demeanor. "Ah, Captain! Come on in! Just the man we were hoping to see."

Rhodes decided to take the bull by the horns. Why pretend to be friendly when they obviously weren't?

"Why did you order the doctors to alter our behavioral protocol?" Rhodes demanded. "Now every one of us is malfunctioning. Half the battalion could have lost their lives from this stunt."

"We altered your behavioral protocol because you disobeyed orders on the battlefield, Captain," General Hyde replied.

Rhodes spun around to stare at the woman. *"You* did this? Who the hell are you?"

"We are the officers in charge of the Battalion 1 project," Colonel Neff replied.

"I thought General Brewster was in command of the Battalion 1 project," Rhodes replied. "That's what he told me."

"He's in charge of operations," Colonel Neff replied. "We're the governing body."

"Then you can order the doctors to put our behavioral protocol back to the way it was," Rhodes snapped. "You can't expect us to fight anybody the way we are."

"We can't do that until we satisfy ourselves that you really will follow orders on the battlefield," General Hyde replied. "General Kaufman ordered you to stay in position with the platoons and hold the Aevod Gap. You disobeyed that order. You risked the safety of...."

"I didn't risk the safety of anything except the Emal," Rhodes interrupted. "General Kaufman was operating under a misunderstanding of battlefield conditions. He refused to listen to my recommendation even when I offered to share the evidence from my SAMs that the Emal were about to breach the Gap. Three platoons would have gotten wiped out if the battalion hadn't acted when it did. The whole beach could have gotten wiped out if the Emal overran that gap."

"You are still part of the regular Legion, Captain," General Brewster chimed in. "You still have to obey orders even when you don't agree with them. General Kaufman was the one making battlefield decisions on Ohait, not you....."

"I won't do anything to risk my subordinates nor will I do anything that unnecessarily jeopardizes other Legion personnel. You wanted Battalion 1 to fight this war in ways the ordinary Legion can't. What's the point of me being hamstrung by people who don't have access to the SAMs' intelligence? What's the point in me having this technology at all if I'm not going to use it?"

"The point is for you to add your strength and firepower to the regular Legion's efforts," General Hyde told him. "I'm sure General Kaufman had information you didn't have...."

"And I'm sure he didn't have information I did have. You were the ones who gave me this technology for good or bad. I'll use it as I see fit. If you don't like it, you can send a real robot in my place next time."

He walked out of the room and headed back to the barracks. He couldn't tell if this smoldering fury in his chest came from the doctors' adjustments or because he really did hate these people for putting him in this position.

Those bastards! Who the hell did they think they were—telling him to obey orders?

Even regular Legion soldiers had to think for themselves before they carried out an order. Every Legion soldier was responsible for making sure an order didn't jeopardize their fellow soldiers.

Every soldier had a duty to uphold the honor of the Treaty of Aemon. That's what being part of the regular Legion meant.

His last words rang in his ears. He said them in the heat of the moment. Now he realized with a kind of fatal certainty that they were truer than true. He wasn't a robot.

He returned to the barracks and sat down on the edge of his capsule. The barracks didn't feel right without Dietz and Thackery. Even Dietz had become a part of this group.

The rest of the battalion kept their voices down when they talked at all. Most of them just went to their capsules and sat down getting ready to go into their conversion cycles.

Rhodes looked forward to shutting his eyes even for a few seconds. Anything would be better than thinking about this.

He turned to pull his feet onto the mattress when Rhinehart jumped up. He'd been sitting down, too, and about to lie down.

He jerked from one direction to another. "I'll kill you, you son of a bitch!!" Rhinehart bellowed. "I swear I'll fucking kill you!!"

Oakes, Rhodes, and Lauer converged from all sides. "Rhinehart!" Rhodes yelled. "What's wrong?"

"YOU SON OF A BITCH!!" Rhinehart thundered and tried to take a swing at Rhodes.

In that moment, Rhodes made eye contact with Rhinehart—or tried to. Rhinehart didn't make eye contact. He looked straight through Rhodes.

Rhodes lunged out of the way. Lauer and Oakes took their chance to dive in and grab Rhinehart by the arms, but Rhinehart's size and strength overpowered all three men.

Rhinehart swung his elbow, threw Oakes off, and fired his scourge gun, but he fired it into the wall. Rhinehart didn't try to shoot any of his comrades.

"RHINEHART!!" Rhodes bellowed. "Look at me!"

"You son of a bitch!" Rhinehart made another dive—for open air. He tried to snatch something out of thin air.

"Interface with Rocky, Fisher!" Rhodes ordered.

"I can't!" Fisher called back. "He's blocking me! He won't let anyone interface."

"Something's wrong with the SAM."

"YOU BASTARD!!" Rhinehart roared and tried to take another swing.

Rhodes thought he understood now. Rhinehart was trying to attack Rocky for some reason, but Rhodes couldn't see the SAM to figure out what the problem was.

Oakes and Lauer threw their weight against Rhinehart to restrain him. His struggles and theirs tipped all four men over. They landed hard on the floor trying to wrestle Rhinehart into submission.

His weapon went off again, but Lauer pinned Rhinehart's arm down. The shot skidded across the floor and hit Dietz's capsule instead. The shot didn't damage anyone.

The medical team charged in. "What's going on?!" Dr. Irvine cried.

"Shut him down!" Rhodes snapped. "His SAM is malfunctioning!"

The medical team surrounded Rhinehart. Rhodes, Lauer, and Oakes had to back off, but at that moment, another gunshot exploded across the room.

Rhodes barely had time to see where it came from before Henshaw's scourge gun went off pointing at her head.

She dove out of the way so fast she knocked herself over backward. Her other hand shot to her right wrist. She actually fought to push the gun away from her own head.

She screamed and that sound electrified everyone in the room. Rhodes rushed her, but Coulter and Fuentes got to her first.

Rhodes seized Henshaw's wrist. "Stop, Georgie! Don't do this!"

"I'm not doing anything!" she shrieked. "He's trying to kill me!"

"WHO?!!" Rhodes yelled back.

"Koen!! My SAM is trying to kill me! I can't stop him!!"

Rhodes pounced on Henshaw's arm trying with all his might to drag her weapon away from her head. She used her left arm as best she could to help him, but the SAM controlled her mechanical right arm. It was too strong.

Rhodes strained his joints to the breaking point. Coulter and Fuentes grabbed Henshaw to pry her arm away, too.

They bent her elbow down one millimeter at a time until, without warning, the resistance holding her arm up gave way. Her arm unfolded under all that pressure.

Rhodes and the others had been pulling her hand away from her head with such force that her arm shot out at full length and the scourge gun went off right in Rhodes's face.

Chapter 35

R hodes opened his eyes and groaned. He was lying in another capsule. It looked like the same capsule he'd been lying in when he first woke up at Coleridge Station.

He was back in Dr. Neiland's lab, but she wasn't here. He didn't see anyone. He was all alone.

He felt like absolute shit—a sure sign that he'd been in a conversion cycle for a long time. That made sense if he got shot in the head.

Poor Georgie. He felt sorry for her. She probably blamed herself for this when it wasn't her fault at all.

Rhodes looked around. He didn't see Fisher anywhere. That was strange....or maybe Fisher was making himself scarce to give Rhodes time to wake up.

He collapsed back on the mattress fighting down the usual wave of nausea. He'd become so reliant on Fisher these last few weeks.

What would Rhodes do if Fisher tried to kill him like that? Rhodes didn't want to believe Fisher would do anything like that. Fisher had only ever tried to help Rhodes.

Fisher wouldn't be able to stop himself. Any random malfunction might cause Fisher to snap. It happened time and again. How long would it take before the same thing happened to Fisher? What would Rhodes do then?

He didn't want to think about it. The thought made him shudder.

Now he had to deal with this whole glorious disaster. Oakes. Rhinehart. Henshaw. Fuentes. Coulter. Thackery. Lauer. None of them got off without some catastrophic problem.

The only person on that list who hadn't suffered some meltdown was Lauer, but he would. It was only a matter of time.

Rhodes knew that now. These implants didn't have to malfunction. Their very existence conflicted too deeply with the battalion's humanity. No one could go through this without suffering some life-changing problems.

The malfunctions were just the icing on the cake. They were the symptom. The implants themselves were the disease. The only cure was death.

In a way, General Brewster shutting down the project would be a blessing in disguise. Rhodes actually looked forward to the day.

He made up his mind right then and there. The threat of Brewster shutting down the project would never make any decisions for Rhodes ever again. He would never let anyone hold that threat over his head.

If Brewster decided this project was too dangerous and too problematic, if he decided to shut it down along with everyone in it, so be it. He sure as hell wouldn't get any argument from Rhodes.

Rhodes finally pried his limp carcass off the mattress and sat up. Rhinehart lay in another capsule nearby. Henshaw lay in another farther down the floor.

Rhodes didn't see Dietz or Thackery anymore. Were they out of the lab now?

Just then, Fisher expanded himself from the corner of Rhodes's vision. Fisher must have made himself small to hide from Rhodes. "How are you feeling, Captain?" Fisher asked.

"Awful," Rhodes grumbled. "How long have I been in here?"

"About a month. Rhinehart and Henshaw have been in here the whole time, too. No one wants to reactivate them until someone figures out what went wrong with their SAMs."

Rhodes snorted, but he did it quietly to himself. Something went wrong with their SAMs, all right. Something was always bound to go wrong with their SAMs.

"I've been thinking about how to correct their malfunctions," Fisher went on.

"What have you come up with?" Rhodes asked.

"Well....nothing yet—but I've been thinking we might be able to correct it if we interface with them."

"Good luck, pal," Rhodes muttered. "You would be as likely to get infected with whatever is wrong with them."

"Then Rhinehart and Henshaw will be taken offline. We can't let that happen."

"What would you do if you could interface with them?" Rhodes asked. "What *could* you do? What could any of us do?"

"I don't know. Maybe something happened that reset Rocky back to the way he was when he first came online. Maybe that's why Rhinehart lost it and tried to kill him."

Rhodes looked down at his hands. "I don't see what's so bad about the way Rocky was back then. He looked like a regular SAM. There was nothing about him that would trigger Rhinehart."

"Nothing we could see. Maybe the SAM had some feature that set off a stress response in Rhinehart. Maybe the two things are related somehow."

"Assuming you're right and assuming we could interface with Rhinehart and Rocky and assuming we could convince Rocky to turn back into a Khikvid, what would stop this from happening again sometime in the future? Any malfunction or battlefield injury could make Rocky switch back. The way he was might be his default voice and appearance. He did say at first that he couldn't change. He might switch back without warning. Then we'd all be in exactly the same situation with Rhinehart trying to kill his own SAM."

"What other option is there?" Fisher asked.

Rhodes glanced across the lab at Rhinehart asleep in his capsule. He actually looked peaceful like this. His blonde hair, boyish features, and oversized body looked almost angelic.

Maybe it would be better to shut Rhinehart down right now. He never had to wake up and deal with this shit ever again.

Rhodes shook those thoughts out of his head. He already ordered the whole battalion not to think or talk that way about each other.

Rhodes couldn't start thinking about putting down his subordinates. He could fantasize all he liked about putting himself down, but not them. He owed them better.

"So what's your plan on how to deal with Koen?" Rhodes asked.

"I don't know," Fisher murmured. "I don't know what's wrong with Koen."

"I don't see any explanation for anything that goes wrong with any of us," Rhodes muttered. "Besides everything."

"I'm beginning to agree with you Captain," Fisher murmured. "Perhaps it would be better if the battalion never went back into battle."

Just then, the door opened and Dr. Irvine came into the lab. Rhodes stiffened for a second. He relaxed when he saw that it was neither Dr. Neiland nor Dr. Montague.

Rhodes didn't trust Irvine any further than he could throw him, but anyone would be better than Neiland.

"How are you feeling, Captain?" Dr. Irvine asked. "I'll just take some readings on your implants to make sure they're functioning correctly."

"They seem to be," Rhodes replied.

Dr. Irvine raised his eyebrows over his device. "And your SAM? Is he functioning correctly, too?"

"He seems to be. He doesn't seem like he's changed."

"Does he look the same—no appearance changes?"

Rhodes studied Fisher's face. "No, he looks the same."

"That's excellent. You should be clear for release as soon as you feel strong enough to stand up and walk back to the barracks."

"What about Rhinehart and Henshaw?" Rhodes asked. "How long do you plan to keep them in here?"

Dr. Irvine shrugged. "We have no way of correcting whatever malfunctions caused this latest incident."

"Why can't you just readjust our behavioral protocol back to the way it was?" Rhodes asked. "That should solve the problem."

"We already did. We adjusted it while you were asleep." Dr. Irvine bent in to study Rhodes. "Do you feel different than you did after the adjustment?"

Rhodes thought about it. "I guess I do. I guess I feel calmer—and the memories aren't there anymore. I mean, they aren't as invasive as they were. I can still remember everything, but they don't bother me the way they did after the adjustment."

"That's excellent. Then you're free to go."

"What about Rhinehart and Henshaw? They should be free to go, too. Why aren't you waking them up?"

"Their SAMs malfunctioning had nothing to do with the behavioral protocol...."

"Of course it did! Everyone in the whole battalion went nuts after that adjustment. The incident with Dietz and Thackery happened because of the adjustment."

"This was different. Rhinehart threatened his SAM before the adjustment, so it couldn't have caused him to threaten it again now."

"Are you sure about that? Maybe he had a malfunction then that didn't get resolved. Maybe he only coped with it because his SAM looked and sounded different. Then, when the SAM returned to its original appearance, it triggered the malfunction again."

"We aren't detecting any malfunction in him or his SAM. Henshaw, on the other hand—her SAM definitely malfunctioned and that had nothing to do with the behavioral protocol. Her behavioral protocol doesn't affect her SAM at all."

"So you don't know why Keon tried to kill her—or me?"

"We have no idea. We've searched his programming and we can't find anything wrong with that, either."

Rhodes compressed his lips to stop himself from saying what he really thought. These doctors and technicians obviously didn't know what the hell they were doing.

They were playing with fire, but it was actually worse than that. They were playing with loaded guns. The doctors and officers were just too stupid and arrogant to realize that's what they were doing.

Rhodes wasn't getting anything done in here. He stood up and headed back to the barracks.

"I still think we can correct them by interfacing with them," Fisher murmured in Rhodes's ear on the way there.

"But we would have to wake up Rhinehart and Henshaw in order to interface with them," Rhodes pointed out.

"True," Fisher replied.

"Which means we'd need authorization from someone higher up the chain of command to release Rhinehart and Henshaw to us. Is it really worth that? What if someone else gets hurt—or killed?"

Fisher didn't get a chance to answer before Rhodes walked into the barracks. Dietz and Thackery were there.

It threw the whole battalion into another confusion or readjustment. Dietz and Thackery were back. Rhinehart and Henshaw were both still gone.

Rhodes didn't say much to either Dietz or Thackery. Rhodes made up his mind to let Dietz show himself one way or the other.

If he really was a violent, dangerous murderer in disguise, he would reveal his true colors sooner or later.

Maybe this last conversion cycle changed him. Maybe getting his behavioral protocol adjusted back to something closer to normal would make Dietz a productive member of the battalion now. Rhodes could only hope.

He decided to give Dietz a chance. Rhodes had to put up with Dietz one way or the other. If Dietz proved himself, who was Rhodes to argue?

Rhodes had to rework his whole concept of reality when it came to dealing with Thackery. Getting shot in the head definitely changed her.

She'd always acted so bouncy and delighted by the whole Battalion 1 project. She said at first that she should have signed up for this. She might even have paid for it.

Now she sat hunched at the table glaring at everyone. She curled her lip in disgust at the sight of her comrades. She even glared at Fuentes.

She kept gulping every few seconds and scraping her facial implants across her shoulder like they irritated her.

She looked and acted exactly the way Rhodes and the others had been looking and acting all this time. She didn't get it until now.

Rhodes hesitated to go over to her, but he couldn't just ignore her. He stopped by the table. "How are you doing, Alyssa?"

She dragged her one good eye up to meet his. Her expression turned even more horrifically disgusted when she looked at him. "I tried to kill Georgie," she husked.

"You didn't try to kill her—and you didn't kill her. You got mad at each other—and she feels the same way about you getting shot. She can't get over the guilt that she was fighting with you before you got shot."

She cast another revolted glance around the barracks. "This.....this is a nightmare."

Rhodes sighed. "Yes, it is."

She gulped again. "My father.....I didn't remember him until.....He died when I was little. I forgot all about him. Now I can't get him out of my mind....."

"The behavioral protocol adjustment did the same thing to all of us."

"I'll never....I'll never be able to leave here.....I'll never have a normal life." Her eyes skipped around the room a little faster. "I didn't realize....I didn't think it would be like this....." She panted faster in rising agitation. "I gotta get out of here....I can't be like this....."

He swiveled around the table and rested his hand on her shoulder. She immediately jerked away and snarled at him.

"We're all going through the same thing," he murmured. "We're all struggling to come to terms with this."

She snorted, but she didn't look at him. She kept glaring at everyone and gulping down disgust at the sight of her comrades.

Rhodes backed away and went over to his capsule. He couldn't help her. He couldn't help any of them. He couldn't even help himself.

The doctors had adjusted the behavioral protocol back to the way it was, but at what cost?

Chapter 36

C olonel Kraft strolled into the barracks and looked around before he spotted Rhodes sitting at the table with Dietz, Lauer, and Coulter.

Fuentes sat at the computer terminal doing something. He worked on it all the time now.

Oakes spent a lot of time by himself these days. He spent most of every day either walking around the station or just sitting in isolated spots away from everyone.

Thackery sat at the other table. She kept as far away from everyone as she possibly could without ever actually leaving the barracks.

She glared and wrinkled her nose and lip at her comrades as much as ever, but she glared and wrinkled her nose at the surroundings just as much.

She kept scraping her face across her shoulder and grimacing when the metal scratched against metal.

Rhodes and the others cut her a wide berth. None of them tried to talk to her and she never initiated any conversation.

Rhodes, Lauer, Dietz, and Coulter no longer played The Ship, The Captain, and The Crew. That kind of light-hearted entertainment no longer seemed to fit what this battalion was all about.

They talked about other subjects when they talked at all. They talked about life in the Legion, campaigns they'd been on, people they knew, and different jobs, ranks, and posts they'd held in different parts of the Treaty of Aemon Cluster.

Their conversation occasionally ranged to their lives and families back on Preinea, but not often.

The battalion members spent most of their time interfacing with each other's SAMs. The SAMs shared their conversation. No one in the battalion hid anything from each other or the other SAMs anymore.

Even Thackery interfaced between Koenig and the other SAMs. She listened to every word they said to each other.

No one wanted to take the chance that one of the SAMs might malfunction without anyone realizing it.

If a SAM malfunctioned—or if a person malfunctioned—everyone wanted to know about it right away with no delay because they hadn't been interfacing at the time.

Even Oakes stayed interfaced with the others even while he was out of the room. He let the others keep track of where he was and what he was doing.

He even let them listen in on his conversations with Dash just to make sure everything was working the way it should.

Dietz sat with Rhodes, Lauer, and Coulter. Dietz joined in their conversation, but not as much as he used to. He had become much quieter and more reserved.

Rhodes didn't understand why, but Dietz never did anything to cause concern. Rhodes sensed the rest of the battalion keeping as close an eye on Dietz as Rhodes did. They would have pounced on him if he so much as cracked a grin at the wrong time.

He didn't. Either he really knew how to behave or he must have changed. Rhodes couldn't tell which it was, but his decision to give Dietz a chance seemed to be paying off—for now.

Rhodes never let his guard down around Dietz. Their interface gave Rhodes a bird's-eye view straight inside Dietz's head.

Rhodes watched Dietz like a hawk. The whole battalion kept Zen under a microscope to make sure he didn't feed Dietz any more wacky ideas.

Colonel Kraft took in the scene with one glance and wandered over to the table. He was the first member of the Coleridge Station staff to set foot in the barracks since Rhodes got shot.

"I'd like a word with you, Captain, if you don't mind," Kraft began.

Rhodes didn't look up. "Whatever you have to say to me, you can say in front of these people. I'm sure whatever you have to say affects them as much as it affects me."

Kraft compressed his lips for an instant and then blurted out, "All right. If that's the way you want it, I have an idea about how to correct the malfunctions in Rhinehart's and Henshaw's SAMs."

Now Rhodes really did look up. "You do? What's your idea?"

"We'll need you and your SAMs to interface between them," Kraft replied. "You and the other SAMs will be able to detect any malfunction. If you can't, you'll be able to see whether the SAMs are functioning correctly. You all know these SAMs better than we do—better than the doctors do."

"What did I tell you?!" Fisher crowed. "You see? I'm not crazy after all."

"We would need to wake up Rhinehart and Henshaw for that," Rhodes told Kraft. "Are you prepared to take that risk?"

"The brass doesn't want to, but I think it will be worth it if we can get Rhinehart and Henshaw back. The only alternative is to leave them offline indefinitely. None of us wants that. I mean, if it doesn't work, we'll have to take them offline anyway. Then we won't have lost anything. We have nothing to lose at this point. That's the way I see it."

"I told you so!" Fisher exclaimed again.

"You can stop saying that now," Wild rasped. "We heard you the first time."

"So....do you have authorization from General Brewster to wake up Rhinehart and Henshaw?" Rhodes asked Kraft.

"Yes, I have it. I just needed to make sure all of you were on board. I mean.....if anything goes wrong, Rhinehart and Henshaw could malfunction again. They could....you know.....try to kill one of you again."

Rhodes glanced around the circle of faces. Fuentes wasn't working on the terminal anymore. He looked up and listened to the conversation. So did Thackery.

Rhodes checked the interface with Oakes. He was back at the loading dock, but he listened to the conversation with Kraft.

"I'm in," he told Rhodes. "It will be worth it if we can get Rhinehart and Henshaw back. We stopped them once before. We can stop them again."

Rhodes looked up at Kraft. "All right. We'll do it."

"Don't you need to discuss it amongst yourselves first?" Kraft asked.

"We just did. When do you want to wake them up?"

Kraft blinked at him and then shrugged it off. "As soon as possible—maybe this afternoon if you aren't too busy."

"We aren't busy. Just tell us when you want us to be there and we'll be there."

"Uh....okay. How about three o'clock this afternoon?" Kraft asked.

Rhodes nodded. "That sounds good. We'll be there."

No one said anything until he left. Oakes stood up from the loading dock and started walking back to the barracks. He walked faster than he usually did.

"Rhinehart and Henshaw better not try to kill anybody again," Murphy growled.

"If I'm right about Rocky malfunctioning and switching back to his original appearance, then that should be easy to correct," Fisher pointed out.

"Maybe we can get the technicians to reprogram the SAM's appearance before we wake up Rhinehart," Coulter suggested.

"That leaves Koen," Rhodes added. "If he really has turned into a murderous freak, we might not be able to do anything about him. He'll just keep trying to kill Georgie until he succeeds."

"Then what will we do?" Coulter asked.

Rhodes shrugged. "I don't see that we'll be able to do anything. We can't leave her in a conversion cycle for the rest of forever. It would be better to take her offline."

"I can't believe we're even talking about this," Murphy husked. "I can't think of taking anyone offline."

"I guess we're about to find out," Rhodes replied.

Just then, Oakes came back. The group talked about Rhinehart and Henshaw until it was time to go down to the lab.

Colonel Kraft met them there and everyone gathered around the two capsules. Rhinehart and Henshaw hadn't moved since Rhodes woke up.

Dr. Irvine attended them. Rhodes didn't trust the other two doctors. He'd already made up his mind never to let Dr. Neiland lay a finger on him ever again.

"Can you change Rocky's appearance?" Rhodes asked Irvine.

Irvine frowned. "How do you mean?"

"Change his programming so he looks different. Make him look like a Khikvid—and change his voice. Make it softer, lower, and less echoing."

Irvine scowled over his computer equipment. "It isn't protocol to tamper with a SAM's unique identity. They're sentient beings. They have a right to determine their own appearance and presentation."

"Not if their presentation puts us in danger," Oakes pointed out.

"What makes you think Rocky's presentation is putting Rhinehart in danger?" Irvine asked.

"Both times Rhinehart threatened Rocky were when Rocky was using his original voice and appearance. Rocky and Rhinehart were fine after Rocky changed the way he looked and sounded. Just try it—please. I'm sure Rocky wouldn't want anything as superficial as that to put Rhinehart at risk."

Irvine shrugged and worked on his equipment for a while. "Okay. I changed it."

"Now make both SAMs as small as possible. Program them not to speak until we give the word. Let Rhinehart and Henshaw wake up first before they see their SAMs."

"Aren't you supposed to interface with them?" Kraft asked.

"We don't want to interface with them before Rhinehart and Henshaw wake up." Rhodes nodded to the doctor. "You can wake them up now."

Chapter 37

Dr. Irvine passed back and forth between two capsules, tapped on the controls, and both covers opened. Rhinehart and Henshaw took a long time to come to their senses.

Rhodes and his people stood in silence while Rhinehart opened his eyes. The battalion interfaced with him, but none of them could see Rocky. He kept himself small and silent.

Rhinehart groaned and his hand drifted to his head. He squinted trying to see through his puffy eyelid.

Rhodes went over to his bed. "How do you feel, Lieutenant?"

"Captain...." Rhinehart croaked. "What happened?"

"Rocky malfunctioned. You've been offline while we try to figure out how to correct the problem."

"I don't......I don't remember anything....."

"You don't remember what you were doing right before you woke up here? Do you remember anything that happened in the barracks?"

"No. What happened in the barracks?"

"What's the last thing you remember about talking to Rocky?" Rhodes asked.

Rhinehart frowned, shut his eyes, and then scowled at the lab around him. "I remember....I was sitting on the edge of my capsule about to go to sleep. I was talking to Rocky.....and then I wound up here."

"Rocky is making himself small and silent right now. We're going to interface with you and make him big, okay? Then we'll see if he's functioning correctly. Are you ready for that?"

Rhinehart sank back into his mattress. "Sure. Do whatever you have to do."

"At least Rhinehart will be too weak to attack anyone if he has a problem," Murphy growled from the side.

Rhodes, Lauer, Oakes, Dietz, Fuentes, and Thackery all entered the interface. All their SAMs watched, too.

"You can make yourself big again, Rocky," Rhodes ordered. "Let Rhinehart see you."

Rocky expanded. He didn't look like a Khikvid anymore. He was back to looking like a horse. "Here I am," he announced in his higher, softer voice. "It's good to see you again, Dane."

"Hey, pal," Rhinehart husked. "How you doing?"

"I'm doing well, but it's good to be back. We've been offline for a long time."

Rhodes didn't see anything wrong with their interaction. Could the problem be so simple to correct just by changing Rocky's appearance?

Only time would tell. Rhodes turned to Henshaw. She took longer to wake up. She moaned with her eyes closed.

Rhodes and the others interfaced with her, but Rhodes didn't see Koen. Rhodes didn't even see a pinprick that might have been Keon hiding from everyone.

"Where is he?" Murphy asked.

"He doesn't want to face us after trying to kill Henshaw," Wild muttered.

"He must be here somewhere." Rhodes turned to Dr. Irvine. "Can you make Keon bigger so we can see him?"

Dr. Irvine scowled at his equipment. "According to my readings, Keon is already as big as he can get. He should be covering the whole Grid right now."

Rhodes looked around at nothing. "Am I missing something?"

Henshaw stretched on the mattress again. She started to raise her hand toward her head.

He didn't see anything out of the ordinary until Henshaw's SAM started to expand. It hovered to one side of her head and got bigger....and bigger.

Rhodes stared at the image. It wasn't Koen's chubby panda face. This one was a hard starburst of crystalline shards jutting outward from cold, mean eyes. Glass shards made up the SAM's tight, hard lips.

"Who the hell are you?" Rhodes gasped.

"Legacy," the SAM growled in a low, deadly snarl. "And you are Captain Corban Rhodes. I thought I killed you."

Rhodes opened his mouth to say that, no, Legacy didn't kill Rhodes, but at that moment. Rhodes caught a flash of movement in the corner of his eye.

Henshaw raised her arm to touch her head and face. She still didn't open her eyes.

Rhodes didn't think anything of that movement at first. He'd seen countless people do that when they first came out of conversion cycles, especially long ones.

His stunned surprise at seeing a different SAM in Henshaw's interface distracted Rhodes for a split second.

Then he realized she wasn't raising her hand to her head to rub her eyes or run her fingers through her hair. She raised her arm to aim her scourge gun at her own face.

Lauer and Oakes both realized the same thing at the same time. "Captain—look out!" they both yelled.

Rhodes spun around. He was the closest to Henshaw.

He dove on top of her arm and forced it down on the bed. Her long conversion cycle made her weak enough for him to restrain her easily.

"Shut her down!" he yelled to Dr. Irvine. "Take her offline—NOW!!"

Irvine pounced on his controls and scrambled through a rapid flurry of button pressing. Henshaw went limp and Legacy disappeared.

Rhodes slumped there breathing hard. "Jesus!"

"What the hell was that?" Coulter stammered.

"Legacy must have replaced Keon somehow. The SAMs got switched." Rhodes turned to Dr. Irvine. "You have to take Legacy offline and replace him with Koen."

"I can't! Uninstalling a SAM would kill her."

"Then how did Legacy do it?" Oakes asked. "He must have switched them somehow—which means he took Keon offline and replaced Keon with himself. You should be able to do the same thing."

Dr. Irvine shook his head over his components. "I don't even know if we have Keon online anywhere anymore. He might be gone."

"Then you'll have to install another SAM for Georgie," Rhodes replied. "You have to find a way to permanently deactivate Legacy. He'll kill anyone you install him in."

"Give me some time," Dr. Irvine exclaimed. "I've never done this before."

Rhodes stared down at Henshaw. It couldn't be as hopeless as this. She got along so well with Koen. How did this happen?

In that silence, he heard Rhinehart talking to Rocky. They talked easily to each other and Rhinehart laughed at something Rocky said.

Rhodes turned around to look at them. Rhinehart sat on the edge of the bed. He was still smiling from whatever Rocky just said.

"Do you feel okay, Lieutenant?" Rhodes asked.

"Yes, Sir. I feel fine—just still a little weak."

"You'll be all right. Your strength will come back." Rhodes got serious when he turned to the SAM. "Do you remember what happened, Rocky? Do you remember how you and Rhinehart got here?"

"No, Captain. I don't remember anything except....Rhinehart was sitting on his capsule like he said. He was getting ready to go to sleep."

"Do you remember how it was when you first came online? Do you remember how much Rhinehart hated you because of the way you looked and sounded?"

The horse head tilted to one side and its eyebrows furrowed. "I don't remember that, Captain. Rhinehart and I always liked each other."

"So you don't remember Rhinehart threatening you?"

Rocky's eyes shot open. "He did what?"

"He didn't like the way you looked. You caused some kind of stress response in him. He only started liking you when you changed your appearance."

Rocky made a slight sneering expression. "I'm sure I would remember that, Captain."

"My point is that your original appearance caused him problems. I want to make sure you don't revert back to your old default appearance if something goes wrong."

"This is my original default appearance, Captain. I don't have any other appearance I could default to."

Rhodes dropped the subject and turned back to Henshaw. She was still unconscious. "What's the story?" he asked Irvine.

"I found Koen's original activation programming. I just have to isolate Legacy's so I can make the switch."

"It can't be this easy," Wild muttered.

"As soon as you make the switch, I want you to delete Legacy's program—permanently," Rhodes told Irvine.

Irvine only nodded. He didn't act like Rhodes giving orders was anything out of the ordinary. "I will delete it. We can't risk it infecting someone else."

"Can I go back to the barracks, Sir?" Rhinehart asked. "I need to lie down."

"Sure, Lieutenant. You go with him, Coulter."

"Yes, Sir," Coulter replied and he and Rhinehart left.

Rhodes didn't like seeing his battalion getting smaller and smaller. He had to get Henshaw back.

Some computer program either shooting her in the head with her own weapons or causing her to be taken permanently offline—he couldn't accept either of those outcomes.

Rhodes and the others stood around waiting for another half hour before Irvine finally said, "Okay, I'm ready to make the switch. If it works, she should be back to her old self. If it doesn't, she'll be dead."

"Do it," Rhodes ordered.

Irvine tapped his components some more and then approached the capsule to wake up Henshaw. She went through the same groaning process.

Rhodes kept a close eye on her to make sure she didn't point her weapon at anyone.

She eventually opened her eye and her vision swam back into focus when she saw Rhodes. "Captain.....you're okay!"

"I'm okay, Georgie. We figured out what went wrong with Koen."

Her face drained of all color and she looked around. "Where is he?"

"He wasn't the one who tried to kill you. Another SAM removed Keon and replaced him. This other SAM was the one who tried to kill you, but we switched them back. The rest of the battalion and I are interfacing with you. We'll be with you when Dr. Irvine brings Keon online. Are you ready for that?"

She glanced the other way and nodded, but she didn't look ready.

Rhodes dipped his chin at Irvine and Irvine did something on his machines. A collection of grid lines appeared in front of Henshaw and went through the usual series of shapes.

It eventually took the shape of a panda. Black and white fur appeared between the grid lines.

"Keon!" she exclaimed. "You're back."

Keon looked around and saw Rhodes, Fisher, Lauer, Wild, Fuentes, Van, Thackery, Koenig, Dietz, Zen, Oakes, and Dash all staring at him. "Was I gone?"

"You were offline, but you're back now," Rhodes replied. "How do you feel, Koen? What's the last thing you remember?"

Keon frowned. "I remember....we disembarked from the *Ero*.....and Dr. Neiland told us we had to come to the lab for testing. Henshaw sat down on the stool and the technician did something to her head. She started to get really angry....and that's the last thing I remember until right now."

"That's when it must have happened. Legacy must have switched places during the behavioral protocol adjustment."

"What's Legacy?" Henshaw asked.

"Never mind. We can leave as soon as you're ready to come back to the barracks."

"I'm ready now." She grimaced at the lab. "I can get my strength back in the barracks. This place gives me the creeps."

Chapter 38

R hodes glanced around at his people—his battalion. Oakes, Lauer, Rhinehart, Fuentes, Henshaw, Dietz, Thackery, and Coulter.

They had become bonded through hardship and shared pain. They knew each other and each other's SAMs as intimately as they'd ever known anyone.

Rhodes no longer doubted any of these people. Their recovery had been long and painful, but they got through it by supporting each other.

"Is everybody ready?" he asked. "It's go time."

"Ready," Henshaw replied.

Her eyes sparkled and a slight smile threatened to break out on her lips.

Thackery didn't bounce around anymore. She tightened her mouth in grim determination. All her exuberant enthusiasm had evaporated in the last few weeks.

She had become as hard and serious as everyone else in this battalion, but that somehow made her so much more trustworthy and reliable.

Rhodes checked each person and each SAM. This would be their first training session since their malfunctions.

If this worked, the battalion would go back into combat. If it didn't......no one talked about what would happen if it didn't.

"Let's go," Rhodes ordered and all nine dropped into The Grid.

The world went dark. Rhodes didn't understand at first what he was seeing—or not seeing.

Then an explosion flashed in the darkness. It lit up the landscape for one instant and his blood ran cold when he realized where he was.

Mounds of torn metal and debris covered the area. Explosions burst on the horizon and then a bone-crushing boom rocked the night.

A torrential fireball of burning gas erupted directly overhead as a Legion Ravager burst into flame.

At the same instant, lasers spurted from somewhere across the shadowy terrain. The Ravager gave a deep thump, groaned on its side, and detonated with an almighty ka-boom.

That outward flare of fire cast a brilliant glow across the devastated landscape. In that moment, Rhodes saw hundreds of Emal swarming over mounds of trash and debris.

They fired lasers at a long flank of Legion soldiers hunkered behind the rubble piles. He was back on Luluna.

A Legion platoon captain Rhodes didn't know reared up on his knees and yelled down the line, "Move out to the east! Move out! Get out of the line!"

He waved his men forward and they all started inching eastward. Rhodes couldn't see where they were going. It didn't matter.

"What's the objective?" Coulter asked through their interface.

"There's a Ravager on the ground four miles behind the Emal line," Wild replied. "The crew is barely holding the enemy at bay. We have to rescue the crew, bring them back here, and get them on board another Ravager that will take them off the planet to safety."

"Beautiful," Lauer growled. "Coulter and I will pull the same laser lawnmower we used on Ohait."

"We can't do that," Rhodes countered. "Emal lasers brought us down last time. You would make too obvious a target. We need to stay small and low to the ground—somewhere the Emal won't see us."

"How do we do that?" Henshaw asked. "They would always notice something."

"Not if they don't realize we're trying to attack them. I say we use something like the whips we used in the plasma vein. We separate, snake along the ground between the alien's feet, and work our way back through the ranks to the Ravager. The Emal won't see us, or if they do, they won't know we're with the Legion."

"We can cut them off at the ankles," Dietz suggested.

Rhodes snapped alert with a jolt. This was the first hint of Dietz's old self coming back to haunt the battalion.

"I just said this plan hinges on the Emal not noticing us," Rhodes snapped. "If you do anything that draws attention to us....."

"I was just joking, Sir," Dietz murmured.

Rhodes glared at him, but they didn't have time to discuss it further. The aliens crawled over another mountain of trash nearby and hammered the battalion's position.

Everyone ducked. The enemy surrounded the hill with dozens of guns.

"We gotta go now!" Rhodes yelled. "Remember what I said! Stay low and stay out of sight. Keep on the ground and don't draw attention to yourselves. Use The Grid to locate the downed ship. We'll converge there and work out a way to lift off the crew."

Oakes said, "Yes, Sir."

Rhodes didn't wait any longer. He shrank his grid lines to a thin filament, dropped to the ground, and took off slithering straight for the Emal line,

The aliens bombarded the hill, but the battalion wasn't there anymore. Legion soldiers fired from covered spots. Their Jackhammers flared and gave the aliens something to target in the darkness.

Fisher brought up The Grid of the area, but Rhodes already knew the place too well. "The downed crew has enough power to keep their fusion charges and Vipers working. That's it," Fisher reported.

"Just show me how far out we are."

Rhodes concentrated on winding his way through countless Emal legs, feet, and ankles. Each alien had multiple legs. The creatures crowded the terrain for miles to the rear.

Thick swarms of aliens surrounded the downed Ravager. The aliens attacked the ship with laser rifles and carved into its hull.

The crew fired into the horde and slaughtered dozens of aliens with every shot, but the crew couldn't defend the ship against so many. The Emal just moved in and replaced their fallen comrades with more laser-armed aliens.

Another explosion went off somewhere to Rhodes's left. He checked all his people and interfaced with their SAMs. He could monitor their progress through The Grid.

They made it to the halfway mark. The Emal numbers thinned here, but they got thicker when the battalion closed on the Ravager.

Rhodes's attention narrowed to the spot on The Grid where his own body snaked closer to the objective. Just one more mile.

"How do you want to lift off the crew?" Fisher asked.

"I guess we can always change into ships and fly the crew out of the....."

Rhodes broke off when a flash of light caught his eye coming from the left again, but this was no explosion.

His fury started to rise when he saw a long, thin whip of laser light snapping in the darkness. It looped around the Emal's ankles, brought them to the ground, and then went to work cutting the aliens to pieces.

More aliens tried to get away at the same time that they tried to rush to the spot to attack the thing. They couldn't figure out what it was.

The whip cracked here and there bringing down one Emal after another. All the Emal spun around to face the whip, but they couldn't get near it with so many bodies in their path.

Their fallen comrades created an impassable barrier to stop them from interfering. The whip cleared a space of dead Emal around itself, landed on the ground, and shot away toward the fallen Ravager.

"Son of a bitch!" Rhodes snapped. "Everyone converge on the Ravager now. Hurry! Leave it, Rhinehart!"

Rhinehart had veered toward the laser whip to help out. He broke off at Rhodes's word and the rest of the battalion rocketed away to the ship.

"Coulter—Lauer!" Rhodes ordered. "Cut your lawnmower around the ship and clear some space. The rest of you converge and form a vessel big enough to evacuate the crew. Rhinehart—you stay with me to defend them!"

"Yes, Sir," Rhinehart replied.

Rhodes blasted out of the mayhem, used his grid lines to change himself into Rio, and took off at high speed toward the Ravager.

All the aliens surrounding him jumped and then swung their laser rifles to bombard him, but the battalion got the jump on them.

Coulter and Lauer joined their lasers together, zoomed around the Ravager, and carved a path to flatten the aliens. Rhodes and Rhinehart soared around the ship plastering the enemy with scourge gunfire to drive the surviving Emal farther back.

Henshaw, Fuentes, Oakes, and Thackery bombed into the circle and slammed down on the ground in a pile. Their grid lines merged and they changed themselves into a modular transport vessel.

"Get the crew out, Fisher!" Rhodes ordered. "Get them on board now!"

Fisher's interface activated and he contacted the Ravager's bridge staff. The crew came pouring out of the ship and charged on board the transport.

Coulter and Lauer kept burning around and around the ship to hold the alien horde at bay. Rhodes and Rhinehart pivoted from side to side blasting any Emal to pieces the instant they showed their faces.

The last few stragglers left the Ravager and the combined battalion transport craft rocketed into the atmosphere. Emal lasers followed the ship and bombarded its underside every step of the way.

Another explosion went off somewhere on the transport. "Go, go, go!" Rhodes ordered. "Get off the planet!"

Lauer and Coulter pulled up. Rhodes only waited long enough for them to zoom upward into the night sky. Then he and Rhinehart launched right behind them.

Lasers fountained from the surface and one of them hit Rhinehart's wing. He roared in pain, toppled sideways, and one of his engines exploded. He started to drift downward toward the planet's surface.

Rhodes altered his grid lines instantly, turned back into his normal shape, and fired his boosters. He snatched Rhinehart by the wrist and launched into the atmosphere taking Rhinehart with him.

Rhodes had half a second to see the laser whip still snaking and snapping among countless aliens down there....and then Dietz shot away, turned back into his normal shape, and blasted skyward to catch up with the battalion.

The group left the battle behind and slowed when they made it into orbit. Rhodes slowed enough, let go of Rhinehart's wrist, and turned to face him. The two men hovered in space with their boosters holding them up.

"Are you okay?" Rhodes panted. "Did you get hurt?"

"I'm all right," Rhinehart gasped. "I guess gunshots don't do any damage in the training session."

Rhodes looked around just as the transport pulled up next to them. Henshaw, Thackery, Oakes, and Fuentes broke apart, reformed into their own normal appearances, and turned their gaze down toward the battle on the ground.

"The crew is gone," Henshaw murmured. "I guess we achieved the objective."

"You did great—all of you," Rhodes told them.

He fell silent when Dietz whizzed into orbit and slowed to rejoin the group. Rhodes clamped his mouth shut and glared at Dietz, but Rhodes didn't say anything here.

He left The Grid and returned to the training room with the rest of the battalion.

"What the hell is wrong with you?" he snapped at Dietz. "I told you not to do anything to attract attention. You went and did exactly what I told you not to."

"I was trying to create a diversion so you could get the crew out," Dietz countered.

"Did you hear me tell you to create a diversion?" Rhodes spat.

"Well, you couldn't get the crew out any other way."

"That isn't for you to decide. The last time I checked, I was the one in command of this battalion, not you. You made that suggestion before we started and I shut it down. We could have gotten all the way to the ship without the aliens seeing us, but you had to go and blow our cover. You could have gotten Rhinehart killed. Do you realize that?"

Dietz's eyes darted around the circle. Everyone glared at him.

"I was just trying to help, Sir," he mumbled.

"The only way you're gonna help us is by doing what you're told," Rhodes snapped.

"Or by taking a bullet to the head," Lauer growled.

Rhodes didn't correct him this time. "If you ever pull a stunt like that again, I swear to Almighty God I'll leave you behind. Is that clear? If you ever put any of us in danger in a real battle, I'll leave you behind and you can take your chances with the enemy. Don't you ever pull that shit again. You're alive right now because of me. Don't make me regret that."

"What does that mean?" Dietz asked. "Why am I alive right now because of you? You never did anything for me."

Rhodes stopped himself from telling Dietz that Rhinehart, Lauer, and Oakes wanted to put him down for trying to kill Oakes—and nearly killing Thackery.

Rhinehart made the decision on Rhodes's behalf. "If you pull something like that again, I *won't* leave you behind. I'll make sure you never make it off the planet alive. Just remember that."

He turned on his heel and marched out of the training room. The others glared at Dietz and then followed Rhinehart one after the other.

Rhodes waited until last. He left Dietz standing there and everyone pretended not to see him follow them back to the barracks.

The tension started to dissolve when they walked in. Rhodes went back to the table to sit down with the others. Thackery didn't glare at everyone as much now. She was starting to relax....a little.

The group barely walked in the door before General Brewster and Colonel Kraft showed up. "That was another outstanding training session," General Brewster began. "I can see you've all worked out your malfunctions. You're back to optimal functioning....."

"I wouldn't call it optimal," Rhodes interrupted.

"It will have to be good enough," Kraft replied. "We just got word. The Emal are attacking another planet in the Zavil system. They're bombarding cities and slaughtering the population. We need to deploy you right away. You'll transport there on the *Ero* first thing tomorrow morning."

Chapter 39

Rhodes paused on the landing bay threshold. The 249th, the 278th, and the 217th Platoons were back on board the *Ero*. Why did he delude himself into thinking it could be any different?

The soldiers nearest the entrance stopped what they were doing to turn around and stare at Battalion 1. The battalion had fought side by side with most of these men on the shelf on Ohait.

Rhodes gritted his teeth and stepped out onto the floor. The captains and lieutenants in charge of the three platoons were busy handing out weapons to everyone who didn't already have them.

That created another barrier between Battalion 1 and the regular Legion soldiers. No one in Battalion 1 carried a weapon—or any gear—or wore any body armor. They didn't need it.

Rhodes walked over to Captain Vernick. "Any word on where we're going or what's waiting for us down there?" Rhodes asked. "Everyone is keeping this hush-hush."

"They're keeping it hush-hush from us, too. I'm telling all the men to prepare for another bloodbath like Luluna."

"I can't wait," Rhodes muttered.

Vernick grinned at him. "I'm sure you and yours will be fine."

"How do you want to play this?" Rhodes asked. "Do you want us to go in with you....or separately?"

"I really couldn't tell you. I don't know anything about the terrain down there or even where the enemy is."

Rhodes pursed his lips, but just then, Fisher showed him The Grid of the planet Sulia. "The Emal are laying waste a city on the northern continent. They just made landfall here—on the Brokix peninsula."

"Where is the *Ero* planning to land?" Rhodes asked.

"Here—outside the city of Thaklia. The city is still relatively intact. The Ravagers are evacuating the population before the Emal get there. Then the Legion plans to defend the city to stop the Emal from advancing any further."

Rhodes became aware of the rest of the battalion and all their SAMs listening through the interface.

Vernick stood in front of Rhodes listening to him carry on a conversation with someone Vernick couldn't see or hear.

Rhodes had to explain all this to him, too. The platoons needed this information as much as Battalion 1 did.

Rhodes glanced around. "Do you have a computer terminal here?"

"Over here." Vernick led the way to the side of the bay, pulled a corporal toward him, and dug around in the boy's backpack before he found a remote device.

Rhodes pulled up the chart on the device and went through all Fisher's information so Vernick could see it.

"That complicates things," Vernick muttered. "We have to fight our way through the city just to engage with the enemy. Why don't they drop us off on the side facing the peninsula?"

"We can get in front of you," Rhodes offered. "We might be able to slow the aliens down until you get into a more favorable position."

Vernick made a face. "I don't like throwing you in front of a gun—again."

"You don't want to get caught with your pants down in the middle of the city without being able to see the enemy coming." Rhodes pointed to a spot on the far eastern side of the city. "We'll rendezvous here. We'll hold them here until you come. Then you and your men can set up fortifications and hold the aliens outside the city. That will work better than fighting house to house and building to building."

"Have it your way," Vernick told him. "You'll have to contact me if your line breaks and the aliens get inside the city. Just don't let them surprise me if they do get past you."

"I won't." Rhodes found himself smiling at his friend. "Good luck down there."

"You, too. I'll see you on the ground."

"I'm certain of it." Rhodes pointed across the bay. "Pull your men back from the launch doors. We'll leave first and put as much distance between us and you as we can."

"You got it." Vernick took off elbowing his way through the packed bay toward the launch doors.

Oakes glanced around at the nearest soldiers. They all cast suspicious looks at Rhodes and his people.

"Good," Lauer muttered. "I don't want to be anywhere near these guys."

"Get used to it," Rhodes told him. "If we succeed in stopping the aliens outside the city, we'll be fighting side by side with these platoons again."

"Let's get out of here," Oakes agreed. "The sooner we get on the ground, the better."

Rhodes led the way to the launch doors. It took Vernick, Turney, and Upshaw a while to convince the soldiers to back off and make room for the battalion to move closer to the exit.

Rhodes faced the doors. He didn't let himself look at the men he knew. He would rather face the enemy.

He went over The Grid in his head while he waited. He turned it this way and that and examined the battlefield from all sides.

The Emal had already leveled four cities farther east from Thaklia. The aliens had driven more Legion platoons out of those cities. The platoons fought their way backward toward Thaklia while the Emal laid down punishing fire all the way.

The *Ero* thumped against something and an electric wave of tension went through the bay. All the soldiers crowded around holding their weapons ready.

Rhodes checked The Grid again. He and his people were the only soldiers here who knew what was going on outside.

The *Ero* touched down half a mile west of Thaklia. The platoons would have to fight their way all the way through town to get to the east side to meet the Emal.

Emal base ships advanced behind the alien horde. The base ships unloaded devastating laser volleys on the city and detonated buildings from miles away. No way could the Legion platoons survive in there.

Rhodes made up his mind. "We'll get out of town and hold them on the eastern limits. We have to. We can't let the aliens get the jump on the platoons inside the city."

"We won't stand a chance once the base ships show up," Oakes pointed out. "No one can hold the line against them."

"Maybe the base ships will be more concerned with bombarding the city than hitting us," Henshaw suggested. "If we hold them at the eastern limits, the base ships will still be close enough to do plenty of damage."

"Our only objective is to get through to the other side of town and stop the Emal there until the platoons catch up," Rhodes cut in. "We'll decide our next move there."

Another deep thud shuddered the *Ero*. Flashing red lights blinkered on either side of the launch doors.

"Stand by to launch!" Rhodes ordered. "Take off as soon as the doors open! Don't wait around in town. Just get east and engage as quick as you can!"

None of his people had time to answer before the doors cracked. A shaft of sunlight blasted into the bay and a warning alarm went off.

Rhodes didn't give the order to launch. He didn't have to.

He and his people fired their boosters and zoomed out of the bay before the ship touched down. The battalion raced away toward the buildings in the distance.

Another colossal laser smashed into a building on the right. The structure evaporated in dust and debris that pinwheeled in all directions. More bombardments struck all over the city.

Rhodes picked up speed, plunged into the city, and swerved to miss another building going up in a towering column of smoke and ash.

"Watch out, Captain!" Fisher warned.

"Don't worry about that, pal!" Rhodes called back. "I just hope we aren't too late already."

"The Grid indicates the Emal are forming an advanced line five miles out of town! They're waiting for their base ships to catch up."

Rhodes pretended not to hear. He could see perfectly well on The Grid where the base ships were.

He could also see the devastation they were wreaking on the city landscape. Buildings burst all around him.

He could have used his grid lines to change into any shape he wanted. He could have bounced off buildings or burned along the ground chewing through buildings right and left.

Riding his boosters made him go faster. He didn't want to mess around with theatrics.

The Grid showed the platoons approaching the west side of town. They advanced at a snail's pace. They might not get to the east side for hours.

All the more reason why the battalion had to get there. He swerved between buildings bursting apart all around him. The Emal escalated their bombardment as they got nearer. There wouldn't be much of this city left for the Legion to hold.

Rhodes had his orders. He didn't need to know anything else.

He spotted daylight between the buildings ahead. The landscape opened up spreading east. He was almost there.

He made one last check of his people. They and their SAMs were all holding up perfectly. None of them suffered any malfunction—yet.

He erupted past the last building, soared over another six miles of open country, and caught up with the aliens on the planes.

He took a page from Lauer's book, extended twin lasers from both hands, and swooped in low.

He banked sideways and raced up the Emal line cutting down as many of them as he could. He extended his lasers as far as they would go to widen his surface area as much as possible.

He made it a mile north from where he started before the rest of the battalion caught up. He killed hundreds of Emal in one pass, but the aliens must have gotten used to this tactic by now.

He angled southward to head back to his starting point. The rest of the battalion plowed into the alien formation. Each person used The Grid differently to change their shape to the best effect.

Lauer and Rhinehart both stayed airborne, bombarded the aliens, and dodged lasers to plummet back and forth across the battle line.

Oakes unleashed dozens of Viper missiles, drew the base ships' fire toward himself to take the pressure off the city, and then veered in other directions to hit the aliens from angles they didn't expect.

Fuentes and Henshaw took a completely different approach. Both of them dove straight down into the horde, landed on the ground, and whirled in all directions cutting down the aliens nearest them.

Henshaw used her scourge guns. Fuentes used lasers.

The Emal surged inward to attack them, but that only brought them into the path of the two fighters' guns.

Rhodes picked up speed to rejoin the others when one of the base ships hit him from the side. It knocked him somersaulting back toward the front line where he fell down hard right in the aliens' path.

Chapter 40

R hodes floundered back to consciousness and heard Fisher yelling from a long way off. "Captain! Are you injured? I can't tell! The interface is blurry."

Rhodes pushed himself up on his arms. He had trouble seeing and hearing Fisher and everything else around him.

He felt alien hands grasping at him. His vision cleared just enough to see an Emal leaning over him. The creature's eyes glazed over and the cilia around its mouth came disgustingly close to Rhodes's face.

He jolted to get away from it, but the creature held him down and stuck a laser rifle in his face.

He snapped to high alert and discovered dozens more Emal surrounding him on all sides. They all aimed their guns at him, but they didn't shoot. One of them touched his face and its spindly fingers traced the outline of his implants.

That touch sent him into a panic. He reared off the ground, tried to push the Emal away, and then remembered all his weaponry. He raised his arm and fired his scourge gun, but nothing happened. The weapon failed.

He scrambled to think and fired his thermal cannon, his lasers, and again tried his scourge gun. None of them worked.

Terror seized him. He shot to his feet and tried to activate his boosters. They didn't work, either. He was stranded here surrounded by hundreds of aliens all armed with lasers that could cut him to pieces—again.

The memory of his arm getting cut off blasted him out of his mind. He swung his arms to strike at the aliens, but too many of them packed around him. He could barely move.

Another Emal raised its hand and touched his face again. Alien hands groped him all over. He couldn't let this happen.

He punched and threw elbows at the aliens nearest him. He wasn't that far away from the city when the Emal shot him down, but he couldn't even see the edge of the horde to figure out how to get away from them.

Their bodies squashed him between them. A few of them pushed against his back. Others in front of him parted to let him through. Dozens of aliens prodded and propelled him.

He got caught in the tide of arms and hands. They were steering him away—where they wanted him to go. Were they trying to capture him?

That thought pushed him over the edge. He spun around and flailed to get through the mob heading the other way. He had to get out of here at all costs.

At that moment, a fast-moving fighter craft blasted over his head. He didn't have time to see what it was. It was flying too fast—faster than a Legion Predator.

Something snatched him away from the Emal crowd. It yanked him up into the sky by the arm and his mind cleared. The fast-moving fighter craft was actually Lauer.

He zoomed high over the alien horde, banked right and left to avoid their laser shots, and pelted westward across the landscape heading toward the city.

The aliens, the battle, and all the danger moved farther away. The Legion platoons had set up a fortified position on the city's eastern fringes. Lauer rocketed toward them carrying Rhodes with him.

His fear and panic faded and Fisher's voice switched back on.

Rhodes didn't realize until that moment that there had been something wrong with Fisher. The image of his face had been glitching and he stuttered back and forth the way he did at Coleridge Station.

Now his image stabilized. Rhodes could see Fisher clearly, but Fisher didn't see him.

Fisher faced sideways and talked rapidly to someone Rhodes couldn't see. "I'm trying to get through to him, but he doesn't respond! There's something wrong with the interface! I don't know what caused it! He was fine and then he got shot down!"

"Did the laser damage him?" Wild's voice asked through the interface.

"No, he was fine right up until he woke up on the ground. That's when the interface started cutting out."

"I'm okay now, Fisher," Rhodes gasped. "I can hear you."

"Captain!" Fisher exclaimed. He turned slightly to make eye contact with Rhodes. "I thought we'd lost you."

"I'm okay now, pal. I just....those aliens....."

"Did they damage you?" Fisher cocked his head to one side. "I'm not detecting any malfunction—not anymore."

"The same thing happened to Thackery," Koenig interrupted. "She got surrounded by Emal and her adrenaline levels went off the charts. That's when the interface failed."

Fisher inclined his head the other way. "Captain Rhodes's adrenaline levels were elevated, too."

"They were more than elevated," Rhodes added. "They were through the roof."

Fisher frowned, and in that moment, the interface between Rhodes and the other SAMs reconnected.

The interface picked up Fuentes, Rhinehart, and Coulter all still on the ground in the middle of the alien horde. Thackery, Dietz, and Henshaw had all retreated to rejoin the platoons closer to the city.

Rhodes's interface picked up spikes of terror and desperate battle fury coming from the three soldiers on the ground. None of their SAMs could contact them or help them in any way.

Fuentes and Coulter suffered the worst. Rhinehart did his best to fight his way to Fuentes's position, but too many Emal crowded around Rhinehart, too.

"Let me go!" Rhodes called to Lauer. "We gotta get them out! You go after Coulter. I'll get Rudy!"

Lauer let go of Rhodes's arm and Rhodes fired his boosters. They worked fine now.

He swooped over the Emal and unloaded his scourge guns, but they couldn't clear a path fast enough.

He fired Vipers in a ring around Fuentes's position. Fuentes fought with all his might, but his weapons systems kept shutting down at the worst possible times.

Rhodes's senses kicked into high gear now that the interface was back online. The Emal were just as fascinated with Fuentes's implants as the aliens had been by Rhodes.

Fuentes would have been dead by now if the Emal really wanted to kill him. They tried to push him to the rear, too. They must want to keep and study these strange creatures that just happened to land in their midst.

The idea of getting captured by the Emal almost drove Rhodes out of his mind again, but he had to keep his head this time. He had to get his three subordinates out of danger.

Fuentes's lasers came back online for a split second. He swung around and carved himself a few feet of space—just enough to hold the Emal at arm's length.

Rhodes plunged in at that moment and grabbed Fuentes by the arm. Rhodes launched into the sky taking Fuentes with him just as Lauer launched with Coulter. That left Rhinehart.

Seeing Fuentes safe flooded Rhinehart with relief and all his systems roared back to life. He blasted his boosters and torched a dozen Emal on his way out of the horde. The battalion converged on the eastern fringes, but not soon enough to save the city.

Buildings kept detonating behind the Legion line. The platoons set up fortifications there, but Henshaw was right. The Legion would never be able to save this city. The aliens destroyed half of it before they even invaded.

Rhodes set Fuentes down next to Henshaw and Thackery. "Sir....." Fuentes gasped. "Sir....the interface....my weapons......"

"Did all of you suffer interface failures?" Rhodes asked.

"I didn't," Dietz replied.

Rhodes ignored him. "What happened to you, Georgie?"

"I got overrun and my weapons started shutting down, but they didn't shut down completely. The Grid stayed up long enough for me to see where I was. I rolled out of the horde and made it back here. I didn't need to shoot. Then, once I got clear, my weapons came back online."

"Our adrenaline levels must be what caused the malfunction," Lauer pointed out.

"How are we supposed to keep our adrenaline levels down when we're in battle?" Oakes asked. "Of course our adrenaline levels are higher now than they were in the training sessions. This is real."

Rhodes turned back to the SAMs. "Can you adjust your sensors so the system isn't as sensitive to our adrenaline levels?"

"We can try," Fisher replied. "We won't know if it will work until we actually go back into battle."

"The interface doesn't shut down from *all* adrenaline," Thackery pointed out. "We all experienced plenty of adrenaline during training sessions. There were plenty of times in training when I completely forgot we were even in The Grid. It must be just levels that are too high that interfere with the interface."

"So what are you saying—that we go into a calm, meditative state when we're in the middle of a battle?" Lauer growled. "That would definitely keep our adrenaline levels down."

"I'm saying maybe it just takes the SAMs some time to get used to battle conditions. None of them has ever been in a real battle before except on Ohait. Georgie and I haven't been in a real battle before Ohait, either."

"At least the SAMs can think clearly," Rhinehart pointed out. "At least none of them malfunctioned enough to interfere with our thinking."

"Don't say that," Coulter told him. "You'll jinx us."

"He already said it, dumbass," Oakes interrupted. "Anyway, if this battle is any indication, we just have to make sure some of us stay out of the line of fire long enough to get the others clear—if it happens again, I mean."

"We're in a war zone," Henshaw remarked. "Keeping some of us out of the line of fire might not be possible. In fact, I'm certain it won't be."

Chapter 41

Captain Vernick and Lieutenant Upshaw approached Rhodes behind the Legion fortifications. "How would you like to throw yourselves in front of an enemy weapon again?" Vernick asked.

"Is that the way you ask all the girls out?" Rhodes asked.

Vernick laughed. "Only the really special ones. The brass is ordering us to assault the aliens and drive them back across the planes to get their base ships away from the city."

"That sounds like it came straight out of General Kaufman's mouth."

Vernick made a face. "I'm too low on the ladder to think about whose mouth it came out of. We have to assault the aliens...."

"Which is a suicide mission," Upshaw interrupted.

"Unless you soften them up for us first," Vernick finished. He pointed out at the planes. "We saw the way they flocked around you. They're fascinated by you for some reason. You could come at them from the side—over there. Once they turn toward you, we'll assault from this side."

"Like you did on Ohait," Upshaw finished.

Rhodes squinted at the sky. "It will be dark soon...."

"That's why we want you to go—if you're willing," Vernick explained. "The Emal can see in the dark. If we assault them head on, they'll see us coming. If you assault them from the side, they'll be paying attention to you. They won't see us until it's too late.....See?" Vernick frowned. "Can *you* see in the dark?"

Rhodes had to think for a split second. He definitely saw in the dark during that Luluna training session.

Most of the seeing he did during that session was just using The Grid to tell where he was. Once the shooting started, the explosions gave enough light to see.

"Yes, we can," he replied. "All right. We'll do it. We'll wait for full dark. Then we'll flank the aliens over there, assault them, and draw them away so you can strike."

"Thanks, man," Vernick replied.

Rhodes waited for them to leave. "Was there something else?"

"We're eating dinner over there. Do you want to join us? You're more than welcome."

Rhodes cast a glance toward the soldiers gathering in clusters farther down the line. "We probably shouldn't. We don't eat, so our presence would probably just make everyone uncomfortable."

"You staying over here by yourselves makes everyone uncomfortable," Upshaw pointed out. "They think you're too good for us."

Rhodes made a face. "Just remind them of how they acted on Ohait. That should be enough to explain why we don't think we're welcome. I appreciate the invitation. I would like nothing better than to share a meal with you two. Them? I'll skip it."

"I'm sorry you feel that way," Vernick replied.

"I'm sure you two and Lieutenant Turley are the only people here who are sorry about it. It's better if we keep our distance. Thank you again for the invitation. It means a lot. We'll get ready for the assault."

"How will we know when to strike?" Upshaw asked.

"One of us will fire a Viper into the air to signal you. That should be enough."

"All right," Vernick replied. "I don't like it, but we can do it your way."

"Thank you again. Hopefully, we'll see each other after the assault and we'll all ride out of here to fight another day."

Vernick cracked a grin. "You always were a dreamer. Let us know if you need anything."

The two officers walked away and Rhodes returned to his soldiers. They all overheard the conversation through the interface.

"That was nice of them," Henshaw remarked.

"It was nice of *them*," Rhodes corrected. "It wasn't nice of the rest of the platoons who didn't ask."

"You're right, Sir," Lauer murmured. "It's better if we keep our distance. We aren't them anymore."

"No one is more aware of that than they are." Rhodes sat down with the others to wait.

The sun went down. The Emal kept up their bombardment of the city's buildings, but the aliens didn't advance any further—not yet.

"What do you think they're waiting for?" Oakes asked.

"Who the hell knows what's going on in their minds?" Lauer countered. "Who the hell knows why they do anything?"

"It would be nice to know what they want and why they're doing all this," Henshaw remarked. "What if we get over there to flank them and they attack the platoons instead? The Emal might completely ignore us. Then the platoons would be exposed because we wouldn't be here to protect them."

"Us being here wouldn't protect the platoons," Lauer told her. "We won't make any difference to this war. We learned that a long time ago if we learned anything from fighting the Emal. They'll win and we'll fall back to give them the territory they want. The Legion can't do anything except maybe hope to slow them down a little."

"Then why is the Legion fighting this war?" she asked. "Why waste all the resources and soldiers' lives? Why not just evacuate the territory the Emal want and let them take it?"

"You explain that to your old man and see what he says."

That ended the conversation. Rhodes spent the rest of the evening thinking about Dietz and what to do about him.

Rhodes considered how he could find out if Dietz did anything underhanded during that last battle. Fisher said the SAMs recorded everything the battalion did.

If that was true, Rhodes should be able to go back through the data and find out what Dietz had been doing, where he'd been, whether he even fought the Emal, and the circumstances under which Dietz fell back to the beach.

Did Dietz fight the Emal at all? Was that the reason his adrenaline levels didn't cause him to malfunction the way everyone else did?

The sun went down and the planet fell into darkness. The noise of countless Emal voices drifted across the planes coming from the east.

"I guess now we know what they're waiting for," Coulter remarked. "They can see in the dark. They must be waiting to play their advantage."

"Just keep your adrenaline levels down and try to stay calm," Rhodes ordered. "Think of this as a simulation like the one on Luluna."

"We'll have to keep an eye on each other," Rhinehart suggested. "If someone goes down, one of us can pull them out."

"Good idea," Rhodes replied. "Let's go—and keep quiet."

He checked in with Vernick, told the captain he was leaving, and the battalion tiptoed out of hiding.

The Legion position covered a long line of terrain surrounding the city from north to south. The Emal did the same, but most of the base ships concentrated in the middle on a direct line between Thaklia and the cities farther east.

"How far are we going?" Coulter asked through the interface.

"This should be far enough." Rhodes halted a few miles south of their starting place. The battalion hunkered behind the platoons' southernmost fortifications.

Rhodes couldn't see the Emal from here, but The Grid showed him all he needed to know.

The Emal must have been gearing up for a night assault, too. Their numbers concentrated closer to their base ships. They would be able to break the Legion position and get inside the city.

Distant booms rumbled across the landscape. The base ships fired into the city and buildings exploded in the darkness. They didn't make any flashes of light to show where the two armies were facing off against each other.

"How do you want to do this, Sir?" Oakes asked.

"Let's crawl along the ground the way we did before. We can draw level with the Emal and attack from the side."

"How do you want us to attack?" Thackery asked.

"Once we get into position, we'll need to make ourselves as big and as visible as possible. Use Vipers and lasers. They're more visible. Don't worry so much about killing tons of Emal. Just draw their attention to that side of the battlefield and bring them in to assault us."

"Good deal," Lauer replied and he transformed instantly.

Grid lines covered his body and then they all folded in on each other on the ground. They vanished and left the long, thin, snaking whip slithering along the ground.

The rest of the battalion did the same thing. Rhodes checked on Dietz, but he did it, too. He didn't pull any dirty tricks—yet.

Rhodes really needed to get rid of that asshole, but he couldn't do it now. Rhodes changed his shape and the battalion crawled out onto the open fields.

The noise coming from the Emal got louder. They didn't even try to hide what they were doing.

Distant yells of men shouting floated from the Legion side. It sounded like the platoons were getting ready for an assault, too, but it mostly sounded like the Emal's noise was alerting the platoons that the Emal were about to strike.

Anyone listening might mistake that sound for the platoons preparing to defend themselves. Maybe in some alternate universe the Emal might not realize the platoons were planning a strike of their own.

Rhodes couldn't think about that. He picked up speed and measured The Grid to find out where he was in relation to the Emal.

He should have spent the time deciding what he would turn himself into when he got there. He decided instead to just improvise. That always seemed to work in the past.

The tension built to the breaking point. The noise firing back and forth from both sides set Rhodes's nerves on edge.

If the Emal attacked first before the battalion got into position to spring their diversion, this whole maneuver would be dead in the water.

He covered the last five hundred yards and made one last check of The Grid. Lauer got the jump on everyone by leaving first. He outpaced everyone and drew level with the Emal line.

He didn't wait for his comrades to catch up with him. He snaked between the Emal's legs to a position right in the middle of their ranks.

Then Lauer exploded to many times his normal size. He erupted into a gargantuan shape. The grid lines covered him and reformed into a massive alien.

The thing towered twenty feet tall with long, whipping arms and a laser spurting from each one. Horns sprouted from the creature's shaggy head and a million teeth stuck out of its huge mouth.

Somehow or other, Lauer made the monster glow from the inside. Reddish-orange and yellow light beamed through the alien's outer skin. It couldn't be more visible if it tried.

It threw back its head and let out a thunderous roar of fury before it smashed its tentacle arms down on the ground.

The creature stomped three steps forward. The ground shook under its weight.

It started slashing and swiping its lasers everywhere, but it mostly just hammered its mighty arms into the ground to squash any Emal who got in their way.

The Emal definitely did not see that coming. They sprang away shrieking and jabbering trying to escape from the monster. They took way too long to make up their minds to attack it.

They must have decided that they still had the advantage of numbers since there was only one of this thing.

The Emal flooded Lauer trying to surround him. They fired their laser rifles at him and he spun around roaring and flailing his arms in all directions.

They took the opportunity of him turning his back to swarm him from behind, climbed on top of him, and more lasers covered him all over.

His deafening bellows set off a chain reaction in the rest of the battalion. They raced straight for him, plunged into the Emal ranks, and everyone turned into matching alien monsters. Rhodes couldn't think of anything more distracting than that.

He blasted out of his skin, let the grid lines take over, and he expanded. His arms extended and more appendages sprouted from his sides and back.

He roared at the enemy and stomped and smashed his way through them. More of these alien monsters materialized out of the darkness. Their glow showed Rhodes and the Emal exactly where everyone was.

The Emal surrounded the battalion trying to swarm everyone in hundreds of bodies. Dozens of laser rifles went off all around Rhodes.

He even felt Emal climbing on top of him, perching on his shoulders where he couldn't hit them, and firing their lasers down at him from above.

Their laser rifles couldn't damage him. He roared again, thrashed to his highest height, and whipped his arms across his back to crush the Emal. Their bodies fell, but more Emal flooded to the spot from all sides.

He barely remembered to fire a Viper into the air to signal the platoons to launch their assault.

The missile coiled into the night sky and a groundswell of noise floated across the planes coming from the west.

Rhodes couldn't see anything over there and he didn't have time to check The Grid. He had to keep fighting the Emal to stop them from overrunning him.

He kept his head just enough not to let his adrenaline take over. Fisher pivoted The Grid in front of Rhodes' eyes to show him where the Emal were, which ones were climbing on top of him, and where to hit them to knock them away.

Explosions went off somewhere in the distance. Lasers and Jackhammer fire lit up the darkness farther north. The platoons were assaulting the Emal line. The diversion worked.

At that moment, one of the base ships stopped shooting at the city, swiveled south, and fired its massive laser straight at Lauer.

The shot smashed him in the head and he crumbled under a wave of Emal. The grid lines transformed him back into a man and he collapsed unconscious on the ground.

"Lauer!!" Rhodes bellowed in his extra-loud alien voice. Lauer didn't respond.

Rhodes had to flounder out of his battle fog to interface with Wild. "How bad are Lauer's injuries?" Rhodes asked.

The skull jittered right and left. "They're flanking to the south. They're flanking to the south. They're flanking to the south."

"Wild!!" Rhodes snapped.

"They're flanking to the south. They're flanking to the south."

Rhodes checked The Grid and tried to stomp his way over to Lauer's body. He lay face down on the ground. Rhodes couldn't see Lauer's face.

Rhodes got halfway there before two more base ships fired south at the alien intruders, too. Rhodes dodged one of the shots before it took him out.

The laser hit Oakes instead, hit him somewhere in the chest, and he went down, too.

Dash vanished off the interface and the link went dead. Rhodes couldn't even pick up Oakes on The Grid anymore.

Something about being this big, enraged monster took over Rhodes's mind. He roared in fury, slammed dozens of Emal out of the way, and stormed over to Lauer.

Rhodes spotted Oakes lying on the ground twenty feet away. Without The Grid, Rhodes had to rely on his normal sight to keep track of where Oakes was.

Rhodes saw Oakes moving, but that was all. Rhodes couldn't tell from here how badly injured Oakes might be.

Rhodes bent down to roll Lauer onto his back. More lasers from the base ships blasted over Rhodes's head.

He ducked to avoid them and heard screaming somewhere out of sight. The interface failed again. Koenig, Van, and Keon disappeared.

Rhodes leaned over Lauer. The shot that knocked him out crushed his facial implants. The eyepiece attached to his mechanical eye yawned into a ragged socket with wires and torn metal fragments hanging out of it.

Rhodes tried one last time. "Wild—can you hear me?!"

Wild kept jerking from left to right and back again. "They're flanking from the south. They're flanking from the south. They're flanking from the south."

Rhodes gave it up and cast a desperate glance at The Grid. Fuentes, Henshaw, and Thackery were all down. Dietz and Rhinehart stood over them fighting off the Emal still swarming the area.

The Emal didn't swarm as thickly as they did before. The platoons' assault distracted the Emal back to the main battlefront. They withdrew—partially.

They didn't seem too interested in Lauer and Oakes. Rhodes had to take this chance.

He grabbed Lauer by the wrist and pulled him off the ground. Rhodes stayed in his giant alien form, but he stopped glowing so the Emal wouldn't see him—or they wouldn't be able to see him as well.

He stormed over to Oakes and picked him up, too. This alien form gave Rhodes plenty of arms to carry both men and still keep shooting at the enemy.

"Bring them here and follow me!" he yelled to Dietz and Rhinehart. "Fall back!"

Rhinehart and Dietz looked around. The battalion couldn't fall back to the Legion position. Too many Emal, platoons, and explosions blocked any retreat in that direction.

Rhodes threw caution to the wind and headed in the only direction left for him to go—west behind the Emal line.

More Emal flooded eastward to join the attack against the platoons. The two armies locked on the planes with all the remaining Emal heading that way.

They abandoned the battalion and left a clear path for Rhodes to lead his people out of danger.

Chapter 42

Rhodes threw Lauer and Oakes down behind a low rise and jumped down there after them. "You're still an alien, Captain," Fisher told him. "Turn yourself back into your normal shape."

Rhodes had to think about it before he remembered. He transformed back into his normal shape just as Dietz and Rhinehart showed up with Fuentes, Henshaw, and Thackery.

All of them had taken hits from the base ships' laser cannons. Henshaw was completely unconscious with part of her ribs blasted out.

A wicked slash carved through Thackery's skull implant. Rhodes didn't see any severe external damage, but her behavior told him something serious must have gone badly wrong.

She jerked her head to the left again and again. She didn't blink. She kept opening and closing her mouth again and again without making a sound.

Fuentes's mechanical right arm had been torn off by some force. Wires and broken mechanical rods hung from the joint.

Rhinehart carried the arm in one hand. Dietz appeared uninjured again, but Rhodes decided to give Dietz another pass for getting Thackery and Fuentes out of danger.

"Where's Coulter?" Rhodes asked.

"No idea," Rhinehart replied. "I didn't see him—and he isn't on The Grid, either. Neither is Murphy."

Rhodes could see that they weren't on The Grid. "Can you access any of their SAMs?" he asked Fisher.

"I'm trying to. Van is still there. She's hiding from us."

"Get her back out here. We need to deal with all these injuries and malfunctions."

Rhodes turned to Lauer. He was still out cold, too. Wild kept repeating over and over that the Emal were flanking from the south—which they weren't. They never had been.

Rhinehart squatted down in front of Fuentes and moved Fuentes's severed arm closer to him. Rhinehart put it on the ground nearby.

Rhodes didn't see what the group could possibly do with it, but Fisher intervened. "Hold the arm close to his shoulder. It will reattach by itself."

Rhinehart frowned at it. "How will it do that?"

"Just hold it up. Put the wires and rods together."

Rhinehart positioned the arm where it was supposed to be. The wires snaked out of the gaping hole in Fuentes's shoulder and the rods extended until their fragmented ends touched.

They rejoined and the arm thumped into its socket. It repaired itself, but that didn't help Fuentes. He glanced around the group and out into the darkness.

Rhodes got in front of Fuentes's eyes. "You okay, Rudy? Are you in pain anywhere?"

Fuentes didn't make eye contact. "She's gone. She's gone," he husked. "She's gone."

"Who's gone?"

"I think he means Van," Fisher explained.

"Where is she? Bring her back."

"I'm trying to," Fisher replied. "She won't come."

"Are you saying she can't or she won't?"

"I'm not detecting any malfunction," Fisher replied. "There's nothing wrong with the interface."

"There must be or she would be here right now."

"She's gone," Fuentes panted again. "She's gone."

"She isn't gone!" Rhodes snapped way too loudly.

He tore his attention away from Fuentes. He wasn't injured enough for Rhodes to spend any more time on him.

The damage to Lauer's face didn't repair itself. Rhodes checked on Oakes. Rhodes rolled him over, but Rhodes didn't find any damage to Oakes, either.

There was definitely something wrong with him, though. He huddled in a ball with his chin tucked all the way down on his chest.

"Look at me, Lieutenant," Rhodes ordered.

Oakes's eyes swiveled up, but he didn't raise his head enough to make eye contact.

"What's wrong, Lieutenant?" Rhodes asked. "Oakes—look at me!"

Rhodes tried to pull Oakes up and force Oakes to sit up straight, but Oakes didn't uncurl from his fetal ball. He twisted away from Rhodes and faced the hillside.

Dash hovered off to one side. The SAM turned right and left, too, but he didn't stutter or glitch. His wild eyes darted across the landscape without seeing anything.

He grimaced in terror and his lips shivered with every rapid, panting breath.

"Dash!" Rhodes snapped. "What's wrong with Oakes?'

"They're coming!" Dash whimpered. "They're coming!"

"Dash!" Rhodes barked a little louder. "Did Oakes get hurt?"

"They're coming!" Dash moaned. "They're coming for us all!"

"I don't detect any damage to Oakes's body or his systems," Fisher remarked. "He seems to be functioning normally."

"What's wrong with them, then?"

"I'd say they're afraid, Captain," Fisher murmured. "They've never gotten injured before."

"Can you find Van at all?"

"She's there. She's a pinprick. She won't come out. She's terrified."

Rhodes gritted his teeth. Now wasn't the time for the SAMs to curl up and die because they were afraid.

He turned his attention to Henshaw and Thackery. "The damage to Thackery's head is minimal," Fisher reported. "Koenig is causing her to malfunction the same way Dash is causing Oakes to malfunction."

Rhodes made a strategic decision not to try to get through to Koenig. Rhodes turned to Henshaw and checked her side.

The housing of her chest implants was already starting to close up by itself. Keon was still offline, though.

At that moment, a piercing scream echoed out of the darkness to the east. It didn't come from the battle. It came from where the battalion had just been carrying out their distraction.

Rhinehart shot up and looked in that direction. "Coulter is out there! He could be scared, too. He could be injured or lost in the dark." He hunkered down behind the hill and turned to Rhodes. "Let me go out and get him, Sir."

Rhodes checked The Grid and interfaced with Rhinehart. He was right. Coulter had taken refuge behind another swell farther southeast.

"All right. You can go," Rhodes decided. "Just be careful and stay interfaced with the rest of us. Don't take any unnecessary risks and make sure you make it back in one piece even if it means you have to leave Coulter behind. We can't afford to lose anyone else tonight."

Rhinehart dipped his chin once. "Yes, Sir. I'll be careful."

He changed himself back into one of those slithering snakes, coiled out of the hollow, and vanished into the night.

Rhodes turned back to the people in front of him. He had to take a few seconds to decide which of them to deal with first.

He decided to tackle Dash. "Dash—look at me!" Rhodes snapped. "Dash!!"

Dash's eyes barely grazed Rhodes's face. Rhodes would have liked to grab the SAM and shake him, but Rhodes couldn't do that.

"Listen to me, Dash. Oakes is in danger. You're the only person who can get him to safety. Listen to me, Dash! You have to snap out of it. I know you're scared, but Oakes is in trouble. You want to help Oakes, don't you?"

Dash barely nodded before he went back to scanning the darkness and panting in terror.

"You have to get Oakes out of here. Understand?" Rhodes went on. "Can you do that? I need you to push through this fear and get Oakes back to the Legion. That's all you have to do. The Emal are all over there fighting the platoons. You can do this, Dash. I know it's scary, but I believe in you."

Dash nodded again. His eyes traced north toward the Legion position. He didn't come out of his terrified trance, but at least he heard and understood.

Rhodes turned to Oakes next. "Listen to me, soldier," Rhodes murmured in his ear. "I know you're scared right now, but this is just a malfunction. You're feeling your SAM's fear. This isn't you. You're a fighter. You can pull out of this. You can get yourself to safety. You can fight back. You've done it before. You can do it now."

Rhodes looked around to see Dietz and Fuentes listening. Fuentes screwed up his face in an agony of determination, but plenty of the old anguish came through anyway.

"Van is making you more afraid than you should be," Rhodes told him. "Try to put your fear aside just long enough to get back to the Legion position. Understand?"

Fuentes nodded down at the ground. That left Thackery.

Koenig was making himself invisible, too. Thackery didn't respond at all when Rhodes tried to talk to her.

"There has to be a way to hack these SAMs and straighten them out," Rhodes muttered.

"I could try to shut them down the way I shut down Fuentes," Fisher suggested. "It would affect all of you and it might even make the problem worse. I could wind up knocking them all out. Then we'd be stranded here."

"We can't risk that."

A deep boom of gunfire and explosions made Rhodes glance over the hilltop toward the battle. The Emal were starting to push the Legion platoons into the city.

Dusters burned back and forth across the battle unleashing seekers and breaker bombs on the Emal. This was turning into another nightmare horrorscape exactly like Luluna.

Chapter 43

Rhinehart came back with Coulter. Rhinehart had to wrestle Coulter down into the hollow and pin him against the hillside to hold him in place so Coulter wouldn't bolt back out into the night.

He sobbed and moaned in terror, tried to break free from Rhinehart's grip, and jerked in all directions trying to see enemies who weren't there.

"Is he injured?" Rhodes asked.

"Not that I could tell," Rhinehart replied. "He tried to fight me off, but he's too scared even to use his weapons."

"We have to fall back to the Legion position," Rhodes decided. "We need to lift off so we can correct these malfunctions. We can't accomplish anything else down here tonight—and Lauer needs medical attention."

"The *Ero* is still on the ground west of the city," Fisher told him.

"How do you say we get there?" Rhinehart asked. "We can't fight our way through all that. You, me, Dietz, and Fuentes are the only ones here with working boosters. We couldn't carry everyone at the same time."

"No, you're right, Rhodes replied. "And I wouldn't feel right about leaving them unprotected, either."

"One of us could stay," Fuentes offered. "Or more than one of us could stay....while the other one carries everyone to the *Ero.*"

"It would be super helpful if we could get one of those Dusters to come and pick us up," Rhodes remarked.

"One of us could change ourselves into a Duster," Rhinehart suggested. "I'm the biggest and the strongest. I could do it."

"Your boosters might not be able to carry everyone." Rhodes straightened up. "You, me, and Fuentes can combine ourselves into a Duster." He looked around again. "Coulter, you help us. Coulter—can you hear me?"

Coulter didn't respond. Rhinehart made a face. "This is stupid. What's the point of going into battle with these SAMs if they're going to malfunction at the worst possible time?"

"We just have to get everyone out of here. Let me just check....."

Rhodes stuck his head up to check that the Emal were all far enough away. They were too busy pushing the platoons into the city streets. None of the Emal gave Battalion 1 a second glance.

"It's clear," Rhodes told the others. "Let's go. We can make the Duster out here....."

He climbed up the nearest rise. The hollow behind it wasn't big enough for a Duster.

He got as far as the upper slope. He didn't even make it to the top before another shot from one of the base ships smashed into him with almighty force.

He hit the ground with a brutal thump. His head swam for a second and he wavered out of consciousness for a minute.

When he came back to his senses, Rhinehart's face hovered in front of Rhodes's eyes. Rhinehart yelled in Rhodes's face, but Rhodes couldn't hear anything.

Fisher hovered there, too. He kept fizzing out in a tangle of grid lines, glitching, and stuttering from side to side.

He reformed a dozen times, changed back into a random squiggle of lines, and reformed, but only for a few seconds before he glitched again.

In those few seconds when Rhodes could see Fisher clearly, he saw Fisher's mouth moving. A scratchy sound came out of the image. Rhodes caught random words here and there, but they got lost in the static.

"Fisher....." Rhodes croaked.

Fisher stuttered sideways and made eye contact with Rhodes for a split second before Fisher's grid lines scrambled again.

Fisher's eyebrows raised and his mouth moved rapidly like he was trying desperately to tell Rhodes something important.

"Fisher...." Rhodes stammered again. "Fisher....what's wrong?"

Rhodes already knew what was wrong. That laser must have damaged Rhodes's implants. Fisher was malfunctioning.

Cold dread seized Rhodes's heart. He couldn't function without Fisher. Rhodes had become dependent on his SAM as a confidante and companion more than anything else.

Rhodes had also become dependent on Fisher's information. Fisher could access so much more information through The Grid than Rhodes could.

Fisher relieved Rhodes from a hundred responsibilities a day. Fisher's assessment of every situation had become as valuable or more to Rhodes than his own opinion. He'd come to trust Fisher in ways Rhodes never thought possible.

He had to get Fisher back at all costs, but he couldn't do that here. Rhodes couldn't even hear Rhinehart. The damaged interface must be interfering with Rhodes's hearing, too.

Rhinehart kept pushing his face in front of Rhodes's eyes and yelling silently. Rhodes read the same desperate panic in Rhinehart's face. Rhodes wouldn't be able to do anything without Fisher.

Rhinehart glanced around the hollow and his features hardened. He was the last one still functioning normally—besides Dietz.

Rhinehart pinched his lips, narrowed his eyes, and raised his head to look over the hilltop toward the battle. Rhodes read his expression as plain as day, but Rhodes couldn't help Rhinehart.

Rhodes's brain kept fading out. Each blur coincided with Fisher turning back into squiggly tangled grid lines. Both malfunctions cleared at the same time, but each episode only lasted a few seconds before the system glitched out again.

Rhodes hauled himself off the ground with an effort. He tried to speak again, but his brain wouldn't connect.

He pointed toward the east. He tried to link one thought to another. The *Ero* was over there. Then he pointed at Rhinehart and east again.

He wanted Rhinehart to use his boosters to fly over there and get help. Rhodes couldn't think of any other solution.

He couldn't manipulate the grid lines well enough to help anyone. He didn't trust himself to fly anywhere, much less hold a shape long enough to keep the battalion alive.

Rhinehart shook his head, turned away, and said something to Dietz and Fuentes. Rhodes's thoughts went fuzzy again. He couldn't think clearly enough to understand what Rhinehart was saying or deciding on behalf of the whole battalion.

It didn't matter as long as someone took over.

Rhinehart pointed at different people. He ignored Rhodes while Rhinehart gave orders to Dietz and Fuentes. They went through the group rounding everyone up.

Rhinehart slung Lauer's body over his shoulder. Dietz and Fuentes pulled Oakes, Thackery, and Coulter to their feet.

Fuentes tried to pick up Henshaw and failed. Dietz pushed him out of the way, picked her up himself, and slung Henshaw over his shoulder, too.

Rhinehart, Dietz, and Fuentes herded everyone out of the hollow and headed up the slope. Oakes, Thackery, and Coulter stumbled and fell over a lot. The others had to stop and pick them up.

Rhodes tried to get his brain working well enough to get to his feet. Fuentes came over to him and put out his arm to help Rhodes up.

Rhinehart climbed to the top of the slope carrying Lauer and guiding Oakes in front of him. Rhinehart steered everyone southeast—away from the battle.

Rhodes floundered to his feet, but before he could move, a Viper spiraled out of the atmosphere from somewhere beyond sight. It hammered into the ground twenty yards from Oakes and Rhinehart.

Both men toppled from the impact and the shockwave knocked everyone off their feet.

Rhodes pitched across the ground. He barely hauled his senses into focus long enough to see a Legion Ravager plummeting out of the atmosphere.

Catastrophic laser fire from the Emal base ships pounded the Ravager from the high clouds all the way to the ground.

Those shots deflected off the Ravager's hull and spiked into the hills surrounding the battalion.

Rhodes tumbled over himself trying to orient his mind. Rhinehart. Rhinehart was the only person who could get everyone out of this.

Rhodes couldn't stand up under the continuous bombardment. He could barely see straight.

He took advantage of brief flashes of lucidity to crawl out of the hollow to where Rhinehart lay.

Oakes and Lauer sprawled on the grass. Rhodes couldn't take the time to check on everyone else.

Rhodes rolled Rhinehart over. Most of his facial implants had been smashed in even worse than Lauer's. Rhinehart didn't respond. Rhodes couldn't access the interface to see if Rocky was still online or not.

Rhodes looked up just long enough to check the state of battle. He had to get to the *Ero*.

He had to get someone—anyone on the Legion side to come and bail out the battalion. They couldn't survive out here much longer.

In that moment when he raised his head to look around, another ship pelted out of the mayhem. It came from the north—out of the thickest chaos over the battle lines.

Fisher took that moment to fade out into squiggly lines again. When he reformed into his own face, another SAM floated in front of Rhodes's eyes. It was Rio.

Rio studied Rhodes with deep interest. Rio's mouth moved, too, but Rhodes couldn't hear anything.

Rhodes blinked.....and another SAM materialized on The Grid in front of his eyes. He couldn't concentrate on the battle with all these SAMs getting in his face.

He needed to concentrate on the battle to find a way to get the battalion to the west side of town, but right then, another person stuck his head in front of Rhodes's eyes. It was Dietz. Rhodes had completely forgotten about him.

Dietz tried to yell at Rhodes, too, but Rhodes couldn't hear a thing except the confused jumble coming from Fisher.

Without asking permission, Dietz grabbed Rhodes and dragged him out of the hollow by main force.

Rhodes became aware of everyone else in the battalion lying on the ground. Some of them moved. None of them stood up. Dietz was the last man standing.

Rhodes stumbled, but Dietz didn't let him go. Dietz dragged Rhodes out into the open—right into the path of Emal bombardment.

Rhodes went into another panic thinking Dietz was either trying to kill him or leaving the rest of the battalion behind.

Rhodes's brain didn't function well enough to understand until the strange ship touched down in front of him. It was one of the battalion's Strikers.

Dietz muscled Rhodes to the ship. Rhodes's limbs didn't function well enough for him to climb into the cockpit.

Dietz wound up grabbing Rhodes around the ribcage with both arms, lifting him up, and physically dumping him into the seat.

Dietz yanked Rhodes where he wanted Rhodes to go and shoved Rhodes down into the cockpit. Last of all, Dietz seized Rhodes by the face and jammed his head back against the prong that locked him into the seat.

A blast of electric power smashed Rhodes in the head—and his thoughts cleared. The volume switched back on. The tangled grid lines covering Fisher's face disappeared.

"I'm contacting the other Strikers," Rio reported. "They're coming in to collect the rest of the battalion."

Rhodes sighed in relief. "Thank you so much, Rio. You don't know how good it is to see you." He turned to Fisher. "Are you okay, pal? I'm so glad you're back."

"I'm okay now, Captain. Your Grid is still malfunctioning, but you'll be able to fly. You just won't be able to transform the ship or yourself."

"I don't care as long as we get out of here." Rhodes activated The Grid—or maybe Rio did it for him. "Will we be able to correct the other SAMs' malfunctions by interfacing with their Strikers?"

"We can only try it," Rio replied. "Here they come."

Four more Strikers swooped out of the night. They had to wheel backward to shoot at the Emal before the Strikers came in to land.

Rhodes felt fine now—or fine enough to get the hell out of here.

He scrambled to the ground and helped Dietz load Oakes, Fuentes, Thackery, and Coulter into their ships. The Striker SAMs interfaced with Rhodes so he could give them orders to take everyone back to the *Ero*.

The rest of the Striker formation hovered over the city trying to fight their way through the bombardment to get near the battalion.

The first four ships blasted into the cloud and disappeared. Rhodes checked the state of battle.

The Emal were still far enough away, but the base ships kept targeting the Strikers to stop them from flying that far behind the enemy line.

The next four had to back across the planes unloading all their firepower on the Emal position.

Even then, the four Strikers could only inch backward one painstaking step at a time before they made it to the hollow.

Two Strikers touched down. The other two stayed airborne to defend what was left of the battalion.

Rhodes and Dietz hauled Henshaw and Lauer to their ships. Neither of them revived when Rhodes locked them into the prongs.

Those two took off and stood guard with Rio while the last two Strikers landed.

Rhodes and Dietz had to work together to drag Rhinehart into the cockpit. He weighed a ton and Dietz wasn't the biggest guy in the world.

They finally locked Rhinehart in. "Go!" Rhodes told Dietz. "Get on board and get out of here! Get back to the *Ero!*"

"What about you?" Dietz asked.

"I'm coming right behind you! Go!"

Rhodes pushed Dietz away. He took off running for his Striker, dove into the cockpit, and blasted away with the others.

Rio came back down, picked up Rhodes, and another wave of relief flooded him when he locked in with his SAMs.

"The base ships are targeting the city again," Fisher reported. "They aren't targeting the battalion anymore."

"Why not? Is the Legion putting up any defense?"

"Not an effective one. They're....."

At that moment, a different weapon hit Rio from behind. The Striker made it as far as the city's eastern fringes—right over the Legion position.

Dietz's Striker, Baron, Rhinehart's Striker, Zion, and Lauer's Striker, Elio, flew right in front of Rio.

Rhodes dropped into The Grid to check what the Emal were doing. He didn't see a thing before what looked like a net of forked lightning hit Rio in the tail.

The blast crackled all around the ship and The Grid shorted out. Rhodes had half a second to see the same net surround the other Strikers. Then everything shut down and he blacked out.

Chapter 44

R hodes woke up lying on his back in some dark, shadowy chamber. Distant slams echoed in the darkness.

He made the mistake at first of thinking he was waking up after a long conversion cycle. He tried to raise his arm, but he couldn't move.

The feeling of being restrained sent him into another wave of panic. He struggled against whatever was holding him down, but he couldn't lift his arms, his legs, or even his head. He could turn his head, but he couldn't pick it up off the surface beneath him.

He looked around in frantic desperation—and saw the rest of the battalion lying on tables. They formed a line on either side of him....and then Rhodes saw a bunch of Emal wandering around.

They passed back and forth between the tables doing something or other. The aliens murmured to each other in their own language. Their eyes gleamed out of the darkness when they turned in Rhodes's direction.

The rest of Rhodes's companions turned their heads to look at him. They were all awake now, including Lauer and Henshaw.

Wires still hung out of the open ragged hole of Lauer's mechanical eye socket. The other side of his face—the human side of his face—registered all the panic Rhodes felt right now.

Rhinehart struggled the most, but not even he could break whatever invisible force held him down.

Fisher and the other SAMs were all back to full functioning. "What the hell happened?" Rhodes husked.

"The Emal captured us," Fisher replied. "They used some kind of electric discharge to ground Rio and the other Strikers."

"Are they okay? Are the SAMs okay?"

"I don't know," Fisher murmured. "I can't interface with them. I don't know what happened to them. We hit the ground and the interface failed. I came back online here. You and the rest of the battalion were already here, restrained."

"We gotta get out of here...."

"We don't even know where we are," Fisher pointed out.

"We must still be on Sulia. We must be on one of the Emal's base ships."

"I assumed that, but we can't be sure. I can't use The Grid outside this room."

Rhodes tried to use The Grid, too, and ran into the same problem. "What do the Emal want from us?"

"Based on the way they were acting during the first battle, I'd say they're interested in your implants. Here they come. I think we're about to find out."

A few Emal came over to Rhodes, discussed something amongst themselves, and then one of them fingered the implants on his face.

He jerked away from their touch, but the other two Emal seized his head and held him still while that one alien explored the implant all the way to the edge of his skin.

He struggled, but the Emal turned out to be a lot stronger than they looked. He couldn't put up much resistance lying flat on his back. They held his head easily.

"Leave him alone!" Rhinehart bellowed. "Get away from him!"

His outburst drew the Emal's attention to him. They turned away from Rhodes and surrounded Rhinehart's bed instead.

He panicked for real when they started touching him. "GET YOUR HANDS OFF ME, YOU STINKING BASTARDS!!" he roared. "GET AWAY FROM ME!!"

They ignored him, held him down, and he burst into high-pitched, broken screams when they touched his implants.

"Lieutenant!" Rhodes called out. "Lieutenant—look at me!"

Rhinehart couldn't look with the Emal holding his head straight.

"I'm here, Lieutenant!" Rhodes yelled. "I'm here!" He turned to Rocky in the interface. "You have to calm him down! His adrenaline levels could cause another malfunction."

Rocky was already trying to reassure Rhinehart, but it all went south when the Emal stepped back, held another murmured discussion, and then bent over Rhinehart again.

This time, they tried to wedge their fingers under his implants and pry them out of his skin. He screeched in pain and then burst into mindless, wordless roaring.

One Emal leaned directly over his head trying to dig its fingernails under the implant. Rhinehart fought back as best he could. The aliens completely ignored his screams.

Thackery compressed her lips to stop them from trembling and turned her head away gulping down sobs.

Henshaw lost it completely, burst into tears, and she started screaming, too, just from the sight of what they were doing to Rhinehart.

Rocky kept trying to talk to Rhinehart, but not even Rhodes could hear Rocky over the noise.

The Emal failed to get the implant off. That one alien stood back and held another long, detailed conversation with his colleagues.

Rhinehart collapsed on the table and broke down in sobs. Blood trickled from his implant and ran down both sides of his face.

"I'm here with you, Lieutenant," Rhodes choked. "We're all here with you. You aren't alone."

Rhodes didn't know what else to say, but he had to say something. If the Emal really wanted to take the battalion's implants, Rhodes wouldn't be able to do a thing to stop it.

He couldn't let this happen. He had to do something.

"You gotta help me, Fisher," Rhodes husked.

"What would you like me to do?" Fisher murmured back.

"We have to get out of here. You said you couldn't use The Grid outside this room. See if you can figure out how they're restraining us."

"These tables emit some kind of electromagnetic field. The power source is under the floor and enters the table from underneath, so there are no exposed wires or anything like that."

"Then we have to defeat this field. Can you locate the power source?"

"It isn't in this room. I'm sorry, Captain. I'll do what I can to...."

He broke off when a different group of Emal came over back to Rhodes. His stomach turned when one of the aliens laid out a bunch of shiny metal tools on a tray next to his head.

Oakes turned his head in Rhodes's direction and strained his neck like Oakes was trying to get up. He barely had time to say, "Captain...." before the Emal bent over Rhodes, grabbed their tools, and wedged them between his chest implant and the organic flesh of his lower rib cage.

He roared in pain and then just let himself scream as they pried, cut, and dug into his flesh and bones trying to unseat the implants from his body.

He felt himself starting to break down. He couldn't take this.

He heard Fisher trying to talk to him in the distance, but Rhodes couldn't hear Fisher over his own screams. Ripping pain spiked through Rhodes's body.

He had a flashback of Poole's death. Rhodes actually envied Poole then. What a fool Rhodes had been even to think that.

Without warning, another brutal crack of electricity went off somewhere. It hit Rhodes in the head exactly the way it did when Fisher shut down Fuentes, but it didn't knock Rhodes out.

The Emal standing over him folded right there and hit the floor, unconscious. Their tools fell out of their hands and clattered on the hard stone floor.

Rhodes collapsed back gasping and groaning in agony. His body writhed in torment. He couldn't move even to roll onto his side. He just had to take it.

"Captain!" Fisher yelled in his ear. "Captain—can you hear me?"

Rhodes couldn't answer right away. He blinked stars out of his eyes while he struggled to catch his breath. Searing pain kept spiking across his ribs every time he inhaled. He didn't dare to use The Grid to check how bad the damage was.

A bunch of other Emal came over, bent over their fallen comrades, and murmured to each other. They gestured at Rhodes and then at their unconscious friends.

Rhodes heard his people yelling at him and demanding to know if he was okay. The SAMs did the same thing.

He caught his breath while the Emal carried their friends away. "What did you do, Fisher?" Wild asked.

"I set off an electric discharge from the captain's fusion generator. I electrocuted the Emal. You should do the same thing. If they try to remove anyone's implants, electrocute the Emal to protect yourselves. We can't let these aliens even try to remove anyone's implants."

"I should have thought of that," Rocky murmured.

Fisher interfaced with Rocky. "I'm not detecting any permanent damage to Rhinehart's implants. The wounds around his eye implant will heal, but the captain is right. We have to get out of here."

"How?" Oakes asked.

Fisher turned back to Rhodes. "The captain's injuries are much more severe."

No one asked for a more detailed explanation. Neither did Rhodes.

"Could we use a discharge from our fusion generators to short-circuit these tables?" Coulter asked.

"I don't think these tables are conductive enough for that," Fisher replied.

"We could try it," Henshaw suggested.

"I already checked when I set off this charge just now," Fisher told her. "The current doesn't pass through the table."

"How does the field hold us down?" Thackery asked. "What's emitting the field?"

"I don't understand it. Believe me. I'm as anxious to get the battalion out of here as you are."

"If we're on one of the base ships, then we're close enough to the Legion," Lauer pointed out. "We can get off this ship and get across the planes to Thaklia. That's all we have to do."

"The problem is getting off the ship," Thackery replied. "Assuming we're on a base ship on the same planet."

Rhodes pulled himself together as well as he could. "If we keep electrocuting the Emal, they'll either leave us here or try to kill us to get rid of us. They only captured us for our implants."

The rest of his people turned to look at him. He read in their faces how bad his injuries must be. He might not survive long enough to get off this ship—if the battalion was even on a ship.

"We need to come up with another plan," he told Fisher. "Something other than electrocuting all the Emal."

"Why not electrocute them all?" Coulter suggested. "Then we'd be alone on this ship. At least we would be safe and they wouldn't try to...."

He trailed off when more Emal came back—a lot more Emal. They surrounded every table.

Rhodes panicked again when four of them leaned over his head. He saw their tools moving toward his facial implants and screams echoed down the line of tables.

Fisher let off another agonizing thump of electricity. The Emal standing closest to Rhodes fell to the floor, but just as fast, another group of Emal moved in to take their places.

These aliens wore some kind of protective suits. The suits covered the aliens' arms, bodies, and feet. The suits insulated them.

Fisher tried one last time to electrocute them, but nothing happened this time. Two Emal bent over Rhodes's face and wedged their tools between his eye implant and his nose.

He screamed himself hoarse. So did everyone else. Pain flooded him and he spiraled out of his mind. He couldn't think about what the Emal were doing to him and his people.

His eye implant started to pull away from his skull. He thrashed in brutal agony even though he knew it wouldn't do any good.

At that moment, a ray of blinding sunshine shafted through the ceiling directly above his head. It split the shadows and all the Emal looked up.

At that moment, Rio appeared on the interface in front of Rhodes's eyes. "Hold on, Captain! We're getting you out of here!"

Rhodes was too out of his mind with pain to answer. Another slash of sunshine split the ceiling open and then a huge section of it peeled back to reveal the broad sky outside.

The Emal panicked, spun away from all the prisoners, and tried to race out of the room. None of the aliens were armed.

Rhodes caught one glimpse of the battalion's Strikers swooping back and forth across the sky out there. They unleashed lasers and thermal cannons on the ceiling to carve it to pieces.

Without warning, some bizarre shape like a giant spider dropped out of nowhere, slammed into the ceiling, and used its many jointed legs to rip torn hull sections out of the way.

Rhodes realized in some distant part of his mind that he really was on some kind of ship. He was on the planet Sulia—right outside Thaklia where the Emal captured the battalion in the first place.

The spider thing ripped the whole ceiling off and daylight blasted into the chamber. The Emal located their laser rifles somewhere and opened fire on the creature.

The monster's many arms sprouted weapons and fired into the chamber to gun the Emal down.

Rhodes experienced another wave of panic when the creature leapt right down inside the ship.

Rio read his mind. "It's Elio, Captain! He's going to get you all out. Just hold on!"

The monster stormed through the chamber hunting down all the Emal. Something wasn't working right inside Rhodes's head. The Emal trying to tear his facial implant off must have damaged him. He was malfunctioning again.

"Hold on, Captain!" Fisher told him. "We're going to take you to the *Ero.* The crew will be able to give you medical treatment."

Rhodes didn't want to believe that. He couldn't cope with any more disasters today.

He couldn't tell which of these sensations were caused by his pain or which might be his implants malfunctioning. Nothing made sense even though he could understand everything going on around him.

The alien monster came back on all its legs and stopped next to Lauer's table. Grid lines covered the monster, but it didn't change into a person or a ship. It was neither.

Lauer bellowed in pain when the monster tried to lift off the table. Elio couldn't dislodge Lauer from the table no matter how hard Elio tried.

"Pull back!" Rio ordered. "Bombard the base ship from the outside! Elio—you have to find some controls to release the field."

Elio stormed through the chamber doing something Rhodes couldn't see. He heard crashes out of sight and then, like some kind of miracle, the field holding him down evaporated.

He tried to sit up, but he couldn't move. Groaning and sobbing sounds drifted down the line of tables.

Elio came back, planted himself next to Lauer's table, and picked up Lauer's body in the monster's many jointed arms.

Lauer hung limp and bleeding while Elio vaulted through the hole, perched there on the ragged edge of torn metal, and changed back into a ship, but with multiple arms still cradling Lauer.

Elio lowered him into the cockpit. The cover closed and Rhodes lost sight of Lauer.

The other Strikers came down to land one after another. Elio's Grid turned him back into the same monster.

He sprang down into the chamber again and again, lifted each member of the battalion out of the base ship, and deposited each person into their own Striker cockpits.

"I'm coming to get you, Captain!" Rio told him. "We're getting you out of here."

Rhodes couldn't move. He was too grateful and relieved to see all his people leave one after another.

Elio delivered Rhinehart to Zion and then Rio landed on the base ship's upper hull. Elio jumped down and scooped up Rhodes in his arms.

Rhodes finally relaxed. He was almost free. He didn't even have to fly the damn ship. Rio would do it for him.

Rio would take Rhodes back to the *Ero*. Rhodes really didn't care anymore what happened after that.

Elio sprang out of the hole. Rhodes was the last member of the battalion to escape.

Elio put him in the cockpit and the prongs locked onto Rhodes's back and head. He dropped into The Grid and saw the whole battle in every gruesome detail.

The Emal had invaded Thaklia. The ragged dregs of the surviving platoons fought street to street, but they couldn't slow the aliens' advance.

The next instant, Rio launched into the sky and took off with Rhodes on board. The Strikers left the battle behind and rocketed away westward to where the *Ero* sat waiting for them.

End of Book 1.

Keep Reading

Battalion 1 Series: Book 2: The Unwinnable War

When a deadly alien invasion turns against Battalion 1, Captain Corban Rhodes and his team will have to summon all their grit and resources just to stay alive, but that's the least of their worries.

With the Battalion 1 project suffering continuous malfunctions and setbacks at every turn, the battalion will face its greatest challenge from within their own ranks. Is someone in Battalion 1 a traitor to the cause, a dangerous psychotic killer, or just another tragic victim of this disastrous experiment gone wrong?

Battalion 1 will have to dig deep and pull it together to save the galaxy from an unwinnable war looming on the horizon. With everyone in the battalion barely keeping their sanity, they will have to depend on each other more than ever when they face their biggest test of loyalty and maybe pay the ultimate price just to live long enough to fight another day.

You can find it at your favorite book retailers.

Sign Up Once--Get all Theo Mann's free books including brand new releases

S ign Up Once--Get all Theo Mann's free books including brand new releases

Commander Layton Raines was just doing his job when he got shot down on the battle defending his platoon's retreat. His whole life changes when he wakes up in the hospital implanted with cybernetic limbs, but Raines is nothing like anyone else who has ever gone through the Battalion 1 project.

With the fate of the galaxy hanging in the balance, the future will depend on the one man who has never been good with authority, following orders, or staying within the lines. With the mission in jeopardy and Battalion 1 pinned down by overwhelming odds, it will take a miracle to save their lives. It just might take a mutiny to throw out the rule book and forge a path no one has ever taken before.

Sign up at www.theomann.com to read it for free

About Theo Mann

I write 70 books per year—and yes, before you ask, all these books are my original creative work. Nothing written under my name is AI-generated or ghostwritten because I write better than AI and any ghostwriter out there.

People don't read fiction for entertainment or to escape from reality. People read fiction to see their humanity reflected in another person's character and story.

This is my promise to you. When you read my books, you'll see your own humanity reflected in the characters and stories. I take this commitment to my readers very seriously. My books are an intimate form of communication between us. I would never disrespect my readers by turning that over to a machine or another writer. This is my bond between me and you as my reader.

I write 20,000 words per day as my daily work output. If anyone with a public platform would like to challenge me to prove this in a controlled environment, feel free to contact me on this website's contact page.

I worked as a professional ghostwriter for fifteen years. Now I'm on a mission to set a Guinness World Record by writing 700 books over the next ten years and 1400 books over the next twenty years, all originally written by me. See my website for the full book list.

I'm also the author of *Proof for the Existence of God* and the *Crimes Against Fiction* blog. You can find all my nonfiction work at www.crimes-against-fiction.com.

If you have a story idea, or if you would like me to explore a series in more depth, or if you'd like me to explore a character by writing a spinoff series about that character or world, leave me a message on my website's contact page. I answer all reader emails, so ask me anything, tell me what you liked and didn't like, and let me know where you'd like your favorite series to go. I would love to hear your ideas and find out what you'd like to read next.

Find out more at www.theomann.com.

Also by Theo Mann (so far)

www.ingramcontent.com/pod-product-compliance
Lightning Source LLC
Chambersburg PA
CBHW071850220626
47052CB00002B/46